MINNESOTA MOONLIGHT

BECKY MELBY
CATHY WIENKE

BARBOUR
PUBLISHING

Walk with Me © 2008 by Becky Melby and Cathy Wienke
Dream Chasers © 2007 by Becky Melby and Cathy Wienke
Stillwater Promise © 2008 by Becky Melby and Cathy Wienke

ISBN 978-1-60260-635-7

Scripture taken from the HOLY BIBLE, NEW INTERNATIONAL VERSION®.NIV®. Copyright © 1973, 1978, 1984 by International Bible Society. Used by permission of Zondervan. All rights reserved.

This book is a work of fiction. Names, characters, places, and incidents are either products of the author's imagination or used fictitiously. Any similarity to actual people, organizations, and/or events is purely coincidental.

Cover design: Kirk DouPonce, DogEared Design

Published by Barbour Publishing, Inc., P.O. Box 719, Uhrichsville, Ohio 44683, www.barbourbooks.com

Our mission is to publish and distribute inspirational products offering exceptional value and biblical encouragement to the masses.

 Member of the
Evangelical Christian
Publishers Association

Printed in the United States of America.

Dear Readers,

Thank you for picking up *Minnesota Moonlight*. Though Pine Bluff, Minnesota can't be found on the map, it captures the essence of so many small historical towns in the Land of 10,000 Lakes. As you soak in the fall colors along the St. Croix River with Sydney, scale a water tower with April, or agonize through a snow storm with Sara, it is our prayer that their stories will touch your heart and stir your soul.

If we could distill a single theme running through all of the books we've written, it would be this: God is the Author of second chances. In *Walk with Me*, *Dream Chasers*, and *Stillwater Promise* you will meet people struggling to move on in spite of the scars of their past. We have drawn on thirty-plus years of trying to follow the Lord, an equal number of years of being friends, and a combined total of seventy-three years of marriage to weave these tales of faith and love.

We'd love to hear how our stories have touched your life or how we can pray for you. Please contact us through Barbour Publishing or at www.melby-wienke.com or beckymelby.blogspot.com.

Rich blessings,
Cathy and Becky

WALK WITH ME

Dedication

To the Pearl Girls
Eileen, Lee, Patti, and Mary,
my precious online sisters-in-writing and critters extraordinaire--
your insight, encouragement, and prayers are invaluable.
"As iron sharpens iron, so one [wo]man sharpens another." Proverbs 27:16
Love you all,
Becky

To Sandy
for being my champion and showing me acceptance.
I love you, Sis.
Cathy

And to Faith Cathleen, my daughter—
I'm praying for your prince, Baby Girl.
Love you more,
Mom

A special thank you to Bill, Jan, Carrie,
Paulette, and Cynthia for awesome editing and support.
And to Tom for sharing his story.

Chapter 1

Only a few October tourists still wandered the streets after ten. Through the window, Sydney Jennet watched two of them, a young couple holding hands on a bench beneath a streetlamp. Their muted laughter lent a bittersweet sound track to her Friday night mood.

Hugging her coffee mug to ward off the night chill seeping in through the walls of the old building, she stared at her reflection in the glass door. Her face was superimposed across gold lettering that spelled out PINE BLUFF, MINNESOTA—CHAMBER OF COMMERCE & TOURIST INFORMATION.

Assessing her image in the window, she felt a measure of satisfaction. Her hair newly layered and she hadn't slacked off too much since running her fourth marathon in June. All in all, not bad for twenty-nine—at least when she was wearing a turtleneck sweater. Subconsciously, she tugged at her right sleeve, pulling it over a raised scar.

Lifting the hinged door in the marble countertop that ran the length of the room, she walked toward her computer. The glow from her monitor was the only light in the dark-paneled room with its high pressed-tin ceiling. The building, which had originally housed the Pine Bluff State Bank, had been restored to its 1884 decor. Behind her, the bronze door of the original bank vault stood open, revealing stacks of old canvas money bags, now stuffed with newspaper just for show.

After finishing her weekly newsletter to chamber members, she opened the file on the upcoming holiday craft fair. She'd typed three words when her cell phone rang. Sydney smiled at the name on the caller ID screen and opened her phone. "Hi, Col."

"I know where you are." Her best friend's voice was gently accusing. "I see your car."

Sydney could picture Colleen Hatcher, hands on her ample hips, peering from her bay window on the bluff overlooking Main Street and the St. Croix River. "You have nothing better to do on a Friday night than spy on me? Go snuggle with your man. It's date night."

A loud "Huh!" accompanied Colleen's laugh. "Let me describe date night after six years of marriage: Two kids asleep on the living room floor, hubby snoring on the couch, popcorn everywhere, including on my man's belly, cold pizza on the coffee table, and I'm watching VeggieTales—*Minnesota Cuke and the Search for Samson's Hairbrush*, to be exact—for the hundredth time, all by myself.

Eat your heart out, single girl."

Sydney swiveled her chair and put her feet on the corner of her desk, one red boot crossing the other at the ankles. "And after painting that heartwarming picture you're going to try to talk me into a blind date with the new physics teacher?"

An exasperated sigh whistled in Sydney's ear. "How did you know?"

"The guy with the popcorn in his navel beat you to it. Stu stopped down here after school."

"And. . . ?"

"And I told him that while I usually jump at the chance to date guys with IQs forty points higher than mine, I think I'll pass on this one."

"Syd, don't close your mind. Alvin's a nice guy."

"Alvin. . .isn't he a chipmunk?"

Again the frustrated sigh in her ear. "Would you get serious for a minute? Are you at your computer?"

"Yes."

"Open your wedding file and tell me what I'll be wearing for your fall wedding. That'll give you a whole year to fall in love with Alvin."

"A year to get used to marrying a chipmunk."

"Humor me, girlfriend. I'm setting an Alvin-meeting mood here. Open the file."

Sydney laughed. "I don't need to open it. You'll be wearing copper satin. . . and I'll be wearing running shoes."

"I'm ignoring you. What's summer?"

"Peach silk."

"Spring?"

"Brown taffeta with an apple green sash."

"That's my favorite. We'll have to fast-track this romance."

Sydney shook her head. "Oh, I'll fast-track, all right. That's where the running shoes come in."

"You don't make my matchmaking job easy."

Sydney tilted her head back, smiling at the ceiling. "Yenta, Yenta. Why did I ever make that deal with you?"

"Because you trust me?"

"Because I was temporarily desperate. I've given your job to God now."

"Fine. Then the cruise will be a celebration instead of a reward."

Headlights rippled across the back wall before darkness flooded the room once again. Sydney's laughter echoed off the walls. The "cruise," Colleen's reward for finding the love of Sydney's life, was really a weekend on a Mississippi River houseboat. "Either way, you win, right?"

"Uh-huh. Now let me tell you what I know about Alvin Scheffler. He's thirty-three, never been married, has a miniature poodle named—"

"Hold on." A beep sounded in her ear, and she looked at the display screen.

"Hey, it's my dad. Go wake Stu and snuggle; I'll call you tomorrow." Without waiting for a response, she clicked over to her father.

"Syd, Mom just got a rescue call. There's a fire at the LaSalle Street apartments I'll meet you there."

ଚଠ

Only a squad car and two volunteer firefighters had arrived ahead of her. By the sound of the sirens, the fire trucks were no more than a block away. Sydney parked two houses down and ran toward the apartment building. The window of the one unoccupied apartment in the second story of the fourplex was broken. Flames were clawing at the window ledge devouring the shingles and the shagbark hickory tree whose trunk butted against the roof.

Please, God, let everyone be okay. Sydney's gaze frantically scanned the front yard until she spotted the group of people behind the sign that read SANCTUARY THREE. A volunteer firefighter she recognized was running away from them. "Everyone's out," he yelled.

Still, she counted heads. Sara Lewis stood in the yard, one child in her arms, the other clinging to her leg. "Everyone all right?" Sydney screamed over the sirens.

Sara nodded, eyes brimming. "We're all okay." The sirens silenced as two trucks pulled into the yard. A woman darted across the street and handed Sydney an armload of blankets.

"I was watching TV," Sara said, "and I heard a noise upstairs. When I opened the door, I could smell smoke. I got everyone out and ran across the street to call 911."

Sydney wrapped a blanket around the shoulders of the elderly woman standing next to Sara. "Are you okay, Gwyneth?"

With a wide-eyed stare and a slight nod, Gwyneth Chapel answered, "I've got twenty-three scarecrows for the craft fair on my dining room table. Will they be okay?"

"I hope so, Gwyn. I don't think the fire touched your apartment." Sydney handed a blanket to Ronny Middleton, the boy who lived above Gwyneth. Though Ronny stood eye-to-eye with Sydney, he had the mind of a kindergartner. Jessica, his seven-year-old sister, stood two feet away, shivering. Sydney put her hand on Jessica's head. "Where's your daddy?"

"He's at work."

"He leaves the door open," Sara added. "I check in on—"

"Mouse! Mouse is in there!" A look of horror froze Ronny's features. Instinctively Sydney reached out and put both hands firmly on his shoulders. "The firemen will get him out."

"I hafta get him!"

"No, you don't."

Suddenly Sara screamed. *"Jessica!"*

Sydney turned in time to see Jessica leap onto the front porch and open the front door. Her heart stopped, then slammed against her chest. "Jessica!" Her scream blended with Sara's. "Help!" She took a step toward the porch then looked back at the firefighters unloading their equipment. Had anyone heard her? Her legs felt like lead; her breath came in gasps. But she had to get in there.

She felt her way into the entryway until the toe of her boot smashed into the bottom step. She groped for the railing, found it, and blindly took two stairs at a time. As she reached the top, Jessica thudded into her. Sydney felt the warmth of the pet rabbit they called Mouse. Just as a firefighter opened the front door, a flash of light lit the stairway. Sydney scooped up Jessica and the rabbit and ran down four steps, handing her over to the firefighter. As she darted ahead of him to hold the door, Jessica's piercing wail shot out of the blackness.

ॐ

Sydney stood at the base of the ambulance steps, watching her mother hang an IV bottle above Jessica's head. The green trim on Mattie Jennet's EMT jacket reflected the overhead light as she motioned for Sydney to come in.

Stepping into the cramped space next to the gurney in the ambulance, Sydney looked down at Jessica's loosely bandaged leg. The little girl's face contorted. "It hurts," she whispered.

"I know, honey. Mattie's giving you something for the pain."

"I saved Mouse."

"You sure did. Your big brother thinks you're a hero." She bent down and kissed Jessica's forehead, then looked up at her mother, her eyes asking questions she didn't want to voice.

"She'll be fine. No sign of smoke inhalation. If she needs any grafting, it won't be extensive."

"What happened?"

"That old curtain above the front door melted and a piece fell on her leg." Sydney cringed.

Her mother leaned toward her. "Are *you* okay?"

Sydney had been thoroughly checked over; the question had nothing to do with her physical state. She turned away from her mother's eyes, fighting to keep her breathing steady, willing the flashbacks to stay at bay. "I'll go check on everyone else."

Halfway across the lawn, her father met her, worry darkening his eyes. Without a word, she fell into Eldon Jennet's arms.

Sydney stayed wrapped in her father's embrace as she watched the firefighters. Before long, steam rose like a gauzy curtain from the roof. Sydney rested her head on her father's shoulder as she stared at the smoke hovering in the bare branches above the streetlight.

Chet Saunders, Pine Bluff's fire chief for over twenty years, approached them with his hands in the pockets of his black-smudged jacket. He looked at

Sydney with concern. "Are you all right?"

Sydney nodded.

"This has to be hard for you. Like re—"

"Syd'ey! Eldon! Where's Mattie?" Ronny ran toward them with his stiff-legged gait, holding his pet rabbit in outstretched hands.

Sydney pulled away from her father. "She went in the ambulance with Jessica. What's wrong?"

"Mouse isn't breathing! You gotta do CBR on him!"

Taking the rabbit in both hands, Sydney ran two fingers along its neck and looked helplessly at her father. Eldon Jennet put his hands on the boy's shoulders. "Ronny, I'm sorry. Your bunny's dead."

"No! Jessica saved him!"

Sydney's throat felt suddenly tight. "He probably breathed in smoke and his little lungs just couldn't handle it."

Tears poured down Ronny's cheeks. "Can Jessica handle it?"

Sydney put her hand on Ronny's face, tilting his head to make him look in her eyes. "Jessica's not going to die, Ronny. She got burned, but the doctors are going to fix her and she'll be fine. Do you understand?"

Ronny nodded and held out both hands. Sydney gently slid the rabbit from her hands to his. "I'm so sorry. Mouse was a good friend, wasn't he?"

The boy nodded. "A really good friend."

"You can pick out a new bunny at our house."

"Today?"

"Today."

Slowly Ronny shuffled away. Eldon Jennet shook his head sadly then looked at the fire chief. Gesturing toward the building, he said, "We replaced most of the old wiring, but not all of it; that's the only thing I can figure could have caused a fire."

Sydney swiped her hand across both cheeks and took a shaky breath. She pointed to the second-story window where glass spikes poking from the window frame caught the orange light of the rising moon. Against the charred interior, they glowed like jack-o'-lantern teeth. "No one was living in the upstairs apartment yet."

Chet's eyes followed his crew as they folded hoses and carried ladders away from the redbrick row house; then he glanced at Eldon Jennet. "You're the manager?"

"Our church owns three apartment buildings," Sydney answered. "Dad manages them."

The fire chief's left eyebrow rose. "This is the place where the convicts were moving in?"

Eldon Jennet sighed. "*Ex*-convict. Parolee, actually. It's part of the Sanctuary housing and mentoring program we started three years ago. We intend to open up space for reintegrating more parolees, but we're starting with one. He's supposed to move in on Monday."

Chet looked at Eldon out of the corner of his eye. "There's been some pretty loud opposition to your new program."

Sydney's hands went to her hips. "Certain people need to get their facts straight and get a life."

"Syd..." Her father's warning came with little force. "They're just people who want to protect the community. The facts are getting a bit twisted, though."

"The guy was in for murder, right?" Chet asked.

It was Sydney's turn to sigh. "Accidental manslaughter. The editorials make him sound like an ax murderer." In truth, she knew nothing more than that about the man her father had chosen as the first candidate for the reintegration program. But it didn't matter; Eldon Jennet believed in the project. And Sydney believed in her father.

Chet took his helmet off and tucked it under his arm. "People overreact when they're worried about their kids." He appeared ready to say more but stopped as Ronny approached them, the rabbit still in one hand, the other holding the hand of the elderly woman who lived below him. "Gwyneth said Mordecai started the fire."

Sydney cleared her throat. "Ronny, take Gwyneth to my car. I'll take everyone to our house for now."

"Good idea," Eldon said. "Sydney will make you some raspberry tea, Gwyn."

Gwyneth nodded. "That's exactly what I said to Mordecai last night. 'I'll make raspberry tea,' I said. But he said, 'No thanks, Gwyn dear.' I don't think Susanna likes it when he calls me 'Gwyn dear.' But that's silly that she gets jealous like that, don't you think?..." Her voice faded in the cold air as Ronny led her across the yard.

"Who's Mordecai?" Chet looked bewildered.

"Mordecai Tate was one of Pine Bluff's first residents," Sydney answered. "He and his wife, Susanna, built the mercantile in 1853."

"1853? And she just talked to him?"

"Mm-hmm."

"Oh brother. She sees a dead guy?"

"She sees him and Susanna and their three children."

"Oh brother."

The sound of tires spitting gravel made the three of them turn in unison. A black Durango made a wide turn around the fire truck and came to an abrupt stop just behind it. The door flew open and a stocky man in a gray shin-length coat got out. Sydney let out a barely audible hiss.

Her father stepped forward, extending his hand. "Hi, Floyd. Had a bit of excitement here tonight. Your mother's fine; she's in Sydney's car."

Floyd Chapel nodded, shook Eldon's hand, then Chet's, and finally extended his hand to Sydney. "Everyone else get out?"

Sydney's jaw tightened at the feel of the puffy, leather-gloved hand against hers. She simply didn't like the man. "Ron Middleton's little girl has burns on her leg. Everyone else is fine."

"Thank God for insurance. Looks like a setback for the reintegration program, though."

Sydney took a step forward, but before she could volley her first word, her father's hand on her wrist stopped her. Eldon Jennet, whose long legs, gray-green eyes, and thick brown hair Sydney had inherited, was still an imposing man at fifty-four. He dipped his head to look squarely into Floyd Chapel's bulgy pale blue eyes. Sydney watched as her father deployed his best weapon. He smiled at Floyd, and the stout little man was immediately neutralized.

"I imagine you've already put this on the prayer chain and called an emergency congregational meeting for tomorrow morning," Eldon said.

"Well, I. . .had my wife call Pastor. He's on his way."

"People will rally round as soon as they know there's a need. We'll find temporary homes for everyone."

Floyd's pudgy hands moved to his hips. " 'Might not be so temporary. The smoke damage alone will take weeks to clean up, and the upstairs apartment will have to be—"

Eldon clapped a hand on Floyd's shoulder. "That's why it's such a blessing that we've got get-it-done men like you on the deacon board."

Floyd stiffened. "You'll call the corrections department, I assume. We can't find another place for that man on such short notice." His protruding eyes narrowed. "It's just a confirmation of what most of us have known all along. This program wasn't God's will in the first place."

Chapter 2

The Greyhound bus stopped with a hiss of brakes and the door folded open. As Trace McKay touched the sidewalk with boots that felt stiff and strange, yet triggered haunting memories, he took a long, sweet breath. Frying bacon, fresh-cut grass, burning leaves—Saturday smells. Laced around it all was the scent of pine sap. To Trace, it was the smell of freedom.

As the bus pulled from the stop, he took a paper from the pocket of the dark blue jacket he'd put on for the first time three hours ago. Even with his once-favorite gray hooded sweatshirt under the jacket, he shivered. Not from cold so much as nerves.

The paper was damp from fingering it with sweaty hands. He opened it and read the address he'd glanced at a dozen times on the two-hour ride from St. Cloud. *1725 E. LaSalle St., Apartment 3.* Arguing with the jitters in his belly, he looked up and down the street, taking in the town he'd soon be calling home and praying it would feel that way.

He'd expected someone to meet him, but no one was waiting at the stop. A street sign several yards in front of him said he was on the corner of Main Street and Minnetonka Avenue, but he had no idea where to find LaSalle Street. As he looked south toward what appeared to be the business district of Pine Bluff, a woman stepped out of a building and headed his way. She was tall; he guessed about five-nine, with long slim legs. She wore a short denim jacket, new-looking jeans, and red cowboy boots. As she got closer, rhinestones along the front pockets of her jeans sparkled in the sunlight. A red turtleneck peeked out above the fashionably worn jacket. She was in front of him before he had time to step from the bus stop. She smiled then looked away. She was several strides past him when he found his voice. "Um, excuse me. I'm looking for LaSalle Street."

She stopped, her thick dark hair swinging forward, skimming her shoulders. "Two blocks west." She pointed away from the river. "I imagine you're headed for the museum; it's two blocks down Main—take a left on Marquette, then right on LaSalle Street."

Her eyes squinted in the sun. He couldn't tell if they were actually gray or just a muted green and wished he had more time to study them. When he couldn't think of a way to keep her there, he simply said, "Thank you."

"You're welcome."

Her scent reminded Trace of rain on a spring morning, and it lingered after she left. He stared at her back until she turned at the next corner, wondering if

14

the town was small enough that he'd see those boots again.

As he stood there getting his bearings, a falcon whistled overhead, bringing his thoughts back to the place he'd just left. The old water tower at the St. Cloud Correctional Facility was a historic landmark that for years had been inhabited by two peregrine falcons. He brushed off the eerie feeling and looked around. What hit him first was color. Two-, three-, and four-story redbrick buildings flanked sidewalks that curved gracefully up the hill to his right and down toward the tea-colored St. Croix River on his left. Streetlamps with frosted pineapple-shaped globes were painted a dark, shiny green. Slate blue, rust, burgundy, and forest green trim surrounded doors and windows of buildings that dated back to the late 1800s. Brass kick plates glinted in the late morning sun. There was nothing accidental about the harmonizing colors. Pine Bluff was a town with a plan.

The corner where he stood seemed to mark the point where the residential area stopped and the business district began. The redbrick buildings south of the intersection housed storefronts on the ground level. Gift shops, boutiques, candy stores, bakeries, cafés, and coffee shops were laid out like a banquet table designed to tempt tourists. As a group of middle-aged women in red hats and purple sweatshirts giggled past him, Trace wondered what the town would be like under a blanket of noise-muffling snow and hoped that winter here meant fewer people and a slower pace.

He looked north, then west, wishing he'd been thinking clearly enough to ask the woman for more specific directions. Though he had no idea how close his apartment building was to the museum, he decided to take the route she'd recommended.

There were no front yards here. Sidewalks butted up to front steps and even foundations. Occasionally a two-foot strip of grass ran like a moat between pavement and building. Clapboard, brick, and stone houses had been built so close together that often they were actually touching. Here, too, color seemed almost overpowering. He'd seen so little of it in the past thirty-six months.

Main Street curved southeast as it ran down the hill, following the contour of the river. Just before turning left on Marquette, he caught a glimpse of the Wisconsin side of the St. Croix, the riverbank thick with pines and dotted with copper and bronze oaks and gold maples. He walked two blocks and turned right. The smell of burning leaves grew stronger with each step, and he looked around for smoke. When he reached the brick row house with a wide front porch, he saw where the smell was coming from.

There were no burning leaves.

A four-foot-wide hole, surrounded by splintered wood and ripped shingles, gaped like an angry sore on the left side of the roof. Below it, a window was shattered and the brick was striped with soot. Judging by the smell of wet, charred wood and the tire tracks on the lawn, the fire had happened only hours ago. Trace pulled out the address he'd memorized and willed the paper to say something different. But the numbers on the paper matched the gold numbers nailed above the porch. 1725 E. LaSalle Street.

This was home.

&

Sydney slipped into the emergency church meeting several minutes late. She'd decided to walk even though she'd been late getting out of the office, and it had turned out to be a pleasant choice. She chastised herself for not taking an extra few minutes to give the man at the bus stop a guided tour to LaSalle Street. It was her job, after all. Though history students from the University of Minnesota were frequent visitors and tourists flowed through Pine Bluff like the St. Croix River itself, most were over sixty or under twenty—and very few took her breath away.

Her thoughts meandered between the man's unbelievably blue eyes and the drone of voices around her. Eighteen members had shown up for the meeting; not bad for a small church on a Saturday morning.

A woman whose husband had died just six months ago volunteered to take in Sara Lewis and her girls. Several people offered to cover the cost of Ron Middleton's stay in a Cambridge hotel for as long as Jessica, his daughter, was in the hospital there. Gwyneth, of course, would stay with Floyd and his wife. Eldon and Mattie offered to let Ronny stay in Sydney's brother's bedroom until Jessica was out of the hospital. He wouldn't be home from college until Thanksgiving. The deaconesses agreed to arrange for meals, and the youth group offered to collect clothing. Eldon reported that he had contacted the insurance agent and arranged for a clean-up company to come in that afternoon to assess the fire, smoke, and water damage and had asked two contractors for estimates.

Quickly and efficiently, Floyd Chapel ticked through each item of business until just one glaring unasked question remained. Sydney stared at the back of her father's head, sure she could read his thoughts, not surprised when he rose to his feet. "Our first parolee will arrive on Monday. He'll need a place to stay."

"Do you know what you're asking, Eldon?" A vein on Floyd's left temple pulsed, and his face seemed to swell as it turned crimson. Sydney looked at her mother, wondering if Floyd was on the verge of needing her expertise in CPR.

Silence descended. Heads turned from Eldon to Floyd and back again.

"Yes, Floyd, I know what I'm asking. I'm asking someone here to open their home to 'the least of these.'"

"That all sounds very kind and generous. . . ." Phyllis Lincoln's poppy orange dress ballooned onto the empty chairs next to her. "We all know Jesus wants us to care for those who are down and out, but not if it means putting our children at risk. Bringing an ex-prisoner into the community is risky enough; asking someone to put him up in their home is ridiculous. And bringing dozens of these men into this little town is simply preposterous. A program like this should be in Minneapolis or St. Paul, not Pine Bluff."

The woman sat back, her arms folding across her ample chest.

Sydney leaned forward to stare at the veteran Sunday school teacher. Phyllis Lincoln had taught her "Jesus Loves Me" and "The B-I-B-L-E," and Sydney had the utmost respect for her commitment and knowledge, but at the moment she wanted to deck the woman. *Good thing nobody told God not to do anything to put* His *child at risk.*

"We do have to be wise and cautious, Phyllis, but we also have to go on faith that God led us to offer this man our support and a place to start over and that He will protect us."

The flesh above Phyllis's elbow jiggled as she wagged her finger at Sydney. "In a perfect world, that would be true. But facts are facts, and the truth of the matter is that people in this church are letting their views be known by letting the offering plate pass them by. If we don't do something about it soon, there won't *be* a Sanctuary program. We won't even be able to pay our electric bill!"

"But—" Sydney swallowed her response when Floyd's clipboard banged the table.

"We've voiced all these feelings months ago." The vein on the side of Floyd's head pulsed. "The vote to implement this program was a close one, and many of us are thinking that the fire is God's way of making it crystal clear that this is simply not His will. I think it's time to put it to another vote."

Amid murmurings of agreement and whispers of dissent, Eldon Jennet stood up. His demeanor quieted the room. "Or," he said, smiling his disarming smile, "it may just be that we are being presented with an opportunity to serve in a whole different way—not at arm's length." His gaze swept the room and landed on Mattie. After a quick glance in Sydney's direction, Eldon turned back to Floyd.

"My wife and I will take him in."

A small gasp escaped Mattie Jennet's lips before her hand slid over her mouth.

৪৩

Movement drew Trace's eyes from the broken window to the porch. A man in bib overalls stood with his back to Trace, rocking rhythmically back and forth as if in a trance. Trace walked up the sidewalk and two wooden steps. "Hello!"

The figure continued to sway. Trace walked closer. "Excuse me!"

"Land o' Goshen!" The man jumped back, hands in the air. The first thing Trace noticed was the watering can in the man's right hand. The second thing he noticed was that the man was a woman. A miniature woman with a face like a shriveled apple and silver hair so thin and wispy her pink scalp showed through.

"I'm sorry. I didn't mean to scare you." Trace held out his hand. "I'm Trace McKay. I was supposed to move into one of the apartments here."

She didn't take his hand. Her eyes narrowed. "So you're one of the outlaws, huh?"

Trace stared at the woman, unsure if he should laugh or be offended. "I'm one of the men in the reentry program."

The woman snorted. "Just a whitewashed way to say ex-con. Guess we're neighbors, then. I'm Mrs. Chapel. Call me Gwyneth."

"Glad to meet you, Gwyneth."

The narrowed gaze studied him. "One of my best friends spent some time behind bars. Levi Tate. . . Got arrested on this very porch for stealing the blacksmith's horse; maybe right where you're standing. Just two days ago he was telling me about that day, all because of you."

"Me?"

"Just because some people can't see Levi doesn't mean he doesn't hear things. With all the hullabaloo about the church taking in outlaws—"

"I'm not an—"

Around the corner of the building, someone was singing. The woman turned. "Ronny! Come meet one of the outlaws."

She stepped toward the porch railing, giving Trace a full view of the red geraniums she'd been carefully watering. . .the red *plastic* geraniums.

Chapter 3

Trace looked over the little woman's white head, anxious to connect with someone who wasn't a few crayons short of a box. What he saw was a husky boy in his teens with blond hair that swirled in every direction. In the boy's arms was a brown and white lop-eared rabbit. Stepping onto the porch, the boy held out the animal, and Trace had no choice but to take it. It was soft and warm in his hands.

Trace's hope of talking to someone with more clarity than Gwyneth Chapel disappeared when he looked into the boy's eyes. "That's my other mouse," the boy said.

"Um. . .that's a rabbit," Trace said gently.

"Yup. And he's Mouse, too."

"A mouse is little. Rabbits are big."

"Yup. My other mouse is bigger."

Gwyneth reached out to pet the rabbit. Her hand looked like crumpled tissue paper. "Hi, Mouse," she crooned.

Trace looked from her to the boy, wondering for a split second if he hadn't been better off behind bars.

"Are you living here now?" he asked Gwyneth.

"Well, yes and no. I'm sleeping at my son's house, I guess. Don't seem to have a choice in the matter, though if they think I'm staying there permanent, they got another thing coming. All my things are here, but the smoke from the fire is all over everything. The fumes could kill you, you know. I told Mordecai to give up that pipe. But it really doesn't matter, I guess. You can only die once, you know."

Trace stared at her, blinked twice, but the picture didn't change. Looking down at the rabbit, he gazed into clear red eyes. Visions of *Alice in Wonderland* leaped into his head. Maybe the rabbit could tell him what to do next. He handed the animal back to the boy.

"Can either of you tell me how to get to Pineview Community Church?"

Gwyneth nodded. "Mattie goes there. So does my son. Can't say as it's done him any good. It's just down the road from the pastor's house."

"Do you know how to get to the pastor's house?"

"It's on the street with those pine trees that grow straight up like telephone poles."

Trace pulled an envelope out of his pocket. "Jefferson Street. Can you tell me how to get to Jefferson Street?"

"Can't say as I can. Ronny, do you know how to get to Mattie's church?"

Ronny nodded. "In Mattie's van."

As Trace looked from the boy with the red-eyed "mouse" to the little woman's crinkled cheeks, the absurdity of it all suddenly hit and he started to laugh. Easy, natural. . .and free, something he hadn't done for a long, long time. Without knowing or seeming to care what was so funny, Gwyneth and Ronny joined in.

After wiping his eyes with the back of his hand, Trace pulled the letter out of its envelope. "Do you know Eldon Jennet?"

Gwyneth smiled, showing a gap between two teeth. "That's Mattie's husband."

"That's Syd'ey's dad," Ronny added.

"Can you tell me where he lives or works?"

"Eldon doesn't work," Gwyneth answered. "He's a writer."

Eldon Jennet would love to hear that.

"He grows rabbits, too," Ronny added. "That's sorta work, I guess. That's where my Mouse comed from."

"Where does he live?"

"In that white house with the green roof," Gwyneth said.

Trace pressed his lips together. "Well, it was nice to meet you both. I think I'll go back to town now." He waved and stepped down to the sidewalk.

Gwyneth picked up her watering can.

"I know where Syd'ey works," Ronny said.

"Cindy? Who's Cindy?"

"She's. . .she's. . .Eldon is her dad."

"Where does she work?"

"In the place with the red door."

"O–kay. . .I'll go look for Cindy in the place with the red door. Thanks." Trace took two more steps down the sidewalk when he heard the boy's voice behind him once again.

"Mouse and me will show you."

<p style="text-align:center">&

Sydney stood just inside the back door of the church next to her mother, waiting for her father to finish his conversation in Pastor Owen's office. After glancing at her watch, she tapped the toe of one red boot on the carpet. "If he doesn't get done pretty quick, you'll have to do lunch without me. I told Colleen I'd be back at the office by noon."

Her mother nodded, but the straight line of her lips and the way her eyes burned a hole into the paneling made Sydney wonder if she'd heard a word. Mattie Jennet leaned against the wall, highlighted hair tousled, arms folded, legs crossed at the ankles, and under-eye circles proclaiming her lack of sleep. Sydney knew exactly what she was thinking. The same thoughts were buzzing in her head.

After a few more minutes, a door opened down the hall and Eldon came walking toward them. He stopped two feet away, looking like a puppy caught chewing a slipper. He lifted both hands in surrender. "I know, I know. . ."

"Do you?" Mattie uncrossed her arms and legs and straightened up like an officer addressing a private, even though she was a full foot shorter than the man she was nailing with her eyes. "I keep thinking of Floyd's question—'Do you know what you're asking, Eldon?' Do you? You've got a single daughter to think of—and a wife, for that matter. We don't have a guest room, we only have one bathroom, we—"

When Eldon put his large hands on his wife's shoulders, the hardness in his wife's eyes softened. It was a phenomenon Sydney had noted often. It seemed as if her father's touch, or a quiet word, had a way of melting her mother against her will. It stirred a longing in Sydney. *Lord, I want that someday.* And then, as always, she repeated her vow to be patient and wait for the man God would bring her. . .someday.

"I can't explain it," Eldon said. "I just felt the Lord reminding me of what I'd just said: 'Whatever you did for one of the least of these brothers of mine, you did for me.' I know it looks like a rash thing to do, but I think it's a faith step. I'm going to ask you two to trust me on this."

Mattie nodded, appearing resigned, if not totally convinced. Sydney agreed with even less conviction. Her father pulled her into a three-way hug. "We're not even sure this will be allowed. Owen left a message at the correctional center; they're trying to contact the person who makes these decisions. Maybe we're concerned over nothing. Let's talk it through over pizza. Do you have enough time?" He looked at Sydney with apologetic eyes when she shook her head no.

"Then we'll drop you off at the chamber and bring you lunch." He ran his knuckles across her cheek. "We'll get through this, Syd."

&

Sydney walked in the back door of the chamber of commerce building, hung her coat on a hook, and poured decaf and French vanilla creamer into her tan mug with the face of a cocker spaniel on the side. She walked up behind Colleen, who was talking with both hands, as usual, waving brochures in the air with her pudgy arms as if she were conducting an orchestra. Her black pageboy hair swung in time to her gestures. On the opposite side of the counter stood John Nelson, town chairman and owner of the Ben Franklin store, still known by locals as the Five and Dime, though nothing but gumballs had been sold for less than a quarter in forty years.

Sydney winked at John and mimed every move Colleen made until John couldn't hold back his laugh.

Colleen stuck her nose in the air. "You and that feisty lady with the red boots had best remember that you're not paying me for this, John."

While appearing to restrain his grin, John's balding head nodded. "The town is forever indebted to you, Mrs. Hatcher."

Sydney nudged her friend's rounded left hip. "Go home and feed your kids, whiner, unless you want to get stuck helping me with posters for Pumpkin Fest." To John she said, "As the Chamber Gold Sponsor of the Month, John, you need to be aware that Mrs. Hatcher here only volunteers so she'll get an invite to our New Year's Eve party. Pathetic, isn't it?"

The door behind John opened, and Ronny walked in carrying his new rabbit. Behind him was a man in a navy blue jacket. . .a man with impossibly blue eyes. John nodded to all of them, said he'd let the women get back to their work, and left.

Ronny stepped toward the counter with the man behind him. Colleen whispered good-bye then leaned close to Sydney's ear. "Yum."

You can say that again. She tore her gaze away from the man's, taking in details she'd missed when she met him on the street. He was about three inches taller than she was, maybe touching six feet. His hair was so short she couldn't define the color, but he carried the style off nicely. She extended her hand to the man, surprised at the softness of his hand. Though he wasn't tanned, he had the look of someone who'd spent a lot of time outdoors. "Sydney Jennet, chamber director. Welcome, again, to Pine Bluff."

ᛒᏉ

He no longer believed in coincidence. This was Providence. It took willpower to let go of Sydney Jennet's hand. "Trace McKay. Thank you, again."

"Ronny is our official tourist greeter. I hope he and Mouse have been helpful." She winked as she said the last word.

Trace smiled and returned the wink, surprised at how natural it felt to enter "the dance." Mouse. That was the rabbit's name? "Ronny's been very helpful."

"Are you just visiting?"

She was the daughter of the man heading the reentry program, but clearly she didn't know who *he* was; that was awkward. But then again, he could have fun with it.

"No. Actually, I'm hoping to find a job and stick around for a while."

"Wonderful. I can give you a list of hotels, rental properties, and real estate and tell you a bit about the area if you're interested. Just ask and I'll try to answer."

Trace felt his pulse quicken. He was rusty at this, but it certainly appeared as though she was flirting with him. Not brazenly, just in a light and teasing way. *"Just ask,"* she'd said. *Hmm. . .* "I guess if I'm going to live here, I need to know everything."

Sydney Jennet opened a brochure and spread it on the counter. It was a full-color map of the town with every business labeled. "Where should I start? Shopping? Tourist attractions? Businesses that might be hiring? Schools? Do you have a family?"

Was she hoping the answer was no?

"No."

She smiled. Trace almost expected her to say, "Good."

"Well, let me point out—"

Ronny waved his hand between them. "I'm going home, 'kay?"

Sydney Jennet smiled and reached out to stroke the rabbit's head. "If you wait a bit, I'll share my lunch with you. Why don't you and Mouse take a short walk?"

" 'Kay." He walked out the front door.

"Where was I?" Smile lines fanned out from the corners of enormous gray-green eyes. "I guess I was pointing out the main attractions. Over here on the north end of Main. . ."

Trace listened for the next ten minutes, asking questions about the history of Pine Bluff and how the demographics changed with the seasons. She was just getting to a list of hotels and bed-and-breakfasts when the door opened behind him. Sydney looked up from her brochures and smiled at the tall, middle-aged man who walked in with a cardboard pizza box in his hand. "Hi, Dad."

So this was Eldon Jennet, the man in charge of Trace's immediate future. Trace held out his hand, ready to introduce himself, when Sydney did the honors. She remembered his name.

Eldon Jennet was obviously caught off guard. "Mr. McKay. . .welcome to Pine Bluff. I don't know how we mixed. . . Well, I imagine you're wondering where you're going to be staying."

"I'm on it, Dad." Sydney pointed to the lodging brochures fanned out on the counter.

"You're on it?" Mr. Jennet appeared immensely amused. "Then you've already told Mr. McKay that he's going to be living in our basement for a few weeks?"

The shock on Sydney Jennet's face was a look Trace was sure he would never forget as long as he lived.

Chapter 4

Where is he?" Sydney's stage whisper carried above the whistling teapot.

Mattie turned around and pointed toward the basement door.

"It's a mess down there." Sydney hung her jacket on a hook. "A cot in a cold, smelly basement can't be any better than a cell."

Mattie dropped four tea bags into a lime green ceramic pot and closed the lid. "We'll fix it up."

Sydney kicked her boots toward the back door and reached into the cupboard for a mug. "I smell chamomile. Is that to calm my nerves or yours?"

"Both."

"You and Dad get anything settled over lunch?"

Mattie sighed. "Anything we settled got undone when we found out the guy was already here. Nobody seems to know how that happened; some glitch in the system our taxes pay for. Anyway, there's not much to talk about now. We'll make do."

"I talked to Colleen on the way home. She said I could bunk with one of the kids for a few weeks. He can have my room."

"We're not going to uproot you because of our decision."

"*Our* decision? You didn't have anything to say about it!"

Mattie shrugged and gave a straight-line smile. "It's the one-flesh thing, honey. After thirty-four years you take responsibility for each other's actions."

Steam rose from the tea that Sydney poured into two mugs and carried to the table. When something crashed in the basement, tea splashed over the edge of both cups. "Where's Dad putting him? Under the ping-pong table?"

"Ronny's helping; that could explain the noise. They took the table down and they're clearing a space for the cot and a chair." Mattie's fingers drummed the sides of her cup. "Hey, guess I don't have to do my Sanctuary rounds tomorrow."

Sydney smiled. "That's seeing the glass half full. Instead of a ten-minute visit at each apartment, you get two tenants living with you. Much easier that way."

"You have Wright Avenue this week?"

"Wright *and* State Street. Audrey's not doing well with her fibromyalgia, so I told her I'd cover both buildings." She sighed and rubbed the back of her neck. "I'm getting a bit swamped with Christmas stuff at the office."

"Already?"

Sydney nodded. "As soon as the craft fair is over, it'll be nonstop. The cookie walk, tree lighting ceremony, breakfast with Santa, Christmas Comes to Pine Bluff...I love my job." The sound of shattering glass rose from the basement, and both women cringed. "What else have you found out about him?"

"Not much. He doesn't seem to be the talkative type. We should probably quit calling him 'him.' He has a name."

"Kind of a cool one. It's different."

"He's been exceptionally polite, but I think he's really uncomfortable with this arrangement."

"At least that gives us some common ground. This is going to be beyond awkward." Sydney hid behind her mug. "He's not what I pictured."

"He's not hard to look at, is he?" Mattie's left eyebrow arched. "Hmm..."

"Not a chance. I thought your standards for a man for me were even higher than mine."

Mattie lifted her mug and tapped it against Sydney's. Her eyes sparkled with the laugh she was stifling. "They get lower as time goes on."

"You're despicable."

"Seriously, he seems like a genuinely nice guy."

"With a record."

Mattie set down her mug and fixed her eyes on her daughter. "Don't let that define him in your mind, Syd. We're going to be living under the same roof. Give him a—" Mattie turned toward the sound of footsteps on the basement stairs.

Ronny was taking one deliberate step at a time, holding Mouse in one hand and the railing in the other. "Mattie, me and Mouse are going to see the other rabbits. He misses his friends."

"Just close the barn door when you're done."

Eldon Jennet ducked to clear the doorway; the man behind him just cleared it. Sydney gripped her mug as she looked up at Trace McKay. He was wearing one of her father's faded blue T-shirts, one that Sydney had just washed and folded the day before. It occurred to her that he'd been carrying a half-full paper bag under his arm when he came into the chamber office. Was that all he had with him? She stood and offered the men coffee, needing to do something to busy her hands. Trace nodded and said, "Please," the left side of his mouth lifting slightly more than the right, revealing a dimple. A scar dented the right side of his upper lip. Eyes that had appeared a deep blue when he was wearing his jacket now seemed to reflect the dusty shade of the faded shirt.

Sydney walked around the island in the middle of the kitchen and took two more mugs down from the cupboard. Her hands were clammy, and she began to wonder if she'd remembered deodorant in her rush to get dressed before the meeting. Two hours earlier she'd bantered back and forth with this man with breezy confidence. Now, knowing who he was and what he'd done and that she was going to be passing him in the hall in her bathrobe with bed head and a naked face, she couldn't think of a thing to say, witty or otherwise. She filled the cups, set them in front of the men at the table, and said the only thing that came to her mind. "Cream or sugar?"

"Black is fine. Thank you." He made eye contact with her until she sat down.

All four kitchen chairs were filled, just the way they'd been before her brother, Zack, had left for college. It was familiar and comfortable yet frighteningly strange at the same time. *Somebody say something!*

"Your dad says you're a runner."

With those smoky eyes fixed on her again, it took a sip of tea for Sydney to comprehend the question. "Yes. I get a little lazy once it starts getting cold, though."

"She ran her fourth marathon in June," Eldon said.

Trace cocked his head just slightly to the side. His bottom lip pressed against the top one, pushing it out a fraction. Both eyebrows rose in a look that communicated he was impressed. "Grandma's Marathon?"

It struck Sydney as odd that he knew, as if being in prison should have isolated him from all news of the outside world. She nodded.

"I guess if you're crazy enough to run in June, Duluth is the place to do it. Did you run the Twin Cities?"

"No. That first weekend in October is crazy around here with fall colors at their peak. The day of the Twin Cities Marathon is our biggest tourist day of the whole year. I ran it once before I was director of the chamber, though."

"What do you think about for twenty-six miles?"

Mattie sputtered, clamping her napkin over her mouth.

"*Mom. . .*" There was warning in Sydney's voice.

"You okay?" Eldon asked. When Mattie nodded, he asked, "What was that all about?"

Sydney could feel Trace McKay's amused gaze even though her eyes were locked on her mother's mischievous grin.

"I asked her the same question after her first marathon," Mattie offered.

Trace's dimple deepened. "And. . . ?" He looked at Sydney and not her mother for an answer.

"And I was twenty-one at the time."

"And. . . ?"

"And I said I was admiring certain. . .aspects. . .of God's male creation as they ran in front of me."

Amazingly, the dimple got even deeper. "Being able to appreciate nature is a gift."

"Would anyone like a cookie?" Sydney turned toward the island and grabbed the rooster cookie jar, wondering what she'd do next if it were empty.

"Yes!" Eldon answered a bit too emphatically, pulling the head off the rooster before Sydney set it down. Taking a handful, he pushed the jar toward Trace. "Snickerdoodle?"

Trace took a cinnamon-covered cookie and stared at it, then held it up to his nose and closed his eyes. "Heaven," he said, his eyes still closed, "probably smells like this." He took a bite, chewing slowly. When he opened his eyes, Sydney half expected to see tears in them. Instead, his lip tipped up on the left. "I don't know how to thank you for making a place for me here." He turned to Mattie. "I know it's an inconvenience. I'll help out wherever I can; just hand me a dish towel or a spatula."

In unison, Mattie and Sydney said, "You *cook*?"

"I may have a relearning curve, but I've been on my own since I was sixteen, so it was pretty much cook or starve. I was a galley cook on a riverboat one summer. As far as I know, there wasn't a single case of food poisoning."

Eldon rested his hand on Trace's shoulder. "You're making me look bad, boy. The joke with these women is that I haven't figured out how to open a raw egg yet."

Mattie shook her head. "It's not a joke. In his defense, however, he makes some mean maple syrup." The phone rang, and she jumped up to answer it, then handed it to Eldon. "It's the correctional center." Eldon took the phone into the living room.

Mattie tapped the palms of her hands together. "Well, let's see. . .what's next? Guess I'll go get hamburger out of the freezer."

Leaving Sydney alone with *him*. Once again, her brain malfunctioned, and once again, he took the lead. "If it's not good news, I may need to get all that hotel info from you."

"What would keep them from approving this?"

Several seconds passed. A slow smile tilted his mouth and fanned thin lines from the corners of his deep-set eyes. "You."

"*Me?*" Sydney leaned forward, squeezing her mug.

"Well, me, living in the same house with a single woman."

"But you're not a—" *Open mouth. Insert foot.*

"No, I'm not. But some things are just standard. And then again, it may depend completely on who your dad talks to. If he gets some official in the middle of a golf game, he may okay anything."

"They approved of you living in the apartment building, and there would have been a single mom with two little girls downstairs from you. They had to have checked that out."

"They would have. That gives me some hope."

Silence. Sydney stared at her cold tea. The first few questions that came to her mind had to be discarded. *So what did they feed you in prison? Did you get that little scar on your lip while you were there? How, exactly, did you accidentally kill someone?*

"What kind of work did you do before. . ." *Just say it, make it seem natural.* ". . .you were in prison?"

"I was working on a Great Lakes freighter. I dropped out of high school at sixteen and got a job on the Mississippi. When I was eighteen I got hired by a company in Duluth that helped me get my GED and then paid my tuition at the Chapman's School of Seamanship in Stuart, Florida."

"They must have seen a lot of potential in you." *And then you let them down and now I just pointed it out. . . . Dumb.*

Trace's expression seemed to reflect Sydney's thoughts. "Yeah, I guess they did. One of the owners kind of adopted me. After I got my captain's license, I spent a couple of years working for a transatlantic company, making regular runs from Jacksonville, Florida, to the Mediterranean. I logged a lot of hours and learned just about everything there is to know about the workings of a ship. I'd just gotten my thousand-ton license, and I'd been back with the Duluth company for about six months, just weeks away from commanding my own cargo vessel, when. . .everything changed."

"Will you go back to it?"

His gaze dropped to the floor then rose to meet Sydney's. "As a felon, I may have trouble getting my license reinstated. That decision will be up to the Coast Guard. On top of that, I'd have to get approval to cross state lines. Can't jump ship every time we cross into Wisconsin." He smiled, but the pain in his eyes was piercing.

"I know several men from town who work on the St. Croix. I'm sure it's not as exciting as the Great Lakes or the Mississippi, but I could check on job openings if that's something you'd be interested in."

"Right now I'd take a job at McDonald's. Your dad is confident that the church will hire me to help with the reconstruction at the apartment building, but that won't last long. I've got the training to be a harbor pilot. I'd even be happy on a tour boat crew. I just want to get back on a boat."

"I'll see what I can find out."

Eldon walked in and gave Trace a thumbs-up. "It's tentative. Have to wait until the powers that be make an official decision sometime next week, but the lady I talked to didn't seem to think it would be a problem with you staying here for a few weeks."

"Thank you. Is this. . .going to be any kind of risk for you? Are people going to be down on you for taking me in? I guess what I'm asking is what caused that fire. Seems a little too coincidental."

With a tired sigh, Eldon sat back in his chair. "No one's discounting that possibility. There have been opposing voices, but I know these people, and I honestly think they're just that—voices. I don't think any of them is capable of arson. My gut feeling is that it was outdated wiring. We should have the fire chief's report by the end of the week. To answer your original question, no, this isn't posing any kind of threat to us. What I can't be sure of is how you'll be treated in this town. It would be easier to blend in during the summer; Pine

Bluff can be a cliquey little semi–ghost town in the winter."

Sydney's eyes must have shown her surprise. She'd inherited her critical nature from her mother; Eldon's cynical words were out of character. "I'm just trying to tell it like it is," he said.

Trace reached for his third cookie. "I understand. I'm hoping to earn respect in this town."

As Sydney stood and walked toward the coffeepot, nothing came to mind that she could voice. Pine Bluff was a tight-knit community where just about everyone was related to someone. Trace McKay had no idea how hard it might be to earn respect.

So Sydney kept her thoughts to herself, and it was her father who filled the silence. "With that attitude, I think you will."

Chapter 5

W onderful supper." Stuart Hatcher set his plate in the sink and picked up his keys.

Colleen shut the faucet off and lifted her face for his kiss. "Syd made the lemon bars."

"You've outdone yourself, Syd."

"So you're not sick of me yet?"

Stuart laughed. "Hmm...let me think...built-in babysitter, someone to keep my woman company so I can have guy time, dessert every night... I'll let you know when you've worn out your welcome." He took his jacket off the doorknob. "So what are my wives up to tonight?"

Colleen set a box labeled SCRAPBOOK SUPPLIES on the kitchen table. "Darning your socks and ironing your shirts, dear."

"That's a good little harem." The door to the garage squeaked as he opened it, whined again as he closed it, still in the kitchen. "You going to be hiding out here Saturday night, Syd?"

Sydney picked up a glass from the counter and slid it into the suds-filled sink. Did he really have to put it like that? "I'll watch the kids, if that's what you're asking."

"Actually, I had something else in mind."

"Such as?"

"Snickerdoodles."

A tiny ripple of queasiness wormed through Sydney's middle. "Snickerdoodles?"

"Yeah. I invited this new guy in town to come over and play pool."

ॐ

Hospital. Resale shop. Snickerdoodles.

The list circled Sydney's head as she drove home from work on Saturday afternoon. Wet brown leaves covered the road. The sky was blackening, promising yet more of the drizzle that had fallen all morning. In spite of the things she needed to cross off her list before the end of the day, her foot barely touched the accelerator. She wondered what she'd say if she got ticketed for driving too slow.

Lights were on in the house when she pulled into her driveway, even though it was just after one. Through the window, she could see her mother setting the table for lunch. The television cast a blue glow on the walls of the living room. Fall was her favorite time of year. Cozy, homey...gearing up for the holidays.

But it couldn't be homey with a stranger under her roof.

Something had to give. She couldn't be "hiding out" at Colleen's every night. She had an excuse this week—Stuart, who coached wrestling at the high school, had a string of meetings this week, and she kept Colleen company while he was gone. But next week. . .well, she could always find work to do at the office.

The way Stuart portrayed it, you'd think she hadn't been home at all in the past five days. That wasn't exactly true. Monday night she'd had dinner at home. . .and Trace had helped her with dishes. Why didn't he watch football like most men?

He'd been polite, interested in the family, the town, what Sydney did for fun. Nothing about him hinted that he'd been in prison for three years. Maybe that was exactly what was making her so uneasy. If he were an angry, hardened, tattoo-plastered ex-con, the boundaries would be clearly defined. But Trace McKay was none of those things. Trace McKay was a regular guy—maybe a few steps up from regular.

ဆ

"I don't want you going alone."

Sydney stared at her father, bristling at his words yet touched by the concern in his eyes. She didn't want to go alone either. "I'll have Ronny with me."

"You know what I mean."

"Jessica's expecting us. I'll be fine." She held out her hand for the keys to her father's truck. "Anything else you want me to get at Goodwill?"

"Just a bed and a lamp." The keys were still in his hand.

"Dad. I'll be fine."

"It may hit you harder than you think. If Mom and I didn't have to be at—"

"I'll go with her."

Sydney whirled at the voice behind her. Her father smiled. "Thanks. I'd appreciate it."

The keys passed Sydney's outstretched palm. . .and landed in Trace's.

ဆ

The handle on the truck door was smooth and cold. Trace's hand pressed around it as he gazed along the driver's side of the dark blue GMC Sierra. He opened the door for Ronny, who eyed him as he had all week, with curious caution. The screen door whined and he heard Sydney's footsteps.

"I don't mind driving," she said for the second time as she rounded the tailgate.

Trace's glance took her in, from the shoulder-length brown hair tickling her face in the breeze to the short denim jacket over a red hooded sweatshirt and well-worn jeans tucked into cowboy boots. The reconnaissance took only seconds but produced a smile. "Neither do I."

He liked the feel of keys in his pocket again—another reminder of freedom even though it wasn't his truck and it wasn't his town. He got in and waited for her to open the passenger door, thinking she probably had enough spunk to refuse to ride with him. She took her time. *Are you making a statement, Sydney Rose?* He played the name in his head. He'd read it on her nameplate at the chamber of commerce office. Sydney Rose Jennet. Did anyone call her that?

When she got in, her smile looked painful. Trace put the key in the ignition and stared at her. "I'm not sensing a lot of faith here."

"About those relearning curves you mentioned..."

"That's only for cooking. Driving a car is like riding a bike; you never forget."

Sydney latched her seat belt and pulled it tight. "How long has it been since you've driven?"

Two years, eleven months, twelve days, and about eighteen hours. "Not quite three years," he said.

She looked at him for only a moment before nodding and pulling what appeared to be a grocery list out of her jacket pocket. As she studied it with more intensity than a grocery list deserved, she said, "Turn left out of the driveway."

He still hadn't turned the key. With his fingers on it and his eyes fixed on the shed in front of the truck, he said, "You're safe with me, Sydney." He meant it in every way she could possibly take it.

☙

No, no, no. I am so, so not safe with you. It took the first mile and a half to regulate her pulse; then Sydney stole a quick look at his profile. He might not have drawn her attention in a crowd, not unless he'd smiled at her or momentarily fixed his eyes on her. It wasn't the way he looked so much as the way he looked *at her* that was causing her synapses to misfire.

But there were things about him that were flat-out annoying, too. She'd seen flashes of arrogance. Refusing to give her the keys and the "You're safe with me" line fit into that category. And was he being sarcastic when he said he wasn't sensing a lot of faith? Jabbing at her Christianity? Where did the guy stand on God anyway? Her father would know the answer to that by now; he'd spent a week with Trace. And while she was on the subject of her father, her extremely overprotective father, why in the world had he put her in this position, essentially alone with a man who was at best a stranger, at worst... She couldn't let her mind touch the terrifying possibilities.

Ronny's hand shot over the middle of the front seat. "There's Mattie's church."

Trace nodded. "Nice and close."

Sydney glanced at him then back at the complex of white clapboard buildings. "It's a good walking distance."

"Or in your case, running, I imagine."

"Sometimes. Hard to make good time in stilettos, though."

Trace laughed. "I'd pay to see that."

"Were you raised in a church?"

"Nope. I can count on one hand the times I've been inside one." He proceeded to do just that. "My grandpa's funeral, a funeral for a kid who got hit by a car when I was in fourth grade, and three friends' weddings. I was best man for two, so I guess if you count rehearsals, I'd need both hands."

So he wasn't a Christian yet. That explained why he hadn't gone to church with them last Sunday. He'd been recommended by a chaplain with Prison Fellowship Ministries; the pastor must have seen a glimmer of hope in Trace. Sydney had a responsibility here.

Lord, grant me the right words. "We have two services tomorrow, at nine and eleven. You're welcome to join us."

He didn't answer. Sydney watched the clock change from 2:48 to 2:49. "I didn't mean to be pushy. I just wanted you to know we'd love to have you. Maybe it would be easier to wait until after you've had a chance to meet some of—"

"What service do you go to?"

She took a moment, hoping to sound casual. "We're there for both, but I teach Sunday school and Mom and Dad are on the worship team during the first."

"Then I'll go to the second."

Sydney hoped her exhale wasn't as loud as it sounded in her head. They passed a sign for the Pine Bluff Feed Mill.

"How many people live in this town?"

"Four thousand seven hundred ninety-nine year-round residents. Closer to five thousand during tourist season."

"Four thousand seven hundred *ninety-nine*? Couldn't they have rounded it up so you could put forty-eight hundred on the population sign?"

"Actually, our population sign needs updating. It reads four thousand seven hundred thirty-seven, but there will actually be forty-eight hundred Pine Bluffians on Tuesday when Amy Monroe has her C-section, unless someone beats her to it."

Trace turned his head slowly to look at her. "Is that part of your job—knowing everybody's business?"

"No, it's just one of the perks."

"I see. Other than keeping tabs on the residents and giving directions to strangers at bus stops, what does a chamber of commerce director do?"

"I conduct monthly meetings, write newsletters, welcome new businesses to town, solicit members, attend grand openings, cut ribbons, work on innovative ways to get businesses networking, update the Web site, pay bills, plan the annual fund-raiser, help run Clean-Up Day. . ." She stopped for a breath and to stare at Trace's smile.

"I'm almost sorry I asked."

"Oh, that's just the tip of my iceberg. I also dictate four thousand seven hundred ninety-nine social lives."

Tilting his head slightly to the left, he glanced at her. "I'm sure they're indebted to you for that. So what occupies Pine Bluff society all year?"

Exaggerating her professional voice, she began a rundown. "The year begins with an ice-sculpting contest at Founders' Park; then we have the Valentine's Day two-dinners-for-the-price-of-one specials at all area restaurants, the Easter egg hunt, Mother's Day style show, City-wide Cleanup, Fourth of July parade, Maxwell Street Days, holiday craft fair, Pumpkin Fest, and more Christmas festivities than you'd really care to hear about."

"Wow. Somehow I pictured you just handing out Welcome Wagon baskets or something. Sounds more like you run this town."

"I leave a few details for the mayor. It makes him feel useful."

"That's generous of you."

They rode in silence for several minutes, accompanied by Ronny's off-key humming. Trace stopped at a crossroad, then shifted smoothly from first to second gear. Sydney watched his knuckles whiten as he shifted, accelerated, and shifted again. He held it at fifty, but the sense of power under control reminded Sydney of a racehorse at the starting gate. "It's fifty-five along here, and there isn't another crossroad for four miles. It's a pretty quiet stretch of road."

He glanced at her with a gleam in his eyes. "Are you tempting me to break the conditions of my parole?"

"Of course not; I'm merely giving you the facts on this part of the county."

Trace laughed and added pressure to the accelerator. "I don't know, woman; you go from being afraid to get in the truck with me to begging for a thrill ride."

Sydney smiled but didn't answer as she watched the speedometer climb over sixty.

A gasp rose from the backseat. "You're breaking the law!"

Trace grinned and eased on the brake. "It was fun while it lasted," he muttered. He set the cruise control. "I've missed that." His voice was almost reverent.

"Driving or speeding?"

"Both. But my speeding days are over."

"It'll do ninety." Sydney looked at him then back at the windshield. "That's a confession, not a suggestion."

"Kinda figured you were the lead-foot type. The red boots are a dead giveaway."

Sydney bit down on the inside of her bottom lip. "We'll be going south on 35 to Cambridge." Out of the corner of her eye, she saw Ronny begin to rock back and forth. This was his second trip this week to visit his sister. He'd come home agitated and full of questions after the first. Sydney reached between the seats and set her hand on his knee. Until they reached the hospital, she'd focus her attention on him, grateful for the reprieve.

34

Her discomfort with Trace McKay was fading far too quickly.

ဆ

The smell. She'd been bracing for it on the elevator ride to the third floor, telling herself that this time she wouldn't let it get to her. This time she'd stay calm and focused and smile for Jessica.

It didn't work. As always, the smell wrapped around her, covering her face like a clinging blanket, like being wrapped in filmy plastic. The harder you breathe, the tighter it clings.

She'd been here many times since she'd occupied a bed here. To attend burn support group meetings, to visit children at the request of her doctor. And every time, she fought the smell, fought the flashbacks. Maybe it was harder this time because she knew the little girl with her leg wrapped in gauze. Maybe it was harder because of the man who walked beside her, his hand just barely touching the small of her back as she stepped close to Jessica's bed. She felt his eyes searching her face, making her wonder just how visible her panic was.

"Hi, Jess. How are you?" She bent and kissed the top of the girl's forehead.

"The medicine makes it not hurt so much. Did they have medicine when you were in the hospital?"

Sydney laughed, making eye contact with Trace. "Yes, even way back then they had medicine."

"They took skin off my one leg and put it on the other. It looks kinda like waffles."

Waffles. Sydney's throat tightened. She knew exactly how that looked. The technology that turned a piece of skin into mesh that would stretch over twice the amount of space was incredible. But the scars it left were unmistakable. Would Jessica have the courage to wear shorts? A bathing suit? Would she accept it or let it unravel her sense of self? Sydney vowed to do all that she could not to let that happen. "Isn't it wonderful how doctors know how to do that?" She hoped her smile hid all that was churning inside her. "We brought you something."

"Really?" Jessica's face lit with a smile that crinkled her nose.

Sydney pointed to the bag in Ronny's hand. "You can give it to her now."

Ronny held out the bag. "It's a rabbit. But just a stuffed rabbit. Syd'ey put a bandage on his leg so he could be your friend."

ဆ

Trace had assumed he'd just be waiting in the car. But Sydney had invited him to come and meet the little girl who'd been burned. As he followed Sydney and Ronny into the hospital atrium, it ripped at him to think that in some twisted way he might be responsible for this little girl's pain. Was it arson? Was someone trying to keep him out of Pine Bluff?

They turned toward the elevators, and Sydney pushed the button. Her hand was shaking. She smiled at Ronny over her shoulder, but Trace wasn't buying the cheeriness. What had happened to her?

He'd seen the scar. She wore her sleeves long, but there were times, like now when she reached for the button, that a bumpy ridge showed just above the bones of her wrist. And he hadn't seen her yet without a turtleneck. How extensive was it, and what horror had she gone through?

The smell hit him first when they stepped off on the third floor. He'd worked with a guy years ago who'd been horrifically burned. The smell of the burn unit was one you didn't forget.

For the next half hour he studied her, sensing her gaining victory over past demons as she concentrated on Jessica. When Ronny and Jessica's father showed up unexpectedly and offered to take Ronny with him, Trace knew the exact moment Sydney realized she'd be alone with him on the ride home. He saw a flash of fear, another emotion she reined in with lightning speed.

Somehow he was going to make her trust him.

Chapter 6

Hi, Lorraine. We're looking for a bed."

It wasn't until that moment, when the Goodwill store manager's trifocal gaze went from her to Trace and back again, that Sydney actually thought about the fact that she was bed shopping with a tall, handsome stranger in a place where gossip scattered like bird shot. The woman didn't move, didn't point, didn't say a word. She was waiting for an introduction.

"Lorraine, this is Trace McKay. Trace, Lorraine Krause."

Trace extended his hand. "Glad to meet you, ma'am. Sorry about the cold hands; I think I'll have to pick up a pair of gloves while I'm here."

"We've got lots to choose from." Lorraine giggled, a sound Sydney had never heard come out of her. "You know what they always say. . .cold hands, warm heart!"

"Well, I hope that's true of me," Trace answered, and beneath Lorraine's thick layer of face powder, a pink glow rose to her cheeks.

Does the man flirt with everyone? The door opened behind them. Out of the corner of her eye, Sydney saw Gwyneth Chapel. She reached out and gathered the little woman in a hug. "Are you settling in at Floyd's?"

Gwyneth waved her hand as if swatting a fly. "My son's got some quirks, but he takes good care of me. Now if Mordecai would just stop causing problems. . ."

Sydney could see the corner of Trace's mouth tilting up. "What kind of problems, Mrs. Chapel?" he asked.

Through squinting eyes Gwyneth stared at him, apparently trying to place him. After a moment she nodded. "The ex-con," she said, more to herself than to Trace. "Mordecai started the fire in *your* apartment." She poked at his chest with a gnarled finger. "He'd best watch his back when you're around. Not that he could get any more dead than he is, of course."

"How did he start the fire?"

"Well, you don't have to say it like that! He didn't do it on purpose, you know. Actually, it's all my fault, I suppose. I never would have let him smoke if I'd thought someone might get hurt. That poor, dear little girl. . . He was in the front yard and he didn't want to come in. He had his pipe, you see, and all he wanted was a good smoke. I've tried to tell him to quit. People get lip cancer from pipes; it can eat away a whole side of your face. . .or worse. But every time I warn Mordecai about that, he reminds me that he's already dead."

In spite of eyes that sparkled with mirth, Trace managed a voice that came off as perfectly serious. "Not much to worry about once you've achieved room temperature."

Equally solemn, Gwyneth nodded. "Precisely. Mordecai doesn't stop by to visit much once it starts getting cold, so that was a bit out of the ordinary. And he came without Susanna, too; that was strange. I asked about her health, thinking she might have gotten that bird flu everyone's talking about; she's such a frail little thing. But he reminded me that she was dead, so of course she couldn't catch the flu. It was the flu that killed her, after all, back in 1917. Did you know more people died of the flu than in the war that year? So I told him I'd make tea for us if he thought Susanna wouldn't mind. She gets jealous of me sometimes, you know, which is so silly since I'm twenty years older than Mordecai."

Sydney watched Trace's Adam's apple rise and fall and bit her lip. She didn't dare make eye contact with him. Gwyneth stopped to pat her straight, feathery white hair with both hands. "But then again, he died before I was born, so am I really older than he is?" She looked at Trace, waiting for an answer.

A vein on Trace's forehead stood out, and he appeared in danger of detonating. Thankfully, Lorraine walked up and steered Gwyneth toward a display of Depression glass. Trace slipped behind a seven-foot-tall armoire and Sydney followed, finding him almost doubled over in laughter. Sydney let out the laugh she'd been fighting to hold in. Accustomed to Gwyneth's stories, she found it was the look on Trace McKay's face that was her undoing. When he finally came up for air, he gasped, "She's priceless!"

Lorraine peeked around the armoire where they were standing with their hands over their mouths, like two naughty preschoolers. "Can I help you two find something?" Lorraine asked.

"We're going to look around in the back room. Do you know if you have any single beds, Lorraine?" She hoped the emphasis on "single" wasn't too subtle.

"At least two. One's got a white headboard with gold flowers. Maybe that's not what you were hoping for?"

Sydney sidestepped the inferred question. "Anything can be painted. We'll go see what you've got."

As they threaded their way through the maze of shelves and racks to the back room, Trace whispered, "I can only guess what's going through that woman's head right now. Tempting to mess with it a bit."

Stopping in front of a maple headboard, Sydney pulled it out from the wall, ran her hand along the top, and smiled demurely at Trace, all the while making sure Lorraine was still within hearing distance. "What do you think, Trace? This will look nice in our apartment, won't it?"

"A perfect choice, Sydney Rose. Let's take it home."

❧

Trace took off his new gloves and wiped his eyes before putting the truck in gear. Beside him, Sydney was doing the same. Lifting the bed frame into the pickup had been almost impossible with the spasms of laughter that kept overtaking them both. Drawing a calming breath, Sydney turned to him. "That was so mean."

"And so fun."

"It'll be all over town by Monday."

"Does that bother you?"

She appeared to mull it over, then grinned at him. "No." She pointed to another resale shop.

"You're not the kind to care much what people think." He framed it as a statement but knew she'd answer.

"As long as my conscience is clear before the Lord, that's all I care about. No, that's not completely true. I'm not an approval addict, but I couldn't handle lies."

"Other than little white ones you start yourself, of course."

Sydney nodded, but her expression had turned serious. "This town can be vicious."

Trace pulled away from the curb. "Are you saying that for my benefit?"

"Mm-hmm."

"I guess I'll just have to follow your motto. As long as my conscience is clear before the Lord, people can say what they want. Pleasing Him is all I really care about."

Once again, the look on her face was one he knew he'd never forget.

℘

Trace waited in the basement until he heard the Jennets leave for church. Mattie had said the coffee would be on and she'd leave bagels on the counter. He turned on the wrought iron lamp he and Sydney had found at the second resale shop and opened his Bible. As always, it fell open to Psalm 55 and the highlighted words: *"My heart is in anguish within me; the terrors of death assail me. Fear and trembling have beset me; horror has overwhelmed me. I said, 'Oh, that I had the wings of a dove! I would fly away and be at rest—'"* But he didn't linger on that page, hadn't for many months. Instead, he turned to Psalm 100 and read: *"Enter his gates with thanksgiving and his courts with praise; give thanks to him and praise his name. For the LORD is good and his love endures forever; his faithfulness continues through all generations."*

The steps creaked as he walked up in bare feet, carrying the button-down shirt he'd picked up yesterday. Sydney had assured him jeans were acceptable, but he hated the thought of walking into church in these jeans, the same ones he'd been wearing the night he was arrested. He'd burn them and the boots, as soon as he'd made enough money to afford new ones.

Shaved and dressed, he walked around the kitchen and living room with a cup of coffee. It was the first time he'd been in the house alone. Mattie had an artistic eye. The color scheme in the kitchen reminded him of Easter baskets.

Every corner of the living room invited relaxation. Trace picked up a framed picture of two girls in long dresses and carried it to the window, staring at a younger version of Sydney, in a red and gold geisha girl type of dress with a stand-up collar. Even then, she'd been striking. He recognized Colleen Hatcher, a few pounds thinner but just as spunky looking, standing next to Sydney and smiled. The interaction he'd witnessed between Colleen and Sydney last night had all the elements of a stand-up comedy routine. All they'd been doing was serving pizza and snickerdoodles, yet he and Stuart had been close to rolling on the floor in laughter more than once. Memories of the evening gave him a thread of courage. The Hatchers had welcomed him and had done their best to assure him that he'd fit right in at Pineview Community Church. Setting the frame back on the shelf, he headed for the door.

He needed the courage. Now he wished he'd gone to church last Sunday. Eldon had invited him, but he hadn't felt ready and he was sure the church wasn't prepared for him. He'd thought it better to show up after they all knew he was here. In retrospect, the element of surprise may have given him a better chance to make good first impressions. As it was now, a week's worth of rumors had probably ripped through Pine Bluff like a shock wave. Whatever he was walking into, he was sure he wasn't ready for it. Squaring his shoulders, he locked the door behind him and walked across the yard toward the road.

The morning frost had melted and the red line on the thermometer nailed to a giant oak was kissing fifty. Trace filled his lungs with the scent of wet dirt and the distinct odor of the cow barn across the road. He heard turkeys gobbling somewhere in the distance. The road curved and a field of ripe pumpkins came into view. He stopped when he got close, marveling at the contrast of bright orange against the brown earth, stretching out for acres in front of him. *Lord, what a world You made.* He imagined that his heightened senses would accept all this as normal before long, but he was in no hurry to lose the childlike wonder that made every experience seem like a first. It wasn't all the result of three years in a monochromatic seven-by-twelve cell. Much of it had to do with what the apostle Paul wrote to the Corinthians: "Therefore, if anyone is in Christ, he is a new creation; the old has gone, the new has come!"

The Trace McKay who stopped on a country road to gaze at a field of pumpkins on his way to church on a sunny October Sunday was not the Trace McKay the bars of the St. Cloud Correctional Facility had closed on three years earlier. He was, in fact, a new creation, and every atom in his being felt the difference. But the closer he got to the church, the more he doubted that anyone would see him as anything but a cold-blooded murderer.

∽

The music had already started when Trace walked into the sanctuary. The lights were dim, and his eyes hadn't adjusted from the sunlight. When he didn't spot the Jennets, he took a seat in a back pew. The words to the worship songs were projected on a screen; Trace was surprised that he knew the first three from CDs and Prison Fellowship services. But singing along with live music and women's voices was entirely different from anything he'd experienced in St. Cloud. As a soloist sang a stanza of "How Great Is Our God," the hair stood up on Trace's arms. He was grateful for his spot in the shadows at the back of the church where no one could see him fighting emotions.

When the music ended, the worship leader told everyone to turn and greet the people around them. Trace hadn't expected this. In seconds, five people lined up to shake his hand. When a man in a dark suit and Buddy Holly–style glasses said, "You look so familiar," Trace swallowed hard and couldn't think of what to say. Before he had the chance to look too foolish, Sydney came up on his right, redirecting Buddy Holly's attention.

"Hi, Sol. How's the new job?"

By the time the man finished answering, the music was playing again and they were told to open their hymnals. "Thanks," Trace whispered.

"No prob." Sydney bent down and picked up a red-covered book, found the right page, and held it in front of Trace, not handing it to him, but offering to share it. Trace hesitated only a moment, then grabbed onto it with one hand. As her left hand dropped to her side, it brushed against his.

Concentrating on the sermon was a battle. He liked the pastor immediately; the man talked as if he were sitting at his kitchen table chatting over coffee and yet managed to get across truth with amazing directness. When Trace was able to focus on Pastor Owen's words, he swung from feeling nailed to the pew with conviction to laughing at his anecdotes; the man was truly gifted. But there was a major distraction less than two inches from Trace's right arm, wearing a fragrance that was earthy and spicy and just subtle enough to make him want to lean closer.

Two inches to his right was exactly where his thoughts were when the sermon ended and announcements began. But his focus jerked to the front of the sanctuary when the pastor asked for visitors to stand and introduce themselves. Trace's heart slammed against his ribs, and his mouth went dry. He felt his throat constricting and knew nothing would come out if he tried to speak. The man in the Buddy Holly glasses turned around and nodded at him. Just as Trace thought he was going to pass out, Eldon stood up in the second row and gestured toward the back.

"I'd like to introduce our new houseguest. Trace McKay will be staying with us until his apartment is ready, and I hope you all make him feel welcome. Trace?"

Sydney nudged his elbow, and somehow he found enough strength in his legs to stand, wiping his palms against his jeans as he did. Was it his imagination, or did the whole room suddenly freeze? It lasted only a moment, and then heads began to turn and necks stretched in succession like Minnesota Twins fans doing the wave. Trace sat down. The man with the horn-rimmed glasses was still staring, still nodding. Was he recalling a three-year-old newscast, suddenly realizing why Trace looked so familiar? Sydney's right hand slid beneath her left arm and squeezed his elbow, and the blood rushed suddenly back into his head, along with the words he'd said to her yesterday: *"People can say what they want. Pleasing Him is all I really care about."*

&

Phyllis Lincoln, in a bright green dress and huge yellow earrings, chugged toward Sydney and Trace like a John Deere tractor at half speed. It didn't take much of a stretch to picture steam pouring from her ears. "This can't be good," Trace whispered.

Sydney looked up and down the crowded sanctuary aisle but couldn't see an easy escape. Stretching her lips into a smile, she reached out...and out...to hug the woman. "Good morning, Phyllis. How's your knee healing?"

"As good as it's going to get. Can I talk to you, Sydney?"

"Sure."

"Alone?"

"I want to introduce Trace to Pastor. Will you be around for a while?"

Trace turned away from her to shake an outstretched hand. That was all the "alone" Phyllis seemed to need.

"I tried to catch your father after the meeting. And then I tried getting Pastor on the phone. . . . Anyway, this living arrangement is ridiculous, Sydney. I've seen your house. He's not staying in Zack's room, is he?"

"We've fixed up an apartment in the basement."

"But still. . ." Phyllis lowered her voice, but Sydney knew it wasn't low enough. "I can't imagine how you and your mother can sleep at night."

A tiny something in the recesses of Sydney's brain snapped. She pictured herself at about six, sitting on Phyllis's now-artificial knee and reading Bible stories. "Actually, Phyllis, I slept like a baby last night. It's amazing how peacefully you can sleep when you know you're doing God's will. I went to sleep thinking of all the 'love one another' verses you taught me in Sunday school."

Phyllis huffed. "I'm not talking about love, Sydney. I'm talking about safety and common sense. You can love without putting yourself at risk."

"Like Jesus did?" The shocked indignation on Phyllis's face provided kindling for Sydney's fire. "I think love is one of the riskiest things we can do, and if more people would—"

A hand clamped on her upper arm from behind. In one smooth movement, Trace stopped her words and held out his hand to Phyllis. His crooked smile was wider than Sydney had seen it yet, his eyes dancing. The man was absolutely oozing charm.

"I'm Trace McKay; I don't think we've met."

Phyllis's red lips parted, closed, then parted again. Finally, she squeezed out, "Phyllis Lincoln."

"Did I hear Sydney say you were her Sunday school teacher?" His words were crusted with sugar.

"I taught for forty-eight years."

"Forty-eight years? What a gift. Imagine all the lives you've touched, all the souls that will be in heaven because you loved them enough to teach them the truth. If some kind person like you would have gone out of her way to take me to Sunday school when I was little, I may have come to know the Lord at a young age and I never would have set foot in a bar. My life would be so different today."

"Well, I—"

"I hope to teach Sunday school someday. If I can keep one child from living in darkness the way I did for so many years, it will all be worth it. I'd love to sit down with you sometime. I'm sure you could teach me so much."

The yellow earrings bobbed as Phyllis nodded and reached in the patch pocket of her John Deere dress for a tissue. Dabbing her eyes, she said, "I'd. . .like that, son."

Chapter 7

Y ou're amazing. You're a magician!" Sydney put her canvas bag in the back of her parents' car and held out her hand for Trace's Bible. After slamming the car door, she nodded toward the road and they started walking. She hadn't taken the time to analyze her motives when Trace said he wanted to walk home and she said she'd join him. It was partly that she loved to walk and wanted to savor the few remaining nice days, but she also had to admit that she loved the adrenaline rush of rattling the orderly lives of the "Phyllises."

"More like a snake charmer."

Sydney laughed and nodded. "My dad refers to the Phyllises as people who were baptized in pickle juice."

It was Trace's turn to laugh. "My grandmother, my father's mother, was a pickle juice Bible thumper."

A car drove past. Two little faces were plastered against the side window. In the car behind it, a woman stared, her lips in a tight straight line.

"Were you close to your grandmother?"

"I only saw her a few times. She died when I was pretty young, but she left a lasting impression. She was about the same size as your Phyllis, and she always smelled like Bengay. I remember this smothering sensation when she hugged me. She made oatmeal cookies that tasted like menthol and were so hard I lost a tooth eating one, and she talked about Jesus. No, she *yelled* about Jesus. I was too young to understand it, but whoever Jesus was, I knew He was scary. Years later I realized that was why my dad hated Christians. I'm sure my grandmother had a good heart, but she shared the gospel with a sledgehammer and chased her own son away."

"That's sad. But *you* weren't scared away for good, I'm gathering."

Trace kicked a rock and watched it bounce several times and land in the ditch. "I guess I was a little too cryptic yesterday. I was enjoying your attempt to convert me."

"There's a very sadistic side to you, isn't there?" The minute she said it, she regretted the words but didn't know how to undo them.

Trace seemed to read the look on her face and shook his head. "Let's get one thing clear, okay? I don't want anyone pussyfooting around me. If you've got something to say, just say it. And feel free to spread that message around."

"I'm guessing you got a lot of that this morning."

A hiss escaped through pursed lips. "I read a book in St. Cloud about personality types."

44

Before he could explain, a car slowed beside them and the window rolled down.

Sydney walked over to the window and Trace followed.

The man behind the wheel appeared to be in his mid-twenties. His hand extended toward Trace. "Jack Larsen. Glad to meet you. Have Syd bring you to our singles group next week." The man waved and drove off.

"You were saying?" Sydney prompted.

"The book categorized people as either otters or golden retrievers—like that guy who just stopped—or beavers or. . .something else."

"Lions."

"Yeah. I've had a lot of time to study people in the past three years, and I made up my own categories. There was kind of a shortage of cute little otters or golden retrievers in prison, but there were plenty of barracudas and vultures, with a few armadillos and chameleons thrown in."

"And what about here?"

"Phyllis is a rhinoceros."

Sydney sputtered. "That's perfect!"

"Thankfully, she was the only one who came charging with horns. People were mostly distant or nauseously nice. There were a couple of house cats who kind of circled around for a while; when they saw the retrievers being friendly, they figured it was okay to get closer."

"I saw the pastor's daughters come right up to you. They must be golden retrievers, too."

Trace smiled. "With a little lion thrown in, I think. Very confident girls. They invited me over for dinner next Sunday and said they knew it would be all right with their parents. I've never met kids like that; somebody's showing them the real deal."

"Their parents are the 'real deal.' Any barracudas?"

"A few giving me the eye from a distance. Out of that whole crowd, there was one kid who did it right. I don't remember his name; longish hair, pierced eyebrow. He walked up and said, 'Hey, I hear you just got outta prison. So how'd ya kill somebody?'"

"That would be Shane Chapel. Gwyneth's great-grandson."

"He looks like a work in progress."

Sydney laughed. "That pretty much says it. His father was abusive; his mom left him with his grandparents years ago, and no one knows where she is. So you *want* people to be as blunt as Shane? 'So how'd ya kill somebody?' is the *right* way?"

"It's what everybody's thinking. Why not be honest and just say it?" When Sydney only shook her head, he said, "It's what *you're* thinking."

Sydney folded her arms across her chest. "I was asking how you became a Christian."

"But you're wondering how and why I killed a guy."

He was right, of course. "It's none of my business."

"Of course it is. I'm living in your house."

"Dad said it was a bar fight, but you didn't mean to. . .really hurt the guy. I don't need details."

"I want to give you the details. Is that a problem?"

There was that tone again, confrontational, egotistical. "No. It's not a 'problem.'" Did he think she was too refined, too delicate to handle the details?

Trace stopped walking.

Sydney was a step ahead before she realized it. When she turned to face him, he was looking down at his boots. "I'm sorry. It's been a long time since I had a civilized conversation."

Sydney nodded. "Another learning curve."

"I guess. Maybe you can civilize me." He looked up, staring into her, through her, and all she could do was nod. "I'd like you to hear the truth from me," he said.

"I'm listening."

Trace started walking again. "I wasn't a drinker; I stopped for a beer after work once or twice a month when my ship was back in Duluth; that was it. It was a buddy's birthday and we took him to this bar and grill. I ran into a girl I'd gone out with a few times. She told me she'd gotten back with the loser she'd dated before me. That's about the time I saw this splint on two of her fingers. She made up some lame excuse, but I knew he'd done it. I just walked away.

"Awhile later the boyfriend comes in. It was obvious he was drunk. The girl said a few words, pointed my way, and the guy starts yelling at her. I couldn't hear a thing over the music, but I could tell he was just reaming her out. And then I noticed that his hand was over hers on the stool and he was pressing down on her fingers, the ones with the splint. You could see she was in so much pain she was ready to faint, but she wasn't even trying to pull away." Trace ran his fingers through his hair. His hand seemed to be shaking. "I didn't think about what I did next. I just walked over and told him to get away from her. Before he had a chance to say anything, *she* told me to get lost. Why I didn't, I'll never know—but he stood up and screamed at me, and I punched him. Just once. But the guy was so wasted he fell backwards and hit his neck on the back of a chair. He was dead when the paramedics got there."

Sydney's steps had slowed, and finally she stopped. "But wasn't that self-defense?"

Trace shook his head. "My lawyer tried, but the guy never did anything but yell at me."

"But you were defending the woman."

"Her life wasn't in danger—at the moment, anyway. And she told the police she had no idea why I just walked up and punched her boyfriend."

They walked without talking for several minutes. His honesty had brought up even more questions. She'd seen documentaries on prison life. What had he been forced to do to survive? How had it changed him?

"You came to Christ in prison?" she asked softly.

"I'd been there about six months when I started going to the Prison Fellowship meetings. My cell mate talked to himself 24/7 and pretended like I wasn't even there. It was starting to make me a little nuts, so I went to a meeting to get away from him; at least that's what I thought. I planned on just sitting there and watching weird religious people for something different to do."

He laughed. "I really expected everyone to be yelling about Jesus like my grandmother did. The whole thing just blew me away. The music, the quiet way the pastor talked, the attitudes of the inmates who were claiming to be 'saved.' I didn't have a clue what saved meant, but I was ready to sign up for it. They had free Bibles, and I took one and started reading and asking questions. I saw guys fall on their faces sobbing and crying out to God to forgive them, and I kept wondering if it was going to happen to me. But all of that came much later. The best way I can explain my salvation experience is that I woke up in the middle of the night and I just knew it was the truth."

"Was it harder, being there, as a Christian? Were you ostracized for it?"

"Everybody's ostracized by somebody for something in there. I got beat up only once"—he pointed to the scar on his lip—"for telling somebody why I was a Christian. But overall it was so much better. If you're a loner, you're in danger. Belonging to the Jesus freaks was much healthier than any other group. Anger would have eaten me alive if it weren't for the guys I was with."

Trace kicked a rock to the side of the road. "I regret everything that happened that night in the bar. It's in my head every minute, and I'd do anything to undo it. But the worst night of my life led to my salvation."

Sydney stared at the house a hundred yards ahead—the house she'd lived in most of her life. She stared at the green shutters, the split-rail fence that surrounded the front yard, and the white-painted footbridge that spanned the irrigation ditch. She'd had twenty-nine years of an almost idyllic life, and yet somehow she envied the man beside her who had been convicted of murder. He had a testimony that would make people listen. "You need to share your story. People need to hear it."

He was quiet for a moment. "Maybe someday. I'm no public speaker, but if God wants me to talk someday, I suppose He can overcome that."

A flock of geese flew over, and Trace looked up. His eyes were on the squawking V moving south when he said, "Thanks for walking with me."

"Couldn't have you getting lost."

"Or attacked by barracudas."

Sydney laughed.

Trace stopped when they got to the bridge. "Why did you?"

"Why did I what?"

"Walk with me." Trace crossed the six-foot bridge and held his hand out to her. "Knowing that people will talk. . .it was a gutsy thing to do."

Staring down at his hand, the answer was clear in her head. Taking one step onto the bridge, she laid her hand in his. "Maybe I'm just a docile, trusting golden retriever."

His eyebrows shot up, and a rich, deep laugh followed. "I think not."

Chapter 8

Sydney's alarm went off at six thirty on Monday morning. Without turning on a light, she navigated the semidarkness on autopilot, sitting up, bending over, pulling her running clothes out of the basket under her bed. The threadbare waffle-weave gray shirt she'd been wearing to bed every night for four years snagged on the back of her earring, and she fought with it while fishing around for her Nikes. Red and gray plaid pajama bottoms landed squarely in the wicker hamper with a kick.

Sixty seconds later, still in the dark, she was putting her hair in a ponytail as she stepped onto the stairs. She stopped when she heard Trace's voice below her.

"...inherited that from my father, I guess."

"Your parents live anywhere near?" her father asked.

Sydney padded down three steps, cringing when the old wood creaked.

"I never actually had 'parents,' not in the plural sense of the word. My dad left when I was about three. Last I knew, he was a blackjack dealer at the Bellagio."

"Las Vegas?"

"Yeah. Makes me proud."

"Ever see him?"

"Every few years. He showed up at my door about five years ago needing money. Haven't heard from him since, but a friend of mine ran into him in Vegas awhile back and he said to say hi and he hoped I was getting along okay in prison."

Sydney eased down four more steps and sat down.

"And your mother?"

"She's down in Mankato. Married her third husband while I was going to school in Florida. She sent me a picture after the wedding and apologized for not inviting me. I'm not sure the new guy even knows I exist. They've got two daughters now."

"Do you hear from her at all?"

"I got Christmas cards the last three years."

"That has to be tough."

Sydney sneaked down to the bottom step. There was a long pause before Trace answered.

"It was. But I've had time to deal with it. I mostly just feel pity for both of them now."

"Can you pray for them?"

"I couldn't until a couple of months ago, but it's getting easier. One of the chaplains told me to expect anger and forgiveness to come in waves, and he was right."

Eldon laughed softly. "That's a good picture. Just when you're feeling victory, another wave knocks you off your feet. It can be a long process. The only thing positive I can say about hours on end in a cement block room is that you have the gift of time to think and pray. How you doing with forgiving yourself?"

"Still working on that one."

"I hear ya. Let's pray before we head out."

Sydney leaned her head against the rough plaster wall, listening to her father's prayer and longing to have his ability to empathize, to walk in someone else's shoes, to understand as if he'd been there himself.

℘

With a last swig of lukewarm coffee, Trace pushed his chair away from the kitchen table. As Eldon Jennet stacked their breakfast dishes in the sink, Trace stared at his back. Everything the man did was imbued with grace. Like a dry sponge, Trace soaked up every word. "I hope I have a fraction of your wisdom when I. . .someday."

Eldon wiped his hands on a paper towel, laughing as he tossed it into the wastebasket. "When you're old like me, you mean?" He took his coat off the hook by the back door and tossed Trace's jacket at him. "Let's get to work."

As Trace closed the back door and stepped onto the gravel driveway, Eldon turned around and held out a bundle of keys. His eyes glittered. "My daughter tells me you have a penchant for speed."

Taking the keys, Trace walked toward the driver's side door. He cleared his throat loudly enough to carry over Eldon's footsteps. "With all due respect, I'm not so sure your daughter has any room to—"

A square of yellow paper, held in place by the windshield wiper, flickered in the breeze. Thickly scrawled words were visible at a glance.

SEND HIM BACK TO JAIL. . .OR ELSE.

Eldon walked around the front of the truck, pulled the paper out, and crumpled it in his hands. His eyes, fixed on Trace, blazed. "We are *not* going to take this seriously. Do you hear me?"

Trace nodded, dread settling like a rock in his gut.

"Let's get to work."

℘

The smell of smoke and charred wood got stronger as Trace followed Eldon up the stairs to the apartment. Opening the door brought a rush of cold, acrid air. The plastic that covered the broken window in the living room rustled as it breathed in and out.

"Kind of eerie," Eldon said, pulling a disposable mask over his nose and mouth.

Trace nodded, doing the same with the mask Eldon handed him. Looking down at the black outline on the wood floor where a couch had been, he thought of how often he used to fall asleep watching TV, and the hair on the back of his neck prickled.

"The church didn't have replacement insurance, so if we want to match the original woodwork and plastering, we have to do it ourselves." The mask muffled Eldon's voice. "I can't see cutting corners on a place with this much history. Unfortunately, not everyone's on the same page, but there have been enough donations to cover supplies." He put his hand on Trace's shoulder. "And your paychecks." He ran his hand along an inside wall of the living room and fingered the edge of a three-foot-wide hole. "Those guys sure love their axes."

They walked through the kitchen, the one small bedroom, and then the bathroom. In the smudgy light seeping through the frosted window, Trace made out turquoise tiles streaked with soot. Eldon took out a square yellow flashlight and aimed it at the light fixture on the ceiling. The paint was brown and bubbled in places; chunks of still-damp drywall hung down in others.

Eldon shook his head. "Not what I expected."

"Doesn't look like it started here," Trace agreed. "The worst damage is in the living room."

"I don't get it." Eldon motioned for Trace to go down the hall toward the kitchen and living room. "We had a cleaning lady come in on Friday morning. She must have been the last one in here. Maybe she was using something flammable."

"And chain smoking at the same time?"

Eldon's eyes crinkled. "Hope she got out," he said dryly.

"Doesn't seem likely that something smoldered for that many hours, but it's possible, I suppose." Trace looked up at the hole above him where firefighters had chopped through the roof.

Eldon pointed the flashlight into the crawl space above the ceiling. The roof joists were black. "No, it doesn't. It had to have started up there, which probably means electrical. We had a few drops of rain before midnight. Maybe lightning..."

Trace stared up at the blackened beams that were covered in deep, grid-like surface cracks. Something in his gut twisted. He'd seen galley fires and engine fires and one on an old tug that had been blamed on frayed wires. He didn't need to wait for the report. This fire wasn't electrical...and it wasn't an act of God.

෨෮

"Stop that!" Sydney turned off the mixer and grabbed the bottle of chili powder from Trace's hand. "Did you even taste it first?"

"Of course." He held out his hand. "Go bake your cake and leave me to my chili."

Her father walked into the room and hung up the phone as Sydney stuck the bottle in her back pocket. "Zach says hi."

He looked at Trace and shook his head. "You're determined to show me up, aren't you, boy? I'm in the middle of writing an article for *The Land*, or I'd be out here helping."

"Sure you would." Trace handed him a spoon. "Taste this and then you can tell Mattie you helped make supper."

"I'm hoping that having you in the kitchen means I'll finally get some manly chili in this house without having to doctor it." He tasted, blinked twice, and grinned. "It's getting there. There's hotter stuff in the cupboard, but Gwyneth's coming for supper, so go a little easy." Sticking a toothpick in his mouth, he winked and left the room.

A guttural laugh came from Trace, and he took a quick step to the pantry cupboard. He dug around until he produced two jars of ground peppers, one habanero, and the other red chili. "Now we're talkin'."

Sydney held both hands over the soup pot. "Remember Gwyneth."

"Mm-hmm. I'll measure carefully." He pulled open a drawer, took out a measuring spoon, and heaped a teaspoon with red chili. "How's this?"

"You'll kill her."

"She'll never know what hit her." He held the spoon over the pot, smiled, and in one smooth motion dumped the chili powder into Sydney's cake batter.

Sydney screamed. "Are you nuts?"

"Not at all."

"You creep! You ruined my cake!" She slapped his arm. Just like a thirteen-year-old. She wasn't at all sure she liked the cutesy, giddy girl that seemed to materialize when he teased her. She didn't like losing control.

"Chocolate chili cake is a gourmet delicacy. There's a famous restaurant in Colorado that serves it."

"Sure there is."

"Here, taste it. Montezuma put red chili in his hot chocolate all the time." Trace took a spoonful and held it out to her.

Sydney pushed his hand away. "You taste it."

"Chicken." He licked the end of the spoon, squeezed his eyes shut, and coughed. "Perfect."

"Uh-huh."

"Taste." He dipped his finger in the batter, pulled it out, and swirled it to catch a drip. There was something artful about the way he moved. His finger rose to her lips. "Trust me."

She didn't really have a choice, did she? Her mouth opened then closed on his finger. Her eyes watered. She sputtered. "You are so not to be trusted."

The side of his thumb brushed her cheek. He laughed and turned back to the chili pot. "Which reminds me. . .I never got a serious answer to my question."

She let her phony look of innocence give her away. She knew the question—"Why did you walk with me?"—and knew the answer. "Which reminds *me*. . . that I need to set the table."

As she reached over her head for plates, Ronny lumbered in. "Gwyneth is here. Can me and Gwyneth make another scarecrow?"

"Are you helping her make scarecrows for the craft fair?"

"Not the little scarecrows. Another big scarecrow with real people clothes. And we can't have a corncob pipe 'cause Mordecai will steal it."

Sydney nodded as she pulled six bowls out of the cupboard. "Okay. No pipe. Are you hungry for chili?"

Ronny shuffled from one foot to the other, his gaze fixed on the floor. "I. . . maybe am. But. . ."

"What's the matter, Ronny?"

"Eldon says your chili is wimpy."

∾

"I don't like that place, Mattie. There's nothing but old people there." Gwyneth put a dollop of sour cream on her chili, as she'd done after each of her three bites. "This chili has a real kick to it."

Sydney handed a basket of soda crackers to her. "These'll take away some of the sting. Trace made the chili."

"It's excellent."

Sydney watched Trace bury his grin in a piece of corn bread. "Wait for dessert," she said under her breath.

"I used to make chili." Gwyneth glared at Mattie. "Before *some*body took all the knobs off my stove."

"So. . ." Sydney didn't dare make eye contact with her mother. "Floyd took you on a tour of Pineridge?"

Gwyneth grunted. "Why do they always name those places after trees, anyway? Just like cemeteries and asylums. Who wants to live in a place that sounds like a cemetery?"

"I think it's to make you feel peaceful," Trace said.

"Peaceful is not what you get with a bunch of old people sitting around in their bathrobes and talking about their kidney stones right in front of God and everybody!"

"I'm sure your family just wants you to be in a safe place."

"My family just wants me out of their house. Not that I want to be there with my crabby son and his puppet wife. My great-grandson's okay, but I don't like his music." She took another bite of chili. "This really is good." She fixed her eyes on Trace, seeming to study him. "I like you. I don't care what my son says about you."

Trace's eyebrows rose. "What does he say about me?"

"He says three years isn't long enough. He says Minnesota should have the death penalty. And he says prison does bad things to a man and if Eldon had a brain in his head, he wouldn't let you anywhere near his daughter."

The phone interrupted the deafening silence. Mattie got up and answered it and handed it to Eldon. "It's Chet," she whispered, but in the sudden quiet of the dining room, everyone heard.

No one attempted to fill the empty space with words. No one pretended they weren't trying to hear every word Eldon said to the fire chief as he walked into the living room with the phone.

When he walked back in, the phone slapped the table. He sank into his chair and picked up his spoon, his eyes focused on his bowl.

"It was arson."

Chapter 9

Sydney turned off her blow-dryer and reached the phone on the third ring, glancing at the clock as she answered it. It was almost one o'clock, and she was already wondering how she was going to fit in everything she had to accomplish and get to the radio station on time.

"Hi, Sydney, it's April. Glad I caught you. I just got off the phone with your pastor, and he had a great suggestion. Would it be possible for Mr. McKay to come in to the station with you? I think it would give people a really positive picture of what the Sanctuary is doing."

Would Trace agree? Should he agree? In light of the fire chief's report, would it help public sentiment for the Sanctuary to "meet" one of the tenants? "I can call him and see what he thinks. If he's not interested, I'll get back to you."

"That would be wonderful. The interview might take longer with both of you. Will that interfere with your schedule?"

"Not at all. I took the afternoon off."

"Are you. . .comfortable? I don't know much about this guy; I certainly don't want to presume. . .or put you in danger." April Douglas laughed, rather nervously for a person who made her living talking to people. "This is awkward."

"It's not a problem."

Sydney said good-bye and hung up, reflecting on how strange it was that her quick statement was true. She decided to stop at the LaSalle Street apartment and ask Trace in person before making her rounds to the two other Sanctuary apartment buildings.

After pushing the speed limit on the way, she took the apartment stairs two at a time.

"God's timing is perfect," was Eldon's response to her question. "The arson thing is going to be all over town soon. The more we can educate people on what the program's all about, the better. Maybe it'll be a start toward getting other churches involved. Take Trace on rounds with you so he's got the big picture."

Eldon kept on sanding a carved piece of crown molding as he talked, and Sydney's eyes were drawn to his hands. Since she was little, she'd loved to watch him work. "April Douglas lives above the chamber office, right?" he asked. "You know her well enough to be confident she'll put things in a good light?"

Sydney nodded. "I know she believes in what we're doing."

"Good." Eldon stopped sanding and turned to Trace. "Think you can find a few positive things to say about the program?"

Sydney looked at Trace. He was holding a sledgehammer, one end in each hand, his knuckles blanched white. He was grimacing like he'd just bitten into a lemon. *He's scared to death!* Instead of eliciting the empathy she should have felt, the image made Sydney desperately want to burst out laughing. The handsome, confident man whose borrowed white T-shirt strained over muscles pumped from wielding the massive hammer was terrified of a microphone.

৪৩

As she did a U-turn on LaSalle Street, Sydney smiled at her passenger, who appeared to be attempting nonchalance. "It's taped, you know. It's not live radio."

"You said that. Twice."

"You're in good company. More people are afraid of public speaking than of dying."

"That makes me feel so much better. But I'm not afraid of public speaking. I'm afraid of public *not* speaking."

"Do you have a history of 'public not speaking?'"

"Tenth-grade English." Trace angled his body toward her. "Picture a skinny, conceited, loudmouthed class clown. If I sneezed or burped out loud, the girls thought it was incredibly witty. I picked knot tying for my 'how to' speech, something I was totally proficient at. I had it down; I could tie knots standing on my head; I could recite the speech in my sleep. But when I got up in front of the room, I couldn't remember a thing. The only knots that got tied were in my tongue and my stomach. My hands froze on the rope and the teacher finally told me to sit down."

"And that's when you dropped out of school?"

"Yup."

Sydney's eyes widened. "I was kidding. You're not serious."

"That was the final straw. Public humiliation on top of lousy grades and a poor attendance record. I was convinced that I was too dumb for school."

"But you got your captain's license."

He rested his knee on the console between them. "It was the hardest thing I'd ever done. The difference was that I loved it and I had a goal and a purpose for the first time."

"And you found out you were smarter than you thought you were, I bet."

"I guess." Trace shrugged. "You were an honor student—valedictorian or something, right? I saw all the gold cords in your graduation picture."

Sydney laughed. "I graduated sixth in my class. I was second until I took a stupid detour. I was a sophomore, too."

"Go on. . . ."

"You know that verse in Galatians that says that those who are spiritual should restore a brother caught in sin, but 'watch yourself, or you also may be tempted'?"

"Mm-hmm. This sounds interesting."

"When we were fifteen, Colleen decided that, like, chilling with the church dweebs was bogus and hanging with the mall chicks was, like, the bomb."

"Ouch." Trace recoiled. "She hooked a husband talking like that?"

"Oh, like, Stuart was like this majorly awesome dude, for sure, and he was like totally psyched about hanging with Col, you know?"

Trace shook his head. "Gag me with a spoon."

"Exactly. So Colleen becomes a partier and I take it on myself to rescue her. I was a crusader on a mission to save all mall chicks from their doom."

"This is where 'Watch yourself, or you also may be tempted' comes in?"

Sydney grinned. "Like, dude, like, I became a totally gnarly Mississippi Valley Girl. Like, school was so lame and, like, who had time for it, you know? I came to my senses the next fall and worked like a dog making up for my stupidity."

She pulled up in front of a white brick apartment building. Trace was still laughing when he got out of the car. "Mississippi Valley Girl; I would have loved to see that. Thank God most of us grow up, hey, dudette?"

"Word. For sure, dude."

ℝ

The next hour gave Trace another window into Sydney's world. There were four apartments in the building. When they knocked on the first door, a very pregnant woman answered, apologizing profusely for the noise and the messy living room. She invited them in, clearly happy to see Sydney and grateful for the bag of diapers she'd brought. Sydney introduced Trace, scooped up a crying toddler, turned off the television, and cleared a place on the couch for the two of them.

Trace marveled at the way she navigated the twists and turns in conversation. When the woman began making excuses for the state of her finances, Sydney gently reprimanded her, wrapping the reproof skillfully in layers of encouragement. If the woman said something negative about her situation, Sydney gracefully listed off all she had to be thankful for.

After that, they spent fifteen minutes with another single mother. The woman had three-year-old twin boys who appeared to be in total control of the household. Sydney reminded the mother that attendance at Thursday night parenting classes was mandatory.

When they reached the third apartment, the door opened just as Sydney raised her hand to knock. A teenage girl stepped out.

"Hi, Allison. This is Trace McKay; he's making visits with me today."

The girl nodded but didn't look at Trace. Her eyes seemed to cling to Sydney. "Now's not a good time."

Sydney put a hand on the girl's shoulder. "I can't just wait for good times to talk to her."

"She won't answer the door."

"Then go in and tell her I'm here and I'm coming in."

"She's sick."

"Allison...your mom signed the paper agreeing to accountability. Protecting her isn't helping her."

A stare-down ensued, lasting what seemed to Trace like an eternity, but the girl finally gave in. After she opened the door, Sydney gave her a quick hug and thanked her. Amazingly, the pale-faced girl with the pink-streaked hair smiled in response.

※

"I've known prison guards who would look like wimps next to you!" Trace grinned at Sydney as she navigated the radio station parking lot. He'd kept up a steady flow of compliments since their encounter with Allison's mother. "My opinion of you has done a complete one-eighty. A woman of steel and velvet..."

"Stop it." Sydney swiped at the tears her laughter had generated. "I'm just following the Sanctuary training manual."

"Oh no, that can't be taught. You're a natural confronter. What did you major in again?"

"Human resources and industrial relations."

They got out of the car and walked up to the double glass doors. Trace reached for the handle. "I'm serious. You're amazing." He stared at a lone freckle on her left cheek as she walked past him. A kissable spot.

Somehow he lassoed his thoughts as Sydney led the way to the front desk. A young woman, probably in her early twenties, with honey-blond hair came around the corner. "Hi, Sydney." She extended her hand to him. "You must be Trace. I'm April Douglas; glad you could make it."

"Thank you." Trace shook her hand. He couldn't say he was glad to be there, because he wasn't. On top of his trepidation about freezing up in front of the microphone was the worry that going public like this might fuel the fire of the person who'd left the note. But as April Douglas showed them around the station and ushered them to their seats in the recording studio, the steel-like bands in his neck gradually relaxed.

"I'll introduce you both, ask some general questions about the Sanctuary program, and then I'd like some personal testimony." April pointed to Sydney. "I want to know what got your church and your family involved, what the hardships and rewards have been." She turned to Trace. "I know this is all new to you, but I'd like to hear what you felt when you knew you'd been accepted into the program. I want to get your reaction when you found out your new home had been destroyed by fire and how you're adjusting to living with Sydney's family. When we're done, I'm going to give a shameless plea for donations and volunteers, okay?"

"Absolutely." Sydney put on her headphones and leaned toward the microphone, a look of excited anticipation on her face. Trace, on the other hand, wiped his palms on his jeans several times before picking up the headphones on the desk in front of him.

After April gave her intro, Sydney launched into an impassioned monologue about the needs in the community. She talked about the urban ministry in Minneapolis that had inspired several families at Pineview Community Church to start a similar ministry. She described the plight of the single parents, recovering addicts, and families with disabled children in the Sanctuary program. She told of her father's passion to provide a safe and God-centered environment for people just out of prison and beginning new lives. "Humanly, we're selfish creatures, and sometimes it's really hard to love and to give. But think of what we'd do for Jesus if He were here, if He were hungry or homeless."

" 'Whatever you did for one of the least of these brothers of mine, you did for me,'" April added.

"Knowing that you're doing it for Him changes everything," Sydney said quietly.

April let a purposeful silence pass and then turned to Trace. Caught up in Sydney's zeal, he was only vaguely aware that his words were being taped. He answered all of April's questions and then turned away from her and looked at Sydney.

"I grew up without a family, without a church, and without God. I've made a lot of mistakes, one that I will live with every minute of the rest of my life. I didn't deserve a second chance, but I've been given one. What I have experienced here, being surrounded by people whose love for God is played out in everything they do, can only be described as pure, undeserved grace."

∞

"Leave Mouse home this time. Mattie will watch him for you." Trace grabbed a napkin off the kitchen table and handed Ronny a four-day-old piece of chocolate chili cake. "Breakfast of champions." He pointed to the back door. "Put him in his cage. You're going to need both hands for working."

"Can I skip school?"

Sydney laughed. "Good try."

"You can work for an hour and then walk to school." Trace ruffled the boy's hair.

Sydney filled a thermos with coffee, screwed on the top, and handed it to Trace. Their fingertips touched in the process. He thanked her with a nod. "You don't have to do this every morning, you know."

"I know. But I have to do my warm-ups anyway. I might as well be making coffee while I'm stretching."

"Have I mentioned that you look stunning in that?" His mouth tilted, folding in the dimple as he pointed to Zack's outgrown navy blue sweatshirt with Oak Hills Christian College across the front, a faded purple turtleneck, and the gray sweatpants with a hole in the right knee.

Sydney lifted her knee and hugged it to her chest, stretching her quads and enlarging the hole. "They're vented."

"Convenient. Have a good run and do Pine Bluff proud at the office today."

"I will." Sydney nodded toward the back door. "Thanks for taking him. You've got the patience of Job."

"He works hard. . .and it's only an hour."

"Maybe I'll bring lunch to you and Dad."

"I'd like that. *We'd* like that."

≪∞≫

Trace had been mudding and sanding drywall in the bathroom for over an hour when he heard the front door of the apartment open and close. He recognized the pastor's voice. The man didn't need the microphone he wore on Sunday mornings. Trace kept working, waiting for Pastor Owen's head to pop into the bathroom, checking on the progress as he had every few days. The voices migrated from the living room to the kitchen, lowered, and stayed there.

He had no intention of eavesdropping, but with the holes cut in the drywall for the outlets, Trace could hear everything.

". . .don't know if we'll recover from this, Eldon. I've cut my salary. That's between us; please don't repeat it."

"We can't give in to them. This is extortion."

"They have us over a barrel. . ."

Trace heard a sound that he assumed was a fist hitting the card table, a gesture out of character for either man. "How many families are in on this?"

Pastor Owen's sighed loudly enough for Trace to hear it through the wall. "I'm not supposed to be privy to this information."

"But you are."

"Yes. Six families, all 'old guard.' All. . .significant givers."

"I can't speak for everyone, and I'm sensitive to the position this puts you in, Owen, but if people knew what was going on, I can't believe they'd let a handful of people undermine everything we're doing here. I think we need to spell it out to the congregation. The rest of us can dig a little deeper and pick up the slack."

Again, the tired sigh. "Maybe. I've never gone over the heads of the elders, not ever. But two of them are in on this. . .boycott. If I bring it to the church, it will be without their approval."

"We need to follow God, not man."

Owen Larkin laughed. "Thank you. I needed that. Promise me one thing though, okay? I'll make sure Trace keeps getting paid for his work here. Just don't breathe a word of this to him."

≪∞≫

Sydney took the ketchup-smeared plate Trace handed her and stuck it in the dishwasher. "Thanks for helping with supper."

"Haven't grilled out in years. It was fun." He said "fun" in a voice that conveyed anything but.

60

"I'll wrap up the last burger for Mom."

"Can she actually eat after going out on a call?"

"Depends on what it is. If it was serious, she may just head straight for bed."

Trace sighed and reached across her for the dishrag. "Sounds like a good idea."

"Tired?"

"It's been a long day."

Sydney stared at his back as he wiped off the counter and then the table. He'd been quiet all day. Lunch at the apartment had been awkward, and supper wasn't much better. She wanted to say something encouraging, but nothing came to mind. She was sure the word "arson" had been scrolling through his mind all day. When he tossed the dishrag back in the sink, she said, "You know, if someone were intent on driving you out of town, they would have done something else by now."

He gave her a look that felt like icy rain.

"Hey, there hasn't been a lynch mob in Pine Bluff since Ralston Chickering was hung for 'gettin' familiar' with the schoolmarm in 1838."

She'd hoped to get a smile out of that one, but the straight line of Trace's lips hardly qualified. Reaching for the dish towel on his shoulder, Sydney let her hand linger longer than she should have. "There isn't going to be a town vote telling you to get out of Dodge, you know."

She held his gaze with hers, not about to let him turn away until she knew he understood. Just as the eye contact was starting to feel too intimate, he sighed. "I wish. There can be votes without ballots." Brushing the backs of his fingers along her cheek, he gave what could almost be called a smile. "Thanks for trying. Sleep well."

∞

Sydney yanked the sheet up to her chin and sighed. *Twenty-nine-year-old Christian women don't obsess over a two-second touch to the cheek. They don't lie awake on a work night analyzing the look in a man's eyes or the inflection in his voice as he says good night.* She punched her pillow into a ball. *Educated women in their twenties are seasoned; they have a vice grip on their emotions and can turn them off and on at will. They pray about their problems, leave them in God's hands, and drift off to peaceful sleep.*

Yeah, right. The self-chastisement wasn't working. Sydney looked at the clock for the hundredth time in the last ten minutes. 12:18.

That was when she heard the outside basement door two stories beneath her creak open and close with a thud.

Chapter 10

Sydney took a bite of spinach soup with chunks of sage-seasoned pork sausage and smiled at Colleen. They sat in a quiet corner of the Sage Stoppe, which had once been an inn along the stagecoach route between St. Paul and Duluth. The restaurant was now known for its authentic Cornish recipes. The waitresses wore long skirts covered with white aprons and white bonnets called "gooks."

Cutting a thick slice of potato bread, Colleen set it on Sydney's bread plate and began cutting one for herself. They'd each had two already. Colleen leaned in. "Okay, we've covered everything but the really good stuff. So how's your Trace?"

Pointing her knife at Colleen, Sydney tried not to smile. "He's not *my* Trace." But the words did have a nice sound.

"I want all the gooey details about the guy you keep in your basement."

Their waitress stopped and asked if they had room for dessert, forcing Sydney to put down the knife. "Pear and chocolate tart and tea with honey for me."

"Hmm. . ." As usual, Colleen was weighing her choice against Sydney's. Decision making was not her strong suit. "I'll have the toffee and apple crumble, and I'd better switch to decaf now." When the waitress walked away, she added, "And a bite or two of yours, of course. Back to Trace. I haven't had an update in two days. Are you admitting you're in love with him yet?"

"I'm admitting—" Her cell phone rang. She glanced down at the caller ID. " 'Unavailable.' How do salespeople get cell phone numbers?"

Colleen set her napkin on the table. "Hey, take it while I run to the bathroom. Give them a hard-luck sob story when they try to sell you something. That always works."

As Sydney opened her phone, Colleen stood then screwed up her face just to produce a laugh. It did. Sydney's "Hello" was barely intelligible.

Her greeting was met with silence. But not dead silence. "Hello?" she repeated.

"I won't. . ." The rough, muffled voice trailed off. "I won't. . .let him. . .hurt you." The connection went dead.

Sydney was still holding her phone when Colleen returned. She replayed the words.

"Should you call the police?" Colleen put her hand over Sydney's.

"I don't know." Sydney took a swallow from her water glass. "I'll talk to Dad first." She took a shaky breath. "I'm not going to think about it now. What were we talking about?"

"Are you sure you don't want to forget about dessert?"

With a smile she didn't feel, Sydney shook her head. "We don't get a chance to do this very often. I'm not going to let some prank call wreck our lunch."

"Okay, if you're sure. I was asking you if you were ready to admit you're in love with Trace."

Sydney let another quivering breath drift through her lips, trying to recapture the mood she'd been in before the call. "I'm ready to admit that I'm attracted and *dis*tracted enough that I'm seriously considering moving in with you."

"*Mi casa es su casa.* Might not be a bad idea to get out of such close proximity. You two cook up anything new in the kitchen?" Her eyebrows took turns rising.

Sydney ignored the eyebrow gymnastics. "He made meat loaf and baked potatoes last night and wouldn't let me help."

"Wouldn't let you help as in 'You go put your feet up, honey,' or as in 'I don't want a woman in the kitchen while I'm working'?"

"I'm honestly not sure. I don't know how to read him. Just when I think he's pulling away, he'll shock me with something teasing or downright flirtatious."

"Like what?"

"Like this morning. . .I was walking out to the car with three boxes of flyers for the craft fair plus my purse, and he and Ronny were kneeling down by the rabbit hutches. I waved and said good-bye, and the next thing I know, Trace is grabbing the boxes and opening the car door and making this huge goofy scene of teaching Ronny how to treat a beautiful lady."

"He said beautiful?"

"And lady."

"And you flirted right back, I hope."

Sydney savored the last bite of her soup and pushed the bowl aside. "I played along a bit."

"Don't you dare hold back on this one, Syd. Or I'm bringing Alvin over. I want the brown dress with the green sash, and the alarm on your biological clock is going off any minute. I'm holding off on getting pregnant again so we can have babies together."

"I'm not going to be responsible for the spacing of your children." Sydney creased the edge of the napkin against her leg. She didn't like the defensiveness that tightened her shoulders. She'd tried so hard to surrender this area of her life to God's timing. But there were too many people in her life who couldn't seem to do the same.

Colleen tilted her head slightly to the right. "Don't lose your balance, Syd. You have to be ready to accept God's will, but still you have to have hope that He's going to give you the desires of your heart."

Hope. . .she'd let herself give in to it once. Two years had passed since the guy she'd thought herself almost engaged to left her for someone else. Hope hurt.

"And what if Trace is it?" Colleen asked.

The question kept her from leaping off the mental bridge constructed of two-year-old thoughts. Sydney shrugged. "You can't spend three years in prison and not come out with some major issues. Who knows what's lurking below the surface. Is it too much to want a guy without so much baggage?"

"And *you* don't have baggage. . .and issues? I think you're using Trace's issues to keep you from getting close enough to let him see yours."

The words slammed into Sydney. "What kind of psycho-babble is that?"

"It's called truth. You're a five-foot-nine perfect size six with amazing eyes and hair a guy could get lost in, and all you can see is your one tiny flaw. Everybody's got flaws."

"Five hundred square centimeters of flaw is not tiny."

"Posh." Colleen drained her coffee cup and set it down with a thud. "I had thirty extra pounds of flaw the day I got married, forty extra now, and Stu can't keep his hands off me. It's not about skin; it's about attitude."

"Sure, everybody's got flaws, but mine are hidden. Stuart knew what he was getting when he first met you."

"So tell Trace about your little topographical maps and see how he deals with it."

"Yeah, I can work that into conversation real easy. 'Please pass the meat loaf, and by the way, I have skin grafts all over my arm and chest.'"

The waitress appeared with their desserts and tea and coffee. While Sydney busied herself spooning honey into her cup, Colleen continued with a lecture Sydney had heard more than once in the eighteen years they'd been friends. Her tone softened as she helped herself to Sydney's dessert. "When the right guy falls madly in love with you, it isn't going to matter one bit to him. In fact, knowing what you've gone through might just make him love you even more."

∞

"I tried, really." Sydney stared at the black hands of the old bank clock and shifted her phone to the other hand. In two hours she'd head home for a weekend that promised to be too long. Rubbing the back of her neck, she waited for Colleen's response, not sure she was in the mood for encouragement.

She'd left the Sage Stoppe with determination. Colleen was right—it wasn't about skin; it was about attitude. Even if it meant fighting fear every inch of the way, she wasn't going to let her scars hold her back. Whatever it took, she'd let Trace see who she was inside.

Six days later, Colleen's words had evaporated.

"It probably has nothing to do with you. He's in a funk because of the arson thing. Even if he's crazy about you, he has to be questioning if there's a future in this town. Once he sees that everybody's cool with him being here, he can concentrate on you."

Colleen's logic wasn't any different than what she'd been telling herself all week, but it helped to hear it. Trace had been reserved all week. His playfulness was gone, but she hadn't gotten the impression that he was trying to avoid her.

"You're right." Sydney tried to stretch the tension out of her neck. "I wish the guy would just talk."

Colleen laughed. "He's a man, Syd. Just hang in there. What are you doing tonight?"

"Dad's taking us to Captain Cook's for the seafood buffet."

"Ah. . .like a double date."

"Like a double date plus Ronny."

"Maybe Ronny should come and watch VeggieTales with us tonight."

Sydney stretched in the opposite direction, smiling as she did. "Hang it up, Yenta. The Mississippi's going to freeze over soon."

"Then you can take me on your honeymoon cruise in the spring."

Movement caught her eye, and Sydney turned to see her mother framed in the glass door. "Hey, my mom's here. I'll tell you all about our cozy date night tomorrow."

"You just get your flirt on, girl. Bye."

Get my flirt on? Sydney was laughing as she stood and walked to the counter. Her laughter died when she looked at her mother's face. "What happened?"

"Somebody slashed the tires on Dad's truck."

&

Trace and her father must have made a pact. They were both three-star actors at best. After asking God's blessing over their full plates, Eldon began regaling Trace with stories of Christmases past, going back far enough to include Sydney at three, picking her nose during the Sunday school Christmas program. Trace's laugh sounded brittle and rehearsed. Sydney shielded her eyes with her hand and stabbed a corn fritter.

Maybe if someone acknowledged the elephant in the living room, they could talk it out and move on to a genuinely pleasant evening. Sydney had lived with a lot of elephants over the years, but her newfound determination to face her fears was making this charade intolerable. *Let's talk about this. Who's got a motive? Who do we know who's capable of this kind of thing?*

But she held her tongue. And when her crab leg cracker slipped out of her hand and landed on Trace's plate, he grabbed a crab leg and, with more flare than the moment deserved, demonstrated the "proper way" to break it open, citing the years he'd logged at sea as his credentials. As he speared an inch-long piece of crabmeat, dunked it in melted butter, and held it out to her, Sydney looked up to see Floyd Chapel, his wife, and their grandson Shane lining up at the buffet table. The crabmeat lost its sweetness.

Floyd walked over with an empty plate in his hand. Eldon wiped his hand on his napkin and held it out. "Floyd."

"Heard about your truck."

I just bet you did. Sydney didn't possess the ability to paste on a smile the way her mother did.

"Have you met Trace yet?" Eldon asked.

Floyd nodded but didn't offer his hand. Trace appeared to size up the situation and extended his. "Glad to meet you, sir."

Another nod, and then Floyd shook Trace's hand for all of two seconds. Sydney was sure his eyes never quite met Trace's before he turned back to Eldon. "This has to stop," he sputtered. "First the fire, now this. Who knows what's next." He glared down at Eldon. "You have the power to stop this before someone gets hurt, Eldon." His bulgy eyes darted toward Trace then back again. "The church is counting on you to put an end to this—now."

§○

Trace wasn't claustrophobic. He'd handled boat cabins too small to change clothes in and kept his sanity for three years in a prison cell. Why, then, did it feel like the walls of his parole officer's office were closing in on him? Maybe it was catching a sickeningly familiar glimpse of a man whose cell had been across from his, a man who'd done time for three counts of domestic abuse for beating his wife. Maybe it was the stench of stale smoke and nervous sweat that permeated the walls. Or maybe it was knowing that he had to follow through on the last thing in the world he wanted to do.

Rubbing the back of his neck, he thought of the sleepless night that had left him feeling worse than if he hadn't tried to sleep at all. He'd gone out for his usual midnight walk, hoping the cold air and prayer time would give him a different perspective, but nothing had changed. Faced with telling Sydney about his decision, he'd been forced to define his feelings for her. He didn't have the luxury of time. What he wasn't sure of was whether or not he should keep the revelation to himself.

The man on the other side of the desk cleared his throat. He was in his midfifties, graying at the temples. Wire-rimmed glasses slid to the end of his nose as he glanced at Trace's file.

Trace sat with his elbows on his knees, fingertips meeting like a church roof, and answered his questions. When Jim Foster finally sat back in his swivel chair and crossed his arms over his belly, Trace leaned back, as well.

"So how's it going with the family. . .the Jennets? Feel like you're fitting in?"

"I couldn't have asked for a better arrangement. They're good people." Trace sighed and rubbed the back of his neck. "Which is why I need to find a different place to live."

"When's the apartment going to be finished?"

"A week or so. But I'm not talking about a different house. . . .I need a different town."

Chapter 11

S he could barely steady her hand to button her jacket. Sydney walked up the steps from the church basement next to her mother, knowing she had to get out the door before she said something she'd really regret. The look on Mattie's face told her she'd probably spouted more than she should have at the meeting.

The morning had started out so beautifully. Sharing a hymnal with Trace, his rich voice blending with hers. The sermon was on friendship, using the example of Jonathan and David, and Trace had taken notes. At one point, when Pastor Owen read from Ecclesiastes, " 'A cord of three strands is not quickly broken,' " Trace had winked at her.

And then they'd announced a short members-only meeting.

Reaching the top step, Sydney glanced at her mother. "I'm walking home." She put her Bible in her canvas bag and hiked the bag onto her shoulder.

"Good idea." Mattie gave her just a hint of a smile. "Don't bring this up at home."

"Are you"—she lowered her voice as two boys ran past them—"kidding?" It wasn't exactly the tone she should be using with her mother. "Trace would hightail it out of here if he knew."

Mattie nodded. They'd reached the front door. There, sitting on the step, was Trace. "Oh no," she whispered.

"Please tell me no one was heartless enough to tell him." Sydney pushed open the glass door. "Hi!"

He stood, flashing the same fake smile he'd used in the restaurant. "Thought I'd hang around and see if you wanted to walk with me."

Mattie slid the canvas bag off Sydney's shoulder. "See you two at home."

Sydney squeezed her mother's elbow. Mattie had spoken more loudly than she needed to. Phyllis Lincoln, waddling toward the car waiting for her at the front door, turned and glared.

"Thanks, Mom."

Sydney held out her hand to Trace. "Let's go."

He looked down at her hand then up at her face. With a grin that actually reached his eyes, he took her hand. "Making a statement, are we?"

"Yes. But that's not the only reason."

"I'm glad." He led the way to the road. "How'd the meeting go?"

"Oh, you know, like church meetings always go. Boring."

"What was it about?" He was searching her face. She could feel it, even with her eyes on the road ahead.

"Just budget stuff."

He didn't respond to that. They walked in silence for almost a quarter mile. And then his pace slowed. "Tell me the truth, Syd."

Unexpected tears made her turn from his smoky blue eyes.

His thumb rubbed the back of her hand. "I know what's going on."

Sydney stopped. "Who told you?"

"I overheard. I know the church is in trouble because of me. I won't let it go any further."

"What do you mean?"

"I have a couple leads on jobs. As soon as I find a place to rent, I'm leaving."

"Where?"

He ran his hand over his eyes. "One's in Taylors Falls. The other's in Stillwater."

Neither were all that far away. Still, she didn't trust her voice and only nodded.

"I've been thinking about the sermon." His hand shifted, and he laced his fingers through hers. "I've never had a 'covenant relationship' like the pastor described—where you vow to love someone as yourself, and you're willing to sacrifice your own goals and comfort for the other person." He squeezed her hand. "So I got to wondering. . .can you have that kind of relationship if you live an hour apart?"

&

The Vikings game was on downstairs. Mattie was making cookies. Sydney said she was going upstairs to take a nap, something she never did. Thankfully, no one commented. She wrapped herself in a quilt, curled up in her papasan chair, and shut her eyes. Every sentence that came to mind started with "Too." Too soon. . .too fast. . .too sweet. . .too scary.

Trace's words about a covenant relationship had looped through her head all afternoon. She hadn't given him the kind of answer he was probably looking for. She'd agreed to stay in touch, agreed to still see him. He'd asked her if she thought that once he was out of the Sanctuary program, people would have a problem with them seeing each other. She didn't have an answer. Too uncertain. . .

There were so many unknowns. She needed time. She had a busy week ahead, gearing up for the craft fair. She'd be gone almost every night and wouldn't cross paths with Trace often. Maybe that alone would help her think. Maybe it was a good thing he was leaving.

But it didn't feel like a good thing.

&

"Thanks anyway, but I'll just stay home and knit scarves like all the other old maids do on Friday nights." Sydney turned onto Wood Road and smiled as Colleen's raspberry sputtered through her cell phone. "Yuck. You got my ear wet."

"Come with us. . .*please.*"

The idea of spending the evening at Chuck E. Cheese's pizza place with Colleen and another mom from church and their combined total of five kids under six just wasn't tempting. Her parents were going out for catfish with some friends. Ron had picked up Ronny and all of his things after school. Jessica had been released, and they were moving back into their apartment. Stuart had invited Trace to a high school wrestling coach meeting. The aloneness would be welcome.

"I really do need some downtime. It's been a crummy week."

"Has Trace said anything more about moving?"

"He was looking for apartments in Stillwater online last night. His parole officer has to approve of everything, so it may take awhile. Dad's trying to talk him out of it."

"And you?"

"What about me?"

"Are you trying to talk him out of it?"

"No."

There was silence on the other end. She didn't have the energy for another lecture.

"I might become your worst nightmare, Syd. I'm not going to let you run from this guy. You're afraid he won't be able to love you, so you're not even going to give him the chance."

Hot tears stung Sydney's eyes. Her grip on the phone and the steering wheel tightened with each word Colleen stabbed at her. But something held her back from shouting the words in her head. *Who made you an expert? You with your cute, adoring husband and perfect kids and beautiful house. Do you have any idea what it's like to be twenty-nine and single, with everyone looking at you like you're defective, and you're too old to fit in with the singles and too single to fit in with the marrieds so you sit home and watch old movies on Friday nights and pretend that you're happy about it?* Instead, what she said was, "I'll talk to you later."

Her mother was in the kitchen when she came in, kicked her boots at the wall, and threw her keys on the counter so hard they bounced onto the floor. Mattie paused with the teapot suspended over a mug. "Bad day?"

Sydney kicked her keys across the kitchen. "I'm sick of being a target for amateur psychologists. Being single isn't a disorder. It's a choice."

Mattie handed the mug to Sydney. "You need this more than I do." Motioning toward the table, she said, "Sit."

"Where is everyone?"

"Ron just picked up Ronny, Stuart's picking Trace up at the apartment, and Dad should be home in about fifteen minutes. Talk."

Mattie listened to the recap of Sydney's conversation with Colleen and then asked, "But you think she's wrong?"

"Yes." As the word came out, she considered taking it back. She wasn't really sure of anything. "If I was supposed to fall in love with this guy, God would make it clear. There's so much junk going on, too many obstacles. He's got too much baggage."

Without a word, Mattie stood up, walked into the living room, and returned with her prayer journal. Opening it, she pulled out a folded index card. When she unfolded it, an odd-shaped paper fluttered onto the table. Sydney gasped, picking up the paper while she stared at the card in her mother's hand.

"You kept these?"

"I pray for your prince every day."

Carefully Sydney unfolded a string of five paper dolls, not girl dolls with skirts, but boy dolls with crowns on their heads. She'd been about Jessica's age when she'd cut them out. "I remember asking Grandma what I had to do to be a princess, and she said I had to marry a prince. So I asked her if she'd help me find one. That's when she showed me how to make these."

Sydney picked up the index card. At the top, in the swirling, overly embellished handwriting of a fourteen-year-old, were the words MY DREAM GUY. Ten points were numbered below it:

1. *He will be a* real *Christian.*
2. *He will love me just the way I am.*
3. *He will have an awesome sense of humor.*
4. *He will be cute, but not too cute.*
5. *He will have blue or green eyes, not brown.*
6. *He will love kids.*
7. *He won't have emotional baggage.*
8. *He will like old movies.*
9. *He will hate rap music.*
10. *He will love chocolate.*

The list had been a youth group assignment. Holding the card in her hand, she could feel the silliness of being fourteen, still more than a year away from being able to date, giggling with Colleen as they'd written their lists while staring at the boys across the room. The comment about brown eyes was there because of her most recent crush who, she'd discovered, had started "going out" with someone else. She had just heard the term "emotional baggage" and liked the sound of it. And she was still using it.

Sydney sighed. "To be young and dumb again. . ."

"How does Trace measure up to the list?"

"Are you in on this conspiracy with Colleen?"

"Just answer the question."

"He has enough emotional baggage for ten guys."

"He has a lot of hurt in his past; that doesn't mean he's carrying it around with him."

"He might like rap music."

"I highly doubt it." Mattie took the list out of her hand. "He's a handsome Christian with beautiful blue eyes, a fantastic sense of humor; we've seen him with Ronny, so we know he likes kids; he can cook—"

"I don't know if he likes old movies."

"Well, that would be a relationship stopper for sure."

Sydney clutched her mug and glared at her mother. "You and Colleen are both so anxious to marry me off that you're completely ignoring the obvious. The guy killed someone. He spent three years in prison. Who knows what could have happened to him there? His father's a gambler, and his mother hasn't even told her husband that she has a son. All I ever wanted was to find a nice, normal guy and settle down and have nice, normal children. How could a kid grow up healthy if everyone's calling him names because his dad's an ex-con?"

Mattie got up and poured herself a cup of tea in silence. When she sat down, she put her hand on her daughter's arm. "Listen to what you're saying. Sydney Jennet, the person who fought harder than anyone to get the Sanctuary program started, who champions unwed moms, homeless men, and kids who need to get off drugs—you, of all people, believe in redemption and second chances. I don't want to sound cruel, sweetie, but I think Colleen's right."

The tears began again. Sydney grabbed a napkin and pressed it to her eyes. "I know all that; I know I'm a hypocrite. But this is my future. Colleen can sound all holy, sitting there with her perfect little life, and you're married to a man every person in town looks up to. Neither of you can understand this."

Looking at Sydney over the edge of her pale green mug, Mattie nodded. "There are no perfect princes out there, Syd. I think it's time for you to have a talk with your father."

&

"Why am I just hearing all this now?" Sydney leaned against the headboard of her parents' bed, hugging a pillow and feeling like a six-year-old. Eldon stood in front of his dresser, looking at her in the mirror. He splashed cologne on his face, put his wallet in his pocket, and turned to face her.

"To be honest, Syd, I didn't want you and Zack to know. I like being the hero in my little girl's eyes. I wanted my kids to see me the way I am now, without that shadow hanging over me."

"But. . .it feels like you lied to us."

"I'm sure it does." He walked over to the foot of the bed, looking down at her. "I always knew that if it came up, I'd tell you everything. And maybe I was wrong; maybe telling you would have been a good thing. But when does a father decide that it's the right time to tell his kids that he put himself through college with his own marijuana farm?"

Her father had been in prison when she was born. What else had he lied about?

Eldon took his brown corduroy sports jacket off the doorknob and sat down on the corner of the bed. "You can't imagine the mixed emotions I had holding my firstborn for the first time. You'd been around for six weeks and I'd only seen pictures. I had so much guilt over leaving Mom alone all those months; it took God and time and a lot of good counsel for us to reconnect."

"I've always looked at your relationship as the ideal."

Eldon touched her face. "It is. . .now. But it wouldn't be what it is today if we hadn't had to fight for it. I've heard Trace say exactly what I've always felt—I would give anything to change that part of my life, but it was that time that brought me to my knees before the Lord."

"So Trace knows?"

"Yes."

"And this is why you pushed for parolees in the Sanctuary?"

Eldon nodded. "I'm sorry, honey. I'm sure it must feel like betrayal, like I'm not the man you thought I was."

Sydney stared at her father's shoes. That was the bottom line. He wasn't the man she thought he was.

Her head hurt. She needed time to process, but he was looking at her, wanting something. She couldn't give sudden absolution, couldn't say it was all okay, it didn't matter.

Her father reached across the bed, resting his hand near hers but not touching it. "What I hope you'll realize someday is that I wouldn't be the person I am today if it weren't for my mistakes." His hazel eyes searched her face. "And the same is true of Trace."

Sydney hugged the pillow closer and shut her eyes against the sting of tears. "I just. . .need time."

"I know." Her father leaned toward her and kissed the top of her head, then stood. He stepped toward the door.

Sydney took a shuddering breath. "Dad?"

"What, honey?"

"It's not just *his* past. . . ."

"It's yours, too?"

"Yes," she whispered.

He sat back down. "You want a man's point of view?"

"Of course."

"You are a beautiful woman, Syd, and your scars don't take away anything from the whole package. But even if you hadn't been blessed with physical beauty or if you had scars over half your body, it's not the way you look but the way a man feels about you that makes the picture in his mind. In spite of the way we try to appear on the outside, we're fragile creatures with delicate egos. A woman who can make a man feel respected and needed and desired is going to win his heart. Most of us face rejection in some form every day, and to know that there's that one woman who looks up to you means everything."

His hand cupped the side of her face. "Haven't you ever seen a good-looking guy with a woman who's just so-so and wondered what he's doing with her when he could have any woman he wanted? It's because he feels at home with her; he can be himself and be sure of her love. In his eyes she's beautiful."

Her father turned the gold band on his left hand then looked once again in her eyes. "When I see your mom standing in front of the mirror and complaining about wrinkles and bulges and gray hair, I know she thinks I'm just patronizing her, but I can say with all honesty that she is still the most beautiful woman in the world to me." Eldon's eyes glistened, and he blinked hard. "I want that for you. I want some man to look at you and not comprehend why you don't see yourself the way he sees you." He put his fingertips beneath her chin and raised her head. "But you have to give him the chance, Syd."

Chapter 12

After her parents left for the restaurant, Sydney made a sandwich and curled on the couch with her laptop. An hour later, she'd finished the final floor plan for craft fair booths, drafted a flyer for Breakfast with Santa, and roughed out an agenda for the December chamber luncheon. She closed her computer and walked into the bathroom, lit only by a night-light, and started running water in the tub. She stared at the bottles of bath salts that lined the wall, wondering what aromatherapy scent matched the strange mix of peace and sadness in her. Deciding between Mandarin Ginger and Lemongrass Lavender seemed too difficult, so she added a scoop of each, thinking she'd probably end up smelling like a fruit compote.

As the steam rose and filled the room with a unique but inviting scent, Sydney unbuttoned her blouse, facing away from the mirror the way she always did. As she reached the fourth button, Colleen's words echoed in her head. *"It's not about skin; it's about attitude."*

Closing her eyes, she lifted a prayer without words, a prayer that was sheer emotion—the dormant cry of an eleven-year-old girl whose dreams of beauty had melted in the flames. Slowly she pivoted and stared at her reflection in the dim light.

This is who I am. This didn't happen outside of Your knowledge, did it, Father? Help me to accept it, Lord, to stop hiding and embrace Your plan for me. Help me to believe that someone could love me in spite of this.

She eased into the tub and let the water run until the blanket of bubbles reached her chin. *Father, forgive me for trying to protect myself instead of trusting You to take care of me. Forgive me for letting fear run my life. Help me not to run away or run ahead of You, Lord.*

An hour later she woke to find the water barely lukewarm. After putting on a pair of clean sweats, she went up to bed, grateful that the house was still empty and she didn't need to talk to anyone. It was just before nine when she crawled under the quilt her great-grandmother had stitched by hand. She was asleep in less than thirty seconds.

When the now-familiar thud of the basement door woke her, she slid out of bed and walked to the window. In the light of a nearly full moon, she could see Trace walking toward the barn. Without taking time to think through what she'd do if she found him, she grabbed her running shoes from under the bed.

Zipping her goose-down jacket as she ran, she reached the barn just as Trace sauntered around the corner toward the woods. A rock spun out beneath her toe. Trace turned and stared at her. The moonlight and the mercury vapor light on the pole in front of the barn made it bright enough to see his face, but it was too shadowed to read his expression.

"Sydney?"

"Hi," she stammered. "I couldn't sleep."

He walked toward her. "Welcome to the club." He held out his gloved hand to her. "Want to walk?"

"I. . .don't know. What do you do out here every night?"

"I walk. And pray. It's so quiet in the house; I'm not used to it, and it kind of gets to me sometimes. It's a different kind of quiet out here." He dropped his hand and stared up at the stars. "I want to enjoy it all I can before it gets too cold."

Sydney nodded, staring up at the star-sprinkled sky and watching her breath rise and drift in the still air. She pulled her gloves out of her pocket and put them on, then held out her left hand to Trace. "Let's walk."

The weeds were high behind the barn, but Trace's nightly walks had trampled down a narrow path. He motioned for Sydney to go ahead of him. "Single file until we get to the woods." He stepped aside and let her pass. "Mmm. . .you smell good."

"It's a new scent I'm trying. It's called Fruit Salad."

"Delicious."

When they reached the woods, he took her hand again. There was a wide path between the trees, cleared years ago for her brother's four-wheeler, but they had to walk slowly in the soft light that filtered through half-bare branches and dappled the leaf-covered ground. Trace pointed to a rabbit that ran across the path.

"You know, it's good for me to watch you enjoying little things," Sydney said. "I take so much for granted."

"We all do. Having it taken away for a while was one of the biggest blessings I got out of being incarcerated. Everything seems intensified. The stars look brighter; the air smells better; I hear things I never used to pay attention to, like the sound of the leaves when I walk."

"What did you miss most?"

"Freedom. Sounds obvious, I suppose. But I never thought of it before I didn't have it. Not just major things like being able to decide what I want to do when, but things like not being able to choose what brand of deodorant I want or buy my favorite gum. I'd find myself thinking of the strangest things at the strangest times. When I'd be out in the yard at St. Cloud at this time of year, I'd think of all the bonfires I used to have with friends and how stupid I was not to absolutely relish roasting a hot dog on a stick and pulling the burnt shell off a marshmallow. I'd wake up in the middle of the night dreaming about fresh-squeezed orange juice or waffles that you could actually cut with a fork."

Such simple, daily things. As she tried to imagine life without the things she took for granted, she suddenly pictured her father, alone in a cell, missing out on the daily changes of his wife's pregnancy, agonizing over the shame he'd brought on her and his unborn child. His words replayed in her mind: *"What I hope you'll realize someday is that I wouldn't be the person I am today if it weren't for my mistakes. And the same is true of Trace."*

Not in spite of their mistakes, but *because* of their mistakes. It would take awhile to absorb what she'd just learned about her father, but this one thing she believed with all her heart: God was in the business of making all things new. She smiled at Trace. "What else?"

"I've never cared much about what I wore, but I'd lie on my bunk and think about how good it would feel to put on a white dress shirt and a pair of khakis with a belt. I'd try to picture myself with hair down to my shoulders, maybe even a ponytail. . .just because I could."

Sydney cringed. She couldn't picture him with a ponytail. But there was so much she didn't know about him. "Do you like rap music?"

Even in the dark she could see the confusion on his face. "Where did that come from?"

"I just. . .need to know."

Trace shook his head. "I don't suppose I'd understand women any better if I hadn't missed those three years in the real world."

"Probably not."

"So here you are walking with me again, and I still don't know why you agreed the first time."

"No, you don't." She smiled at him and pointed to an opening between the trees that led into a plowed field. "How was the meeting tonight?"

Trace laughed. "Smooth subject-shifting. The meeting was good. Stuart's put together a solid team of coaches."

"Are you going to be helping him?"

"Unofficially, from the bench, for as long as I'm here. I don't think the school board would approve of me."

"If they heard your whole story, they might realize you're exactly the kind of role model those kids need."

Trace smiled at her and squeezed her hand. "Thank you for the vote of confidence."

"Well, it's true. Kids think they're invincible. They need to hear the truth about where they could end up if they keep taking risks with drinking and drugs. You're a straight shooter, and they'd listen to you. I don't think God put you through three years in prison for nothing, Trace." Her voice was getting more passionate with each sentence, and he seemed to find her highly entertaining. "You're not listening."

He laughed. "I'm listening. I appreciate all the compliments, but the truth is that no parent is going to want me around their kid."

"That's garbage!"

"Well, I'm not going to be around long enough to find out."

Sydney let go of his hand.

He stopped walking and turned to face her, taking her hand in both of his. "I'm not moving to China, Syd."

"I know," she whispered.

"And you're not sure you want me to stay anyway, are you?"

"I. . .think being here is good for you."

"But is it good for you?" His hands tightened on hers. "Would it scare you, Sydney Rose, if I said I'm falling for you?"

Chapter 13

*W*ould *it scare you. . . ?"* he'd asked. Why was everyone suddenly accusing her of being scared? It took a moment for the rest of his sentence to traverse the nerve path to her brain. *"I'm falling for you."*

She *was* scared, of course. In spite of the fact that she'd dreamed, imagined, and rehearsed this moment since she was fourteen, she was terrified. "Yes." She held his eyes with a steadiness she hadn't possessed the day before. "But not for the reason you think."

With just the slightest movement, he nodded. His fingertips touched her sweater just below the hollow of her neck. "Because of this?" he whispered.

"My father told you?"

"No. I didn't ask; I've been waiting for you to tell me."

Sydney's pulse was drumming in her ears. She couldn't remember how to breathe.

"What happened?" Trace's voice wrapped around her like a hug.

"I was eleven. It was the day Zack was born. Dad had just put in the dormer window upstairs and he'd filled the burn barrel with scraps. He was getting ready to burn it when my mom went into labor. After they left for the hospital, I thought it would be fun to surprise him by burning everything."

Her right arm moved in toward her middle, and she covered it with her left. "What I didn't know was that he'd poured gasoline on the wood. . . ."

Trace's hand rested on her shoulder.

"My sleeve went up in flames so fast I couldn't even think what to do. I screamed and ran—the worst thing you can do. My grandfather ran out and tore a sheet off the clothesline and wrapped me in it." She stopped, deliberately slowing her breathing. "I had three surgeries for skin grafts. I have. . ." She looked Trace in the eye then turned away, brushing her hand over the top of her jacket. "I have scars. . .all over. . .on the right side."

The groan that came from Trace startled her. She had only a moment to think of running back to the house before his arms slid around her and held her tight. Minutes passed. And then he whispered, "I am so, so sorry."

She thought he'd let her go then. He was sorry he couldn't love her the way she was. Wasn't that what he was saying? But his arms stayed. His lips brushed the top of her head. "Eleven is such a. . .transition age. Especially for a girl."

Sydney swiped at her face and nodded against his chest.

After awhile he took her hand and they started walking again. "So what has it done to you, Syd?"

She looked at him out of the corner of her eye, not sure what he was asking. "If you expect me to say something like 'What doesn't kill you makes you stronger,' I can't."

"I don't want to hear what you think you're supposed to say. I want to hear the truth. How has it affected your sense of self, your confidence?"

"A lot. In some areas."

He smiled in a way she'd seen before, a way that said he was hearing all that she'd left unsaid. "Your love life?"

Sydney returned the smile that had just a hint of teasing in it. "My lack thereof."

"Why?"

Why? Quoting her father, she said, "Because men are visual creatures."

Trace laughed. "True. To a point. Looks may grab our attention. . . ." He stopped and faced her. His gloved fingertips traced a line from her temple to her chin. "Yours grabbed mine at the bus stop." He drew his hand away. "But it's not the only thing that does. And it takes something much deeper to hold it."

They began walking again. Moments passed before Sydney found the voice that had disappeared with the touch of Trace's fingertips. "Some men don't care what's inside if they don't like the wrapping."

Trace pulled back a branch and let her step ahead of him. The grass in the meadow was knee-high and painted silver in the moonlight. "I take it you've met a few of those."

"Two of them." She thought of Colleen's lecture. "The rest I guess I've run from before I could find out what they'd do."

"Tell me about the two."

Sydney sighed. "When I started high school, I was still wearing a pressure garment on my arm to reduce scarring, and after that I wore long sleeves and high-necked shirts. I had a merciful guidance counselor who got me out of taking swimming when I was a junior. In some ways, hiding my scars probably made things worse. Colleen told me a couple of the rumors she'd heard; one said that my whole body looked like alligator skin. Anyway, I had guy friends, but I didn't date."

Sydney fingered the strings that dangled from the hood of her jacket. "There was a girl in my dorm in college who was bald because she'd had surgery and chemo for a brain tumor, but she never wore a wig. Her confidence inspired me to give up my turtlenecks. That lasted about two weeks; I couldn't stand everyone staring or trying to act like they weren't. So I covered up again, but then a new guy at school who I had an insane crush on finally asked me out. He was constantly telling me how beautiful I was, and it made me feel deceptive."

She flashed a quick glance at Trace, unable to handle the intensity of his gaze for more than seconds. "After our third date, he was talking about how many kids we were going to have, and I knew that before things got any more serious, he had a right to know about my scars. So I showed him my arm. He was very kind and said he was so sorry I had to go through all that. But that was the last time he told me I was beautiful."

She took a breath to steady the unexpected quiver in her voice. "Within a month he'd transferred to a private school."

"And you've been afraid ever since."

Fear. It was working its way into every conversation. "Yes."

"It would be hard to let yourself be vulnerable after that."

They walked in silence for several minutes.

"The other one was just a few years ago. I was living in St. Paul, working in human resources at Minnesota Mining. This guy asked me out, and I decided to tell him all about my accident on the first date. I showed him the scars on my arm and described the rest of them. It didn't seem to faze him. We dated for two years. I didn't admit it at the time, but I always had this feeling that he was scanning the horizon, on the lookout for something better to come along. There always seemed to be something missing in our relationship. I worked really hard at denying it, but deep down I knew what it was." She ran her fingers along her upper arm. "About the time I was expecting an engagement ring, he told me he'd found someone else."

"Mmm." Trace slowed. "Is that why you're living back at home?"

Sydney wrinkled her nose at him. "I would *not* leave a good job over a man. About six months after he dumped me, the company downsized by seventeen hundred employees. My only satisfaction was that they let him go before me."

"Can I be honest?"

"I. . .guess."

"The first guy was a jerk." He flashed a smile. "But maybe the second one left for completely different reasons. Maybe you simply didn't have enough in common. Isn't it possible that it had nothing to do with your burns?"

She didn't have an answer.

Trace filled the silence. "Can I ask you another question?"

Again she said, "I. . .guess."

"What was your first impression of me? At the bus stop—or when I walked into the chamber office, what was your first thought?"

How honest do I have to be? "That you were. . .you had a nice smile."

"Come on—you're killing my ego here."

Sydney looked up at him then concentrated on her footing on the uneven turf. "I thought you were extremely handsome, and I was hoping you were single and you weren't just passing through."

His smile was self-conscious. "That was more than I was asking for, but I'll take it."

"Was there a point to your question?"

"Yes, but I lost it. Okay, it's coming back to me. What happened to all those thoughts when you found out who I was?"

She thought back to the almost physical shock she'd felt. "I was. . . surprised."

"That's polite."

"I was stunned."

"And. . . ?"

This wasn't something she wanted to say out loud. "Disappointed."

Trace nodded. "Would you have had the courage to get to know me if you hadn't been forced into it? If I hadn't ended up in your house?"

As the truth registered, Sydney looked over at him. "Probably not."

"I guess all I was trying to say was. . .I kind of understand your fear."

The sound of rustling grass made them stop and look to the right. Two does bounded across the clearing less than a hundred feet in front of them. Sydney glanced at the deer then studied Trace's face as he watched them with childlike wonder.

"Let's head back before you get cold," he said.

They didn't talk the rest of the way. As they came around the side of the barn, Trace stopped and took both of her hands in his. "You have a way of getting me off track."

"I do?"

"You do. Half an hour ago I was working up the guts to ask you out."

"You were?"

He nodded. "I finally have enough money to take you out for supper if you don't mind sharing fries."

She laughed but didn't answer. Taking him by the hand, she led him to the circle of light beneath the utility pole. Taking off her gloves, she handed them to him. Slowly she unzipped her jacket and pulled the neck of her sweater down to three inches below her collarbone. In spite of the sting of tears in her eyes, she forced herself to watch his face.

His eyes narrowed, and he shook his head slowly. "I'm so sorry, Syd." And then he took off his right glove, brought his fingers to his lips, and touched the spot just below the hollow of her neck. Involuntarily, Sydney took a sharp breath, her eyes widening, searching his. The acceptance she saw there weakened the wall she'd hidden behind for so long. She closed her eyes, and a tear slid from beneath her lashes and onto his hand. His arms closed around her. Against her hair he whispered, "Will you go out with me, Sydney Rose?"

Chapter 14

Trace opened his eyes on Saturday morning and stared at the clock. Sure he was dreaming, he blinked twice, but the time didn't change. He'd slept until after nine, something that would have been impossible in prison. After walking with Sydney, it had taken him well over an hour to fall asleep. He kept going over and over the things she'd said and the way he'd responded, wondering what she'd seen on his face when he looked at her scar, questioning if he'd said enough to make her understand that he wasn't repulsed, that he hurt for her.

Instead of pushing him away, her vulnerability had touched something deep inside him, a primal kind of urge to protect her. If anything, it had made him want to touch her all the more, to kiss away the pain of years of stares and rumors and self-doubt. Rubbing his hand across his face, he swung his legs out of bed. *Lord, help me to take every thought captive. I want to honor You and wait on Your timing.*

The floor above him creaked, and the smells seeping down through the crack beneath the door were tantalizing. Grabbing clean clothes, he took the stairs two at a time. With a wave at Mattie, he darted into the bathroom, finishing his shower before the water had completely warmed.

Tossing his dirty clothes to the bottom of the stairs, he smiled at the two women who had their backs to him in the kitchen. "Morning, ladies. Put me to work."

Sydney turned and handed him a long-handled spoon. Her hair looked like it had only been quickly brushed. She wasn't wearing makeup, and her eyes had a look of morning softness. *Guide my thoughts, Lord.*

"Sleep well?" she asked.

"Eventually."

She nodded, as if she'd experienced the same sleeplessness. "Orange juice is in the freezer. Sorry, it's not fresh-squeezed."

The fact that she'd remembered his comment tasted better than a glass of juice ever could. He smiled at her, only then noticing that the long-sleeved navy blue shirt she was wearing had a slightly scooped neck. He didn't try to hide his stare as he looked at the raised weblike scar that stretched across her chest and toward one shoulder. Taking the spoon, he smiled at her. "Thank you," he whispered, his eyes fixed on hers, making sure she understood it had nothing to do with the spoon.

As he pulled a pitcher out of the cupboard, Eldon came up behind him and clamped one large hand on his shoulder. "What did I tell you about making me look bad?"

With the spoon in one hand and a smiley-faced Kool-Aid pitcher in the other, Trace turned and held out both objects to Eldon. "That's the last thing I'd ever want to do. Orange juice is in the freezer."

Mattie's laugh was loud and long. Digging an apron out of the back of a drawer, she tied it around Eldon's waist and told Trace where to find the camera. Eldon's answer was to act completely oblivious to her. As he scooped the juice concentrate into the pitcher, he turned to Trace. "I hear you're getting the grand tour today."

Trace nodded. "Unless there's something you need me to do."

"Oh no." Eldon gave a roguish smile. "The last thing I'd ever want to do is keep you from a fun-filled day of sightseeing with our walking encyclopedia here."

Ten minutes later, the table looked like a Norman Rockwell print. After meticulously filling each square in his waffle, first with butter and then with Eldon's homemade maple syrup, Trace looked up to see Sydney staring at him, an amused smile on her face. He smiled back. "Food should be an experience."

With two hands, she held out a platter of sausage patties. *"Bon appétit."*

Eldon sat down and folded his hands. "Heavenly Father, thank You for this meal and the blessings You have showered upon us this day and always. Thank You for Your care and protection. You know the concerns of our hearts, Lord; help us to leave them all with You and trust You to light our paths and guide our steps. In the name of Your precious Son, we pray, and we live. Amen."

Trace took his first bite of waffle; the taste was indescribable. Suddenly it all seemed overwhelming. Sydney remembering that he'd dreamed of waffles and fresh-squeezed orange juice, Mattie putting her hand on his back so naturally as she set the syrup on the table. . . Just as he took a long, steadying breath, Eldon said, "Can you pass the butter, son?"

Trace tried to swallow, but his throat felt constricted. His eyes suddenly brimmed with tears he couldn't stop. Grabbing a napkin, he pretended to be choking, dabbing his eyes, swallowing hard, and then coughing. Mattie stood up, ready, he knew, to administer the Heimlich maneuver. If he could just get his emotions under control, the scenario would be comical. He held up his hand, signaling that he was all right, and headed for the bathroom.

Head down, gripping the edge of the sink, he took three deep breaths then turned on the water and splashed his face. It wasn't that he'd never shed tears; he'd cried buckets in the two months after turning his life over to God. But nothing before or since had made him feel like this. Breaking down under the enormity of God's grace and mercy is one thing; falling apart over waffles is another thing altogether.

But it wasn't really the food; it was the family, the motherly touch on his back, the trust in Sydney's eyes, and a single word. . .*son.*

೭ಾ

"Pine Bluff's first permanent structure was erected in 1838, twenty years before Minnesota became a state. . . ."

Trace pulled the truck out of the driveway and arched his eyebrow at the woman in the red boots sitting next to him. "I think I'm getting what your dad meant."

"Oh, you have no idea. I worked as a tour guide every summer for six years."

"Oh boy."

"And if you interrupt me, I have to rewind to the beginning."

He gave her a baleful look.

"Just kidding."

"Go on. I guess there are worse things to pass the time. Fingernails on chalkboard, Chinese water torture. . ."

"Which reminds me. . .we have to make a pact to live in the moment today."

"Meaning. . .?"

"Meaning that for one day we don't talk about any of the bad stuff going on around us."

"I'm with you, Pollyanna. Keep tour guiding."

Sydney laced the fingers of her red leather gloves and angled in the seat to face him. With a deep breath, she began. "Pine Bluff is steeped in history and rich with homespun tales. Oh. . .and by the way, lunch is on me."

"But I asked you out."

She waved his protest away. "Seventy-five percent of our well-kept nineteenth-century buildings are listed in the National Register of Historic Places, and many of the elegantly restored homes are open to the public for tours. Several of these homes are occupied by descendants of the original owners, who will gladly regale you with tales of days gone by. A few even claim that on a still, dark night, Mordecai and Susanna Tate, two of the founders of Pine Bluff, may sit on the porch and sip tea with you. While never proven, these legends have certainly not hindered tourism."

"Wait. Gwyneth isn't crazy after all?"

"No. Gwyneth isn't the *only* crazy one."

"Do you believe the legends?"

"If I say no, I lose my job; if I say yes, you think I'm crazy. I plead the fifth. Actually, I think the power of suggestion is a strong thing, and good for business."

They stopped at the chamber of commerce office. The back door was unlocked; Sydney held it open for Trace. He sniffed as he walked past her. "Smells like fresh paint."

"Shane Chapel, Gwyneth's great-grandson—the kid you met the first time you came to church—is doing some work for us. My dad hires him to mow the grass at home and anything else he can come up with." She lowered her voice. "We have an agenda—to show him what real Christians act like. I hate to think what he's seeing at home. Floyd isn't role model material."

"You really don't like that man, do you?"

"I repent of it constantly, but no, I don't." She nodded toward the door that led to the front office. "Go say hi to Shane; I'm going to look at the mail."

The floor along the walls was covered with drop cloths. The boy was standing near the top of a twelve-foot ladder.

"Hi, Shane. Don't know if you remember me."

Shane looked down, nodded, and went back to pulling an edger just below the ceiling. "I remember."

Trace walked through the opening in the front counter and scanned the black-and-white photographs and framed newspaper clippings on the wall. Pictures of lumberjacks, logjams, and an old sawmill dated back to the late 1800s. "This town has quite a history."

Moments passed. Trace wondered if Shane had even heard him. Then the boy pointed toward a glass-front cabinet. "My great-grandma wrote a book."

Trace walked to the cabinet and picked up the paperback displayed on a book stand. The picture on the cover gave him an almost physical jolt. A little girl with straight hair and bangs and an enormous bow on top of her head sat on the step of the apartment building where he was supposed to be living. Across the top was the title *Growing Up in Pine Bluff*. "Gwyneth Monroe Chapel" was printed at the bottom.

The book was full of pictures interspersed with anecdotes. He flipped to the front of the book where a stern-faced Susanna Tate stood behind her seated and amused-looking husband, Mordecai. Trace was engrossed in the first page when the ladder creaked.

"How long you on probation?"

This was the honesty Trace had said he wanted. At the moment he wasn't so sure. "Ten years."

"Hmm."

Shane stepped down from the ladder then walked through the counter and into the back room. Trace heard Sydney tell him he was doing a good job.

"Thanks," Shane replied.

"Did you talk to Trace?"

"Yeah." The sound of a paint can being pried open followed. "You like him?" Shane asked.

"Yes. As a matter of fact, I do like him."

৪০

The formal tour began on the north end of Main Street and took two full hours. Sydney pulled Trace into every gift shop and candy store. By noon he had sampled eight varieties of fudge and four kinds of salsa and had tasted freeze-dried strawberries for the first time in his life. He'd also been introduced to more than a dozen people and discerned instantly which ones knew who he was. The most remarkable part was that Sydney didn't seem to care about the reactions. If anything, the rebel in her was actually enjoying the quickly covered looks of trepidation or even the blatant curious stares as she introduced Trace as "a friend of mine."

Around twelve thirty, Sydney looked at her watch and asked him if he was hungry yet.

Trace laughed in response. "You're like a little Jewish grandma. I haven't gone ten minutes without food in my mouth since I got up this morning."

"Eating a little at a time throughout the day is supposed to be the best way to keep your weight under control."

"I don't think that rule works if your main food group is fudge."

"Fine. We'll have a healthy meat and vegetable lunch." She pointed toward the sandblasted sign for Founders Park a block ahead of them. "Go find us a picnic table and I'll meet you there."

Trace shot a distrusting look her way but did as he was told. She was back in fifteen minutes with two grocery bags. Out of one she pulled a bag of charcoal and a can of starter fluid; from the other she took hot dogs, buns, potato chips, marshmallows, graham crackers, and Hershey bars.

Reaching for Sydney's hand, he pulled her down onto the bench beside him. Gripped with an emotion he couldn't even label, he put his hand on the side of her face, feeling the softness of her cold skin. "You have no idea, Sydney . . . All this. . ." He pulled his hand away and swept it toward Main Street. "It's all just everyday stuff for you. I don't think you have any idea what it means to me. The last few weeks. . .just being in your house, with your mom taking pictures, watching you folding clothes, helping your dad feed the rabbits. . .it's like visiting a foreign country, but feeling like. . ."

"Like you belong?"

Looking down at the ground, Trace nodded slowly. "I didn't want to say that. But yeah, it's like—"

Sydney's cell phone, sitting on the table just behind them, rang at full volume and startled him.

Sydney grabbed the phone and looked at it. "It's just Mom. I'll call her back in a minute."

"Answer it. I'll get the grill going." He stood, realizing the timing was perfect. If he didn't curtail the schmaltz, Sydney was going to get a truly distorted view of him.

Sydney bent her head over the phone. "No, you did the right thing," he heard her say. "We'll be right there." She closed her phone and stared at him, her eyes wide, her face pale. "Somebody. . .spray-painted on the side of the barn. . . ." She looked away from him. "It says 'Killer.'"

Chapter 15

Trace was hefting the suitcase she'd loaned him into the backseat when Sydney walked out of the house. She set a bag of groceries on the floor behind the driver's seat and slid in, waiting for him to get in and shut the door. "Where am I taking you?" She fumbled with the key.

"My PO found a place. They use it for witness protection. He thought it might be better if no one knew where I was, at least for now, so he's going to meet us at St. Paul's Church in Braham and drive me there. Very clandestine, hey?"

"Very." She didn't like his casual attitude.

"Actually, that's his church. He's planting tulip bulbs."

Sydney backed up and pointed the car toward the road. "You're not taking this seriously."

Trace leaned his head against the headrest. "It isn't going to do anyone any good to overreact. I'm getting out of here; your family won't be a target after it gets around that I'm gone."

"I'm not worried about us. What if it doesn't stop when you leave? What if they find you?"

"You think you know who's behind this, don't you? Gwyneth's son?"

"And his cohorts."

"What's his motive?"

"Societal cleansing."

"That's pretty strong. Isn't he some kind of leader in your church?"

Sydney took her eyes off the road long enough to cock her eyebrow in Trace's direction. "He's an accountant, so of course he got voted to be a deacon in the church. People don't seem to see his twisted legalistic ideas. I don't think he believes in grace *or* forgiveness."

"An eye for an eye. . ."

"Exactly."

Trace turned toward the side window. "We need to pray for that man."

Involuntarily, Sydney's fingers tightened on the steering wheel.

"Whatever has him so angry, you know it's eating him alive." Trace shifted in the seat to face her.

"How. . .how can you think like that when you're the object of his anger? I mean, I know you're right. But how do you get to that point?"

"I guess all the time I stewed in my own anger showed me how toxic it is.

I feel sorry for people who don't know there's a way out." He reached across the seat and brushed a strand of hair from her face. "There isn't always a person involved. We can get locked into anger over an. . .event."

The air rushed out of her lungs, and for a moment she couldn't remember how to fill them again. He was talking about *her*. She'd never thought of herself as angry. Scared, yes—afraid to believe in happily-ever-after, yes—but angry? Her lips parted, but her protest never materialized.

Trace's open hand brushed the back of her neck. He lifted his hand, letting her hair slip through his fingers, then did it again. It was hard to keep her thoughts on the road. When he stopped, his hand rested on her shoulder. "I don't know," he said. "I've tried to imagine how you must have felt. You were eleven, probably just starting to think about boys and clothes and makeup." His fingers trailed down her arm, down the jacket sleeve that hid her scars. "And then something happens that makes you question everything about who you are and what your future holds. I think I'd be angry."

A psychologist studying her body language at that moment would certainly side with Trace. Her knuckles whitened; her spine wasn't touching the back of the seat. She'd laid so much down in her prayer of surrender a week ago, but maybe it was just the tip of the iceberg. "I've never. . . I don't know."

She heard him take a deep breath and let it out slowly. "If things were different, we'd have time to sort through all this. But we don't have time. I'm just wondering if part of the reason you pull back from me is because you don't think you deserve happiness. I may be way off base on this. . . ." He stopped, and Sydney had the feeling he was gathering courage. "Is it possible that you blame yourself for your accident?"

They were driving through a replanted forest area. White pines stood like sentinels in perfectly straight rows that stretched as far as she could see. Were they planted by hand? By high school kids on Earth Day back in the seventies? Irrelevant questions delayed the answer to the one Trace had asked. She counted the rows as they filed past the window.

Did she blame herself? Not in so many words. But how often had she relived the moment. . .striking the match, lowering it to the wad of newspaper she'd thrown on top of the wood. . .the roar. . .deafening. . .engulfing. . .panic. Why hadn't she smelled the gasoline? Why didn't she drop to the ground and roll the way she'd learned in school?

Did she really believe she didn't deserve happiness? "I don't know," she whispered.

Trace's hand slid over hers on the steering wheel. "I'm asking because I've had the same thoughts about myself."

She looked at him then back at the road, but it was long enough to read a sadness that shouldn't have been there. "Maybe we're both guilty of believing a lie."

"Maybe this is a good time to start believing that we both deserve some happiness." He pointed to the street sign where she needed to turn. "I'm willing to give it a try if you are."

Turning the corner, she saw the church on the left. The ride had gone too fast. "I'm willing. Will you call me?"

"Every chance I get. Did you know your dad loaned me money for a car?"

"No." Sydney smiled. "But that's my dad for you."

Trace nodded. "This place isn't within walking distance of anything. I couldn't accept a job without a car. I'll buy a phone with my first paycheck."

Jim Foster, the parole officer, was waiting for them in the church parking lot. Trace rolled down the window and introduced Jim to Sydney.

Bending down to look in the window, Jim nodded at Sydney. "If you need to get in touch with him, you can contact me." He walked around to the driver's side of his car and got in.

Trace's right hand brushed her cheek, then conformed to the back of her head as he leaned toward her. There was no resistance as he drew her closer and his lips pressed against hers. After a moment, he touched his lips to her cheek and then her ear. "Save the marshmallows," he whispered. "We're still going to have that picnic."

⁊

Like magic, the Pineview Community Church budget was back in the black by the following Sunday. Sydney volunteered for the nursery during second service. There were too many faces she didn't want to look at. Though she didn't have facts, she was pretty sure she knew at least some of the people who had withdrawn their giving for the past two months. The only word that came to her mind as she rocked a sleeping infant was "unconscionable."

Colleen's head emerged over the half door of the nursery. "Hiding out?"

"Uh-huh. I might punch somebody if I go upstairs."

"Refreshing to hear someone being honest. Not a lot of that around here lately. How you doing?"

"I can't say 'fine' now that I've got the honesty thing going, can I?"

"Nope."

"I'm. . .doing. One day at a time. I feel like I'm waiting for something, but I don't know what. When are we going to know if it's safe for Trace to come back? We don't know if the jerk who slashed the tires just doesn't want church money supporting him, or doesn't want him in town, period."

"Can I be hyperspiritual for a minute?"

Sydney laughed. "Go for it."

"I think you should be grateful for this time. I think it's just what you need. It's already helped you define how you feel about him, hasn't it?"

"If feeling like a body part has been lopped off without anesthesia is called defining, then I guess you're right."

Rust-colored oak leaves drifted lazily in the afternoon sun and landed on the algae-covered water at the edge of Pokegama Lake. Trace pulled up the hood of his sweatshirt. Though the sky was cloudless and sunlight dappled the surface of the lake, the air was crisp, the November breeze whispering of winter.

His hand slid into the back pocket of his jeans. He'd finally earned the money for a cell phone. Almost an hour had passed since he'd left his first message for Sydney.

In the two and a half weeks that had passed since he'd left Pine Bluff, he'd talked to her only twice, both times from a pay phone while she was at work. Neither conversation had done much to counteract his battle with doubts. Had she had time to think more clearly without him around? He tucked the phone away and stepped onto the path. Each step on the pine-needle carpet released the scent of Christmas. Where would he be in a month? Still here, celebrating the holidays alone? He could go to his mother's—shock her husband and kids by showing up at the door. The thought brought a sneer. It didn't even remotely paint a "home for the holidays" scene. The only place he wanted to be was a place he couldn't go.

Threading through his gloomy thoughts, a loon cried—hauntingly fitting. Trace stopped, peering through the branches until he spotted the black head and white-dotted body near the middle of the lake. Leaving concentric ripples, it dove, disappearing from sight. Moments passed before it surfaced then floated for several yards. Suddenly another cry, high and eerie, drifted over the water. A flap of heavy wings, a clumsy running start into the wind, and the bird was airborne.

The Lord had blessed him with so many visual messages here; the loon's takeoff provided yet one more object lesson. This one spoke of hope. Breaking into flight may be a struggle, but God would lift him up and set him free. . .in His time.

Pulling a handful of soft green needles from a white pine, he crushed them in his hand. If God ever blessed him with a family, his kids would live the Christmases he'd only imagined. Try as he might, he couldn't ward off the vision of Christmas with the Jennets—a grown-up version of a little boy's dream. Did they have a candlelight service on Christmas Eve like the one his grandmother took him to once? Did they open gifts on Christmas morning, still in pajamas? Knowing what he did of Mattie, the house would smell of cinnamon, cloves, and cranberries. The counter in the spring-colored kitchen would be crowded with ham or a stuffed turkey, real mashed potatoes, homemade pumpkin pie. . .

His stomach growled, bringing him back to Pokegama Lake and his present reality. As he turned around on the path, he reached in his sweatshirt pocket for a granola bar and headed toward the cottage.

The furnished one-bedroom cement-block house had a western view of the lake. The back of the structure had a flat roof, the front pitched steeply over a porch. The house had everything he needed, including a fieldstone fireplace. There were seven other square buildings just like his. The guys next door, three kids who were attending Pine Technical College, had invited him over for pizza the night before. They were all going to school for gunsmithing, which made for interesting conversation. This morning, Trace had gone for breakfast in Pine City with them and bought his phone while he was there.

Once again his hand slid into his back pocket. Had he accidentally silenced it instead of putting it on vibrate? He knew the answer and didn't let himself look. When he reached the dilapidated dock twenty yards in front of the cottage, he bent to pick up the battered toolbox he'd left there and walked over to the boathouse, where a flat-bottomed boat was upturned on three sawhorses. He'd found the boat beached against the roots of a cedar tree, camouflaged by branches that kissed the water. Kip Nearing, the guy who owned the property, didn't know how it had gotten there but had offered to pay for the supplies to make it lake-worthy. Trace had hung four trouble lights from the middle beam in Kip's run-down open-sided boathouse, making it possible to work after dark. The little skiff was a godsend, filling his evenings and weekends, but the dropping temperatures stiffened his fingers, and he knew it wouldn't be long until he'd have to give it up. He hated the thought of winter in this place, his only neighbors three trigger-happy twenty-year-olds.

Power tools would have saved time, but since his goal was filling time rather than saving it, the old rosewood-handled spokeshave, hand sander, plane, and chisels he'd found in the ancient toolbox suited him fine. He'd put several hours into cleaning off years of rust and corrosion. When he was done with the boat, Kip could probably make a pretty penny selling the tools on eBay. Methodically he scraped at the old paint, watching the curls of weathered green float to the ground. Engrossed in the rhythm, he almost didn't notice the vibration in his hip pocket. When he did, the plane clattered to the ground.

Chapter 16

"Hello?" He hoped the absurd panic that rose as he fumbled with the phone wasn't evident in his voice.

"You have a phone!"

Closing his eyes at the sound of her voice, Trace sat down on an upended crate. "I do."

"It's good to hear your voice." She cleared her throat.

"You, too. What have you been up to?" He wished something wittier had come to mind. "Anything new in Pine Bluff?"

"Not much. The craft fair went off without a hitch; Gwyneth sold all her scarecrows. Oh, we have a new batch of bunnies, and Ronny named one Trace."

"I'm so honored. Hope he hasn't got red eyes."

She laughed. "They're called ruby eyes. But this one has blue eyes. Really looks a lot like you."

"Thanks."

"So are you feeling settled in?"

"Yeah." He laughed. "I was pretty much settled in as soon as I hung my three shirts in the closet and put my socks away."

"So it was fully furnished?"

"Right down to towels and silverware. Definitely a God thing. But I'll have to leave if they need to use this for the witness protection program."

"Is that why I can't have details?"

"Mostly. But it's also to protect you. . .and me. There's a possibility. . ."

He wanted to take the words back as soon as he'd said them. He didn't want to worry her more than she already was. But she wasn't a child; the thought had probably already crossed her mind. Her father had certainly voiced it. "There's always a chance that the fire and the tires. . .weren't done by somebody from Pine Bluff."

"Somebody. . .from your past? The family of the man—"

"Yes." He didn't want her to say it.

She answered with silence, and he groped for words to reassure her. "Syd. . ." Only one thought came to mind. "I wish you were here."

Again, silence. Sydney blew her nose. She was crying. He waited.

"And I wish you were here," she whispered. He had to cover his other ear to hear her. "How will we know if it's safe for you to come back unless you come back?"

"You're playing on my loneliness, woman."

"Well. . .isn't that the truth? I think you need to come back and draw the culprits out of hiding."

A hint of playfulness danced in her words, and he hated that he had to dash it. "I won't take that chance."

She sighed. "I know."

"So how 'bout we change the subject?"

"Okay. Tell me about your job. Just don't give me enough detail that I'll be able to hunt you down."

He smiled at her sarcasm. "Don't you think the element of intrigue just adds a unique dimension to our relationship?" He'd almost said "friendship," shifting gears at the last second.

"I'd rather have the element of face-to-face for dimension."

I love your boldness, Sydney Rose. "Me, too. But let's make the best of this, okay?"

"Okay. Twenty questions?"

Unsure what he was getting into, Trace agreed.

"Is it a minimum-wage job?"

"No."

"Are you using the skills you learned at sea?"

The girl should be a reporter. "Yes."

"Does it involve you being on the water?"

"No." If she'd asked if it involved him being on a boat, his answer would have been different. The tugs he was overhauling were dry-docked.

"Are you working with tools?"

"Yes."

"Are you working with wood?"

"No."

"Are you fixing things?"

"Yes."

"Do you think of me while you're working?"

"Constantly."

∞

The cottage next door was a mirror image of his, but the comparison ended with the matching floor plan. Foot-deep piles of dirty clothes, empty soda and beer cans, and fast-food wrappers littered every room. The dorm room smell unearthed a jumble of memories, some he treasured, some he wished he could bury forever. Trace waded through the mess to the bedroom. Monday was paintball night for the boys, and they'd told him he was welcome to use their computer. He marveled at their trust. It seemed he'd become somewhat of a hero in their eyes after sharing his story over pizza. He'd felt a Holy Spirit nudge to be open with them, but when all of their questions focused on the events in the bar and his time in prison, he wondered if they'd even heard the part about God doing a complete one-eighty with his life. At best, he'd planted a seed.

Sydney had done her part to lift him onto the pedestal, though of course she didn't know it. Al, James, and Carl had naturally asked about Trace's "women." He'd been careful to point out that there was only one and to extol her unseen qualities, her sense of humor and faith, but the boys were, of course, more interested in the physical. Trace had no problem talking about that aspect either, but they were clearly disappointed with his G-rated answers.

As he typed in Al's username, Top Gun, he pictured Sydney waiting for the instant message icon to pop up on her screen. Unfolding a crumpled piece of notebook paper, he cleared a space on the cluttered desk and smoothed it out. Like a scene from *You've Got Mail*, he rubbed his hands together, warming them in preparation. After all the "Hi, how are you?" stuff was out of the way, he had something to tell her.

> TOP GUN: *I saw a bear today. Actually two.*
>
> REDBOOTS: *Seriously?*
>
> TOP GUN: *Yup. Heard a crash about an hour ago. A little black bear was trying to get into my garbage can.*
>
> REDBOOTS: *And Mama. . . ?*
>
> TOP GUN: *Watching from the edge of the woods. I stayed inside.*
>
> REDBOOTS: *Thank goodness.*
>
> TOP GUN: *How was work?*
>
> REDBOOTS: *Busy day. Worked on details for the Christmas parade. How was work for you?*
>
> TOP GUN: *Productive. Came home covered in grease.*
>
> REDBOOTS: *Ah. . .another clue!*
>
> TOP GUN: *But you don't know if it's axle grease or bacon grease!*
>
> REDBOOTS: *True. Colleen says your new phone might have a GPS track ing device.*
>
> TOP GUN: *Smart woman.*
>
> REDBOOTS: *So it does??*
>
> TOP GUN: *No.*
>
> REDBOOTS: *Ah, well. . .I convinced her I wasn't a man chaser anyway.*
>
> TOP GUN: *Man chasing isn't always wrong. Supposing the man wants to be caught?*
>
> REDBOOTS: *Are you speaking hypothetically, Mr. McKay?*
>
> TOP GUN: *Not in the least.*

❧

"Looks good, Shane."

It was just after four and Shane had been painting the back room of the chamber office for over an hour. The boy looked down at his shoes, then back at

Sydney. In a move that was completely out of character, he reached out and gave her a stiff, two second hug. "Thanks for asking me to do it."

Colleen clattered through, juggling signs for the Christmas parade. "You look like roadkill, girl. Did you talk to Trace *all* night?"

"Maybe." Giddiness fizzed inside her like ginger ale. Beyond a doubt, a teenager had shanghaied her body. "We chatted on Instant Messenger a bit. . .if four hours counts as a bit."

"Wow. And here you were complaining that he didn't talk. Stu wouldn't have that many words in a year. What in the world did he say?"

"He saw a bear yesterday."

"Hmm." Colleen laid the signs on the counter and lifted the hinged door on the counter. "Get to the good stuff." She sat in the chair on the other side of Sydney's desk and motioned for Sydney to occupy her leather chair.

"If the good citizens of Pine Bluff only knew how I spent my time." A sound like an empty paint can hitting the floor drew their attention. "Shane's painting."

"You're good for that kid. He needs a mom figure."

"I'm not *that* old. . .not quite."

"Back to the good stuff. . ."

Sydney tapped her nails on the side of her coffee mug. Trace had been amazingly transparent last night. Instant messaging seemed to allow him to be more courageous than he was on the phone. He'd told her about a dream he'd had of lying on the ground in a bed of pine needles, watching the clouds with her beside him. And then he'd typed, "You fit perfect in my arms, you know."

She hesitated. She'd never had secrets from Colleen, but this was different. "He wrote a poem for me."

"Seriously?"

Reaching down to her purse, Sydney pulled out the piece of copy paper she'd printed it out on. "Don't laugh, okay? It's a bit on the mushy side." It was almost verbatim the way Trace had prefaced the poem. "Here goes. . . *In the quiet, I think of you. In the wind I hear your sigh. Every morning—*' " Her cell phone rang. It was Trace.

Colleen shook her head and laughed. Sydney handed her the poem, watching her expression as she opened her phone. "Hi."

"Hi, yourself."

With a wistful sigh, Colleen set down the poem, picked up her keys, and left. Sydney swiveled in her chair, raising her feet to the top of her desk. "Just a minute—I'm settling in."

"You still at work?"

"Just wrapping things up."

"Want to walk with me?"

"Huh?" Irrationally, she looked toward the front window.

"It's gorgeous out—at least it is here. Have you got comfy shoes on?"

"Yes."

"Then grab your jacket and go outside and pretend I'm holding your hand."

෯

Curled in the papasan chair in the corner of her room, waiting, as usual, for the phone to ring, Sydney watched the elongated shadows creep across the hardwood floor until they covered the scarred planks. Dusk was descending earlier every day.

The smells from the kitchen foreshadowed tomorrow's feast. Zack would be home on Thanksgiving break in a few hours, but the usual excitement eluded her. Trace would spend the day with some neighbors; that was as much as he would tell her. The secretiveness was wearing on her. Whether it came from Trace's overzealous need to protect her or from orders from his PO, the measure of caution seemed extreme. She wanted him safe, of course, but if there was a vendetta against him for what had happened three years ago, wouldn't they have found him by now? And if someone just wanted him run out of Pine Bluff, he'd never be able to come back until they found out who it was. She'd been half kidding when she suggested flushing the culprits out of hiding, but how else would they get to the bottom of this?

After all this time, she was sure no one followed her, watching her every move. She was pretty sure Trace knew that, too. By the time the phone rang, a plan was taking shape in her head.

Chapter 17

The plan had all the elements of a movie scene...if only she had a satchel of money on the seat beside her instead of a pumpkin pie in Tupperware.

Parking on the left side of Colleen's driveway at 2:35 on Thanksgiving Day, she scurried through the garage and into the kitchen.

"It's Syd the Super Sleuth!" Stuart waved from the couch where he was parked with his father and a massive bowl of Chex Mix. On the flat screen, the Vikings' quarterback threw an interception. Stuart moaned, then turned back to her. As Sydney took off her gloves, Stuart grinned. "Your trench coat is on the kitchen table. I got a deal on a revolving license plate, so you should be good to go."

Sydney walked into the kitchen and stopped short. Stuart wasn't kidding. Enormous dark glasses, a tan fedora, and a trench coat filled half the table. The man was crazy. But she was grateful for his craziness. Borrowing his car was Stu's idea, just an added precaution on the off chance that someone really did hope she'd lead them to Trace. She stuck the hat on her head, retraced her steps, and interrupted the game. "You're bizarre."

"I try."

"Thank you." She walked out before the serious shift in her voice embarrassed him.

With one child on her hip and the other one perched on the counter, Colleen was loading the dishwasher. She answered Sydney's "Hi" with a "Shh!" Pulling the shade down over the kitchen window, she whispered, "Are you sure no one followed you?"

"Other than the big black van with the AK-47 hanging out the window, no one." Sydney held out her hands to two-year-old Morgan and kissed her on the cheek. "Maybe I should take her along for cover."

"Sure. Whatever." Colleen waved her dishcloth. "I'll send her Super Soaker along. Are you in a hurry? Dumb question, I suppose. Are you in a hurry for a secret rendezvous with a gorgeous man?" Closing the dishwasher, she said, "I'm putting a wire on you."

Sydney laughed. "That would be for your vicarious pleasure, not for my protection, right?"

"Right. I'm so jealous." Wiping her hands on her jeans, Colleen placed a set of keys in Sydney's hand. "Watch your back, girl."

8○

The road narrowed and turned to gravel. Sydney's confidence vanished with the pavement. The idea of meeting in a neutral place had seemed like the perfect plan until now. When she'd found the resort on the Internet, she hadn't realized it was on a dead-end road. Her tires stirred a plume of dust that blocked her rear view. Spying the sign for Rock Haven Resort half a mile ahead, she turned into a U-shaped driveway and drove around until she faced the road. She waited two minutes, three; not another car in sight. She knew she was being a bit melodramatic, but she'd rather be foolishly overcautious than take a chance on not being the only one to rendezvous with Trace in this remote setting. Continuing on, she passed the sign, rounded a curve, and saw Whitebark Lake spread out before her, gunmetal gray beneath a heavy sky.

Another hundred yards and the lodge came into view, the A-frame front all glass and rough-cut cedar. An idyllic setting for a honeymoon. That wasn't a thought she should be entertaining. Sydney eased Stuart's Suburban between two parked cars and turned off the engine.

Where was he? There was the sign: Birchwood Trail. He said he'd be waiting at four fifteen. She looked down at the clock. She was eight minutes early. She pulled down the visor mirror, touched up her lipstick, played with the collar of her white turtleneck, and tried to shake the jitters.

She looked down at the clock—a minute had passed—then back at the sign. And then she saw him getting out of a tan car, looking around. He was seven minutes early.

Even from twenty yards away, he looked amazing. Three and a half weeks had lengthened his hair, and his face was no longer pale. Her chest tightened as she opened the door, stepped out, and cinched the belt on the trench coat. She knew the moment he spotted her. Because he started running.

Before he reached her, she slipped on the hat and sunglasses.

Trace stopped in his tracks and burst out laughing. Covering the last few feet in huge strides, he grabbed her hand and led her, giggling and barely keeping up, to the entrance of Birchwood Trail, where arching oak and birch limbs and thick underbrush cut off the view of the lodge. He stopped, turned, and stared at her. Slowly he removed her sunglasses and hat and tossed them to the ground. His arms engulfed her and hers slid beneath his jacket. His fingers raked through her hair, lifting her face to his. As his lips pressed against hers, she felt the thudding of his heart. When he pulled back, his crooked smile was wide. And then he kissed her again, his lips traveling from her mouth to the tip of her nose, then to her forehead. Against her hair, he whispered, "Face-to-face is definitely better."

She grinned up at him. "But a little intrigue doesn't hurt."

He bent and picked up the hat and glasses. The glasses he folded and stuck in his pocket; the hat he set back on her head. "I kind of like that look, Sherlock." His smile softened, and his eyes seemed to devour every inch of her face. "I missed you."

"Me, too."

He held out his hand. "Got your walking shoes on?"

She nodded. "I'm catching on that that's a requirement around you."

"Good."

The trail began to rise almost immediately. Man-made steps curved up and to the left. Trace was breathing hard before they reached the top. "Guess I'd better buy myself a pair of running shoes. You're in way better shape." His eyes flickered from her face to her toes and back in a split second. He smiled approvingly. "*Way* better shape."

There was a clearing at the top. Trace stepped behind her and pointed toward the western edge of the lake. "Sunset is at 4:34."

Sydney wriggled in his arms to stare at him, then looked from him to the leaden clouds that covered most of the sky. There was no sun. Only a narrow ring of blue was visible above the trees. "You, sir, are an optimist."

"I am." He stretched out his left arm so that his wrist emerged from his jacket. He held his watch in front of her face. "Six minutes. Don't blink."

She leaned against him, relishing the warmth, the feel of his rough chin on the top of her head. Neither of them spoke. Slowly a rim of bright orange descended from the pewter clouds, stippling the water. It lasted only minutes, the sun disk slipping behind the trees, brushing the clouds with gold.

Trace's arms tightened around her. He rubbed his lips on her cheek. "There's a fireplace in the lodge."

&

Sydney slipped off her shoes and tucked her feet under her as she leaned against Trace. Four freestanding fireplaces in the lodge atrium allowed for intimate conversation groupings. Cuddled together for the past hour in the center of a rounded sectional sofa, hugging mugs of hot chocolate as they stared into the fire, Sydney was sure they looked like all the other couples enjoying the holiday together.

Trace bent forward and scooped a handful of peanuts from the dish on the coffee table. "Ever wonder what things would have been like for us if we'd met years ago?"

"What-ifs can make you crazy." Sydney took a peanut out of his hand. "But think about it—you wouldn't have been a believer; I still would have been in career mode, clawing my way to the top. . . ."

"I can't picture that."

"It's a bit of an exaggeration, but not much. I've changed since I came back home; my life has slowed way down, and I like it."

"And Pine Bluff is a better place because of you. Did they kick somebody out of the position when they heard you were available?"

Sydney laughed. "Yes."

"I was kidding. They really did?"

"Gwyneth was the director before me. She was starting to lose it, but she was hanging on to the job for dear life. They convinced her that she needed to mentor me into the position so that she could be freed up to write her memoirs of growing up in Pine Bluff."

"I saw her book. She was still pretty coherent just a couple of years ago, huh?"

Sydney swirled the hot chocolate in the bottom of her mug. "She's an intelligent woman with a head full of history that's starting to spill over into reality. I just hope we can convince her to move to a safe place where she can make scarecrows for the craft fair and bring Mordecai his corncob pipe and make raspberry tea for Susanna and just live peacefully in her distorted little world."

She pulled away from the warmth of Trace's arm and looked up at him. "Speaking of distorted little worlds...when are you coming back home?"

His eyes closed, and a long sigh rushed through his lips. She'd used the word "home" purposely to elicit an effect. It worked.

"I need to talk to your father, I guess, or maybe the pastor. I'm not convinced that the church funding the reintegration program was the only issue. Maybe I'm just not wanted in that town." He pulled her close again and kissed the top of her head. "We need to make some decisions, Syd."

An icy finger of fear slid along her back. "What do you mean?"

"What if I can't ever set foot in Pine Bluff without putting you at risk?"

"Then we meet somewhere else, like this."

"We can't spend the rest of our lives sneaking around."

Sitting up straight again, Sydney set her mug on the coffee table. "Then I move. Back to the cities where nobody knows who you are."

"What if being associated with me means you're not welcome in your own hometown? What if you couldn't go home for Christmas? What if it puts you and your family in danger?"

Sydney turned, looking him straight in the face. "Remember the sermon on covenant relationships? Well, I'm willing to make a covenant with you, Trace McKay. In spite of all my fears and all the unknowns, I'm willing to risk it because—"

Now she'd done it. She wasn't about to be the first one to say it. Trace was grinning at her, waiting. "Because you love me?"

"Yes." It was barely a whisper.

He leaned forward, his lips finding hers and lingering. His hands rose to her face; she felt the heat from his palms. He kissed her lips, the tip of her nose, then eased back, his hands still on her face. "Sydney Rose, I don't deserve you, and I don't know what's around the corner for us, but I am madly, passionately, crazily in love with you, too."

છે

Minutes passed in silence. Trace stared into the fire, wondering if Sydney had fallen asleep. He stretched his arm until he could see his watch. It was getting late, and he was already worried about her making the drive home alone. But there were things they still needed to talk about. He eased away from her to look at her face.

"I need you to know what the future holds for me. I need to spell it out."

The fear was visible on her face.

"I'm looking at probation for another ten years."

"What exactly does that mean?"

"I can't leave the state without permission; I have to report to my PO on a regular basis. Jim is a really decent guy who respects the fact that I'm not a risk, but if I move and I'm assigned to someone who sees things differently, I could have to submit to random drug testing, inspection of my home without notice, psychological testing. . .who knows. Hunting with your dad and your brother is never going to be an option, because I can't own a gun."

The weight of the facts settled on his chest. Was the truth hitting Sydney equally hard? "I'm not asking for any kind of an answer tonight. But before we go any further, you need to ask yourself if you could handle that."

He was glad she didn't answer quickly. He hoped she'd take the time to look at what a future with him could cost her. What she did next threw him off guard. Sitting up, she crossed her arms and grabbed the bottom of her turtleneck sweater. Slowly she pulled it over her head. Beneath it was a pale pink tank top. It was the first time he'd seen her without long sleeves. With a look in her eyes that made him want to fall in, she stretched her right arm in front of him. "Before we go any further, you need to ask yourself if you could handle *this*."

Lifting her hand, he slowly ran his fingertips across the raised crisscrossed scars, then kissed her arm, inch by inch, from her wrist to her elbow. Looking up, he kissed the path of a tear on her cheek. "You are so beautiful."

Chapter 18

Something wasn't right. At first glance, everything in the boathouse appeared to be just the way he'd left it when he'd gone to meet Sydney, but it didn't *feel* right. He brushed the back of his hand across his forehead. Maybe his imagination was just in overdrive with his thoughts so channeled on the girl in the red boots.

Trace pried open the can of Regatta Red bottom paint. One last coat, a day to dry, and he'd be ready to try her out. Over the glossy white enamel on the flat stern he'd lettered *Rose Red*. The little skiff would be christened in Sydney's honor, even if she couldn't be there to crack the bottle of Mountain Dew against the *Rose*'s bow.

The paint slid over the primed flat bottom like butter on toast. The pungent smell of the paint and the rhythmic strokes flooded his senses with long-stored impressions. His first job had been painting tugs on the Mississippi. Sixteen years old, with no one to answer to, no one to care if he came home at night, he'd done pretty well for himself, finding a job and a room to rent. The crew he worked with was a rough bunch, most of them three times his age or more, but the old salts with nicknames that reminded Trace of the Seven Dwarves had taken him under their wings; it was the closest thing to family he'd ever experienced.

The persistence of several of the men eventually led him to Duluth and then on to get his captain's license. He could still hear Rusty Jay, a grizzly little man in his sixties: "You're too smart for this. Someday when you're captaining one o' them two-hundred-foot mega-yachts for some snooty celebrity with a yappy poodle, you remember your old friends, hey?"

Is that where he'd be now if life hadn't veered off in a course beyond his control? Just as the familiar shackles of regret coiled around his gut, a thin bead of red dripped off the ferrule of his brush. Trace reached blindly toward the rag bucket just below him under the sawhorse. His hand found only air. Using the tail of the shirt that stuck out beneath his jacket, he stopped the line of paint before it marked the spotless white top of the hull. Setting the brush on the paint can, he looked beneath the sawhorse. The bucket was gone.

A list of plausible explanations came to mind. The boathouse was open-sided, after all. Anyone could have access to it. Still, he couldn't stop the shift in his mood. Finishing as quickly as he could, he sealed the paint can, cleaned up, and headed for the cottage.

Near the corner of the house, about ten feet from the back door, was the five-gallon bucket, tipped upside-down below his bedroom window.

Trace opened the screen door, and a paper fluttered to the ground. In blue marker were the words: *Don't come back.*

&

Sydney closed her phone and set it on the table next to the papasan chair. The digital display read 11:26, but she knew that trying to sleep would be futile. There'd been an edginess in Trace's voice, though he'd tried to deny it. At one point he'd interrupted her and said he wanted to listen to something outside. Just the bear cub or a raccoon, he assured her, but she was sure she'd heard the slam of a dead bolt.

At least three times she'd asked him if he was sure he hadn't been followed home. Nothing he said took away the fear that was building in her. Pulling the down comforter off the bed, she wrapped it around her, then did something she hadn't done since she was a little girl. She got down on her knees to pray.

&

A hissing sound. That's what woke him. Trace held his breath. There it was again, air rushing like a leak in a tire. Easing bare feet to the cold floor, he padded to the door and listened. For a moment there was nothing, and then a wail. . . a cat. . .screeching like something had landed on its tail. Trace let out the breath he'd been holding and laughed out loud. *Get a grip.* In St. Cloud, he'd fallen asleep with the backdrop of guards hauling screaming inmates to solitary, and now a catfight was jangling his nerves. He crawled back in bed, shivering under two wool blankets until he fell asleep.

Thud. Something banged on the roof and bounced, each thud getting softer until he heard it hit the ground. Blinking in the dark room, Trace tried to clear his head. A pin oak stood less than ten feet from the side of the house. A week ago, during a storm, acorns had bombarded the roof. Though the night was still, that's probably all it was.

He hadn't told anyone about the note. If he called the police, would they really take it seriously? Trace had enemies; every guy just released from prison had enemies. But if someone had followed Sydney to him, how much danger had he put her in?

Another hiss. It had to be the cats again. Sitting up, he looked at the clock—1:42. What he needed was some fresh air to clear the spooks from his head—and to assure himself that no one was out there.

He dressed in the dark and, flashlight in hand, opened the back door slowly. A full moon hung in the star-splattered sky. His breath hovered, white mist in the motionless air. Two shafts of light arced across the boathouse roof and the side of the boys' cottage.

Chills crept like cold fingers beneath Trace's shirt. Instinctively he edged close to the house, peering around the corner. His pulse hammered in his ears. And then he heard voices.

"Shh! Shut up and grab the keg. I got the rest."

A car door slammed. Muffled footsteps came toward him.

Trace breathed a sigh of relief. "Hey, guys."

James, all six gangly feet of the boy, jumped. "Man! Freak me out, why don't ya? What're you doing out in the middle of the night?"

Before Trace could answer, a rattling like a child's wagon came from behind James. Trace aimed his light toward the sound. It was just what it sounded like. Al, pulling a beer keg in a little red wagon, grinned at Trace. "Party?" He walked between Trace and James, opened his back door, and turned on the patio light.

Trace smiled back. So much for his stealthy venture into the night. "No thanks." It was a relief to have someone to talk to. "You guys seen anybody nosing around here today?"

Al nodded. "We saw a black SUV, one of those big expensive ones, cruising up and down like it was lookin' for somebody. We were expecting this one guy, but I guess it wasn't him 'cause he would have called if he wasn't sure what house was ours."

"What time?"

"It was just startin' to get dark. Looked like a couple people in the front seat. Didn't get a good look at 'em, but we were wondering what they were up to."

Jim tapped his knuckles on Trace's shoulder. "Hey, if somebody's buggin' you. . .if you ever need help, we got your back."

&

"I hated to wake you." The edge was still in Trace's voice.

"I wasn't sleeping." Tucking the phone under her chin, Sydney rose from her knees, where she'd found herself for the second time in three hours. "What's wrong?"

"I need to ask you something."

Sydney wrapped the blanket around her shoulders and walked stiffly to the window. Something in his voice made her not want to ask. "What?"

"Do you know anyone who drives a big black SUV?"

Sydney's stomach knotted. "Like a Durango?"

"Maybe."

"Floyd Chapel has a black Durango. Have you seen it?"

"The kids next door. . ."

Sydney pulled back the curtain. The mercury light on the utility pole washed the frost-coated barn roof in pale yellow. It was a scene that usually flooded her with a sense of security. But as she listened to Trace, a strange fusion of relief and dread swept over her. Now they knew for sure who was behind this. When Trace finished telling her about the boys seeing the vehicle, she had the distinct impression there was more.

"What aren't you telling me?"

He cleared his throat. "There was a note."

She waited for him to continue, but he didn't. "What did it say?"

His silence lasted too long. Finally, he answered. "It said, 'Don't come back.'"

"Okay." Sydney ran her hand over her eyes. "Are you calling the police, or am I?"

"There isn't enough to tell them yet."

"Yes, there—"

"Syd!" Her mother's voice rose up the stairs. "Syd, wake up! Ronny's missing."

∞

Tired of pacing and waiting for the phone to ring, Trace walked out of the cottage for the second time. He prayed better outside.

Thick mist hovered over the lake, veiling the full moon. Frost covered the lawn, and only rabbit tracks broke the expanse of crystal-coated grass. He stood on the cement patio, taking deep breaths, trying to calm the racing in his mind. Why was all of this happening at the same time? He should be in Pine Bluff, helping with the search for Ronny. Sydney would be in her car by now, combing every street.

Ronny's dad had come home from working overtime at his second-shift job. Jessica was spending the night with her aunt, and Ronny was nowhere to be found. *Lord, protect him. Let them find him soon.*

He'd given in and given Sydney the address of the cottage but told her not to call the police yet. Not that she would listen. But for all he knew, he'd need her to make the call before the night was over. In a way, he was glad she was caught up in hunting for the boy. Otherwise, it would have been just like her to show up here.

He needed to walk. Pulling his flashlight out of his jacket pocket, he turned the corner. In the circle of light, dark footprints broke the expanse of white. The light swept up the cement block wall of the cottage. Spray-painted in foot-high red letters were the words STAY AWAY, KILLER.

The hissing sound. . .this explained it. He looked around. Was he being watched? He tried to picture Floyd Chapel's overweight form hiding behind a tree. What was the man capable of?

Taking the side stairs to the low wood-planked front porch in one stride, he arced the light from the floor to the overhanging roof. A two-seat glider rocker with threadbare cushions butted up against the house; in one corner a broom, the bristles worn to nubs, leaned against the back side of a wrought iron trellis. The planks groaned beneath his feet as he crossed to the front steps. Looking down, his right foot stopped in midair. A splash of Regatta Red paint spattered the bottom step. *The boat.* What had they done to his boat?

Stepping over the bottom step, his boot hit the ground and he looked behind him. His stomach tightened; he dropped to one knee, aiming the light at the step, close enough to confirm what he already knew.

It wasn't paint.

SO

The moon was higher now, rising out of the fog. Trace crossed the narrow dirt and gravel road in front of the cottage and stepped into the woods. He'd only bow-hunted for deer twice, but the same antsy adrenaline buzz had a grip on him now as he tried to walk with silent steps. A stick snapped under his boot, the sound bouncing off the cedars and birches that closed him in. The lowest branches on the ramrod-straight white pines were several feet above his head. Finally, he found a pin oak, its leathery brown leaves curled but still clinging, with a limb low enough to hoist himself up. Straddling the limb, he leaned against the trunk. It wasn't quite the vantage point he'd hoped for, but he was hidden and comfortable enough to sit for hours if need be.

He half expected a Pine Bluff squad car to drive up, lights flashing, sirens blaring. The thought had no more than formed in his head when a pair of slow-moving headlights lit the road below him.

A second later, a gunshot cracked the night air.

SO

In spite of the cold, the palms of Sydney's driving gloves were damp. She held the printout map close to the dome light and put on her turn signal. She passed the first cottage. Trace had said it was the fifth one.

"One. . .two. . .three—" A gunshot rattled the car windows.

As Sydney slammed on the brake, a strange gravelly scream, faint through the closed windows, rose from her right. And a man ran across the beam of her lights.

Trace.

Get down! She wanted to scream at him. Instead, she crept ahead, straining to see him. Suddenly he stopped, looked up, and yelled something. She stopped the car, got out, and ran toward him, expecting at any moment to hear another gunshot. He walked out of the light from her headlights and into the blackness between two houses. Again he yelled.

"Al! Put it away!" Trace waved both hands over his head. "It's okay; they're friends."

The boy with the gun stood outside the blackness under a yard light. Slowly he lowered the rifle. "I wasn't shootin' at them! I was scarin' the bear." Beyond him, at the edge of the light, a cub paced, lifted his nose, and bellowed. "Thing must be deaf." The boy pointed toward the roof of the cottage he was facing. "What are they doing on your roof?"

Sydney followed the beam of Trace's flashlight. Two terrified faces peered over the edge of the roof. She gasped. "What in the world?"

Trace whirled to face her when she spoke. She glanced in his direction then back to the roof.

Beneath wildly swirling blond hair, the boy's face was a mask of terror. "Syd'ey! Get away from Trace! He's a killer!"

∽

Trace had a moment of wondering if he was in the middle of a bizarre, disjointed nightmare. A redneck gunsmith shooting in the air, a little old lady in bib overalls, and a boy a few crayons short of a box perched on his roof while the girl of his dreams materializes out of thin air and slides into his arms—it had to be a dream. He pulled Sydney close, breathing in the scent of her but keeping his eyes on Ronny and Gwyneth.

Sydney swiveled, turning away from him but not out of the circle of his arms. "It's okay, Ronny. You know Trace. He's my friend; you know he would never hurt me." She turned, staring into Trace's eyes for the space of a heartbeat. "I trust him."

Gwyneth's head shook back and forth. "That's not what Shane said. He said he turned into a bad guy in prison and he's going to hurt you. We're keeping him from coming back to town."

"He killed somebody, Syd'ey."

"I know, but it was an accident; he didn't mean it. Come down and he'll tell you about it."

"We can't." Gwyneth stared at her, as if that were enough of an answer.

"Why not?"

"Because my great-grandson cut his leg."

"Shane is with you?"

"Of course. He drove. He's passed out like a baby. He got cut on a nail and I wrapped it with his undershirt, but if that bear smells blood, he'll swallow us whole."

As if on cue, the cub bawled again. Trace tightened his hold on Sydney and bent down until his lips touched her ear. "Now can I laugh?"

In the distance, a siren wailed.

"Finally." Gwyneth shook a gnarled gloved finger over the edge of the roof. "I told Mordecai to call the authorities hours ago. Finally, someone believed him. Just because he's dead is no reason not to take him seriously. Why, there was one time..."

Sydney's hands molded over Trace's forearms; her shoulders pressed against his chest. "Now you can laugh."

Chapter 19

Give the man the benefit of the doubt. This whole mess has to have humbled him."

Sydney swung Floyd Chapel's front gate open, gave Trace a wry smile, and said, "I'll believe it when I see it."

Floyd answered the door, nodded, and stepped aside for them to enter.

"I'm sorry!" Ronny blurted the words before Sydney and Trace had their coats off. "You're not bad. We shouldn't have tried to scare you." He appeared on the verge of tears. "We was just gonna put firecrackers in the chimney. It wouldn't of hurt you."

Sydney stepped aside as Trace reached out and placed his hand on Ronny's shoulder. "You were just trying to protect Sydney. I'm glad she has people watching out for her."

"So you're not mad?"

"Have you asked Jesus to forgive you for what you did?"

"Uh-huh." Ronny's head bobbed. "Lots and lots of times."

"Then He's forgiven you, and I forgive you—"

Behind Ronny, Floyd cleared his throat. "Come in. Ronny, hang their coats on the hooks."

They followed Floyd to the living room, where he gestured to an empty love seat. Velma, Floyd's wife, seated in a straight-backed chair, nodded as they walked in, making only fleeting eye contact with Sydney.

Floyd took the empty chair between Velma and Gwyneth. Shane, in shorts with a wide bandage around his thigh, sat on a couch, his eyes riveted to the floor. Ronny sat down beside him.

"How's the leg?" Trace asked.

"He had twenty-six stitches this morning," Floyd answered. "He'll be fine."

Trace nodded. "Shane, I need an explanation."

The boy didn't move.

"What it all boils down to"—Floyd leaned forward and folded his hands—"is that I need to be a little more careful who's listening when I shoot off my mouth." Sydney couldn't decipher his expression. Not quite smile, certainly not remorse.

Beside her, Sydney felt Trace lean forward. He had to be sharing her thoughts. *He's actually making excuses for his grandson?*

Floyd appeared surprised that neither Trace nor Sydney responded. "I'm a man of convictions," he finally continued. "My grandson's got the same fire in him. He just decided to act on his."

Was she really reading this man right? Was he actually proud of his grandson? Sydney scanned the Chapels' doily-accented living room, her gaze landing on Velma. Sitting with her hands on her lap, her gray sweater matching her hair, the woman stared at her feet, just like her grandson.

Slowly, Shane's posture stiffened. His head lifted, and he glared at Floyd with a look that terrified Sydney.

"You just don't get it, do you?" The boy's hands tightened into fists. "This has nothing to do with your convictions. Your convictions are all talk. You never *do* anything! You talk about what happens to men in prison. You talk about how they come out angrier than when they go in. Did you really think I didn't know who you were really talking about?"

Shane's hands parted, and he gripped the couch cushion on each side of his legs. "Do you really think I don't know my father's locked up? Do you think I don't know it's because of him my mom left? I was little, but I remember. I remember the screaming and the hitting and—" His face distorted, but a ragged breath seemed to restore his control. "And you didn't do. . .anything! We lived under your roof. Your own daughter—and you didn't call the cops; you didn't do anything. All because you didn't want anyone to know. All because you—"

Floyd stood, and Shane's entire body rocked back reflexively, just an inch or so, but the reaction spoke volumes.

"You were a child. You don't know what you're talking about." With that, Floyd left the room.

Silence echoed. Velma folded her arms over her sweater. "Are you going to press charges?"

Sydney had never heard the woman string that many words together. Before she had a chance to say more, Floyd stomped back into the room.

"Of course they'll press charges, Velma! Your grandson thought he could take the law in his own hands. And now he's going to jail just like his good-for-nothing father, and when he comes out, he'll be a real criminal."

Velma crumpled; her hands covered her face and her shoulders shook. Floyd stood behind her chair, hands on hips, clearly unmoved.

"Velma." Sydney tried to block out the image of the man behind her. Beside her, she could sense Trace struggling, like she was, not to lash out at Floyd. "Listen to what Trace has to say, Velma. Please."

Trace rested his elbows on his knees. "I've talked to Eldon about the truck tires. We prayed about it this morning. Shane, I guess the answer to that question is up to you. You're seventeen; you'd be tried as an adult. There may be no way around it because of some of the other things you've done, but I don't want to see you go through that. We'd be willing not to press charges for the vandalism if you'll work with us."

The anger and fear in Shane's eyes seemed to soften with what Sydney read as hope. "What do you mean?"

"There'd be some community service involved, but mostly we'd just be spending time with you, sharing our stories. It'll be a lot of God talk and what they call tough love. You might be able to avoid going to jail, but I think you need to hear what it's really like to be locked up. Maybe we'll even take a trip to St. Cloud. Frankly, I want to see you scared, so scared that you'd never even think of committing another crime."

Trace rubbed the back of his neck. His tension was almost palpable. "Shane, I don't want to act like I get what you've been through, but maybe I do on some level. My dad wasn't abusive, but he left when I was three. So I kind of understand the anger. And there's another thing I want to say." Trace looked up, directing his words at Floyd. "Criminal behavior is not hereditary. It doesn't matter what your father did; you can make right choices and break the cycle. My dad's a gambler; I decided years ago that I wasn't going to be anything like him. You're the one who decides what kind of person you're going to be."

"So you wouldn't press charges?" Shane looked more like a scared little boy than someone who could get tried as an adult.

"Not as long as you cooperate." Trace's tone was firm.

"I will." For the first time, Shane made eye contact with Sydney. "I will. I just...didn't want you getting hurt...like my mom."

Sydney had been vacillating between wanting to lecture Shane and wanting to get down on her knees and wrap her arms around him. "I know. I'm still unnerved that you followed me to get to Trace; it's going to take some time and work for me to trust you again, but I'm trying to—"

"I never followed you."

"You had to. How else did you find Trace?"

Shane's wide-eyed gaze went from Sydney back to the floor. "That poem that you copied. I heard you talking to Mrs. Hatcher about instant-messaging him and how you wanted him to come back. After you left, I picked up the paper and got the username off it. I tried a couple messenger services until I found the guy whose computer he used."

Every time Shane referred to Trace as "he" or "him," he nodded in his direction but didn't once look directly at him. "I chatted with the guy for a while until I worked it out of him that there was an ex-con living next door to him. After that, all I had to do was get myself invited to a party at his house. That's how I got the directions."

In spite of everything, Sydney couldn't help but smile. "Maybe you'll end up a detective someday."

"Yeah." A slight smile played on Shane's lips. "Maybe."

"Why did you get Gwyneth and Ronny involved?"

"The only way I could get the car was to offer to pick up Grandma Gwyn at my great-aunt's house. Ronny came over when I was getting ready to leave, and my grandpa told me to let him ride along."

Ronny nodded. "Mr. Chapel says Shane drives good with me in the car. But I shouldn't have b'lieved Shane about Trace. Shane said we were soldiers for Jesus."

"Christian soldiers, that's what he said." Gwyneth shook her finger at Shane. "Why we listened to you, I'll never know. I hope you're ashamed of yourself."

Clearly he was, though he didn't answer. Sydney wished she didn't have to add to the shame the boy was carrying. "There's another issue that you'll have to answer to the church and the police about, Shane. The fire."

His head jerked up. "I didn't do that. I didn't start the fire."

"Shane. . ." Sydney tried to keep her tone even, but his denial angered her. "There's no use—"

"Fess up, boy." Floyd gripped the back of Velma's chair. "No one else had a motive."

Sydney shivered. Minutes ago Floyd had been defending his grandson to the point of acting proud of his actions. How could someone turn on a person he loved so quickly?

Tears brimmed in Shane's eyes. "I didn't start the fire. I didn't do anything until I saw them together in church and I was afraid. . ." He glanced at Sydney. "Afraid he might do something to hurt Sydney."

"I told you." Gwyneth shook a bony finger at Sydney. "I told you that Mordecai's pipe started that fire. I knew he shouldn't smoke, especially that silly corncob pipe. Those things. . ."

Ronny's head was bobbing up and down. "I told you we needed to make another scarecrow without a pipe, Syd'ey. 'Cause the other got fired up."

Sydney looked from Ronny to Gwyneth. Was there really some truth in the midst of her fantasy? "Tell me again, Gwyn. How did the fire start?"

Gwyneth sighed. "I told you twice already. Mordecai wanted a light for his pipe, and I tried to talk him out of smoking, but he said he'd stay out by the hickory tree and not come in, and when I realized that he really couldn't get cancer from it after all, I lit his pipe for him."

With a frustrated sigh that matched Gwyneth's, Ronny said, "She just maked believe it was Mordecai. It was really the scarecrow we maked and hanged in the big tree for Halloween."

Locking eyes with Trace for a fraction of a second, Sydney asked, "What happened when you lit Mordecai's pipe, Gwyn?"

"*Poof!*" Ronny beat her to the answer. "It went *poof!* and *whoosh!* and all a sudden it distappeared."

Chapter 20

In her wildest imagination, Sydney couldn't have described a Christmas Eve moment quite as perfect as this one. Fat snowflakes, seemingly birthed by streetlamps, drifted onto an almost-deserted Main Street, in no hurry to cover the tracks left by red cowboy boots and steel-toed work boots. With his hand wrapped around hers, Trace stopped and raised his face to the sky. His crooked smile parted as his mouth opened, catching snowflakes. Lacy bits of snow dotted his lashes and landed on his cheeks and melted. He laughed, the sound deep and rich, yet childlike at the same time.

They'd just gotten out of Trace's car, about a block from the chamber of commerce office. He'd been acting strange all day, and every time she'd questioned him about his mysterious expressions, he'd answered with a patronizing smile and the words "It's Christmas." In spite of dead ends, she tried again. "Where are you taking me?"

"It's a secret. Trust me."

Sydney laughed. "You are so not to be trusted."

Trace opened the back car door and pulled out two plastic grocery bags, one lumpy, the other bulging like an overstuffed pillow. He held out his free hand to her. "Let's walk."

They crossed the street and kept walking even when they passed the last building on the river side. Sydney stared down toward the frozen edge of the St. Croix. "Now will you tell me?"

"Maybe."

They walked under a streetlamp and she stopped, staring up at the flakes just as Trace had done earlier. "Did you ever wish you could freeze moments like pictures and relive them over and over?"

His gloved hand reached up and traced the outline of her lips. "I'm freezing this one in my mind." He leaned toward her, his cold lips touching hers.

"Me, too. This is so perfect."

"But it could be perfecter."

She laughed, opening her mouth to the snow. "What could make it perfecter?"

"S'mores." His eyes sparked with mischief.

"S'mores?"

"I owe you a picnic in the park."

"You're nuts."

"Over you." He handed her one of the grocery bags. "Merry Christmas."

Sydney examined the contents of the bag. Hot dogs, buns, paper plates, napkins, Styrofoam cups, chocolate bars, marshmallows, graham crackers. Tears stung her eyes. "It's twenty-three degrees."

Trace opened the other bag. He pulled out her down jacket and a long red scarf she'd never seen before. "Put them on."

"You're still nuts."

"Over you."

A tear lost its grip on her lashes. "Do you know how much I love you?"

Trace pointed to the steps leading down to the river. He took a deep breath that sounded shaky and turned a tremulous gaze on her. "Hopefully enough."

He led her along the lamplit cobblestone walk toward the cluster of pines near the river. About an inch of snow covered the bricks. Snow was still falling, the flakes finer now, like powdered sugar from a sifter. The bells from the Catholic church chimed out "O Little Town of Bethlehem," the notes echoing off the bluff. When they reached the picnic table where they'd attempted their last picnic, Trace pulled a blanket out of the bag and spread it on the bench.

On top of the picnic table, a small grill glowed with red coals. Sydney zipped her jacket. "You sneak."

"Mm-hmm." He pulled out the hot dogs, opened the package, and set four of them on the hot grate. "You can set the table."

Sydney took out two paper plates and two napkins. "Do you want to sit next to me or across from me?"

"Now that's a dilemma. Stare into your amazing eyes or cuddle up next to you. I think I'll opt for cuddling." He sat down next to her.

"Good. I was hoping you'd share some body heat."

His arm slid around her shoulders, and she leaned against him. The hot dogs sputtered, and orange sparks rose to meet the powdery snow. In the distance, the church bells rang out "Silent Night."

All is calm, all is bright. . . . Lord, thank You for this moment, for this man. Thank You for blessing me with the desires of my heart. This was so worth waiting for.

Trace pointed to the bag on the table. "If you get out the buns and shake off our plates, I think we can eat."

"I wish I had a camera. Colleen will kill me for not capturing this scrapbookable moment."

"Not a problem." Trace reached into his jacket pocket and pulled out his camera phone.

He snapped a picture as she took her first bite. Around a mouthful of hot dog, Sydney grinned. "You were right." Her words came out garbled, making them both laugh.

"About what?"

"It could get perfecter."

"We still have marshmallows to roast."

From under the table, Trace produced a long two-pronged fork. "Only one s'more apiece, though. Your family's saving the plum pudding until we get there."

"Did they know what you were up to tonight?"

"Uh-huh. Zack came and started the grill for me."

"Really?" Sydney slid two marshmallows onto the fork. While Trace held it over the coals, she unwrapped a Hershey bar. "You're amazing."

"I know. And it's not over yet."

"There's more?"

"Yup." Trace squished a marshmallow between two graham crackers layered with chocolate and held it to her mouth.

"Mmm. . . What else is there?"

"Don't talk with your mouth full." He assembled his own s'more, took a bite, then set it down. "I can't finish this." He stood, wiping his hands on his jeans.

"You're acting really weird, you know."

"I'm about to get weirder. Trust me?"

"Maybe."

"Good enough." He pulled the scarf from her neck, placed it over her eyes, and tied it at the back of her head. "This'll only take a minute."

She heard his steps. Four or five and then they stopped. A plastic bag rustled. And then a hissing, sizzling sound. The smell was familiar, but out of place. What was it? The steps returned. He walked behind her and slid the scarf from her face.

Sydney blinked. Lights. . .fire. . .on the ground, but not a campfire. Sparklers. Sparklers in the shape of letters. She gasped.

Spelled out in hundreds of tiny explosions of light were the words WILL YOU MARRY ME?

Chapter 21

So let's plan this shindig." Colleen nodded as the waitress set two bowls of clam chowder on the table.

Sydney folded her hands. "Lord, thank You for time together, for a wedding to plan, for answers to prayer that go beyond our dreams, and for this food. Amen."

"Amen. I saw the most amazing wedding dress on the David's Bridal Web site. It had 'Sydney's Amazing April Wedding' written all over it. Stand-up collar, long sheer sleeves, a train a mile long, with little crystals sewn all over the skirt..."

Picking up her spoon, Sydney thought through her answer. She hadn't realized how much her decisions were going to affect her best friend. "Actually, that's a little formal for what I had in mind."

"O–kay. Tell me what you're thinking."

"A simple, intimate wedding."

Colleen's spoon stopped in midair. " 'Intimate' translates 'small,' right?"

"Right."

"Small as in low budget or small as in short guest list?"

"Both."

"But where are you going to draw the line? You know every single person in this town."

"That's basically the reason for keeping it small. Trace has a handful of friends that would come; he called his parents and left messages, but neither one has called back. I can't invite two hundred people if he only has three or four."

"But..."

"I know. But this"—she fluttered her ring finger—"is about a marriage, not a wedding. Trace has no money saved up and—"

"You can't tell me your mom doesn't have a wedding fund with your name on it."

"That's not the point. At our age, I think Trace would feel awkward having my parents pay for the whole thing."

Colleen put a spoonful of chowder in her mouth and shook her head. "Trace is a lucky man. I wouldn't have been nearly so understanding. Okay, so what are we looking at?"

"An afternoon wedding in the chapel, just my family and yours, and then dinner here at the Sage Stoppe."

"What do I wear?"

"How about if I let you pick it out? Something semiformal. Okay?"

Her disappointment thinly veiled, Colleen nodded. "Okay."

⁊

The diamond chip on her left hand caught the light as she typed, making it impossible to focus on the flyer for the citywide Easter cantata. Six days after Easter, she'd sign her name as Sydney Rose McKay. Giving in to distracted thoughts, she clicked on the file labeled WEDDING, the list of dreams that had started in college and found its way to four different computers over the years. It held color schemes and pictures of dresses, cakes, and flower arrangements she'd updated on a regular basis—dreams of the wedding she once thought she wanted. Scrolling down the page marked SPRING WEDDING, she stared at floor-length dark brown bridesmaids' dresses with satin sashes the color of Granny Smith apples; a three-tiered cheesecake covered in smooth dark chocolate with lacy white icing and bright green and peach-toned flowers; a bouquet of lime green and pale orange Singapore orchids; and a white dress, fitted at the waist, with a Mandarin collar, long lace sleeves, and a full skirt and train that would sparkle in the candlelight as she floated down the aisle. . . .

Staring down at her ring, she deleted the file.

On the way home from the park on Christmas Eve, she'd made an easy decision—she didn't need anything in the wedding file except the groom. Trace had neither money nor family, and she wouldn't allow him to feel like simply a necessary player in *her* little-girl dream. Their ceremony would be small, cozy, and *them*. And if Sydney could pull it off, there'd be a few surprises waiting for Trace as he took his place at the altar.

⁊

Nothing was going right. Her wedding day dawned dark and drizzly, and by two thirty, an hour and a half before the ceremony, Sydney was on the verge of becoming one of the hysterical brides who make reality shows so popular. Slamming the phone onto its base in the kitchen, she yelled for her mother. No answer. Of course. Where was everyone? She'd just spoken to a hostess at the Sage Stoppe. The woman was clueless. The tables in the meeting room Sydney had reserved for dinner weren't set yet; the heart-shaped white cake she'd ordered from the bakery hadn't arrived.

For the fourth time in an hour, she dialed Colleen and was shocked to finally hear her voice.

"Where are you? I've been trying to call you!"

"I'm at the church with your mom."

"My mother's at church? Why? We finished everything last night. She's supposed to be here helping me with my veil."

"She found some ribbon she thought would look nice as big bows on the ends of the pews."

Oh no. Sydney's stomach knotted. Her mother's tastes were so far from her own. She pictured country blue and mauve. Weakly she asked, "What color?"

"Kind of a chartreusey green. It looks great with my dress."

"Your dress is teal!" Sydney wasn't a yeller. But some situations required it. "Stop her, Col. Tell her I need her now and then rip them off."

"Okay." Colleen's voice was way too laid-back.

"Your job is to look out for me today. My mother knows I want this simple. I've held her down this long; now you have to take over. Please?"

"I'll send her home. You'll be here at three, right?"

"Right." Her eyes went to the clock. She had to be ready, makeup on, veil in place, in twenty-seven minutes.

"And your dress is already here?"

"Yes. Mom took it over this morning before it started pouring."

"So everything's cool. Sit down and chill, girl."

"Chill? The cake hasn't arrived at the restaurant, my veil isn't on, the—"

"Hey. . .cool it. It's all going to fall into place. Shut your eyes and picture your beautiful dress and your hunky man and relax."

Sydney shut her eyes. "You're right. I can do this." She hung up the phone. *Lord this isn't about the show; it's about the marriage. Forgive me. Focus my thoughts.* She pictured the look on Trace's face when she walked down the aisle in her tea-length white dress. It was classic and simple, and she knew he'd love it. As her anxiety began to melt, her phone rang. Trace. *Thank You.* His voice was exactly what she needed right now.

"Hi." She stood and headed toward the stairs. She'd start on makeup while she talked. "Are you calling to chicken out?"

"Only on part of it."

Sydney's heart slammed against her ribs. Trace's voice held no humor. What else could go wrong today?

"Wh–at part?"

"The honeymoon."

I can handle this. They'd planned three nights at the Rock Haven Resort, taking walks and trying out the little skiff he'd named for her. Maybe something had come up with one of the boats at work. "We have to postpone it?"

"Not exactly."

What was he having so much trouble saying? "What. . .exactly?"

"They didn't hold our reservations at Rock Haven."

Sydney stopped in the living room, staring out at the rain. She was going to spend her wedding night at the Motel 6 in Pine Bluff. "Why not?"

"Because I told them not to." He paused; she didn't try to fill the empty space. "Because my father sent us plane tickets and we're going to Las Vegas and the Grand Canyon for our honeymoon."

"But I thought you couldn't leave the state."

"I got it approved."

"Seriously?"

"Seriously."

Over her squeal, he asked, "Syd. . .how did my father get my address?"

∞

The first thing that hit her when she walked into the bride's room was the three-paneled mirror. Alone in the room, she stared at the incongruent picture she made in faded jeans, pink blouse, and cowboy boots, with pearl drop earrings, her hair in spiral curls, and a finger-length veil.

The second thing she noticed was the padded hanger the seamstress had hung her wedding dress on.

The hanger was empty.

As she reached for the door, it opened. Her mother walked in first, wearing a champagne-colored dress that brushed the toes of matching shoes. Rhinestones lined the neckline. *Oh no.* What happened to the taupe suit Sydney had picked out with her? Next to Sydney, her mother would look ridiculously overdressed.

Mattie gave her a kiss on the cheek. "We want to pray with you before you get ready." She swung the door open, and Colleen, in tea-length teal with strappy brown shoes, walked in. Behind her were Zack and Eldon in black suits with teal-tipped white boutonnieres.

They gathered around her, and before she had a chance to ask about her dress, Eldon began to pray. "Lord, Mattie and I gave our little girl to You years ago, and now we also give her to her husband. Bless them, draw them ever closer to You and to each other, and let their marriage"—he stopped and pulled a handkerchief out of his pocket—"and all that You have brought them through be a testimony to Your grace and mercy."

As her mother prayed, tears fell from Sydney's face onto the gray carpet. She took a tissue from Colleen's hand and whispered, "Amen," after her mother.

When the circle parted, Sydney dabbed at her eyes. "Where's my dress?"

Mattie blew her nose. "I'll get it."

"I'm going to check on the kids." Wiping her eyes, Colleen left the room.

Seconds later, her mother entered, holding a dress hanger above her head. But the dress on the hanger was not Sydney's dress.

It was the dress in her wedding file. Every detail, from the mandarin collar to the pearl and rhinestone swirls on the train. Sydney's hands flew to her mouth but didn't stop the sob that tore from her chest. She sank into a chair, and her father knelt beside her.

"My little girl deserves the dress of her dreams." He swiped at his cheek as he grinned at her.

"But I didn't want Trace to feel—"

"Trace has been in on this from day one. He's about jumping out of his skin waiting to see you. So put on that dress, and I'll be waiting outside the door."

The lace sleeves ended in a point at her wrist, hiding her scars. But she was marrying a man she didn't need to hide from. As she turned one last time in front of the mirror, that thought brought fresh tears. "I have to stop this." She sniffed.

Her mother handed her two fresh tissues. "Wrap them around the base of your bouquet."

"My bouquet! Where is it?"

"Dad has it." Mattie opened the door then stopped halfway. "Have I given you all the advice a mother's supposed to give?"

Sydney gave her a gentle hug. "If not, I know where to find you."

With a few hard blinks, Mattie nodded. "Think you're ready for this?"

"Yes."

As Mattie opened the door wider, she whispered, "We'll see about that."

Her father stood in the hallway, a bouquet of flowers in his hand. It was not Sydney's bouquet of teal and white roses.

It was the bouquet from the wedding file.

"What...?" When words wouldn't form, she numbly took the arm her father offered her and took her first step toward the chapel.

She couldn't take a second step. Her father stood rooted to the floor. "This way, princess." He turned her slowly in the opposite direction. Mattie fell in step on her left, grinning and crying all at the same time.

Her father was leading her toward the front foyer. Halfway there, Zack met them, letting out a long, low whistle. "My sister's a fox!" It was then that Sydney noticed that his boutonniere had changed color. She looked at her father's. His white carnation was now tipped in lime green. Zack held out his arm for Mattie and they walked away, toward the door of the sanctuary.

"Dad... What's going on?"

"The wedding of your dreams, sweetheart."

A swishing sound behind her caused her to turn. Colleen curtsied in a dark brown dress with a satin sash the color of Granny Smith apples. She straightened and pointed at Sydney. "You look beyond amazing. Don't you dare cry." With that, she walked ahead and through the double doors.

Somehow Sydney made it from the foyer to the door of the sanctuary. Every pew was filled. The lights were off; candelabras lined the aisle, and candles lit the platform. The organ sounded the first few notes of the "Wedding March" and everyone stood. Sydney brushed her lips across her father's rough cheek. "I love you, Daddy. Have I told you lately that you're still my hero?"

Her father's eyes closed for a moment, and he took a shuddery breath. "I love you, too. Ready?"

She nodded and fixed her eyes on the silhouette at the front of the church. Each step brought her closer and revealed Trace's crooked smile and the candlelight reflected in his eyes.

Glancing to the right, she smiled at the plump, brassy-haired woman in the front pew. The woman who would soon be her mother-in-law. That, at least, was something she'd actually planned herself. She'd have to wait to hear Trace's reaction to the surprise, but the tears in his eyes spoke volumes.

"Who gives this woman to be married to this man?"

"Her mother and I do."

Her father placed her hand in Trace's. His hand closed around hers. "You are so beautiful," he whispered.

The next few minutes felt like a dream. As Pastor Owen spoke, her eyes wandered from the candelabras to the flowers, to the tears spotting Colleen's brown dress. It was everything she'd imagined, everything she'd convinced herself wasn't important.

And then it was time to face her husband-to-be and fit her hands in his. It had been Trace's idea to write their own vows, his idea to keep them secret until this moment.

His smile sent heat all the way to her knees. This man, who was terrified of public speaking, was doing this for her. He'd known all along that the sanctuary would be full.

"I, Trace, take you, Sydney Rose, to be my wife, my partner, my best friend. Before God and these witnesses, I promise to support you, protect you, and sacrifice for you. I promise to pray for you daily, to do all that I can to encourage and strengthen your walk with the Lord. I will tell you every day for the rest of my life that you are beautiful and cherished and loved. And. . .I promise to buy running shoes and to never, ever put chili powder in your chocolate cake."

Sydney reached behind her for the tissue wrapped around the bouquet in Colleen's hand. When the laughter died, she began.

"I, Sydney, take you, Trace, to be my lawfully wedded husband. For the rest of my life, through all of the uncertainties ahead, I will walk with you. . .because you are a man who cares more about pleasing God than pleasing man, because I love you more than life, and because when I am with you, I feel beautiful. I will walk with you, no matter where God leads us, because you are the man I trust.

DREAM CHASERS

*To Kristen, Holly, Adrianne, and Brittany.
You are the women we prayed for before our sons were born.
Thank you. . .for accepting this family in spite of the Melby Wander and oyster stew, for not being Paper Dolls, but perfect fits for our boys, for adding stockings to our mantel, and for raising our amazing grandkids in the joy of our Lord.
I love you, Becky*

*To Nathan's beloved, Michelle Stempniewski-Wienke. I am so thankful to God for bringing you into our family. Thank you for loving our son. And to Brian's parents, Donald and Beverly Wienke. Thank you for raising my loving husband.
Love you all, Cathy*

*Thank you to Scott Emerson Crosby for sharing his water tower story.
And kudos to Bill for creating the Polar Cap.*

Chapter 1

I'm halfway to the top. No turning back now."

Gripping the rung tighter with her left hand, April quickly adjusted her hands-free microphone. "My knees feel like spaghetti, but I *will* do this." *Eighty-three, eighty-four.* She counted the rungs. *Don't look down.*

Her gaze followed the ladder to the point where the giant steel legs met the base of the water tank. She arched her neck, staring up—and up.

The ladder swayed.

Or had it? April's breath caught. Her heart hammered at her ribs. Hugging the ladder, she waited. "Vertigo. That's all it was. I won't do that again."

Her breathing slowed. She moved one hand and then her foot. "I wish this was television instead of radio so you could see the scripture verses I've written on the backs of my ha—" Her foot slipped. She gasped, heart pounding again, and regained her footing.

Rung by rung, she reached the base of the reservoir. The wind picked up suddenly. Her Minnesota Twins cap bounced against her forehead. Honey-blond bangs pulled free and whipped across her eyes, blocking her vision for a moment and sending a fresh ripple of panic down her back. She focused on her hands. " 'I can do everything through him who gives me strength.' That's the verse on my right hand. On my left, I have—"

The whir of helicopter blades covered her words as a massive shadow blocked the sun, darkening the pale blue surface of the water tower and obliterating her words.

"Well, folks," she shouted into the microphone, "this is why the powers that be at KPOG don't let me do live radio yet!" It was a comment she'd delete before it reached the ears of anyone back at the station.

The helicopter rounded the water tower, giving her a momentary reprieve from the deafening vibration before appearing in her peripheral vision on the opposite side. "Looks like I'm not alone up here!" she yelled over the rhythmic pulse of the blades. The chopper hovered about thirty yards out. Afraid that turning her head would cause another wave of dizziness, she gritted her teeth and slowly looked to her right. . .directly into a camera lens.

The cameraman sat in the chopper's open doorway, his legs swinging in the air. Kneeling beside him was a man with a microphone. A man familiar to most of Pine Bluff, Minnesota—the local cable channel's weatherman.

Seth Bachelor. The sight of him made April's jaw tense and the cords at the base of her skull tighten like steel cables. Why him? Why now, in the middle of her first giant step away from fear?

But April Douglas knew how to hide her personal problems from the camera. She produced a TV smile. "The KXPB-TV news chopper is filming me."

Her hand grasped the rung that ran parallel to the bottom of the bright blue *I* in PINE BLUFF. A catwalk with a railing circled the reservoir. She remembered this spot; she'd been here before, years ago. Here—but no farther. A siren and a blinding spotlight had stopped her.

The chopper edged away. The air calmed, and the noise dropped. But the helicopter hovered at a distance. "It's about time Channel Five decided to use me on camera." Another comment she'd delete before her show.

The presence of the helicopter messed with her train of thought. *Focus. Don't stop.* She moved to the next step. "The verse on my left hand is from Psalm 139: 'Where can I go from your Spirit? Where can I flee from your presence? If I go up to the heavens, you are there.'"

Reading the verse out loud acted like an intravenous drip of boldness, giving her just enough courage to let go with one hand and aim a smooth, controlled parade wave at the camera. For all her fears, performing on camera was not one of them. This was, after all, a chance to show KXPB-TV her versatility and make them sorry they didn't snap her up when they had the chance.

Strength seeped back into her legs, and her hands gripped the rungs with a determination that banished much of her anxiety. It all worked together to propel her faster up the vertical side of the tank to the point where the steel curved toward the top and she had to crawl. The metal rungs bit into her knees, and she couldn't shake the realization that only a skin of steel separated her from three hundred thousand gallons of water—and nothing but air separated her from the ground, 148 feet below.

Don't look down. She kept her eyes on her hands until she reached the last rung. A lightning rod marked the summit.

"I'm at the top! I made it!"

She'd expected to feel nothing but triumph and exhilaration. But instead, an almost palpable sense of aloneness engulfed her. She wasn't supposed to do this alone.

But she had. In spite of her fear of heights, in spite of the fact that her sister wasn't with her, she'd reached the top.

Just like she'd promised.

With a sigh that vibrated the windscreen on her microphone, she smiled. A tear dropped from her chin to the sky-blue metal. Slowly releasing her right hand from the rung, she gripped the bill of her cap, pulled it off her ponytail, and flung it into the air.

"This is for you, Caitlyn!"

∞

"After nine inches of rain in less than twenty-four hours, the Snake River has crested and is overflowing its banks." Seth Bachelor adjusted his headset as he peered through the helicopter window. "Several houses have—" Movement caught his eye. "Look!" He nudged the pilot's arm and pointed. "Somebody's climbing the water tower!" The guys at the station would hate him for the editing they'd have to do on his flood coverage, but this diversion could prove to be newsworthy.

Grappling with the latch on his seat belt, he squeezed through the space between the front seats as the pilot banked and circled the water tower. Over his shoulder, he yelled, "Get the police on the phone. See what they know." He glanced at his watch. The morning news wasn't quite over. "And call the station and tell 'em to get a reporter over here—stat."

In the back, Rick James, the cameraman, already had his lens trained on the tower. Seth turned off his microphone. "Is it a girl?"

Rick had the advantage of a telephoto lens. "Oh yeah. Most definitely."

"How old?"

"Can't tell. Probably teens."

A voice crackled in his ear. "Seth? Merv. Can you go live with this in one minute?"

"Sure can."

The attack of nerves surprised him. He could give a weather report in his sleep, but the metamorphosis from meteorologist to reporter wouldn't be smooth. He cleared his throat again, shouted a few instructions at Jay and then Rick, and said a quick prayer that his brain wouldn't freeze up.

"In spite of warnings from the police and increased fines, some things never change. If it's spring in Pine Bluff, Minnesota, kids will be climbing the water tower. They've been doing it for more than fifty years, and as the end of the school year and graduation approach, we'll see more incidents of this illegal and extremely dangerous—yet time-honored—tradition. What's unusual about what we're seeing here is that this young lady is more daring than most. She's climbing alone and in broad daylight."

Whoever she was, she was in for trouble. "This girl's going to be arrested, and if memory serves me, the fine is likely to be around four hundred dollars." He stared at the girl's jean-clad legs and maroon jacket and the gold hair that whipped around her face. "She's halfway up the tank now. This is where we'd expect to see the spray paint come out, but she's still climbing."

A thought struck him. Was she going to jump? Sure, she'd just smiled and waved for the camera, but what if it was all a ruse? He leaned over Rick, getting a good look at the base of the tower. "There are a couple of people on the ground watching her. One appears to have a camera or binoculars. I'm expecting police sirens any moment. . . ."

But what if the police were staying away purposely so as not to frighten her? Were they actually communicating with her somehow, trying to talk her down?

Maybe it wasn't a camera or binoculars he'd seen after all. Maybe it was a bull-horn. "She's reached the top. I hope what we're witnessing is just a high school prank, but there's no way of knowing what her intentions are.

"I can't imagine what would bring this girl out here in the middle of the school day, knowing she's likely to get caught. I'm surprised that she didn't retreat when she saw our helicopter. You're probably coming to the same conclusion I am—there's a good chance this poor girl is climbing to the top of the water tower with thoughts of jumping. We've contacted the authorities, and you can rest assured that, if they aren't already down there trying to talk her down, they'll be on the scene any moment. Folks, if you believe in prayer. . .now would be a good time. This could be life or death."

&

"What in the world are they doing?" The chopper was closer now, the staccato beat of the blades so loud she couldn't hear herself think, much less transmit. How could a dinky cable television station like KXPB afford a helicopter, any-way? Slowly, she climbed back down to the catwalk. Standing upright, with both hands securely clutching the railing, she drank in the view for the first time.

For a moment, she was grateful for the excuse not to talk; no words came to mind. The panorama that stretched in every direction was a kaleidoscope of color. Flowering crab apple and cherry trees dotted the town like wads of cotton candy. The sky, cerulean and cloudless, seemingly washed clean by days of rain, met craggy bluffs to her left and white pines to her right. To the north, the brimming Snake River, true to its name, wound like an overfed serpent toward its junction with the St. Croix.

Nestled close to the banks of the St. Croix lay the town April was learning to call home all over again. Below the water tower, the high school football field spread out, surrounded by a cinder track. She'd run that oval more times than she could count. Looking down at the miniature runners, she could almost hear the crunch beneath their feet. She located the roof of her apartment and the house she'd grown up in, but when she attempted to find the steeple of her church, the chopper blocked her view. She glared at it, the same thought cycling through her mind again. *What in the world are they doing?*

If they'd hoped to see something dramatic, they must have figured out by now that she wasn't going to be performing any aerial stunts. They certainly had enough footage, though April was confident she hadn't done anything worthy of the six o'clock news.

Pointing to her microphone, she tried to wave them off. What was the universal media signal for "I'm trying to tape here, you bozos!"? Maybe Seth Bachelor had all the time in the world, but she had a radio show that aired at three o'clock. If anything, her attempt at sign language made the helicopter edge nearer. Any closer and they'd rip into the reservoir. She could picture sliding down the newly created waterfall. *That* would be newsworthy. "Go away! Go

126

do your weather thing!"

The catwalk wasn't wide enough for her to maneuver without turning sideways. She inched her way around to the west, hoping that News Chopper Five wouldn't follow her. As she took her third step, the helicopter rose straight up and made a beeline for the river. Silence echoed in its absence.

April drew a deep breath and tried to bring her thoughts back to her reason for being there. Switching on the microphone, she closed her eyes, needing a moment of introspection.

"So this is number one, the first thing on Caitlyn's dream list. As you can imagine, I'm experiencing a lot of conflicting emotions. By God's grace alone, I stared down one of my major fears. There's a sense of victory in that, but I can't help thinking how much fun this would have been with my sister leading the way."

The helicopter looked like a Matchbox toy as it followed the curve of the St. Croix River and angled west along the Snake. Sunlight glinted off the aircraft's side and on the brown and churning river below it. April swiped at another maverick tear. "But life goes on. . .and God has a way of turning tarnished dreams into something beautiful."

Chapter 2

Y ou have *got* to be kidding!" April paced her living room, unable to share even a modicum of her best friend's amusement. "They aired it live?"

"In Technicolor." Yvonne Sondergard fluffed her white-blond curls. "Couldn't really make out your face, but all of east-central Minnesota got a great shot of your Lucky jeans."

With a groan, April plopped her Luckys onto the couch but bounced up again. "What did they say?"

"They thought you were going to deface the tower...or kill yourself."

"What?"

Yvonne pulled a crumpled bag from under the coffee table and took out a tortilla chip. "He started out by saying that you were going to get slapped with a hefty fine when you were arrested."

Another groan emerged. "So everybody who recognized my backside thinks I'm in jail now."

"Yup." Yvonne stuck a chip in her mouth. "These are stale. You'd better make it perfectly clear at the top of your show that you had permission from the city and that the station would have taken responsibility if you'd plummeted to your doom...or leaped to your doom."

A twinge of guilt surfaced. "Yeah...about that...not so much."

"Huh?"

"Never mind."

"Seth was really getting into the drama of a possible suicide and—"

"Seth? You're on a first name basis with the weatherman?"

"Of course. I know the mailman and the crossing guard on the corner, too. What are you so stressed out about?"

"That man—" The phone on the kitchen counter rang. April sighed as she got up to answer it. Her quick trip home for a shower had taken half an hour so far, and she still hadn't had the shower. Her "Hello" echoed her frustration.

"April? I need you in my office. Now."

☙

Jill Berkley's almost-black eyes smoldered. "Why?"

"Because the risk had to be real." April stood in front of her boss's desk, hands on hips.

"Did you even once consider the risk to the radio station? If you'd slipped, and landed in the hospital—"

"If I'd slipped, I would have splattered. There wouldn't have been anything left to hospitalize."

Perfectly manicured hands shot into the air above Jill's short-cropped black hair. "You're impossible!" Her sigh fluttered the papers on her desk. "April. . .you wonder why the board won't give you a live show, and then you go and pull something like this?"

"No one would have known I wasn't wearing a harness if that stupid helicopter hadn't shown up."

"So it would have been fine if you hadn't gotten caught?"

April shrugged. "Yeah. Sort of."

A hint of a smile pulled at the corners of Jill's mouth. "If you weren't so crazy good at what you do, you would have been fired months ago."

"So I'm not?"

Jill shook her head. "Once again, I went to bat for you. But you have to take this seriously, April. Three job applications have crossed my desk just this month. If you take too many chances, the board could run over me like a steamroller and hire somebody to replace you."

"I'll make it up to you."

"Make sure you do. Now go. Put together a show that will knock my socks off and make me forget all the rules you break."

April bowed, hands outstretched, grateful for the thousandth time that her immediate superior was far more friend than boss. She had her hand on the doorknob when Jill stopped her.

"That broadcast is on the KXPB Web site."

"Great." She stopped and turned toward Jill. "No, actually, it is great. I'll copy it and keep it as a reminder of my first big step. I'll just mute the commentary."

"Oh, you have to listen to it. It's highly entertaining. Seth Bachelor is layering the drama until his audience is convinced you're going to jump, and then all of a sudden there's dead silence, followed by, 'We've just received information'"—Jill's voice lowered to a rough impersonation of the weatherman—" 'that this. . .woman. . .works for a local radio station. Evidently this is some kind of publicity. . .campaign.'"

"Publicity campaign?"

"Hey, he didn't say 'stunt.' Gotta give him credit for that."

April closed her eyes and leaned her head against the doorjamb.

"At the end of the news, they showed another clip of your climb and said, 'We now have the name of the lone climber.'"

" 'The Lone Climber.' Think I'll have a T-shirt printed with it."

"The timing was perfect."

"For what? Humiliation? I manage that on my own just fine." She ran one hand through hair still tangled in places from the chopper. "At least he didn't tape me throwing up when I got to the bottom."

Jill shook her head and tossed a mini Mounds bar at April. "They gave a plug for your show. That doesn't happen every day in the Christian radio biz. You may have a much larger audience today, thanks to Seth Bachelor." Jill flipped a calendar with the tip of her pencil. "And you can thank him in person next Saturday."

Bending to retrieve the candy bar from under a chair, April stiffened. "What do you mean?"

"At the citywide cleanup. He's the cochair, and you're interviewing him."

The wrapper on the candy bar in April's hand crackled as her fist clenched. "Get someone else."

"Why?"

"I've got. . .reasons."

"Well, get over them. You're doing the interview."

❧

"April?"

The flat voice coming through her office phone elicited a familiar wave of trepidation. April set her purse back on the floor and leaned against the back of her desk chair. She wouldn't be heading home soon.

"Hi, Mom."

"You should have warned me." A tiny, muffled sob finished her mother's last word.

For a split second, April considered playing dumb. But what was the point? "I didn't think you could get my show since you moved."

An empty space, filled with ragged breathing, followed. April closed her eyes, willing warmth into the cold spot in her chest. Too many guilt-inducing silences, over too many years, had leeched emotion from her soul.

"I drive up to the Goose Creek rest area on Saturdays to catch your show."

The picture of her mother sitting alone in her car, listening to her talk about Caitlyn from the top of the water tower, finally brought a twinge of empathy. "I'm sorry, Mom. I didn't—"

"I can't believe you're exploiting your sister's suffering like this."

Indignation rose like bile in April's throat. "How can you think for a second that I would do that?"

"It's getting you closer to your goal, isn't it? My daughter, the next Oprah."

April's mouth jarred open, but nothing came out.

"Midge told me you were on the news, too." Her mother spat the words. "The weatherman—you do realize he's the one—"

"Yes. I know. I have to go, Mom." Without waiting for a reply, she slammed the phone into its base.

❧

Over the next few days, the calls and e-mails generated by what the station employees were now referring to as "The Water Tower Show" lifted April's spirits from the pit her mother's call had left her in. Jill and the station owners were excited—the new kid on the block was having an impact. On a personal level, the e-mails stirred emotions that had just begun to settle. "Your words resonated in my soul," one woman wrote. She then went on to tell of her son's battle with leukemia. The boy had died just a week ago.

Resonate. That was the reason she'd gone to school—to make a difference in someone's life. But this level of public transparency was going to cost her something. On Wednesday morning, she was in the middle of a reply to the woman who'd lost her son when her phone rang. The young receptionist, usually poised and articulate, stammered over April's name. "I'm sorry. I know you're busy, but I didn't want to put this girl off. She's just been told she has an inoperable brain tumor."

Just listen and share your story. The advice had come from her grief support group. "I'll take it."

She listened. The girl was only sixteen, a year younger than Caitlyn had been. When the girl ran out of words, April spoke the one thing her sister had told her never to say again. "I'm so, so sorry."

"I love your idea." The girl's voice was hoarse with tears. "I don't want to spend whatever time I have left just thinking about dying. I want to live, like you said. . .to embrace life."

"That's a beautiful attitude, Libby. Are you going to make a dream list?"

"For sure. And the first thing on it is to lose my virginity!"

Lord. . .help! It was going to be a long morning.

❦

April recognized the boy with the wild swirls of light blond hair from a story she'd done on the Special Olympics. He was holding up a full trash bag as if it were a trophy fish.

"So why are you helping with Cleanup Day, Ronny?" April held a microphone out to him.

"It's good to make the world cleaner. And I like the hot dogs. And the garbage bags are going to make a huge pile and get bigger and bigger and bigger like a volcano." He pointed to several volunteers in orange vests who were adding their bulging bags to a pile near the entrance to Founders Park.

Thanks in part to April, a picture of the finished "volcano" would make front-page news in the Sunday paper. She'd asked the city for permission to count the bags and estimate the weight. The director of the Pine Bluff Chamber of Commerce had taken her idea a step further and had arranged for all the bags to be dumped into a pile in the park where the volunteers would gather after the cleanup.

"Looks like you've worked really hard. You earned your hot dog." She switched off the microphone. "Follow that path to wash your hands first."

As she watched the boy's attempts to swing his bag to the top of the heap, she thought once again that she wished she were filming a television spot.

"Hey, if it isn't the Lone Climber!"

Yvonne's voice, coming from behind April, brought a smile. Taking in the three-inch heels, white skirt, and the lace that stuck out beneath Yvonne's mint green tank top, April shook her head. "You're a little overdressed."

"As if."

April laughed. The two words needed no explanation. Yvonne didn't own clothes for manual labor. She was a transplant from Minneapolis, having followed her fiancé to Pine Bluff just over a year ago. Like a hothouse plant exposed to the elements, Yvonne wasn't thriving well away from the city. She and April had moved in on the same weekend, meeting as they both carried boxes up the steps to their apartments above the chamber of commerce office.

Stretching her hands out, April threatened to hug Yvonne with her trash-picking gloves and was rewarded with a horrified grimace. She lowered her arms in a gesture of surrender. "What are you up to? Oh yeah, you're singing for a wedding in the Cities, right?"

Yvonne nodded. "It's an evening wedding, but I'm heading in early. The church is only a couple of miles from Nordstrom's. Anything you need?"

"As if." As if she could afford even a pair of pantyhose from Nordstrom's.

"You doing okay today?" Yvonne gave her the kind of look most people reserve for stray kittens or children with skinned knees.

"Yeah. . .no."

"I've been thinking about you this morning, and I couldn't leave without seeing your face. I knew this was going to be a tough day for you."

A year ago, Caitlyn had roped April into helping with the cleanup. In her track uniform like the rest of her team, her sister had looked the picture of health, making it easy to deny her recent diagnosis. They'd talked nonstop as they picked up fast-food wrappers and soda bottles along the highway, laughing so hard at times they had to stand still to catch their breath.

As they'd stood in line for hot dogs, Caitlyn had made a proclamation that would be forever etched in April's mind: "I feel invincible. I'm going to beat this thing."

And she had, for five months. And then she'd gotten caught in a thunderstorm, and two days after that she was in the hospital. A month later, April knew all the hospice nurses by name.

April shrugged and attempted a smile. "Thanks."

"Can I pray for you?" Without waiting for an answer, Yvonne placed a perfectly manicured hand, adorned with three silver rings, on April's arm.

As always, the words she spoke were poetic and cut straight to the heart of the emotions that pressed down on April like a physical weight.

Long after Yvonne left, her prayer remained wrapped around April like a warm shawl. Her friend was a contradiction in terms. A shopping guru who wore nothing but name brands, never went anywhere without makeup, and drove a bright red BMW, she also taught a junior high girls' Sunday school class and worked as program coordinator at the local nursing home. More than once, she'd literally given the shirt off her back to a resident who had admired it, and gone home in a scrub top.

While the "material girl" image had never appealed to April, there was something about her new best friend that she envied. The girl knew who she was. Two years ago, April would have said the same thing about herself. Back when she was twenty-four and starry-eyed. Before her seventeen-year-old sister was diagnosed with leukemia. Before she'd left her job at the television station in St. Paul. Before she'd moved back to the town she'd waited eighteen years to escape.

"Describe yourself in one word" was something she said often in interviews. What word would fit April Douglas on this sunny April morning? Lost? To some extent that fit, but it made her sound helpless and pitiful. She was neither of those. If anything, she'd become stronger, not in herself, but in the knowledge that God could carry her through anything.

Before she found her one word, a girl about April's height, her hair in stubby pigtails, approached her. The girl appeared dressed for a rave instead of garbage duty. Multiple strings of shiny red and black beads hung over her orange reflective vest, and a tight black-and-white-striped shirt showed beneath it. April smiled. "Hi."

"Are you April?"

When April nodded, the girl said, "I'm Libby. I just wanted to say hey and thanks for inviting me to this trash thingy, you know? And I figured you'd want to know that maybe something good came out of all the bad with your sister dying and stuff 'cause I really did listen to what you said about staying pure, and I really do want to do something important with the ti—"

The sound of a motor in high gear stopped her words. April whirled around just in time to see a four-wheel ATV careening around the corner, heading straight for them. Whipping back around, she shielded Libby with her arms while yelling at her to move.

Missing her heels by inches, the ATV plowed into the mountain of bags. Paper and plastic debris exploded from the pile. The ATV slowed to a stop several yards beyond, leaving a wake of litter behind it.

Like a creature from a low-budget sci-fi movie, the driver, dressed from head to toe in black with a full-face helmet on his head, rose from the seat. With hands still on the grips, he half stood and turned. By then, April was within yelling distance.

"You could have killed that girl! You could have killed me! If this is your idea of fun, I can guarantee that you're not going to think picking up all that trash and rebagging it is—"

Black-gloved hands removed the helmet, and April stood face-to-face with the man she'd dreaded encountering today.

Chapter 3

"Are you done?" Seth wondered if there was actual steam shooting out of his ears. "Because I'll just wait until you are, and then I'll explain that the brakes failed and I couldn't stop the stupid thing if my life depended on it—which it did! You're not the only one who could have been killed, lady!"

To her credit, the girl with the goldish blond hair looked appropriately mortified. She moved her sunglasses to the top of her head, as if needing to examine him better. As she stared at him, her expression evolved from anger to shock to embarrassment and then to the most artificial smile he'd seen in a long time. Strained though it was, he was pretty sure the corners of her mouth were pointed more up than down. Not that any hint of it was reflected in her eyes. They were pretty eyes—deep, deep blue surrounded by long lashes. She wasn't wearing too much makeup. Then again, she'd probably spent hours layering on the natural look. He knew from experience that the pretty ones were always stuck on themselves.

Maybe he'd come on a little harsh. He could take the high road here. "Are you two all right?"

The girl who looked like she was dressed for Mardi Gras nodded as she backed away, eyes wide with shock or fear, then turned and ran. The blond gave something closely resembling a nod. Wasn't this where she was supposed to ask how he was? *Your brakes? That must have been frightening! You're not hurt, are you? Should I call 911? Please accept my apology for completely spazzing out like that.*

"You're. . .Seth Bachelor."

Did the woman have lockjaw? Not only did she seem incapable of an apology, she seemed to have trouble forcing words through her teeth. Was her mouth wired shut? Nobody could be that angry over a couple of busted trash bags. Who was she, anyway? Maybe she was the mayor's daughter and the garbage bags had come out of her allowance. He refrained from hurling that one at her. "I am. And you are. . . ?"

"April Douglas."

April Douglas. . .why did the name sound familiar? He'd remember that face if they'd ever met. Her eyes challenged, as if her name was supposed to elicit some response. He rifled through the little black book in his head. Sadly, most of the pages were blank. And if they'd dated even once, even years ago, he would have remembered those eyes. "Have we met?" It was the oldest pickup line in history; he hoped she wouldn't think that was his intention. She was absolutely not his type.

"Not exactly." Her tone was flat. "But I thought we shared a meaningful moment at the top of the water tower last week."

Oh no. Not her. *Lord, You do have a sense of humor.* Not sure what he was supposed to say, he opened his mouth, but she spoke first.

"Can I interview you?"

Interview? Ah. . .this was her way of getting even. She'd probably focus her questions on his qualifications for driving an ATV instead of his cochairmanship of Cleanup Day. Well, he wasn't going to make it easy for her. "Before or after picking up this mess?"

"During."

∞

April shoved a crumpled beer can into a filled bag that sat on the ground. "How long have you been cochairing Cleanup Day?" Head down, she didn't even look at the man in black as she held the microphone in his direction. If her equipment wasn't good enough to pick up his answers, she'd wing it with a summary of the interview.

"Three years. Gil Cadwell did it before me. KXPB-TV has been sponsoring the cleanup since the seventies."

If the leather jacket had buttons, they would have been popping. You'd think he was talking about running the country instead of garbage pickup. "*Co*sponsoring with the chamber of commerce."

He bent over, creating a tempting spot for April to plant her hiking boot. She reeled in the thought. Tossing a wad of newspaper into his bag, he turned, still bent over, and looked at her. "For the past five years, yes."

"But it was originally started by high school students. Yes?" Copying his word, she added her own inflection.

"No. It was started by the Kiwanis Club. They got the kids involved."

Did that little detail really matter? "I heard there were almost two hundred volunteers signed up this year. That's a bit of an increase over last year, isn't it?"

"Two hundred and three this year. Last year there were a hundred and eighty-seven."

The man was a master at splitting hairs. April stood, pressed dirty gloves against the small of her back, and stared at Seth Bachelor's hunched-over spine. "Who provides the food for the volunteers?"

"KXPB supplies the food and does all the recruiting of volunteers. The chamber of commerce donates the bags, reflective vests, and gloves." He stood up. One eyebrow crept a fraction of an inch higher than the other. "Your radio station foots the bill for the portable toilets."

That was it. April tied the top of a half-full trash bag. The toilet comment was the last straw. Not the fact, but the delivery. "Thank you, Mr. Bachelor, for your cooperation." Her bag sailed through the air, missing the weatherman by a good two feet.

ళు

"You know him?" April handed a glass of sweetened tea to Yvonne, who was sitting cross-legged on April's faded denim couch. "How come you never told me?"

"I did tell you."

"You made it sound like you knew him like you know the snowplow driver! You didn't say you *knew* him knew him. How come you never mentioned him?"

"It never came up. He's been in my Wednesday night Bible study for a couple of months."

"He's a Christian?" April didn't try to temper the incredulousness in her voice. "My sympathies to your pastor and his wife." After pouring her own glass of tea, she moved her giant white teddy bear to the floor and sat down on the other end of the couch she'd nabbed from her mother's basement before she moved. "The Larkins must have the patience of Job."

Yvonne's expression turned defensive. "Seth's a really nice guy."

Was she serious? Maybe Yvonne was just overtired from singing and shopping in the Cities. It was, after all, past midnight. April took a gulp of tea and a relaxing breath. Her emotions had been frazzled all day. She hadn't felt good about her show this afternoon and had spent the evening in a mental boxing match.

"Then maybe I met a different Seth Bachelor. I could hardly use anything he said in the interview. It was like he was deliberately condescending, and enjoying it. If I'd said the sky was blue, he would have said it was purple."

"And he would probably have been right. He's the meteorologist."

Yvonne's effort to lighten the mood almost worked. April gave a weak smile and stared at Yvonne. Was it possible she had more than a passing interest in Seth Bachelor? Yvonne was engaged, but until that license was signed, things could change. If that were the case, April shouldn't let her personal issues interfere. "Okay, so if he's not the obnoxious, argumentative know-it-all he appeared to be, tell me something good about him."

"He knows how to dress."

April's iced tea slopped over the side of the glass when she laughed. "You're right. How could I have been so wrong about the guy? His style sense should cancel out all the negatives."

"He's cute."

"A sad waste."

Yvonne lowered her head, staring through curled top lashes. "He's got a headful of Bible knowledge."

" 'By their fruit you will recognize them.' "

"He's really a nice guy!" Yvonne set her glass on the coffee table with a thud. In the silence that followed, a siren screamed below them, heading north on Main Street. "You just got off on the wrong foot with him. He's witty and deep and discerning—he's always got some new insight into whatever we're studying."

Where was his gift of discernment back in October? April sighed and rubbed her hand across her eyes. "Maybe he's got a Jekyll and Hyde thing going on."

Yvonne stood and took her glass to the sink, only ten feet from the couch in the small apartment. "I have to get some sleep." Putting her hands on her hips, she turned to face April. "Come to Bible study with me on Wednesday."

April picked up the white four-foot-high bear and plopped it on the couch next to her. Leaning against it, she curled her feet beneath her. "I have to wash my hair that night."

ॐ

She should have gone to bed. But Snow Bear made an inviting pillow, and she hadn't had the energy to move after Yvonne left. Now, squinting at the time on the microwave in the tiny alcove known as her kitchen, April massaged the kink in her neck. It was 2:32. Two hours of heavy, dreamless sleep in the fetal position and now she was awake, but her right leg wasn't. Dragging herself off the couch, she shook the pins and needles out. Her numb foot slid on something, and she looked down. Her orange vest from the cleanup. Pictures of a day she'd like to forget flashed in her head.

Seth Bachelor was only part of the reason the day had gone wrong—she'd started the morning in a lousy mood. Grief was a strange thing. She'd been upbeat all week, buoyed by the positive feedback from the water tower show. Making arrangements for next week's *Slice of Life with April Douglas* had kept the adrenaline flowing and her time at the station busy. But from the moment she'd opened her eyes the day before, sadness had settled on her chest like a weighted vest.

Thoughts of Caitlyn permeated even the most inane details of her morning. Caitlyn writing HAPPY BIRTHDAY, APE on the bathroom mirror with toothpaste. . .the food fight Caitlyn had started with scrambled eggs because April had used too much pepper. . .trying on wigs and turbans after they'd both shaved their heads before Caitlyn's first round of chemo. And then, reliving moments from last year's Cleanup Day and her sister's words, "I'm gonna beat this thing."

The way April had blown up about the ATV slamming into "her" pile of trash was evidence of her lousy frame of mind. Had she known who the driver was before she yelled, there would have been some sense to her outburst, at least in her mind. But the accident wasn't his fault. The brakes had failed, and he'd deserved some slack under the circumstances. It wasn't like her to go ballistic without first checking out the facts.

Yvonne's protective defense of the man was interesting. "Seth's really a nice guy." She'd said it twice. April had been in a miserable mood at the cleanup, but that didn't explain his bristling responses to her questions. So where was the truth in all the contradictions? Was Seth Bachelor a chameleon, showing his "nice guy" side only when it fit his purposes? Maybe she should show up at the

Wednesday night study after all. . .seeing the other side would be fascinating.

Then again, maybe she should just wash her hair.

&

A low and distant rumble woke April to semiconsciousness. Pale pink light seeped between the slats of her blinds. Dawn. Sunday. What was the rumble? Her eyes shot open; her hand groped toward the nightstand where her cell phone quivered against the alarm clock. "Hello?"

"April? It's Jill. Sorry to wake you. I'm wondering if you'd be willing to do a live coverage."

"Sure. What is it?"

"Two kids from the high school were in a car accident last night. One of them was killed; the other's in critical condition. Some of the students are holding a prayer vigil outside the hospital. Orlando's going to cover the press conference with the highway patrol; I don't have anyone else who can go to the hospital."

"I can do it. Do you have the names of the kids?"

"Yeah. . .here somewhere. . .Dave Martin was the one who was killed. Brock Lewis is the one in the hospital."

"Oh no." Her heart skipped a beat. She sat up, throwing off the covers.

"April? Do you know them?"

"Brock was a friend of my sister's. How bad is he?"

"I don't have details. Critical is all I know. Can you do this?"

Her eyes closed, April lifted a prayer and took a deep breath. "I'll do it."

&

Six o'clock on Sunday morning. The streets of Pine Bluff were silent, though a few hours from now they'd be brimming with early season tourists in search of breakfast. As she pulled out of her parking space and into the alley that paralleled Main Street, April turned on the radio. She preferred silence this early, but knew she needed something to reset her mood dial. KPOG's six-to-nine slot was filled by Nick Joplin, an animated charismatic Christian who'd grown up in Warroad, just south of the Canadian border. Nick could talk faster than anyone April had ever met, though he didn't touch caffeine. "Got a Holy Spirit buzz going on," he claimed.

"It's 6:01 in beautiful downtown Pine Bluff. Daffodils bloomin' by my back door this mornin'. Just gotta praise God for color right now. Thank You, Lord, for all the little added touches. It's got its problems, for sure, but it's a fine world You made us. A fine world."

As always, Nick had her smiling in the first minute. When he played a praise song, she sang along.

Her 2001 Grand Prix knew the route from her apartment to the station and then to the hospital. How many times had she driven that circuit? But this wasn't the time to reminisce. *Lord, let me be a comfort. Let me respect their grief but*

138

find a way to share their story. She turned the music up and sang until she got to the hospital.

She'd expected maybe a dozen teens. . .a small prayer circle near the front entrance. What she saw raised goose bumps on her arms. The grassy area inside the circle drive was full, not just teens but adults and young children. Fifty people, maybe more. . .at six thirty on a Sunday morning.

Father God, be glorified in this place. Let Your presence be felt.

ᘯ

There was something invigorating about Nick Joplin's voice. Seth wasn't the kind who needed three cups of coffee to get moving in the morning, and Nick's voice and choice of contemporary and gospel music fit his energy level. It was a good way to start a Sunday morning.

He was whistling to "Give Me Words to Speak" as he stepped out the back door and dumped an empty dog food can into the garbage. Just looking at the dark green bag that lined the trash can stopped the song on his lips. Trash. He'd picked up more of it yesterday than he'd touched in all of his twenty-seven years. He slammed the aluminum lid harder than he needed to and went back into the house, giving the screen door a shove for good measure. Maynard looked up from his chicken liver hash, reprimanding him for disturbing his breakfast.

"Sorry, boy." Seth ruffled the part-mastiff's ears. "That's what a woman'll do to you."

As he poured a cup of Highlander Grog coffee, his gaze landed on the flashing red light on the kitchen phone. Another reminder of what a woman could do. He'd looked at the caller ID when the call came last night but hadn't picked up the phone. The last thing he needed to hear at the end of a frustrating day was Brenda Cadwell's voice. As he knew it would, a text message on his cell phone had followed in minutes. His answer had been short and not so sweet.

Glowering at the annoying light on the phone, he headed for the bathroom where he turned on the shower radio along with the water, needing the music to keep his Sunday morning mind-set.

It didn't work. Thoughts of yesterday's fiasco flooded his mind. As if failing brakes and exploding garbage bags weren't enough, he had to go and have a run-in with that woman. Sarcastic, defensive, grating. . .April Douglas had been all that and then some. What was it about him that attracted the good-looking ones with attitudes? Where were all the soft-spoken godly women hiding out? And why was self-absorption so in style these days? He'd fallen for the queen of me-centered beauties, literally, and until he found someone who was everything Miss-St.-Cloud-wannabe wasn't, his last name would also describe his marital status.

The shower radio was still on as he wiped the steam off the mirror. Humming to the music, he looked down at the book on the counter, a commentary on the book of Romans. This morning, the adult Sunday school class at church would be studying the last half of chapter 12, the part about showing kindness to your enemies. If there'd been a way to get out of this lesson, he would have, but it was his week to facilitate the discussion. Once again, the thought hit him that God had a sense of humor.

Back in January, when he'd signed the clipboard, he had no idea what the topic would be this week. If the Christian Education Committee knew the extent of his hypocrisy, they'd show him the door.

Seth waited for "Sunday's Comin'" to end before reaching around the shower door to turn off the radio. As he touched the knob, Nick Joplin's voice changed, suddenly somber. "Two local teens were involved in an accident on Highway 65 around midnight last night. David Martin, a senior at Pine Bluff High School, was pronounced dead at the scene. Another senior, Brock Lewis, is in critical condition at Emerson Memorial. April Douglas is live at the hospital where students have been holding a prayer vigil since word of the accident got out during the night. April, I understand you know the young man who was injured."

"I do, Nick, and I have to echo what I've been hearing from the people gathered here this morning. Brock is the kind of guy who never plays favorites; he makes everybody, teachers and students alike, feel. . .like. . . ," her voice faltered, "like a friend." Several seconds passed. "Dave Martin was one of those friends. He and Brock had been buddies since grade school. The kids, the faculty, and the staff are reeling from the loss. Allison Johansen was at the party Dave and Brock attended last night. Allison, I know it's not easy for you to talk right now, but can you give us some idea what Dave would want us to remember about his life?"

Seth stood, towel wrapped around his waist, fingers resting on the radio knob, transfixed by the tenderness in April Douglas's voice.

Maybe he'd been wrong about her.

Chapter 4

Riverdance...at the Orpheum Theater in Minneapolis. She'd waited a long time for this.

April stood in front of her full-length mirror as she blow-dried her hair. On the back of the closet door hung the black dress with white polka dots she'd be wearing tonight. For once, she and Yvonne had agreed on a point of fashion—they were both wearing black and white.

Anticipation of Friday had carried her through a difficult week. She'd gone to the memorial service for Dave Martin on Thursday. She'd never met the boy, but neither had many of the twelve hundred people who had packed the high school auditorium and overflowed onto the football field. The senior class, Caitlyn's class, had filled row after row of folding chairs in the same space they would occupy at graduation just two weeks from now. Sitting in the bleachers, just as she had for so many basketball games, April had tried not to let her thoughts center on her own grief, but it had been an impossible task. In the third row, right behind Dave Martin's family, a single chair sat empty. Caitlyn's two best friends sat on either side.

As of Tuesday, Brock was in stable condition. April had gone to see him after he'd been moved from intensive care. When she'd held her hand out to him, he'd gripped it weakly and smiled through the tears that dampened his pillow. "Caitlyn's whipping Dave at one-on-one up there," he'd said. Through her own tears, April had agreed.

God has a way of taking our tarnished dreams and turning them into something beautiful. She didn't even know where that phrase had come from, but it was becoming a daily chant. She plugged in her curling iron and picked up her digital recorder.

"When Caitlyn and I ordered our tickets for *Riverdance*, we both knew there was a good chance I'd be going without her, but maybe the pretending gave her a few more days, or maybe it just gave her a little more to smile about in the"—the phone rang—"time she had left."

Snapping off the recorder, she lunged across the bed for the phone. "Hello."

"You know I didn't mean that remark."

Almost two weeks had passed since the "My daughter, the next Oprah" comment. April tucked the phone against her shoulder and picked a black bracelet from the jumble of jewelry on her dresser. This wasn't the time for confrontation. Nothing was going to undo the delicious anticipation of a night at the Orpheum.

"How are you, Mom?"

"It's been a hard week."

"I know."

"Do you? Do you know what it's like when your only living daughter doesn't come to see you? Do you know what it's like when your ex-husband calls you out of the blue just to say you were a lousy wife?"

"Dad called?" Sickeningly familiar tension squeezed her abdominal muscles.

"Over a week ago. Not that you care."

Another too-familiar sensation took over. Her pulse picked up speed, and her ribs wouldn't expand enough to take in air. "Mom, I'll call you tomorrow. I have to go."

"You're getting ready, aren't you? You're going anyway, even without Caitlyn."

Fingers choking the receiver, April sank onto the bed. "Yes. I'm going anyway. I'll call you tomorrow." She hit the button that disconnected her from her mother.

Her hair was only partially curled when the phone rang again. The hoarse voice on the other end was only barely recognizable.

"Yvonne? What's wrong? Are you crying?"

"No." A coughing spell crackled through the receiver. "I'm sick."

"What? You were fine this morning!" April glanced at the clock, ashamed that her thoughts were totally selfish.

"I know. It came on so suddenly."

Sure of the answer, she asked, anyway. "Do you feel good enough to go?"

"No. I'm so sorry. But I found someone else to go with you."

April flopped onto the bed, facedown, talking into the spread. "I don't want to go with anyone else."

"I know, but you can't not go, and it would be no fun at all to go alone. Be ready at four, just like we planned. I made five o'clock reservations at JP's for dinner."

"With who?"

Another coughing fit erupted in her ear. She waited as Yvonne wheezed, sputtered, and gasped. "I think I'm going to throw u—" The line went dead.

&

She gave Yvonne enough time to do what she had to do in the bathroom and then walked across the hall. With a warning knock, she turned the door handle. It didn't budge. That was weird. Since theirs were the only two apartments and the door at the bottom of the stairs had a dead bolt, they rarely locked their doors. "Yvonne? You okay?"

Seconds passed, and then a weak voice said, "I'll be fine. Just the flu. I don't want you getting it."

"Can I bring you anything? I've got a can of chicken soup I can heat up."

"No. No foo—"The muffled sound of the bathroom door slamming covered her words.

By three thirty, April had worn a path in the berber carpeting between her bedroom and her front door. Dressed in the polka-dot dress and Yvonne's sling-back black shoes, she paced the living room, talking out loud to the two fish in separate bowls on a table beneath her front window. "She can't leave me hanging like this. Willy, you wouldn't do that to Splash, would you? Of course not, and you guys hate each other." Once more, she walked across the hall, heels clacking on the old wood floor. "Hey, I know you feel like death warmed over, but you have to at least tell me who I'm going with."

She waited, wondering if she could possibly have been heard over the sound of the movie on the other side of the door. She recognized the dialogue and Matthew McConaughey's voice. Yvonne was watching *The Wedding Planner*. Finally, the door opened, but only a few inches. Yvonne's pale face appeared in the crack above the brass door chain. "It's a date. Unlock the downstairs door and have fun." The door slammed in April's face.

∽

This was not good. This was worse than not good. While Yvonne was engaged to one of the most charming men April had ever met, her taste in guy friends was not so great.

Halfway across the hall, a horrifying thought hit like a cherry bomb going off in her head. She wouldn't dare. . . . "Yvonne!" Backtracking, she pounded on the door. "Tell me you wouldn't set me up with Seth Bachelor!"

A weak laugh came from behind the door. "Huh. . .why didn't I think of that? You're so paranoid! It's Friday. Seth does the six o'clock news."

April's fist unclenched and slid along the door as an exaggerated sigh poured out of her.

But her relief was fleeting. Yvonne's New Year's Eve party came to mind in high-def. At least twenty of Yvonne's friends from the Cities had crowded into the tiny apartment April was now locked out of. True, she probably shouldn't have gone in the first place. It was just six weeks after Caitlyn died, and she wasn't up for a party. So maybe, just like last Saturday, her mood had colored her opinions. But still. . .her frame of mind hadn't influenced the main topics of discussion that night. Was brown really the new black? Did one really need live plants in each room to get the right flow of positive energy?

April unlocked the downstairs door, tromped back up to her apartment, shut her door with a controlled *click*, and proceeded to stomp her feet like a two-year-old. In the midst of her tantrum, her gaze landed on the black purse that concealed her digital recorder. She'd planned to record her impressions of *Riverdance* for tomorrow's show, but why not start now? Surely someday she'd want to do a segment on blind dates gone wrong. Slipping the strap of her purse over her shoulder, she dug out her hands-free microphone, hooked the recorder at her neckline, and began to talk as she paced.

"My best friend feels sorry for me. She's never voiced that sentiment, of course, but I can tell. Case in point. . .when she suddenly came down with the flu today—today when we have tickets for *Riverdance* at the Orpheum—she set me up on a blind date with one of her friends. I've been looking forward to this day for months, and now, frankly, I'm scared stiff. I've met her guy friends. Please, no offense to any of you, but you're not my type. I love Yvonne dearly, but her criteria for friend picking are way different than mine.

"So what are my criteria? In my wildest fantasy, what kind of man would stand on the other side of that door when—" There was a rap on the door.

Wiping sweaty hands on her polka dots, April inhaled and opened the door.

"Ooh! Don't you look stunning!"

It wasn't her date. It was her aunt.

"Midge. How nice." April opened the door wider, expecting a lightning bolt at any moment. "Nice" had been a slight exaggeration.

"Just got back from the Cities. Your mom wants a picture." Aunt Midge—all sixty-one round, overenergized inches of her—bubbled into the room. "Ooh . . .where did you get this?" She fingered the hem of April's dress, then, moving faster than her roundness should have allowed, she pulled at the neck and read the tag. "Ann Taylor. Wow. Expensive. But you deserve it, sweetie, and you've got the figure for it. Is Yvonne ready?"

"Did Mom actually say she wanted a picture?"

"Oh, you know. . . ."

"Yeah. How was she today?" No point in letting on she'd just talked to her and knew exactly how she was.

"A little better, I think." Aunt Midge unzipped the jacket of her three-shades-of-pink sweat suit. "We took a walk today, stopped for pie. . .and she actually ate some."

In the weeks since her mother had moved to Minneapolis to "get away from the memories," Midge's answer had never changed. *"A little better, I think."* How many times had she heard it? April hadn't seen any improvement in her mother's clinical depression, in spite of a change in her medication and a new counselor. Leave it to Midge to find something positive.

Midge's cup was not just half full; it was eternally spilling over. But, as irritating as her effervescence could be at times, it was Midge's optimism that had stabilized her mother's downward spiral after Caitlyn's death, something April had been powerless to do on her own. Midge was one of those characters of whom people said, "You just gotta love her."

April managed a bit of a smile. "A daily dose of pie might do her more good than Paxil."

"It might at that. Is Yvonne ready?"

April sank onto the couch and lifted Snow Bear onto her lap. Her makeup kept her from burying her head in the long fur. Instead, she simply clutched him and groaned. "Yvonne's not going."

"What?" Midge dropped onto the cushion next to her. "You're not going alone, are you?" Her pink nails began making circles on April's back.

"I wish." She repeated the groan. "Yvonne set me up with one of her GQ friends."

The nails stopped circling. Midge's round face lit into a grin. "A date?"

"A blind date."

"How exciting! Do you know anything about him?"

"Not a thing. But I've met her friends. They're. . .plastic. All polished and trendy and probably manicured."

Midge pressed her hands together in a prayer pose. "But she wouldn't set you up with a non-Christian."

"No, she wouldn't. But believers in Jesus come in many shapes and sizes. Red and yellow, black and white, real and plastic or uptight. . .you remember, you taught me the song."

Midge laughed then stood. She had a knack for never responding to sarcasm. "Well, stand up and let me get a picture. I'm not going to hang around and spoil Mr. Wonderful's first impression. I'll just lurk in the parking lot."

With a camera flash, a hug, and a giggle, she was gone.

In the silence, April found herself almost wishing Midge had stayed. She turned the recorder back on and finally remembered where she'd left off—her criteria for "Mr. Wonderful."

"I want comfy. I want a guy who enjoys the little things in life, like making a pizza and doing dishes together, or walking barefoot down by the river. I want a guy who doesn't try too hard to impress me. He listens to me and laughs with me instead of bringing me jewelry or flowers or—" There was a rap at the door.

April wiped her damp palms on the skirt of her polka-dot dress, took a deep breath, opened the door. . .and gasped.

Dressed in a black suit, white shirt, and black tie was Seth Bachelor. . . holding a mass of flowers. . .and a box of garbage bags.

Chapter 5

W ow."
Shimmery, honey-colored hair fell softly. . .little black earrings dangled from her ears. And polka dots. . .they seemed to make a statement. Seth held out the flowers, knowing he was supposed to say something more than just "wow" but having trouble getting beyond that single syllable. This shouldn't be that hard. He talked for a living. "You look beautiful."

She appeared to be in shock. He couldn't decipher if it was good shock or bad shock. He held out the box of garbage bags. "I owe you an apology."

The color washed from her face. Her lips parted. "What are you doing here?"

He smiled, trying charm, though he wasn't sure he possessed enough to thaw April Douglas. "I'm your escort for the evening."

"No." She shook her head. "I can't. Not with you. It just. . ." Tears welled in her eyes. "No." The door closed.

Seth stared at the door, confusion tangling his thoughts. What had he done to deserve that? He'd picked up the garbage, and he'd apologized. What was wrong with the woman? Still clutching the flowers, he went down the stairs and out into the parking lot.

He was loosening his tie and debating whether he should throw the flowers under his back tire, when hurried footsteps made him turn around.

"Wait!" A short, forty-something woman dressed in pink toddled toward him. A gasplike sound escaped, and she stopped abruptly. "Oh."

He returned her wide-eyed gaze.

"Oh. . . ," she repeated. A sigh of apparent disappointment followed. "You're April's date."

"I was supposed to be. And you are. . . ?"

"Her aunt. Did she. . ." Her round face crunched into a grimace. "Was she really upset?"

Seth tilted his head to the side. "Yes, as a matter of fact, she was."

"Under the circumstances, Mr. Bachelor, I can't imagine you expected anything different."

"What 'circumstances'? Is she mad because I taped her idiotic climb up the water tower or because the brakes on my ATV failed? Neither are really criminal offenses. Does your niece have a habit of holding ridiculous grudges?"

The little woman's fingers flew to her mouth. "Oh," she said for the third

146

time. "You don't know."

"Know what?"

The woman's top teeth pressed into her bottom lip. "Wait here."

Before Seth had a chance to wonder if he even wanted to, she walked away, disappearing into the building.

∞

"No."

April pulled the backs off her earrings and threw them at the coffee table.

"April Jean, the poor man doesn't have a clue what happened. You owe him an explanation for the way you acted and—"

"Owe him? I don't owe him anything. I owe Yvonne a kick in the shin with her own stinkin' shoes! I bet she's not even sick!" She dropped into her bentwood rocker. Midge knelt on the floor in front of her.

"This might be a step in the healing process." Her voice was low and soft, the voice that had whispered over April on so many sleepless nights.

"Maybe I'll talk to him sometime. Not tonight."

A gentle smile curved Aunt Midge's mouth. "You don't want to miss *Riverdance*. And it wouldn't be any fun to go alone."

"You'll go with me."

"I can't, honey. I have to clean the bank tonight. Yvonne would feel terrible for letting you down if you didn't go." When April didn't answer, her aunt picked up both of her hands. "Do it for Caitlyn, honey."

April pulled a hand free and wiped her face. "You do guilt as well as Mom. Only nicer."

"So you'll talk to him?"

Covering her face with her hands, April moaned. "Okay. I'll talk to him. But I'm going to *Riverdance* alone."

"I'll send him up." Midge got up from her knees, walked to the door, and exited, leaving the apartment door wide open. April listened to the downstairs door close and waited for the creak of footsteps ascending the stairs. A car horn blared from Main Street, a security alarm that wouldn't stop. The noise jangled April's frayed nerves. Her heart rate began to double-time. She didn't want to do this. Nothing either one of them said would change a thing. April didn't subscribe to the idea that wounds needed to be reopened to heal.

The alarm stopped. In the silence, she heard the steps groan. In seconds, Seth stood in the doorway.

"May I come in?"

April nodded.

He set the flowers and the trash bags on the coffee table and sat on the couch. He rested his elbows on his knees and laced his fingers. Waiting.

Clasping her trembling hands, April took a deep breath. Staring into his eyes, the anger seemed to seep out of her, taking with it her strength. Weak and tired, she wanted only to crawl beneath the blanket on the couch. "Do you remember—last year—you took three high school students out to. . .chase a storm?"

He looked puzzled. "A buddy and I do talks to science classes on a regular basis, and several times a year, we take a couple of kids out with us. We're really just tracking, watching cloud formations, measuring barometric changes, not chasing. I'd never put kids in danger."

The anger returned, like starch to limp fabric. Every muscle in April's body tightened. "You put my sister in danger."

"What?" He leaned forward.

"Last year, in October, you took three kids out with you. One was my sister." Her eyes narrowed. "The one with the bald head."

Seth's hands separated, turning palms up. "I remember her."

"Do you remember getting caught in a hailstorm?"

A slight smile showed a dimple she hadn't noticed before. "Of course. But there really wasn't any danger. We were standing in an open field, no trees, no power lines. The storm hit us sooner than I'd expected, so we got wet, but there wasn't any lightning. The hail was small, and we made it to an overpass before it really started coming down. The kids loved it. We were all laughing hysterically." His hands lifted several inches off his knees. "There was never any danger."

April gripped the curved sides of the rocking chair. Her fingers bit into the wood. "Caitlyn wasn't strong enough." A picture of her sister's thin frame and pale face flashed in her mind. "Wasn't it obvious that she wasn't healthy?"

His lips parted then closed. He stared at her for several long seconds. "I thought she might have been anorexic, and she was wearing a hat, so other than how thin she was, we didn't know there was anything wrong with her when we first met her. Besides, that wasn't our call to make. We won't take a kid without a parental permission slip."

"What?" That wasn't the way April had heard it. She started to say that her mother would never have given Caitlyn permission to go, but stopped. What Caitlyn wanted, Caitlyn got. It had always been that way.

"What happened? She was fine when we dropped the kids off at the school." Seth's quiet voice interrupted her thoughts.

"She got pneumonia. She died five weeks later."

Seth's eyes closed for several seconds. He shook his head slowly. "I'm so sorry, April."

Once again, the simmering anger that had been a constant white noise in the back of her mind for so many months drained away. "It wasn't. . .like you said, it wasn't your responsibility." He didn't try to fill the silence. April was grateful for that. She stared at her fish, nose to nose in their separate bowls. "I've been a real jerk to you."

Seth smiled. "Hey, you haven't exactly seen the best side of me." His voice was soft and soothing, a voice more suited for late-night radio than a weather show. "We could make it up to each other by going to see *Riverdance*."

A jumble of conflicting emotions littered April's mind. Her mother had given permission for Caitlyn to go on the storm watch. Yet couldn't Seth and his friend have seen, just from looking at her, that she wasn't up to it? She thought of the way Seth had described it—Caitlyn running from the rain, laughing, breathless, thoroughly enjoying the moment. All this time, she'd silently accused those two men of taking Caitlyn's life. Caitlyn hadn't seen it that way, hadn't once placed any blame on them, nor had she ever expressed any regret for going along. Was it possible that they'd really given her something—a taste of real life, momentary freedom from the constraints of a disease that would probably have won eventually?

April stared at Seth, her answer to his suggestion changing with every tick of the clock. *"You haven't exactly seen the best of me,"* he'd said. She was seeing the best of him now, as he waited, nothing but concern in his eyes. But the other side, the one that had snapped sarcastic answers to her interview questions—how long would it be until she saw that face again? Thanks to her father, she'd experienced more anger in her twenty-six years than some people deal with in a lifetime. Her fear of it was justified.

"Do not fear, for I am with you. . . ." The Bible verse whispered over the tumbling thoughts. She'd climbed the water tower. She'd made a vow not to let fear run her life. If for no other reason, she could do this for Caitlyn. Looking up into dark eyes that seemed to say he'd give her all the time she needed, she ran her fingertips across her bottom lashes. She didn't want to miss *Riverdance*. And it was only one night out of her life. "I guess we could."

∞

Seth stood up, needing something to do while he waited for April to fix her makeup. He panned the small apartment, taking in details that gave clues about the woman who'd done the decorating.

Two round fishbowls occupied a small white table. In each, a single fish, purplish blue with deep red fins waving gracefully, floated near the top of the water, facing the other.

Over the worn blue couch hung a large framed photograph. He recognized it immediately. "Itasca," he said out loud. The headwaters of the Mississippi River. The picture showed a narrow stream dotted with rocks. In that spot, you could wade across the Mississippi.

April walked out of the bathroom, her mascara no longer smudging her eyes. Again, the word "wow" surfaced. He turned back to the picture. "I haven't been there since I was a kid."

"I love that place." There was reverence in her voice. "When I was about twelve, I wrote in the lodge guest book that I'd be back on my honeymoon."

"Douglas Lodge. . .any relation to you?"

"It was named for Attorney General Wallace B. Douglas, who was a great, great, great something of mine."

"So they should let you stay there free on your honeymoon."

April made eye contact for a split second. "By the time I was sixteen, my goals had changed. I wrote in the lodge book that I was going to become a park ranger and live at Itasca State Park. I actually took some classes in natural resource management before I switched to broadcasting."

Seth angled toward her. "What made you change your mind?"

"The money."

He laughed. "You forget; I'm an insider."

She smiled, but there was still something rigid about her expression. "Speaking of which, who's doing the weather tonight?"

"A friend of mine. . ." *My storm-chasing friend who was also with your sister in the hailstorm.* The thought brought the storm scene into focus again. He may have witnessed Caitlyn Douglas's last experience of enjoying life. ". . .a friend from college. He's filled in for me before."

April nodded, her eyes fixed on the picture. He studied her, only too aware of his lack of wisdom where women were concerned. His last relationship had ended much like the two Siamese fighting fish glaring at each other in their separate bowls. Opening both hands, he postured what he hoped was a peace-making gesture. "I know we got off to a really bad start. . . ."

That wasn't what he'd wanted to say. Now he was giving the impression that he wanted to "start" something. "I'm really sorry about the whole water tower thing. . . . From now on, I'll leave the drama to you reporters." Her smile seemed real yet somehow guarded. He gestured toward the flowers and the box of garbage bags. "And I'm sorry about the garbage pile. The brakes really did fake out on me."

"I believe you."

"Could we maybe start from scratch? A whole new beginning?"

"I. . .guess so."

Seth extended his hand. "Hi, I'm Seth Bachelor."

She took his hand. "April Douglas. Thank you. . .for the flowers."

Chapter 6

April glanced sideways at the profile of the man behind the wheel. He had a strong jaw. His hair was short but long enough in front to touch his eyebrow on the right.

He smiled, showing just a hint of a dimple. "I haven't had a chance to tune in to your Saturday show yet. I didn't want to hear what you did with that ghastly interview of me, but I heard your coverage of the prayer vigil. You're good. You don't come off as a vulture."

April laughed, surprised that she could. "I was a little more aggressive when I worked for WCCO."

"You've done television?"

"Mm-hm. Definitely my first love. Even tried to get a job at KXPB."

He turned, surprise covering his face. "When?"

"About eight months ago. I tried commuting from the Cities when Caitlyn started chemo. It was too hard, so I moved back."

"There must not have been an opening at the time."

"Oh, there was an opening, all right." She made no attempt to hide her feelings about the people he worked for.

"Who did you interview with?"

"Some guy with a potbelly. Sorry, I know you work for these people. He was nice about it when he called back to tell me I hadn't gotten the job. He said if it were up to him I would have been hired, but 'the man upstairs' thought I was overqualified and I'd probably move on as soon as something better came along. I don't think he was referring to God."

Seth's mouth formed what appeared to be the beginning of "What" or "Why," but nothing came out. April jumped in. "Maybe we should talk about something else."

"Maybe. Tell me about your sister."

The green sign to April's right said they'd reach I-35 in eight miles. They had an hour drive ahead of them. If she was going to enjoy the night, she couldn't spend too much of it talking about Caitlyn. "She was diagnosed with acute lymphocytic leukemia a little over a year ago."

Seth's hand touched hers then returned to the steering wheel. "I heard you climbed the water tower for her."

April nodded. "She made a list." *When she was in the hospital with pneumonia.* Maybe it hadn't been Seth's fault, but would the thought continue to surface all night? "She called it her dream list. . .things we'd do together as soon as she was in complete remission. We both pretty much knew by then that she wasn't going to make it, but it gave us something to focus on instead of the disease."

"Now you're fulfilling the dreams?"

She liked the way he phrased it. "The day before she died, she made me promise that I'd at least try. It was her way of telling me to get on with life."

"And you're sharing your experiences on your Saturday show, I take it."

Again, his choice of words revealed a sensitive side. "I really struggled over that decision. I'm so afraid that people will think I'm exploiting my sister's tragedy." Her mother's words echoed in her mind. "But I learned so much from her. She made conscious decisions every step of the way. . .not to be fake, to express her anger but not be overcome by it, to accept the inevitable, and to make the most of each day. At a time when you'd expect depression and hopelessness, I saw her relationship with Christ grow into something I envied." She shifted in her seat to face Seth. "I think she'd want people to hear about her journey."

With a slight smile, he nodded. "I think you're right. What else is on the list?"

"This."

He turned toward her, confusion clearly registering. "This what?"

"Tonight. *Riverdance*. Didn't Yvonne tell you?"

"No." He was quiet for a moment. "Then we'll have to make this a very memorable night."

April reached down and picked up her purse, moving slower than she needed to. The night was already beginning to be memorable. Opening her purse, she pulled out a small notebook and a penlight. "Should I read some of it?"

"Some of it? How many things are there?"

"Forty-two." April waited for his reaction, and she wasn't disappointed.

His right eyebrow all but disappeared beneath a lock of brown hair. "Forty-two?"

"They don't all involve danger or expense."

He laughed. "But it sounds like you've got enough adventures to last for years."

Turning to the first page, April smiled, feeling wistful yet lighter than she had in a long time. "I hope so."

∽

"They aren't all huge adventures. A lot of them are pretty tame." She smiled at him. Her body language had transformed over the last few miles, and the more she relaxed, the more striking she appeared.

"Climbing a water tower is tame?"

"Compared to smuggling Bibles to Mongolia."

"Wow. I guess."

"Okay. I'll pick out a few things. . . backpack the Superior Hiking Trail, go rock climbing—indoor or out, visit the Grand Ole Opry, walk barefoot in the Rio Grande, ride motorcycles to the Harley rally in Sturgis, South Dakota. . . .

We decided we'd either find cute guys to ride with or take lessons and get our own bikes."

Seth took a split second to ponder the wisdom of his next statement. "I don't know about the cute part, but I could help you out with that one. I've got a bike, and I've always wanted to do Sturgis."

"Seriously?" Her expression was wide-eyed and little-girlish.

Should he really give her hope of something he might not want to follow through on once he'd gotten to know her better? He couldn't quite imagine that happening. "Seriously."

"I've seen how you ride."

"Funny. Think you can handle ten hours on a Harley?"

Her chin lifted. "You keep the tires on the road, and I'll deal with the saddle sores."

The girl had wit. He liked that. "Ever ridden on one?"

"My boyfriend in college had an Ultra Classic. Unfortunately, I couldn't compete with the bike."

"Maybe if you'd started dressing in chrome...."

Her laugh was so different from the wooden sound he'd heard earlier. "Why didn't I think of that?"

"What's next on the list?"

She turned a page in the notebook. "Have you seen the statue of Mary Tyler Moore at Nicollet Mall?"

"Of course."

"Caitlyn and I used to watch reruns from the *Mary Tyler Moore Show* together. So I took her to see the statue when it was dedicated in 2002. They gave everybody a tam, just like the one Mary throws on the show, but when it came time to throw them, nobody wanted to give them up. We kept ours." She was silent for a moment. "Caitlyn was buried with hers." Again, she took a moment, clearly having trouble steadying her voice. "Anyway, when we were making up the list, we came up with all sorts of places where we could throw hats. From the top of the Eiffel Tower or the Leaning Tower of Pisa—"

"Or the Pine Bluff water tower."

"Yeah. I guess it sounds silly."

"Not at all. Sounds like the stuff movies are made of."

"Hmm...it does." She flipped the page back again. "The next one is 'Watch the sunrise in Sunrise.'"

"Minnesota or Florida?"

Her head tipped to one side. "Minnesota. But maybe I'll add Florida."

"The sunrises might be a bit more spectacular. What's next?"

"Ride the jungle canopy on a zip line in Brazil, ride in a hot-air balloon, make homemade caramel corn and stay up all night eating it and watching Ashton Kutcher movies." Her hand did an elegant little flip. "See, they aren't all huge adventures. The next one, she put in to torture me, just like the zip line and the hot-air balloon and the water tower. I only have two major fears in life, and my sister hit them both."

"Fear of heights and. . . ?"

"Storms."

He glanced at her, trying to read her emotions. Had she been afraid of storms before her sister had been caught in one? Was he inadvertently responsible for her fear?

She rubbed the palm of one hand with the thumb of the other. "Number twelve is chase a tornado."

Seth felt his pulse do a two-step. "So that was something your sister wanted to do?"

"Yes." She said it quietly. "I guess I should tell you. . . . While she was in the hospital after the. . .hailstorm. . .she said it had been one of the coolest things she'd ever done. She only wished she could have seen a tornado."

Clearly, that admission hadn't been easy for her. The realization touched him. "If. . .*when* you decide you're ready to cross that off your list, just let me know."

"Have you seen one? Up close?" He could hear the fear in her voice.

"Up too close a couple of times. Biggest adrenaline rush you could imagine."

"And you like the rush, I take it."

"Love it." Seth felt muscles on the side of his neck grow taut. If he didn't change the direction of this conversation, he'd be poor company the rest of the night. "Anyway, that's a topic for some other time."

"Okay, then let's change subjects again. What do you do for fun?"

Whether it was feminine intuition or her investigative reporter training, the girl had found the key to his egotistical heart. . .get him talking about himself. "Just about anything outdoors. Skiing, winter and summer, taking the bike out—year-round, as long as the roads are clear. I have a dog that takes me walking whenever he can. And I can be talked into cultured things like musicals and concerts on occasion."

"So tonight won't be too far out of your comfort zone?"

Seth ran a finger under his collar. "I'll admit that I much prefer jeans when I'm not working, but I'll dress up for a purty girl any day." He took his eye off the road long enough to enjoy the reticent smile teasing her lips. "What about you? What's a wild and crazy night out for April Douglas look like?"

This time she laughed, full and unreserved. "I read, I go to church—the same church I went to when I was two—I talk to my fish, and once in a great while, Yvonne drags me to the Cities where I reluctantly spend money on non-sale items. Wild and crazy are two words no one has ever accused me of. Well, not wild, anyway. Not yet."

"Mm. . .a hint of intrigue. The lady is mysterious, no?" His Antonio

Banderas impression landed a little flat, but it did widen her smile.

"The dream list is my sister's final kick in the derriere. I've lived a very cautious life until now."

"Why?"

The question seemed to startle her. "Well. . .I guess I've got all the classic firstborn tendencies. Responsible, achiever, too sensible for my own good."

"Was it just you and your sister?"

"When I was five, my mom had a baby. He was killed in a car accident when he was six months old. It was my father's fault. My dad started drinking, and my mother's been in and out of depression ever since. Caitlyn was born when I was seven, and my dad left us two years later. . .the first time but not the last. There were times when I had to be the parent."

"There wasn't any chance for 'wild and crazy.'"

She shook her head. "I tried busting out of my mold once." Her lips pressed together as if trying to contain a smile. "That's when I climbed the water tower the first time."

"The first time?"

"My seventeenth birthday. My one day of teenage rebellion. I woke up that morning and decided I was sick of coloring inside the lines. So I called two guy friends who had climbed the tower dozens of times and told them to meet me there at midnight."

"And you did it?"

"Almost. One of the guys caged me. . .kind of like a human shield. It was all very exhilarating until I got to the catwalk and the cops showed up."

"Busted."

"Yeah. By my own father. He was making one of his rare guest appearances and heard me sneaking out of the house. He followed me and then called a friend of his who was on the police force. They took me to jail, and my dad sat and played cards with the officer while I sat in a cell all night."

"Ouch."

"Yeah. Some fathers might do that to teach a kid logical consequences. My dad did it for a good laugh with his buddy."

Something wrenched in Seth's gut. He had to fight the desire to grab her hand, touch her face, show her in some way that he understood. All too well. "And that was the end of your adventurous spirit?"

He shot a sideways glance at her, long enough to catch the funny little smile that twisted her lips. "I suppose it would have made some kids even more rebellious, but it just made me give up coloring outside the lines. But I've been pushing the envelope a bit at work lately, and I kind of like the freedom. I'm bound and determined to loosen myself up."

Seth stole another glance. "You're an inspiration. I could use a little coloring outside the lines myself."

Chapter 7

Magical. That would be the first word she'd record when she got home. The Celtic rhythms of *Riverdance* still reverberated in April's chest as the lights came up in the Orpheum Theater, and she stared at the massive brass chandelier dripping with Italian crystals that hung from the domed ceiling. From the mural above the stage to the rich Victorian colors of the carpet, the almost-ninety-year-old building whispered of its rich vibrant history. *Caitlyn, you would have loved this.*

April folded her playbill. "Can't you imagine being here back in the roaring twenties when it was all new?"

Seth nodded. "You'd be sitting there in a flapper dress, and we'd be watching the Marx Brothers."

"Did you know that Bob Dylan owned the Orpheum for a few years back in the eighties?"

"Really?"

She nodded. "The Minneapolis Community Development Agency bought it from him and renovated it in 1993."

Seth laughed. "You've done your research."

"I did a talk on it in college."

As she stood, Seth's hand touched the small of her back, light not possessive. "Thank you," he said softly.

She questioned him with her eyes. What was he thanking her for? The ticket? The company?

He answered, "You didn't have to give me a second chance."

The decision had been harder than he'd ever realize. But she had to keep the moment light. "It's hard to say no to a guy who brings garbage bags."

The shallow dimple on his right cheek creased. "Most guys just don't understand how high trash bags are on a woman's list of priorities."

"You're very in tune."

"I try." He gave a comically exaggerated sigh as they stepped into the aisle. "Let's see how I do on the next thing on the itinerary."

"We have an itinerary?"

He nodded. "An incredible night deserves an extraordinary dessert."

❀

"Kuik E Mart?" April narrowed her eyes at Seth but couldn't quite tame the smile that seemed to be becoming a habit. "Our extraordinary dessert is coming from a convenience store?"

Seth winked at her. "I said 'extraordinary,' not 'gourmet.' Wait here." He opened the door then turned back to her. "One question. Strawberry or raspberry?"

"Surprise me."

He got out, walked up to the entrance, stopped, and came back to her side of the car and tapped on the window. April pushed the button to lower the window.

"One more question. You're not allergic to sodium stearoyl lactylate, are you?"

April's brow wrinkled. "I have no idea."

When he returned, he handed her two warm cups that smelled like hazelnut. She set them in the cup holders and took a plastic grocery bag from him.

"No peeking." He started the car and turned onto South Eighth Street. Five minutes later, he turned onto Cedar Avenue, and then Riverside, in the middle of the West Bank of the University of Minnesota campus. April knew the area like the back of her hand but had no idea what they were doing there. He parked in the parking garage just south of Locust Street. Picking up the two coffee cups, he smiled at her. "Follow me."

They walked across West River Parkway to a cement wall that ran along the riverbank. On the opposite side, the outline of the East Bank campus towered over the trees. Lights from the University Medical Center blinked in the darkness. Seth took the bag from her so that she could step over the wall. They sat, hugging paper cups of coffee, staring at the headlights and taillights strung like white and red beads on the bridge that crossed the black Mississippi.

After several minutes, Seth set both of their cups on the ground and handed April a roll of paper towels. "Would you mind opening these while I prepare dessert?"

As she ripped off the plastic, she watched. Out of the bag came two packages of Twinkies, a jar of raspberry jam, and a box of plastic silverware. Seth slathered jam over the top of a Twinkie and held it out to her. "Shortcake, madam?"

Closing her eyes, April savored the too-sweet concoction, all the while trying to put brakes on savoring the moment. "Delicious. And very creative."

"I invented it when I was eight."

"When I was eight, I lived on soda crackers and grape jelly." *Because my mother was too depressed to work, and my father wouldn't send the checks. . . .*

Seth gave her a thoughtful look, giving her time to add more. When she didn't, he filled the silence with stories of his childhood and tales of college misadventures that she was quite sure had been stretched. In between, he asked questions about her favorite memories but seemed to sense when he'd hit on something sensitive for her to talk about.

They talked about weather patterns and life in the media through two beeps of Seth's watch. "Midnight." He threw the Twinkies and jam back in the bag.

"Don't want you dozing through your show."

April picked up the two empty cups. Instead of stacking them, she carried one in each hand as they walked back to the parking garage. Seth opened the car door for her and then walked around the front and got in. He held his hand out. "I'll take those."

She handed him the cups, fingers touching for a fraction of a second. As the dome light faded, his eyes found hers. "Are you busy next Saturday night?"

April's eyes opened, a little too wide, advertising that he'd caught her off guard. She needed time to think. Going with him tonight hadn't been her idea. Was she ready to agree to an official date? "No." The word in her head came out of her mouth, and she suddenly realized what she'd just done.

"Would you be interested in dinner and a truly gourmet dessert? The Melting Pot, maybe? Fondue for two?"

She had a whole week to make excuses. Maybe she'd catch Yvonne's flu. "That would be nice."

Seth's phone on the dashboard in front of her dinged. He reached for it. "Sorry. It's a message from my station manager. I have to check it." He listened to the message, his features hardening in the dim garage light. "Sorry," he repeated. "I have to call him back." He pushed a button. "Merv, what's up?"

The muscles on Seth's jaw bulged. The softness left his eyes. "Okay, so he was late, but he made it." His lips pressed together as he listened. "Hey, take it out on Darren; I'm not his nanny." His right hand slammed against the steering wheel. "When are you going to quit blaming everybody else for your problems? You should be able to deal with things like this without bringing them to me. And I'm not the only one who's taking notice. You'll be looking for another job if things don't start changing." April cringed as exasperation rushed through Seth's pursed lips. "You're a manager. Act like one!" The phone slapped shut.

∞

The magic was gone. The rest of the ride alternated between awkward silence and Seth ripping on the antiquated policies and woeful incompetence at KXPB, and what he was going to do to change things around there as soon as he had the chance. When he parked behind her apartment, April thanked him for the evening. After a quick good-bye, she got out before he could say anything. Locking the downstairs door behind her, she kicked off her shoes, sending one bouncing up to the third step, and trudged up the stairs. As she straightened up after picking up the wayward shoe, she shrieked.

Yvonne stood at the top of the stairs, wearing jeans and sandals and a turquoise blouse. Her hair was styled and her face made up. The overhead light glinted off her teeth as she grinned. "So?" she squealed. "Is he everything I said he was?"

April's eyes narrowed. "He's way too much of what *I* said he was." She opened her door and threw in her shoes. "Why aren't you in bed?" She took a long look at the bouncy curls and pearly pink lip gloss, the perky smile now phasing into confusion. "Why don't you look sick?"

"Because I'm. . .not. Didn't Seth tell you?"

"Tell me what? That my best friend's a liar?" She chucked her purse through the open door.

"He asked me to set up a date with you, and this just seemed perfect." Yvonne's disappointment pinched her features. "I was so sure you two would hit it off and you'd be so grateful that it wouldn't matter that I faked being sick. What happened?"

"You should be an actress. All that retching and gagging and. . ." April's breath came in short, tight gulps. One more word would unleash the torrent brewing inside her. With a final glare at Yvonne, she walked into her apartment and closed the door behind her.

The tears began as she unzipped her dress, clawing at the zipper as if it were the polka dots' fault she couldn't breathe. The dress fell at her feet, and she kicked it toward the closet. Jerking open a drawer, she pulled out a floor-length night-gown, pulling it over her head and hugging it close to her belly, seeking comfort in the softness. But the feel of flannel against her skin roused a sadness that had nothing to do with Seth Bachelor.

Arms wrapped around Snow Bear, she curled on the couch and gave in to tears. . .the sobs of an nine-year-old girl whose father had just said he was never coming back.

The tiniest details were branded in her memory, etched there by her father's rage: lightning flashing through the slats of Caitlyn's crib, striping the faded pink-flowered wallpaper. . .icy rain slapping the window. . .the wind howling, sometimes louder than her father's cursing, sometimes not. . . April had stood beside the crib in her long flannel nightgown, gripping the rungs, singing "The Itsy Bitsy Spider". . .louder and louder to cover the sound of the storm and the screaming in the kitchen. Caitlyn giggled, and April wondered why. Why wasn't she scared?

Looking back now, she knew the answer. Her little sister had never known anything else. She hadn't known a mother who smiled or a daddy who played games. To her, the fighting was normal.

April remembered the smoothness of the painted spindles, the fabric soft-ener smell of Caitlyn's stuffed purple elephant, the hum of the vaporizer in the corner. And as hard as she'd tried to forget, she remembered her father's words, shot at her mother like the machine guns in the movies Daddy liked to watch. The connecting words had eroded over the years, but the bulletlike imprecations remained, shooting to the surface with unpredictable triggers. . .flannel—or a man's fight with his boss.

She hadn't seen or heard from her father since Caitlyn's funeral. There were times she could pray for him. Tonight wasn't one of those times.

Finally, when her tears were spent, April tried to back step into objectivity. Had she overreacted with Seth? Was she being unfair to let Seth's bout of anger overshadow the sensitivity she'd seen earlier in the evening? Maybe. She pulled a fleece throw off the back of the couch. Using the bear as a pillow, she lay down. Maybe she hadn't been fair, but she couldn't risk being around him long enough to find out. She couldn't risk falling for a man whose anger might burn out of control. A man who might leave her.

༄

"I know you had good intentions." April stared past Yvonne, counting the travel mugs on the coffee shop shelf, not quite ready for the honesty of eye contact.

"Does that mean you forgive me?"

In the fog of her exhaustion, even resentment felt like work. "I forgive you." The truth was, she felt betrayed, but she had to respond to Yvonne's motives, not the disappointing outcome.

"Then tell me every detail. . .everything before he got the phone call."

April shook her head. "If I do, you'll tell me I'm being irrational."

"And truth is something you no longer believe in?"

There were thirteen mugs on the top shelf, six stainless steel and seven plastic. "It's just. . .I don't know. . .he's not what I'm looking for."

Yvonne's just-waxed brows tapped her flat-ironed bangs. "Because you're looking for perfect."

"You're vicious this morning."

"Faithful are the words of a friend. Tell me about the rest of the night."

April stared over the rim of her Polar Cap, a frozen cappuccino concoction flavored with mint. "If I could blot out the last hour. . .he was amazing. I was determined not to like him, but I did. He asks questions and makes you feel like he really wants answers. He's interesting. He reads, he travels: There wasn't a second of awkward silence. I was on the edge of my seat as he was describing hot and cold air masses crashing together." She rested the back of her head against the wall. "But my dad was a really nice guy a lot of the time."

"April. . .don't do that. Seth lost his temper—"

"Twice."

"Every guy gets frustrated with his boss. Don't generalize; don't make him into your father."

In the strained silence, Yvonne's phone rang. April counted bags of organic coffee while she eavesdropped.

"We're. . .I'm at Perk Place. . .yeah. . .sure. . .bye."

April opened a packet of sugar, sprinkling it on top of the half-gone Polar Cap. "That was short and sweet."

"Yeah. Just one of the girls in my study. Now, where were we? Oh yeah. We were talking about you generalizing."

"Let's talk about something other than my neuroses. What are you and Kirk doing tonight?"

"Dinner at his folks'."

"Name the kids again."

Yvonne laughed. An only child, she would soon be marrying a man with nine siblings, all with names starting with K.

Ten minutes later, April drained her cup and picked up her purse. "I have to get to the station. I was going to do my show on my experience at *Riverdance*." She sighed and crumpled her napkin, stuffing it into the paper cup. "Maybe I'll do it on changing weather patterns instead."

Yvonne didn't appear to have heard her last remark. Her eyes were focused somewhere over April's head, in the direction of the front door. Seconds later, a woman stood by their table, holding out a vase of tulips. The vase was surrounded by tissue paper. . .and sitting in an empty Twinkie box.

"April? This is for you."

Chapter 8

I want to do a call-in show today." April stood in front of Jill's desk, hands on hips.

Her boss sighed. "We've talked about this."

"How come Orlando gets to do a call-in?" She played the whiny-toddler act to the hilt. "I've been here almost as long as he has."

"Orlando takes questions on hermeneutics. Your listeners are. . .diverse. . . 'unpigeonholeable.' Like I said, we've talked about this."

"I know. I'm going to wear you down."

Jill threw a Mounds bar at her, hitting her in the shoulder. "It's not me you have to convince."

"But you think I could do it?"

"Of course. You know how frustrated I am that we're not utilizing your full potential. It's a liability thing with the board."

April bent to retrieve the candy from under a chair. "I happen to know they're meeting this morning. Do you want to get your name on the agenda, or should I?"

With a barely stifled laugh, Jill held both hands in the air. "I'll do it."

"Yes! Tell them it's just a trial run. And tell them my reaction time is like lightning. The slightest hint of anything unseemly and I'll hang up or hit the obscenity button."

"Okay, I'll talk to them. Get out of here and go work on Plan B, just in case my persuasive powers fail."

"Have I told you lately how awesome you are to work for?"

Another Mounds bar sailed her way. "Go. Pray. Don't waste your silver tongue on me."

Licking chocolate off her fingers, April traipsed into her office and began typing her opening script. The idea had germinated, along with a headache, in the aftermath of her tears. Comments from her water tower show were still trickling in. Out of a listening audience that only numbered in the hundreds, April had heard so many stories of loss and hope. They needed to be told.

Several minutes into writing her opener, she stopped. A nagging thought, like a puppy scratching at the door, had pestered her since leaving Perk Place. *Riverdance.* She fingered a tulip petal, wondering half-consciously why she hadn't left them in the car. She'd told her listeners what she'd be doing on Friday night. She couldn't ignore it like it never happened. That, of course, was only a fraction of the thought. The rest, the part that concerned Seth Bachelor, she didn't have time to act on now. The flowers, and the note accompanying them, demanded a response. At the moment, she had no idea what it would be.

Redirecting her train of thought wasn't hard with the possibility of finally hosting the kind of show she felt God had designed her for. Or close to it, anyway. The real desire of her heart, the one she'd shared with only the people she trusted—the one her mother had thrown in her face after the water tower show—was a dream she'd probably never get close to.

Living in Pine Bluff, her chance of ever seeing her hopes materialize was beyond slim. All through school, she'd dreamed of becoming a television talk show host. Jill's comment fluttered around her as she worked... *"we're not utilizing your full potential."*

There weren't many options open to her when she'd moved back home. One cable television station, and the nonprofit AM Christian radio station where she'd worked as jack-of-all-trades for eight months now. During the week, she was the afternoon disc jockey; in the mornings, she prepared for her Saturday show or played gofer for Jill. It wasn't a bad job, but it wasn't what she'd hoped for.

There'd been an opening for an anchor at KXPB-TV. With her experience, she'd been sure they'd hire her, but that turned out to be the reason she hadn't gotten the job. When they signed a girl just out of broadcasting school, April had been miffed. But maybe the "man upstairs" was right. There really wasn't any reason for her to stay in Pine Bluff now. Caitlyn was gone. Her mom was in Minneapolis. Maybe it was time to move back to the Cities where at least she had a chance of realizing her "full potential."

More than an hour later, she was engrossed in outlining her show when a hand jutted around the door frame. A slim-fingered hand with long red nails. It closed slowly into a fist, and the thumb popped up.

April squealed. "For real?"

Jill's slim silhouette slid into the doorway. "For real. I've convinced them you're the Christian radio version of Rush Limbaugh."

Two hours later, laptop under one arm, April was ready to head into the studio. As she switched off her desk lamp, a single tulip petal floated onto her desk. She picked it up. Red, with lines of yellow rising like sunbeams. She reached in her back pocket and pulled out the crumpled note that had been handed to her by Seth's delivery girl, the "girl from my study" who had called Yvonne at the coffee shop. She read the words that she assumed were handwritten by Seth.

"April—I had a wonderful time last night. I'm so sorry you had to witness that tiff. My invitation for dinner still stands. If you want to join me, just call W-E-A-T-H-E-R-G-U-Y."

Lord, I will deal with this. I'll thank him. I'll forgive him. She tossed the note at the wastebasket and missed. *But I can't have dinner with him.*

℘

"This is April Douglas, and you're listening to *Slice of Life* on KPOG, praising our God in Pine Bluff. If you tuned in two weeks ago, you heard me talk about my sister, Caitlyn, and her dream list—forty-two things that she and I hoped to do together before the end of our lives. My sister didn't live long enough to experience even one of them." April took a sip from her Nalgene bottle. "Caitlyn Renee Douglas died of leukemia on November 12, but she made me promise to at least try to accomplish everything on her list.

"Keeping that promise is going to be possible because of the encouragement and help I'm getting from many of you. I've had offers of backpacking equipment, sailing lessons. . ." April stood her gel pen on end and smiled. "A year's supply of Bridgeman's Wolf Tracks ice cream, and. . ." The words that came to mind weren't the ones she'd planned to say. "I even received an invitation to join a group of storm chasers tracking a tornado. And in return, I want to share my adventures with you."

She segued easily into *Riverdance*. She described the pounding cadence of the Irish jigs and reels, the sweet sadness of the violins, the refurbished opulence of the Orpheum Theater. Several times she used "we" but didn't mention who she'd shared the evening with.

"When the music ended, my first thought was how much my sister would have loved it. But. . .and this is the heart of why I don't want to keep these experiences to myself. . .my thoughts were bittersweet, not morose. I find myself remembering the good times and looking forward to whatever God has in store for me. Caitlyn's short life was a celebration. Even when she began to lose hope, she never lost her gratitude. I want my life to be a testimony to the wonder of God."

Her fingertip traced the edge of the keyboard. Though she'd done a call-in show in college, this was different. "I've been blessed this past week to hear some amazing stories, some tender, some heart wrenching. Today, I'd like to give you an opportunity to talk. Grief is something we'll all experience at some time. We're called to 'Rejoice with those who rejoice; mourn with those who mourn.' Let's do that. Has the Lord led you through the valley and brought you out on the other side? What did He teach you there that might bring encouragement to someone who's still on that dark path? If you have a story to share that may offer hope, or if you're in need of some encouragement, the lines are open. . . ."

The first caller was a high school guidance counselor. "As most of your listeners know, April, Dave Martin, one of our students, was killed last week. He had a lot of friends, and it's been a horrendous loss for them. But these kids are doing some really constructive things with their grief. They're putting together a scrapbook of memories to give to the Martin family, and they've started a memorial fund; the money they collect will be donated to Habitat for Humanity."

An elderly woman called with a story of forgiveness. A year after her husband's death, God had finally given her the courage to face the woman whose decision to drive after too many drinks had cost her husband's life. The two women now met once a week for coffee.

A steady list of names filled her monitor through most of the first hour. The calls tapered off near the halfway point. April leaned in closer to the microphone. "On the other side of this break, I'd like to transition to a new topic. King Solomon gave us some wise words: 'There is. . .a time to be born and a time to die. . .a time to mourn and a time to dance.' My question to you is. . .are you dancing? Are you celebrating the gift of life? If not, why not? What's holding you back from rejoicing in the moment and embracing whatever God brings your way? I want to hear from you after this break."

April looked up to see Jill standing in the control room, once again giving the thumbs-up sign. April smiled her thanks and scanned the screen on her laptop, reviewing the cues that could keep her talking for the rest of the show if no one called in.

Three minutes later, she realized she wasn't going to need any of the cues. She welcomed the first caller. "Hi, Mary Jane. What do you have to share with us?"

"This may sound silly, but one of the ways I celebrate life is by completely ignoring all the rules of fashion."

April laughed. "I hope my best friend isn't listening. You sound like a free spirit, Mary Jane."

The laugh was returned. "Free in Christ. I'm in my sixties, and I'm a watercolor artist. I sell my greeting cards at craft fairs. So of course I love color, and I express that in everything I do, including what I wear. My neon paisleys and purple polka dots are a constant source of humiliation to my daughters, but you know what? I don't care! My grandkids love me just the way I am, and that's good enough for me."

"Mary Jane, you just keep on splashing color all around you, and maybe you'll give some of the rest of us the courage to do the same. Thank you so much for calling."

The hour went too fast. "We've got five minutes left—time for two more calls." She looked at the board. There were three names on the monitor. Frank, Carol. . .and Seth.

She had a choice. She pushed a button. "Hi, Frank. Welcome to *Slice of Life*."

"Thanks. I'm. . .glad I got through." The man sounded out of breath. "I've been listening to you on the last leg of a fifty-mile bike ride. I'm in my late thirties, and about a year ago, I took a long, hard look at my life. I was an overweight armchair quarterback, living vicariously through the flat-screen idiot box in my living room. So I did something that almost got me committed to a nuthouse."

April smiled and shook her head. All these fascinating people lived in Pine Bluff? "What did you do, Frank?"

"I donated my whole entertainment center to the Sanctuary Program."

"Wow! For anyone who isn't familiar with it, the Sanctuary Program offers housing and support for individuals and families in crisis. It's run by Pineview Community Church. Frank, you're an amazing guy. And what's changed in your life because of that decision?"

"I lost forty-one pounds, I've got a girlfriend, and I'm heading to Guatemala on a mission trip next month."

"Fantastic. Any advice to the armchair quarterbacks in our audience?"

"Yeah! God didn't create you to channel surf. Get off your. . .couch and do something purposeful!"

Two names stared at April as she said good-bye to Frank. With a deep breath, she pushed a button.

"Hello, Seth." There had to be more than one Seth among her listeners. "You're the final caller. What words do you have for us to end the show?" At least to her ears, her voice didn't lose a bit of its professional calm.

"Thanks for taking my call, April." Maybe there *was* only one Seth in Pine Bluff. Thankfully, nothing in his tone hinted that he knew her personally. "I've just recently been challenged by a friend's decision to color outside the lines more. I'm a pretty structured guy, but I'm excited about making some changes in my life."

April took a quick sip from her water bottle. "What kinds of changes are you going to make, Seth?"

"Well, for starters, next Saturday night I'm going to have chocolate fondue for supper. I'm all in favor of eating healthy, but sometimes you just have to skip the veggies and go straight for the cheesecake dipped in chocolate. So I've got reservations for two at The Melting Pot, and even if I end up eating alone, I'm going to enjoy coloring outside the lines. As far as final words, I'd just like to give kudos to the watercolor artist who called in earlier. The world could use a lot more polka dots."

Chapter 9

Pushing the door shut with one foot, April set her salad from Burger King on the kitchen counter. Her second Saturday call-in show had just ended, and she was still basking in the afterglow. The first had gone better than she'd dared to hope. In light of the positive feedback from last week's show, two members of the station's board of directors had called Jill, thanking her for "pushing for change" and "believing in that young woman."

She walked over to the fishbowls and pried the cap off the Betta food. "You two are looking particularly ticked off at each other today." She added a pinch of flakes to each bowl. "Didn't you guys listen to my show today? Life is too short to spend it mad at each other." A sudden stab of guilt scrunched her mouth into a grimace. "Do as I do, not as I say. Willy, you want to make a phone call for me?"

She'd put it off for a week, jumping each time any of her phones rang. Apparently, Seth was leaving the next move up to her. Thanks to his corny phone number, she couldn't claim she'd accidentally thrown the note away and lost the number. Staring at the clock, she reassured herself he'd be on set by now and not answering his phone. She dialed and listened, annoyed at the reaction his voice mail message had on her pulse. After the beep, she simply said, "Hi, Seth, this is April. Thank you again for the invitation, but I have to say no."

Feeling the nudge from her conscience turn into a shove, she hung up the phone. At the very least, she could have offered an excuse. Brushing off the thought, she took her salad out of the bag, threw away the plastic fork, and got a real one out of the drawer. She settled on the couch and was engrossed in *The Philadelphia Story* when there was a knock on the door. Yvonne, no doubt, here to bug her one last time about going out with Seth. With a resigned sigh, she paused Cary Grant and opened the door, salad in hand.

"Hi, sweetie!" Aunt Midge filled the doorway in a daffodil-colored sweat suit, holding two cups and her key to the downstairs door in her hand. "I met the girls at Perk Place and thought I'd bring you a Polar Cap. I know how you love those mint things." Midge handed her a cup and walked in. "Go ahead and eat your salad. I had a chicken salad croissant with Sue and Laura. Tried to get your mom to drive up and go with us. She always liked those girls, but. . ." An impending frown suddenly morphed into a grin. "Maybe next time. I really came by to tell you that I loved your show today." Her gaze dipped to the floor. "Oh, that's not true. I just came by because I'm just dying to know if you're going to The Melting Pot tonight."

April held up her salad in answer and sat on the couch, gesturing for Midge to sit down.

"So you're eating a salad now and going out for dessert later?" Midge tilted her head to the right with a look of hopeful expectation on her face.

"I'm not going."

"Honey, you really need to give the man a second chance. . .or third, I guess. From what you've told me, he sounds like a sweet man who just had a little *LOGR* moment."

April's fork stopped in midair. "Logger?" Images of men in red plaid shirts floating logs down the St. Croix came to mind.

Midge giggled. "I just heard it at that women's thing I went to this morning. 'Lots of Grace Required.' Isn't that beautiful?"

"Yes. . .it is."

Midge's gaze went to the TV and then to the microwave. "The weather is on!" Midge scooped the remote off the coffee table and switched from DVD to TV. "I want to take my Sunday school kids outside tomorrow. I need to find out if it's going to rain."

Shaking her head, April flopped against the back of the couch. "That was lame, Midge."

"Shh. Listen to the weather." Midge pointed at Seth, who was perfectly filling out a tan sports jacket. "Look. . .it's raining dimples. . .and the sun is shining in those amazing eyes. . . ."

"Stop!"

"You're right. We should be listening." Midge turned up the volume.

April took a massive bite of lettuce, chewing as loudly as she could. But Seth's voice carried above her chewing.

". . .with Daisy Troop 401 this morning. I had the pleasure of answering questions about cloud formations." A video clip popped on the screen, showing Seth, sitting on a beanbag chair, talking to a circle of little girls. He held a microphone out to a five- or six-year-old with bright red hair. "What's your question, Pamela?"

The camera zoomed in on the freckled face and the crayon-printed name tag that hung around her neck. "My dad said that fog is just clouds on the ground; so how come in the sky, clouds sometimes look like kittens or turtles or something, but on the ground they just look like steamy stuff?"

Sitting at the little girl's eye level, the sleeves of his pale blue dress shirt folded back to just below his elbows, Seth smiled. It was, indeed, raining dimples. April stabbed a crouton and chomped, but she couldn't block out his answer.

"That's a wonderful question, Pamela. Wouldn't it be fun if there were cloud animals all over Pine Bluff on foggy days?"

The little girl nodded.

"Fog forms when the air temperature gets so low that it can't hold the water in it and. . ."

April couldn't drown out the voice, and she couldn't keep her eyes off the screen. Seth's gentleness with the little girl was touching her in ways she couldn't ignore.

Midge turned the volume back down. "Laura's sister's daughter lives two houses down from Seth Bachelor, and Laura asked her what he's really like, and she said that he's just the perfect neighbor and—"

"That's what everyone always says about serial killers."

"April Jean!"

"Sorry."

"You are not going to find a perfect man, you know."

There was that word again. . .perfect. "I'm not looking for perfect. I just want a guy who doesn't have a hair trigger."

Midge wagged her finger. "Any guy with a pulse is occasionally going to lose it."

"I know. . .a LOGR moment." April set her salad on the coffee table, no longer interested.

"I'll make you a deal. If you go out with him, I'll clean your apartment for a month."

A moment of true temptation. A woman who cleaned for a living was offering to scrub her bathroom floor and chase her dust bunnies. April reached over and pulled her aunt into a one-armed hug. "I love you."

"I love you, too. Okay, if bribery doesn't work, how about guilt? I've heard you say that Caitlyn wanted you to do the things on the list because she wanted you to fully enjoy life. You know if she were here she'd be telling you to go for it."

April withdrew her arm. "You tried that once before. That's low, and that's so not like you."

Midge kept her eyes on her coffee cup. "I know. But sometimes the end really does justify the means. You've been moping around this dinky town with almost no social life for way too long. You need to practice what you preach. It's time for you to dance, my dear."

❧

"It's time for you to dance." Katharine Hepburn twirled, her calf-length skirt flowing out from her wasp waist. April pushed PAUSE and stared at the time on the DVD player. Seth wouldn't have left the station yet. *Lord, I need direction. The two people I trust most in this world are pushing me toward this man. I've always believed that there is wisdom in many counselors. Am I being overly sensitive? Is Yvonne right—am I projecting my dad's flaws onto Seth?*

Her eyes were drawn by a flicker of blue. Willy and Splash, in full battle mode, darted and dodged, their fins unfurled to intimidate. The threat seemed so real to them. April had separated them once, putting Splash on her dresser in the bedroom. But instead of finding tranquility, Willy had become hyper-vigilant, and Splash, if a fish can become depressed, appeared lethargic and melancholy. Though it was a love/hate relationship, they were good for each other.

Was the relationship between her Siamese fighting fish a metaphor for her life?

"Rrrrr!" She tossed the remote onto the couch. "Fine!" With a glare at her gridlocked Bettas, April picked up her phone. "Will you all leave me alone if I give him one last chance?"

∞

To say he was pleasantly shocked would be an understatement. After a week of silence, her first message hadn't surprised him. Her second had almost knocked him off his chair. Seth stared at the girl in the teal blouse as he speared a maraschino cherry with a long, two-pronged fork and plunged it into the pot of melted chocolate. "So what are you going to cross off the list next? Salmon fishing in Alaska?"

A little divot formed at the right corner of her mouth. "I think you need to make your own list. I'm hoping to do a day hike on the Superior Trail in a couple of weeks and something low-key this week. . . ."

"Sunrise at Sunrise? Minnesota, I mean."

"Hmm. . ." Pale light from the fixture above their table glinted in her eyes. "Maybe."

He chewed on his next thought for a moment before deciding to abandon caution. "I'll make breakfast."

April appeared to freeze mid-breath, like a kid in a spelling bee. *Could you repeat the word, please?* He decided to give her a way out. "Just a thought."

He pulled his fork out of the pot and slid the smothered cherry onto his plate. "You know, before we get onto something else, I want to explain about that blowup with my station manager." He'd already apologized—twice, if the flowers counted, but he wanted her to know it wasn't a regular occurrence.

April's shoulders lost their rigid lines.

Seth set his fork down. "Merv and I have a long history of getting under each other's skin. The guy's going to end up losing his job. He was out of line, but so was I. I apologized, and so did he. I'm just sorry you had to witness it."

"So this wasn't the first blowup?"

Now this was the thing—well, one of the things—he didn't understand about women. He'd just explained that he and Merv had said their apologies. Over, done, *finito*. Why did women have to dig things up and dissect them after they were dead and buried?

"We've had our disagreements. I've never lost it quite like that before."

"Obviously, you didn't lose your job over it."

Seth did everything in his power not to let his smile warp into a smirk. "No, I didn't."

April stared at him, as if wondering if he was worthy of amnesty.

Her silence made him antsy. "Maybe it's just a guy thing. I didn't waste any sleep over it. I'm pretty sure Merv didn't either."

Finally, she gave the subtlest of nods. "Everybody has logger moments."

"*What* moments?"

"LOGR. Lots of Grace Required."

"I like that. I pretty much constantly require lots of grace." He smiled as he watched April attempting to rescue a drowning piece of marshmallow that had fallen off her fork in the fondue pot. "You don't know how fortunate you are to be working with Christians."

"Actually, I do. I thank God every day for it." The blue-green stones in her earrings ricocheted light. Seth found it hard to stay disgruntled. He put the cooled chocolate-drenched cherry in his mouth.

Wrapping both hands around her coffee mug, April looked at him with an expression that reminded him of a nurse taking his pulse. "What are you doing in Pine Bluff?"

There were a lot of answers to that question, not all of which he was ready to share. "It's a friendly town. I like the energy during the tourist season and the slow pace in the off season."

April's eyes narrowed slightly. "Do you ever feel like you're not working up to your full potential?"

"I guess I don't need the big bucks to feel good about what I do, if that's what you mean." He set his fork down. "That sounded defensive, didn't it? I'm not really sure what you're asking."

"Do you ever feel stifled doing the weather on a little cable station when. . ." Her hand rose to her face, and she peered at him through spread fingers. "I'm sorry. That came out so rude." She dropped her hand to her lap and gave a sheepish smile. "I've been accused of projecting. I shouldn't be putting the junk of my life onto yours."

Seth's chest tightened. She couldn't possibly know her question had caused physical pain. "Then I should ask you the same thing. What's keeping you in Pine Bluff?"

Her eyes focused on the fondue pot on the built-in warmer between them. "I've been asking myself that question all day. My mother moved to Minneapolis last month. She was my reason for staying after Caitlyn died. I love the people I work with, but there's so much more I want to do with my life."

"Could you get your old job back?" Seth leaned against the back of his seat and folded his arms, wondering as he did what his body language communicated.

"Probably. But anchoring was really just a way to get my foot in the door."

"You have higher ambitions? Management?"

She laughed. "No." Staring up at the purple and green pendant light above their table, she said, "Promise you won't laugh?"

"Promise." Seth leaned forward, resting his arms on the table.

"I want to be a television talk show host."

He studied her, imagining her on set, her earrings and eyes flashing in the lights, asking probing questions. He reached across the table and touched his fingertips to the top of her hand. "You'd be good at that. Describe it for me: What does an hour on the prime-time *April Douglas Show* look like?"

The touch seemed to startle her, but she didn't pull her hand away. When she didn't answer, he filled the silence. "Big names, lots of controversial topics?"

Her honey-blond hair swayed as she shook her head. "No actors, no politicians. For years I've pictured a show with a setup like Oprah's. . . ." She grinned and gave a one-shoulder shrug. "How's that for pretentious? I just mean a comfortable setting. No desk like *The Tonight Show*. And even when I'm nationally syndicated"—her smile was accompanied by a raised brow—"I'm only going to have regular people as guests. Real people with real stories of how God is working in their lives."

"Kind of like your radio show today."

"Exactly."

Seth brought his fingertips together. "Then make it happen, April." He looked down at the table then back to her eyes, not voicing the words in his head: *Would you consider starting small. . .say, at a "little" cable station?*

Chapter 10

The clock on the microwave glowed the hour. Four o'clock Saturday morning. An hour and a half before sunrise at Sunrise. April set her camera and digital recorder on top of the blanket in her oversize straw bag.

The only light filtering through the living room blinds came from the streetlamps below. April yawned and slipped a Vikings hoodie over her head. Carrying her hiking boots, she looped the handle of her bag over her wrist, opened the door, and stepped into the hall.

"This is getting serious."

April jumped at the sleepy voice. Whirling around, she laughed. Yvonne leaned on her doorframe, wrapped in a purple satin robe, a towel on her head and lime green spacers between her toes. The smell of nail polish wafted through her open door.

"What in the world are you doing up?"

"Primping. I'm singing for a wedding in Edina at eleven." Yvonne's turban tipped to one side. "I heard about your sunrise breakfast. . .*from Seth*." The insinuation wasn't even close to subtle.

"I. . .was going to tell you." It was true. She was going to tell her. . .after the fact.

Yvonne's hands landed on her hips. "What did you think I'd do if you admitted you liked him? Do you really think I'm immature enough to say I told you so?" Even in the dim hall light, the bulge made by her tongue in her cheek couldn't be missed.

"Yes."

"You're right. I am." Yvonne stuck her thumbs in her ears and wiggled her fingers. "I told you so."

"Who says I like him? I need to cross this thing off my list, and he offered to bring food. Why would I turn down eggs and sausage cooked over an open fire?"

Yvonne laughed. "How many times have you talked to him on the phone this week?" Not waiting for an answer, she shook her head, waved, and stepped back into her apartment. The door closed and then opened just a crack. "I told you so."

❧

The purple LED lights on the dashboard of Seth's Camry gave just enough light to allow surreptitious peeks at his square jaw and the tiny bump at the top of his nose. April settled into the leather of the bucket seat. The outside-temperature display read fifty-four, but Seth had turned on the seat warmer before picking her up. Not really necessary but a nice touch.

Seth's right arm shot across her line of vision. "Moon's coming up."

"Just now?" April stared at the sliver of white nearly concealed by treetops. "It's almost dawn."

"As the moon orbits the Earth, it moves thirteen degrees eastward every night. Thirteen degrees translates into about forty minutes, so the moon rises forty minutes later each night. Once in a while, the sun beats it out of bed."

His look hovered thirteen degrees east of patronizing, but his words landed smack dab in the middle. It was the same tone he'd used to answer the little red-haired girl's question about clouds. April's fingers coiled around the seat belt shoulder strap. She could do patronizing.

"Wow." She batted wide-open eyes. "Is that a getting bigger moon or a getting littler moon?"

"That's a waxing crescent. After the new moon and before the full, it's called waxing. Like dipping a candle, it gets bigger—" He stopped suddenly, pressing his lips into a line. Slowly he turned, locked onto her eyes for a split second, and then focused back on the road. "I just came off like an arrogant snob, didn't I?"

April stifled a sneer. "What tipped you off?"

"I heard your teeth grinding." Smile darts radiated from the outside corners of his eyes. "I am so sorry." He flipped the right blinker and turned onto a narrow country road lined with tall pines. "It's my father's fault."

"What is?"

"The condescending attitude."

"Ah. It's in your DNA."

Tapping his foot on the brake pedal, Seth nodded. "It may be due to nurture instead of nature, but it's sure ingrained. You know that phrase 'Kids learn what they live'?"

Turning in the warm seat, April flipped the shoulder strap over her head and rested her back against the door. Maybe Seth Bachelor had way more in common with her than she imagined.

⟨∞⟩

"Tell me about your dad."

Seth was only too aware that she'd repositioned her entire body to face him dead-on. "Let's just say he was never satisfied with less than perfection. Because of him, I'm a TV weatherman instead of…some other things I could have chosen."

"Is your dad still living?"

Seth nodded. "My folks are in New Mexico. We see each other at Christmas and usually once in between. We get along fine that way."

His headlights bounced off a sign about twenty yards ahead. "We're here."

174

"Tippet House. A bed-and-breakfast?"

The quiver in April's voice made him smile. Clearly, she was questioning his intentions. "We're here for the breakfast part."

Her shoulders lowered. "I thought you were cooking."

"I am."

She didn't reply. He slowed to a stop in front of a Victorian farmhouse smothered in gables, cupolas, and gingerbread trim. Exterior lights illuminated pink siding and pale blue and white molding.

April's mouth parted slightly. "Are Hansel and Gretel here?"

"Let's go see."

They got out of the car, and he took her hand, guiding her along a winding brick path lit by ankle-high copper-shaded lights. The path led to the backyard, past a stone fountain. Water arced over the backs of two bisque-colored swans. Pink light shimmered through the streams.

April hadn't said a word since getting out of the car. Each time he turned to watch her expression, her eyes seemed to get wider. When they reached a gazebo aglow with miniature white lights, he walked up the first step. April stopped. "Seth. . ."

He suddenly realized that, aside from the radio show, it was the first time she'd called him by name. "What?"

"Thank you."

He squeezed her hand. "You haven't even seen the sunrise."

"I can't wait," she whispered.

He motioned for her to go ahead of him up the five steps. When she reached the top step, he heard a sharp inhale and smiled to himself. A round table, covered with a lace cloth, was set for two. Gold flatware flanked rose-covered plates and cups. Light danced from a three-wick ivory candle shielded by a hurricane shade.

Pulling a wrought iron chair away from the table, he gave a slight bow. April sat down, and he handed her a cloth napkin. "Breakfast will be served momentarily, ma'am." As he pulled out the chair opposite her, he heard steps on the brick walk.

Bessie, who had owned the Sage Stoppe restaurant before opening the bed-and-breakfast, ascended the stairs with a large silver tray. Tall and thin, with wisps of straight gray hair springing loose from a tight bun, she was as stoic as her Cornish grandmothers must have been. After resting the tray on a wooden stand, she set two covered serving dishes on the table, followed by a basket, the contents hidden by a linen napkin. With a nod of her head, she picked up the empty tray.

"I owe you my firstborn child, Bessie."

"That you do," she answered and disappeared down the stairs.

Instead of uncovering the dishes like he thought she would, April simply sat, smiling across the table at him. "This is not at all what I expected. You're a man of surprises."

"Is that a good thing?" It seemed to be. She was smiling, after all.

"Usually."

Reaching across the table with both hands, he turned them palms up. "Let's pray." When her hands rested in his, he bowed his head, grateful for a reason to hide for just a moment from those deep blue eyes. "Lord God, thank You for this food, and thank You for the witness of Your majesty we are about to see. Amen."

"Amen." Once again her lashes glistened, but she didn't appear in danger of giving in to whatever emotion was getting to her. She touched the edge of the napkin that covered the basket. "Don't tell me. Twinkies?"

Seth laughed. "Homemade biscuits."

As April lifted the napkin, a rose-pink glow lit the cloth. Orange spears blazed through the eastern sky as the gold orb lifted from the horizon and gilded the valley below them with morning light.

80

"Told you so, told you so, told you so. . ."

April sipped her Polar Cap as she listened to Yvonne's silly chant. Slurping on her straw, she stared, refusing to crack even the slightest smile. "That is so first grade."

The ditty finally came to an end. "But it makes me feel so good." Yvonne broke a scone in half and slathered it with lemon curd. "Details. Don't leave out a single second."

April toyed with the flip menu that displayed Perk Place's catering choices. She'd made Yvonne wait four days until their schedules would mesh so she could share the "details" face-to-face. A few more minutes would only enhance the anticipation. "Do you think any of the people in your Bible study would be interested in a day hike on the Superior Trail a week from Sunday? We could all go to the Saturday worship service at your church—"

"Ahem." Yvonne cleared her throat and held out her watch. "We have to be at Bible study in twenty minutes."

"Who says I'm going?"

"Hah! As if. You're going, even though it's for all the wrong reasons." She snatched April's cup, pulling the straw out of her mouth. "Details."

"He was very. . .creative." April recaptured her Polar Cap. "I imagined sitting at a picnic table eating scrambled eggs seasoned with ashes. But what I got was a candlelit table and *sformatino*."

"Is it contagious?"

"It means 'pie' in Italian. Kind of like quiche, full of veggies and cheese."

"And Seth made it?"

"With his own little hands the night before. The lady who runs the B and B baked it, but—" Her phone, sitting on the table, vibrated.

April stared at the caller ID screen and sighed as she opened her phone. "Hi, Midge."

Even before her aunt spoke, there was a sense of crackling tension in the silence. "April, why haven't you answered your mother's calls?"

A sigh started in the bottom of her lungs. There were four missed calls on her phone since noon. "I couldn't find the time." *Forgive me, Lord.* She could have *made* the time. "She didn't leave a message. I was going to call her later. Is something wrong?"

"I've never heard her like this. She's so upset, and she's not making sense. Her words are slurred, and I'm afraid she took something. Should I call 911?"

April's mouth went dry. Part of her was scared. The other part seethed. "Are you sure she's not just trying to get a rise out of you? What's she upset about this time?"

"You. . .going out with Seth."

"Why?" The seething part took over.

"She says she found out something about him, but you won't answer her calls. She's furious."

"Did she say what it was?"

"No. But, April, this isn't about Seth. . .or you. I'm worried about your mother."

Rubbing her eyes, April nodded. "I'll call."

Why, just for once, couldn't it be about her? She closed the phone and sighed again, looking to Yvonne for sympathy.

"Trouble?"

"Probably just drama, but I guess I can't ignore it. I'm sorry."

"Take your time. I'll meet you at the study, and we can talk after." Yvonne gathered her purse and latte and waved good-bye.

April pressed 4 on her phone and waited. Her mother didn't bother with "Hello."

"Mom. . .settle down. I can't understand you."

"I just found out." The voice coming through April's phone rasped, as if she'd been yelling for hours. "I went to the library and searched the newspaper files."

"For Seth?" Seething might become a permanent state.

"I'm not going to lose another daughter to that man!"

April rolled her eyes. "And what did you find?"

"I'll tell you what I found. Seth Bachelor is married."

Chapter 11

April clutched her Bible to her chest like a shield as she walked up to a stone house with no front yard. Next to the shiny red door with a brass kick plate, a burnished bronze plaque declared it to be on the Historic Registry of Homes. April touched the bottom of the antique door knocker but couldn't make herself use it.

She didn't want to be here. But not showing would have raised too many questions. If she could just shut out the picture and her mother's voice until she got home and had time to sort this through. Her brain felt as though she'd head butted an electric fence. After the jolt had come the fuzzy numbness that wouldn't allow her to formulate a concise thought, let alone a rational next step.

Confront him. That's what she needed to do. But when? And how? If she hadn't taken out a fraction of her agitation on gunning her engine and turning the radio up full blast, she might have done exactly what she wanted to do: March into this house and slap Seth Bachelor's square hypocritical jaw.

How was she going to sedate these emotions and act normal? How was she going to ignore the conversation that kept replaying in her brain?

"The picture is right in front of me, April. I e-mailed you a copy."

"Maybe he's divorced, Mom." Would that have made her feel any better?

"Don't you think I thought of that? There's no record of a divorce."

"What if his wife died?" Why would he hide something like that?

"April Jean, give me some credit for being a thinking human being. I checked the death records."

Still not convinced, she'd run home to check her e-mail before coming to the study. There was the picture. . .Seth in a long-tailed tuxedo, the new Mrs. Bachelor, née Brenda Cadwell, in a scoop-necked dress.

Seth is married. The words became a refrain to every thought. No wonder he'd seemed vague about why he was in Pine Bluff. He was hiding out. Did Mrs. Brenda Bachelor even know where he was? Or maybe they were still together, and he was living a double life. Were there children involved? In three years, they could have had two children. Was he sending child support?

It was all too easy to imagine two little children with Seth's dark hair and dimples. Two little girls, maybe, sitting at the kitchen table, waiting for food that didn't exist, finally rummaging in empty cupboards and a bare refrigerator until they found a half-empty package of stale soda crackers and the remains of a jar of grape jelly.

A car door slammed behind her, zapping her into the present. She tapped the brass knocker against the door.

⅋

They'd saved a seat for her, right between him and Yvonne on the extralong couch. Why hadn't she taken it? During introductions, her smile had made the rounds, landing on each person to Seth's right, hopping over him, and continuing with everyone to his left. He'd seen her talking to Yvonne before the study began, so she wasn't avoiding her. She was avoiding him.

Seth stared across the room at April, sitting cross-legged on the braided rug by the Franklin stove. Her rust-colored blouse brought out the reddish tones in her hair and reflected in spots of color on her cheeks. Not once in the fifteen minutes since she'd walked in had she made eye contact with him. What had he done now?

He sifted through what he remembered of the couple of times they'd talked since their breakfast at Sunrise and couldn't come up with anything she might have misconstrued. Had he inadvertently said something to make her mad? Was she simply losing interest? Had she really ever been interested? Why did women have to be so multifaceted? Just when you think you're getting to know one of them, a whole other side pops up that you didn't know existed. He forced his focus back on Pastor Owen, who was asking them to turn to the thirteenth chapter of Second Corinthians while he read aloud.

" 'Examine yourselves to see whether you are in the faith; test yourselves. Do you not realize that Christ Jesus is in you—unless, of course, you fail the test?' "

A test. That's what he needed. An MMPI for every woman he met. *Hi, I'm Seth Bachelor. Glad to meet you. I'd like you to take the Minnesota Multiphasic Personality Inventory before a single word comes out of your mouth.*

That's the only way he'd be sure of finding someone who really was what she appeared to be. He'd let himself believe that April Douglas wasn't like so many of the women he'd met. She was a straight shooter, not a game player. If she didn't like something, she said so. So what statement was she making by sitting across the room and avoiding eye contact? He'd never been good at reading signals. He needed words. And he'd drag them out of her as soon as the study was over.

Things between them had been precarious right from the start. So what was it about her that made him keep coming back? She was good at letting him talk about himself, asking just the right questions at the right times. But that could be nothing more than her reporter training. She was funny, in the subtle kind of way he loved. Her compassion for others was genuine. He'd seen nothing in her that he'd label egotistical or vain. That alone was worth a ton of points.

He'd felt a bit off balance since the moment they'd met. . .and it wasn't all that bad a feeling. The sudden realization surprised him. In the past, he'd hated unpredictable relationships. The last few weeks had felt a lot like tracking an F5 tornado.

And he was loving it.

Looking down at his open Bible, he willed his mind to stay on task. Pastor Owen was reading verse eleven.

" 'Finally, brothers, good-by. Aim for perfection, listen to my appeal, be of one mind, live in peace. And the God of love and peace will be with you. Greet one another with a holy kiss.'"

A holy kiss. . .it had crossed his mind more than once in the past few days. Apparently he wouldn't be obeying that command any time soon.

He studied her, the way she toyed with the tassel on her bookmark, the uncomfortable-looking straightness of her posture. She'd glued her attention on Pastor Owen and his wife Audrey, appearing to be soaking in every word they uttered. Looking closer, he could tell that her glazed eyes weren't focused. Clearly, her mind wasn't on Second Corinthians.

At least they had that in common.

଼

There was a reason why April had participated in forensics rather than drama in high school. She could give an extemporaneous speech that would make a vegetarian order prime rib, but she was lousy at pretending to be someone else. Her broadcast classes had taught her to tuck her emotions into the cubbyholes of her psyche, but apparently that only worked in front of a camera or a microphone. Her training wasn't coming through for her now.

She realized too late that sitting across the room from Seth was a huge mistake. The thought of sitting close enough to smell his aftershave and feel his body heat had made her woozy. She'd opted for a spot on the floor, but now she was in his line of vision. Though she managed not to look directly at him, her peripheral scanning kept tabs on him. She was pretty sure his eyes hadn't left her face for an entire hour.

So she'd been right to distrust him in the beginning. No wonder the man had anger issues. Sure, there had been teases of the kind of man she'd always dreamed of—attentive, understanding, patient, creative—but none of that mattered now. Unless. . .what if he hadn't really deceived her? What if his wife had died in a different state? Her death certificate wouldn't be filed in Minnesota then, would it? Would the same be true of divorce records? Or what if, even now, Brenda Bachelor lay in a permanent coma, brain-dead from an accident? Maybe an accident that was Seth's fault?

But he would have told her something like that. Or Yvonne would have told her. It's not the kind of thing he'd hide from his church friends, his support system.

No imagined scenario gave him an easy out. The man had been—apparently still was—married.

At least she'd found out the truth before any real feelings for him had taken root. As it was, she might lose a night's sleep, but she refused to lose any tears.

Her neck and shoulders ached from sitting in the same rigid position. She had to move, but it had to be calculated. When her gaze left the front of the room, she couldn't let it sweep across Seth. She leaned back against the free-standing fireplace and turned her head to the left, away from Seth. At that angle, she was staring directly at Trace and Sydney McKay, newlyweds who somehow managed to hold hands while flipping through their respective Bibles.

As director of the chamber of commerce, Sydney collected rent checks from Yvonne and April every month. Over the course of a year, April had gotten to know her well. Just weeks after Caitlyn died, Sydney had announced her engagement. Though they were at very different seasons in their lives, they'd formed a bond, following the apostle Paul's words: "Rejoice with those who rejoice; mourn with those who mourn." April thought back to Trace and Sydney's wedding. Candlelight, a flowing dress encrusted with crystals, pale peach orchids, a wedding cake covered in chocolate and lacy white icing. And the groom, waiting at the altar with misty eyes. . .

April blinked, shocked by the sting of tears.

She looked down at her open Bible and forced herself to read and reread chapter thirteen of Second Corinthians. Verse eight jumped out at her. "For we cannot do anything against the truth, but only for the truth." *Lord, grant me the strength to speak the truth.*

Lost in outlining the speech that would corner Seth into the truth, April was startled by the sound of her name. Yvonne was talking about her.

". . .Remember that we prayed for her after her sister died, and I'm sure a lot of you have heard her radio program, *Slice of Life*, on Saturday afternoons. She's fulfilling a list that she made with her sister, experiences that celebrate life, I guess you'd say, and she's sharing her adventures with her listeners. Anyway, she's organizing a day hike on the Superior Trail for a week from Sunday. Anybody here interested in going?"

Heat flooded April's face. *Not now, Yvonne.* This time, her training came to her rescue, and she smiled and nodded like the cool, calm professional she didn't feel like. "I'm thinking of doing a five-mile loop, starting at Gooseberry Falls. It'll be a slow pace, so even if you're not an experienced hiker, it shouldn't be difficult. If you're interested, just e-mail Yvonne, and I'll get in contact with you." *Now shift the focus to someone else, please.*

"Let's see a show of hands. Who thinks they'd like to go?" Yvonne looked around the room as she asked.

Yvonne's hand lifted slowly, tentatively in reply to her own question, prompting April's mouth to open spontaneously. "You're going?"

Yvonne almost pulled off the look of offense. "I like the outdoors." The circle burst into laughter. Obviously, they knew her well. "So who's going to join us?"

Five hands rose. One of them was Seth's.

Trying her hardest to concentrate on the closing prayer, April found it impossible. Her mind painted pictures of what could have been. . .climbing the rise to Gooseberry Falls, her hand in Seth's, picking their way across the river on lichen-covered rocks, falling into his arms when her foot slipped. . . . The prayer ended, and the room buzzed with a dozen conversations at once. April stood, frantically searching for someone to talk to while she regrouped her resolve. But it was too late. She'd barely gotten to her feet when Seth crossed the room and stopped a foot in front of her. "Can we go outside for a minute?"

This wasn't the way she wanted the scene to play. She'd planned on being the one to say, "We need to talk." She'd planned on being in control. Setting her Bible on an end table, she nodded.

80

"What's wrong, April?" He leaned against the seat of a pale blue and shiny black motorcycle, legs crossed at the ankles, arms folded over his chest, tightening the sleeves of his dark blue T-shirt. He scanned her face, patient once again.

What happened to the fury that she needed to carry this through? Why did her spine turn to Jell-O around this man? She took a deep breath and blew it out, puffing wind into her own sails.

"I think I should be asking what's wrong with you. What's wrong with a guy who's living a lie—or a double life?"

"What in the world are you talking about?"

"Isn't there some little detail you failed to tell me before you asked me out?"

Seth's brow creased. "April, I'm sorry. I have no clue what you're getting at. Spell it out."

Her hands clamped on her hips. "My mother found your wedding announcement."

He stared at her, but she wasn't falling for the blank look. He wasn't even going to defend himself or try lying his way out? Her indignation returned with a vengeance. "Let me jog your memory. You get married, you take a picture, you put it in the paper. . . ." Her voice amplified with each word, but she didn't care. The tears she'd vowed not to shed teetered on her lashes.

Of all the expressions she would have expected from him, a smile was not one of them. Slowly it spread, deepening his dimple, forming little river deltas next to his eyes. April felt heat creep from her solar plexus to her temples. Could blood actually boil?

His hand reached for her shoulder. She jerked away. The infuriating smile didn't fade.

"But sometimes, if your fiancée's best friend works for a newspaper, you pose for the picture, you put it in the paper. . .and you *don't* get married."

Chapter 12

Check your facts; know your sources. The line had been drummed into her in school. She knew it like she knew her own name. Why in the world had she chosen this particular time to listen to her mother? She should have checked the public records. But the picture was evidence. It hadn't crossed her mind to question it. Who took wedding pictures before a wedding?

April's eyes opened, her jaw locked tight. Beneath the pineapple-shaped globe of a streetlamp, the blue on the Harley glowed like Caribbean water. Seth's eyes appeared more black than brown—polished ebony, fixed on hers, holding her captive.

"You...didn't...get married?"

He shook his head. His eyes danced. "Still Bachelor."

He was playing with her, relishing her humiliation, yet the message that came through his teasing smile was unexpected. Grace. He wasn't mad. She'd cornered him like a deranged banshee, but he wasn't mad.

"I came frighteningly close to marrying the wrong woman, but I didn't."

The tears rolled over their banks, topping humiliation with fresh embarrassment. "I'm sorry." She fished a tissue out of her pocket.

Seth stood and took a step toward her. "You and I are getting to be experts at new beginnings, aren't we?"

All she could do was nod.

"Are you up for a moonlight ride?"

Wiping her nose, she nodded again, still fixed on the midnight glint in his eyes. A smile finally unparalyzed her face. "Promise you won't get all astronomical on me?"

"Five minutes of moon phases, max. Maybe ten on Mercury. If we stay up late enough, we'll be able to see it in the northwestern sky." He grinned, turned, and unlatched the trunk compartment, pulling out a half helmet, two black leather jackets, and two pairs of gloves. His own helmet hung from a silver hook beneath the trunk. "Pays to keep a spare." He held out the helmet, but when she grabbed it, he didn't let go. "Before the thought hits your pretty head, this did not belong to my ex-fiancée."

"Thank you." His reassurance hadn't come before the thought, but it did put it to rest.

April walked around to the opposite side of the bike as she zipped the jacket and fastened the strap on the helmet. "I love this color."

"Suede Blue Pearl."

"Anniversary edition, huh?" She ran her hand across the curve of the gas tank.

Seth stopped, one hand partway into a leather glove. "You do know something about Harleys."

April glanced down at the Harley logo, silver wings upturned against an orange and black background. Above the wings was printed 105 YEARS; below them, it said, "1903–2008."

"Yep, I know my bikes."

"I'm impressed." Seth tucked his sleeves into his gauntlet gloves. "Ready?"

"All set."

He turned and reached out for the left grip. His hand stopped in midair. Turning, he grinned at her then touched his gloved fingertips to the anniversary logo. "I really, really hate being gullible. It'll be a wilder ride because of that, you know." He swung his leg over the seat.

April stepped onto the foot pad. Holding onto Seth's shoulder, she hopped on. As he revved the motor, she yelled in his ear. "Bring it on!"

Seth did a U-turn and headed north, out of town. The air that had felt balmy when they'd walked outside now chilled April's cheeks. She wrapped her arms a little tighter around Seth's chest. When the speed limit changed to fifty-five, she felt the gears change. The vibration increased, the motor roared. The road curved as they climbed the bluff. Molding her body to his, she leaned into the turn with him. They flew over the crest of a rise. April's breath caught, and she felt like she'd left her stomach at the top of the hill. The wind rushed, and her eyes watered as they whipped along a straightaway and began to ascend again. Her hair slapped against the jacket collar. The road dipped, and they hit a pocket of cold air. April ducked closer into Seth's shoulders to block the wind.

Yvonne's words came to mind. *"Experiences that celebrate life."* This moment, maybe her first in well over a year, was a celebration.

Seth had asked her if she could stand ten hours on a Harley.

Absolutely.

☙

"I was engaged to the second runner-up in the Miss St. Cloud Pageant."

"Brenda Cadwell."

"Mm-hm."

They sat on an orange blanket embroidered with Harley-Davidson emblems. Below them, the lights of Pine Bluff scattered like diamonds across the valley.

"Very prestigious." April watched his reaction, wondering how the breakup had really affected him.

"Yeah, that's what I thought when I first met her. She was a broadcasting student, shadowing the manager of the station I worked at for a class she was taking. I knew who she was before she introduced herself. I'd seen some of the pageant coverage. I was blown away when she asked me out."

"*She* asked *you?*"

A wry smile pulled at his mouth. "Yeah. Should have seen the manipulation red flags, but I was so caught up in the fact that she'd chosen little ol' me. I was blind right up until a week before the wedding."

"What happened?"

Seth picked up a stone and tossed it over the side of the bluff. It pinged against the rocks, the sound trailing off in the dark abyss. "I got a clue from her sister that there were a few little things she'd failed to mention in the two years we'd dated. Like the fact that she'd maxed out two credit cards and then run up thirty thousand dollars on Daddy's accounts, which she'd promised to pay back. All told, we would have started our marriage sixty-four thousand dollars in debt."

A long, low whistle slipped through April's lips. "All for the wedding?"

"No. Her parents and I covered the wedding bills as they came along. She'd charged clothes, jewelry, makeup, spa services. . .anything to decorate herself. And she'd hidden the debt from me." He pitched another rock. "When I confronted her, she denied it. The debt was one thing. The sin of omission and then the lying was what I couldn't get past. I could only guess at what else she'd forgotten to mention."

"So you broke it off a week before the wedding?"

"Worse than that. I did a credit check on her, and when she denied everything, I wanted to believe her. So I did some research. It took a few days to double-check everything. There was no mistake. I broke up with her an hour before the rehearsal dinner."

"Whoa. I'm picturing a rather angry bride."

Smile lines bracketed Seth's mouth. "I think 'livid' is the correct word. She drew blood when she launched the ring at me."

"Ouch."

"A couple weeks before the wedding, she insisted on having wedding pictures of the two of us taken at a studio. Had to have the right lighting, you know." He shook his head. "Her roommate worked for the paper and sidestepped the usual policy for her, letting her submit a picture early so it would come out in the Sunday morning paper. By the time they thought of it, the paper had already gone to press."

April studied the relaxed set of his jaw. She'd seen him upset enough to know that his jaw muscles usually bulged when he was angry. "You seem to have dealt pretty well with it. I think I'd still be bitter."

"That was the amazing thing. The second I told her I wasn't going to marry her—in front of her parents, by the way—the relief was unbelievable."

"But you weren't miserable with her before that?"

Seth shrugged. "Did you ever have a tag on the neck of a shirt that was stiff and scratchy, and all day long, you're kind of subconsciously aware of it, but you're too busy to focus on it? That's what our relationship was like. On some level, it wasn't feeling right. She wasn't interested in much of anything I like to do. I sometimes wonder if she was interested in me at all, or if she was just addicted to the male attention and any guy would do. Honestly, I think she would have been just as happy dating a full-length mirror."

It was April's turn to pick up a smooth, flat rock and pitch it into the darkness. "I'm glad you found out before it was too late. Do you still have contact with her?"

Seth's sigh carried notes of weariness mingled with frustration. "Only when I have to. Unfortunately, our paths cross often. . .professionally."

"I'm sorry I lashed out at you. I should have checked the facts."

"Forget it. A wedding announcement sure looks like fact. Besides. . ." His fingertip traced the outline of her hand on the blanket. "Your righteous wrath was kind of flattering."

April aimed her smile at the distant lights. "And why is that?"

"Because it just might mean that in spite of all our ups and downs, you're developing some feelings for me."

"And you'd consider that a good thing?"

His arm slid around her shoulders. "I'd consider that a very good thing."

ৰ০

He'd been waiting for the right moment to put his arm around her. When he did, she nestled against his shoulder and looked up at him. Close enough to kiss. Slowly, he bent his head toward hers.

"I hear we're in for a storm tomorrow," she whispered.

The sparkle in her eyes told him she knew full well what he'd been about to do. And he was pretty sure the distraction technique was more to lead him on than away. He'd gladly play that game, and he had just the strategy to make it a short round.

"Thunderstorms are usually instigated by several factors: sufficient moisture, usually at low levels near the surface; a vertical profile in the atmosphere that is unstable, meaning a parcel of air will continue to rise if given a push upward"— he gestured with his hand—"and a mechanism to give the air parcels a push, such as a cold or warm front. Simply stated, moisture, instability, and lift. When these three things come together within certain parameters, we can be pretty sure of a thunderstorm."

Her eyes stayed fixed on his, her bottom lip firmly clamped between her teeth. She wasn't going to cave in as easily as he'd thought.

"It is possible that thunderstorms can arise with just two of the three parameters. . .for example, when there is no surface front or other mechanism to lift the air, but there is great instability and plenty of moisture. If the air parcels rise"—he inched closer and lifted his hand to illustrate—"due to the instability and there is nothing to stop them, a shower or thunderstorm may—"

Her hand reached out and grabbed his in midair. "Okay. I surrender." Her head pressed into his shoulder. "Let's. . ." Her eyes closed. "Let's just. . .talk about tornadoes." Her eyes popped open, her lips spread into an amazing smile.

"O. . .kay. . ."

Her fingertip pressed against his lips, sending prickly sensations down his spine. "Specifically, when do we get to chase one?"

Seth laughed against her finger and then graced it with a featherlight kiss. She lowered her hand but rested it, palm up, on her knee. Saving his kiss? "You do realize, my dear, that there has to be a tornado in the vicinity in order to chase it."

An elbow boxed his right side. "And here I thought you'd create one just for me."

"I would if I could." Her deep blue eyes suddenly seemed a bit too deep, a little too inviting. Folding his legs under him, he turned sideways to face her. "June is the biggest month for tornadoes in Minnesota, so we should have an opportunity soon. I'll introduce you to Darren, the storm-chasing guru. Are you free Friday night?"

"Yes."

"Darren's coming over for pizza. How about if I ask him to bring his family, and we'll make it a five-and-a-half-some."

Her eyes narrowed. "Ah. One child and one on the way?"

He nodded. "Denisha is due in about a month. Wesley is four. . .going on fifty."

"Wesley. . .nice name. Thank goodness they didn't pick a *D* name."

"I tried to convince them to give him my middle name. Darren, Denisha, and Dalton—has a nice ring, don't you think?"

"Your middle name is Dalton?" Amusement danced in her.

"Yeah. . .I don't like it either. I was named for my dad's alma mater in Georgia."

"How. . .significant."

"Just laugh and get it over with."

She did.

"Okay, that's enough. You must be blessed with a very normal middle name."

Once again, she laughed. "It's Jean, and I hate it. It would be perfect if I'd wanted to be a country music star."

"April Jean will be singin' for us t'nite, folks," he twanged.

"Anyway, about the tornado guru. . ."

"Hey, that was a meaningful rabbit trail. We learned something about each other."

"If you ever say my name through your nose like that again, I'll use your middle name on the air the next time you call my show."

"Yes, ma'am." He loved how easily she made him laugh and lose track of what he was saying. "Friday night. . .Darren will cure your fear of tornadoes. There's nothing he loves more than showing spine-chilling videos of his close calls."

"And that will cure me?"

"You'll have chase fever before the end of the night. You'll be begging for the chance to see an F4 up close and personal."

"Right." She stretched her lips in a pretend smile.

He looked down at her hand, pressed against the blanket, and touched the silver ring on her index finger, sliding it back and forth. "I don't know if I've actually put it into words yet, but I admire your courage."

"I'm anything but courageous." She crossed her legs to mirror him, and they sat knee to knee.

"Do you know what Mark Twain said?"

"No. What did Mark Twain say?" Even in the engulfing darkness, he could see the gleam in her eyes.

"That 'Courage is not the absence of fear but resistance to the mastery of fear.' He said, 'Except a creature be part coward, it is not a compliment to say it is brave.'"

"Well then, I guess I qualify. I felt like the lion in *The Wizard of Oz* at the top of the water tower."

"But the point is. . .you were at the top of the water tower." Seth raised his right hand, sinking his fingers into her hair. He felt her take a tremulous breath. As he leaned toward her, he lifted her chin with his other hand. Millimeters from her lips, he whispered, "I think you're very brave."

Her eyes closed; her lips parted.

And Seth pointed. "Look, a meteor."

April's eyes jarred open and then followed the line of his arm to the white trail disappearing into the invisible horizon. She smiled, shook her head just the tiniest bit. "Can't you just call it a falling star?"

"But it really isn't a star at all." He matched her knowing smile. "The streak of light is caused by tiny bits of dust and rock falling into the atmosphere and burn—"

Her fingers sealed his lips, slowly pulled away. Her eyes closed again.

And he kissed her.

Chapter 13

Y ou're listening to Christian R&B on this super sunny Thursday afternoon in beautiful downtown Pine Bluff. This is April Douglas. We just heard a Glenn Kaiser song, 'In the Ocean of His Love,' a personal favorite of mine. Love those acoustic rhythms. Drowning in the ocean of His love... that's where we all need to be, isn't it?"

Words gushed like the St. Croix after a spring rain, in spite of a night full of daydreams in which sleep eluded her. April was in her zone, incredulous, as always, that someone was willing to pay her a salary, be it ever so meager, for doing what she loved. She looked up at Jill and grinned, getting the now familiar thumb in the air in response.

"We're taking a little break from routine in a minute. I'm going to give a little teaser of my show, *Slice of Life*, that's now airing live from three to five thirty every Saturday. I'll take as many calls as we can fit into a five-minute slot. Here's your assignment: In one word, describe how you're feeling today, positive or negative. No holds barred, just keep it family friendly. After that, give me a single sentence to explain why you chose that word. So break out the thesaurus, and let's see how creative we can get. I'll start taking your calls in forty seconds." She pushed the button that played a public service announcement for the local food bank.

Her monitor began filling with names before the break was over. She watched the clock, counting down to the green light, and leaned into her microphone. "You're listening to KPOG, praising our God in Minnesota. My screen is lit with Pine Bluffians ready to share the single word that best describes how they're feeling today. Shane, what's your word?"

"Grateful."

April gave an inward sigh. This was exactly what she'd been afraid of— and the reason she was keeping this experiment to five minutes. An hour of Christianese—*grateful, blessed, happy, thankful. . .*—would be more than she could handle. She'd been hoping for some more nitty-gritty words. "And why did you choose 'grateful,' Shane?"

"Because today is my eighteenth birthday, and thanks to some really forgiving people, I'm having pizza with my youth group tonight instead of celebrating all alone in a jail cell."

Okay, so she'd been wrong. Goose bumps dotted her arms. "Our God is awesome, isn't He?" She swallowed, clearing the roughness the unexpected emotion had brought. "Happy Birthday, Shane. I hope your day is incredible. If you'd be willing to share your story sometime, leave your number with Orlando."

She scanned the list, not the least bit surprised to see Seth in the queue. Was this going to be a regular occurrence? She smiled at her reflection on the monitor. Her listeners would start suspecting something if she took his calls every week. "Melissa, what's your word?"

"Harebrained."

So it wasn't going to be a predictable few minutes after all. "Can't wait to hear your reason, Melissa."

"I've been searching high and low for my dish detergent. My son just found it—right behind the catsup in the fridge."

Five more calls produced five more surprises. Apparently her listeners had taken the thesaurus suggestion seriously. *Magnanimous, exasperated, worshipful, goofy,* and *whimsical.* . .she really could fill an hour like this.

"Now, on to our final caller. Seth, what one word describes you today?" She closed her eyes.

"Breathless. Because I saw a falling star last night and haven't been able to catch my breath ever since."

ॐ

"You did what?" Her mother's voice, high and shrill, made the hair on the back of April's neck bristle.

April scrunched her face at Splash and Willy and turned the volume down on her phone. "You heard me, Mom. I went for a motorcycle ride with Seth."

"But. . ."

"He never got married. They took the picture before the wedding and then called it off."

"And you believe that?"

April rubbed a tight spot on her shoulder. "Yes."

"Baby. . ." It was a term her mother used like a weapon. "I don't have a good feeling about this. Take it from somebody who's been kicked around. . .this man is only going to use you."

"You don't know the first thing about him! All you know is that he's a man. There are good men out there, Mom."

A low huff came through the earpiece. "This is moving way too fast."

"What is? We went out a couple times and watched the sunrise together." *And kissed.* She picked up Snow Bear and twirled between the coffee table and the kitchen counter. This wasn't news her mother was going to hear.

Silence filled the next few seconds. She heard a slow exhale on the other end.

"Why did they call off the wedding?"

"It wasn't his fault, if that's what you mean. Let's talk about something else, okay? Midge said she's hoping you'll join her and Laura and Sue for lunch one of these days."

"Those church ladies don't want to hang out with me. They're just doing their Christian duty. I can't stomach pity."

April stared at Willy and Splash, stuck in their eternal battle-ready positions, and swallowed back the acerbic remarks that burned her throat. Never in her life had she met anyone as adept at eliciting pity as her mother. "I thought you liked Sue and Laura. If you give them a chance, I'm sure—"

A hollow sigh echoed through the phone. "Don't try to distract me, April. Believe me, I understand that you want a man in your life, but you can't just jump at the first guy who talks sweet to you."

"A gentle answer turns away wrath." "Do not repay anyone evil for evil." "If it is possible, as far as it depends on you, live at peace with everyone." She repeated every peacekeeping verse she knew, but her blood still pounded in her temples. *Lord, I don't think it's possible to live at peace with her.* "He's not a sweet-talker. He's just a nice, genuine guy."

"Sure he is. A nice, genuine guy who left your sister in the rain to get chilled to the bone and—"

"It didn't happen like that." April set Snow Bear on the couch and slumped down beside him. She massaged the spot between her eyes that throbbed with every breath. She'd decided not to bring it up, ever, but living at peace didn't always mean biting your tongue. She took a deep breath. "Why did you sign the permission slip for her to go with the storm chasers?"

Silence. A muffled gasp. "I never. . ."

"They won't take minors storm tracking without parental permission."

"But I. . .I don't remember. There were so many papers, insurance forms, medical reports. I don't. . .remember." A soft sob ended her words.

And guilt ended April's internal rage. Deep down, she hurt for her mother. Like simmering magma, that pain was at the center of her very being, sometimes erupting in sympathy, other times in avoidance. She understood pain; she understood betrayal and bitterness. What she couldn't accept was wallowing in it and sucking everyone else in with you.

"I'm sorry. I shouldn't have brought that up."

"So it was my fault." A chilling deadness shrouded her mother's voice.

"No. You gave Caitlyn a gift, just like Seth and his friend did. That was the best day she'd had in a long time."

"But it killed her."

"No, Mom. Leukemia killed her. It would have anyway; you know that."

Another long, quiet stretch spanned the seconds. April chose not to fill it, hoping her words would sink in.

"Thank you." The words were so soft that April wasn't sure she'd heard them.

"I love you, Mom." Not easy to say but true nonetheless.

"I. . .love you, too."

Friday night came almost too quickly. Anticipation and anxiety vied for center stage as April's maroon Grand Prix rolled to a stop in front of Seth's house. It wasn't at all what she'd expected.

She'd pictured him in one of the newer, more secluded homes on the bluff. A home built for efficiency, with clean lines, neutral colors, and minimalist decorating. That would fit him. Instead, she found herself on Minnetonka Street, just three blocks off Main, in front of a small, two-story symmetrical white house with black shutters, probably built in the thirties. Dormer windows jutted heavenward like raised eyebrows, giving the house a welcoming, smiley face appeal. Two brass lights on either side of the door added dimples to the face—just like its owner's.

Seth Bachelor, you are a man of surprises. Grabbing her purse and the pan of brownies she'd baked before work, she got out of the car. As she walked up the steps from the sidewalk to the walkway that led to the house, she assessed her look. Brown wedge sandals peeked out from the hem of her jeans. She'd painted her toenails the exact shade of the two inches of coral tank top that showed beneath a brown T-shirt. She'd used hot rollers to add a bit more curl than usual and wore small turquoise and sterling earrings and a matching necklace. *Not too shabby.* It felt good to feel good. For months, she hadn't really cared.

April stepped between the two sculpted evergreens, twice as tall as she was, that guarded the front door and rang the doorbell. Before the second chime, Seth opened the door. April held out the nine-by-thirteen-inch pan covered in aluminum foil. It gave her something to do in the first awkward seconds when she wondered if he'd kiss her.

He did. Leaning over the pan, his lips touched hers for only a moment, but his eyes loitered. "Wow." He stood back, giving her room to walk past him. "You look amazing."

"Thank you." She wasn't usually the blushing kind, but the capillaries under her skin couldn't seem to stay constricted under the heat of his gaze. Was it proper to tell a man that he also looked—and smelled—amazing? He wore flip-flops, jeans, and a formfitting black Harley T-shirt that appeared to have seen a lot of motorcycle rides. The shoulders were slightly sun-faded, the seams frayed, stirring thoughts of riding behind him without a helmet, hair dancing in the wind, her face resting against the worn-thin shirt. Which would bring her closer to the source of the musky aftershave and the dark stubble shadowing his square jaw line. "Should I put this in the kitchen?"

"Sure. I'll give you part of the tour on the way." He led her through an arched doorway into the living room. White walls, hardwood floors, black couch and loveseat with huge red accent pillows. Above an arched brick fireplace, also painted white, hung a framed black-and-white photograph of a seemingly endless flight of shadowy stone steps, lit by old gaslight streetlamps. In front of the fireplace, a shaggy white rug begged for bare feet.

"Wow." It was her turn to use the word.

Another arched doorway led to the dining room. The walls were bare, the round black table held a square white plate with a cluster of blue and white baseball-sized glass balls. Dishes in the same color, but a different pattern, lined the shelves of a black oriental-inspired china cabinet.

Seth swept his hand toward the doorway to the kitchen. If April's mouth had closed since she'd entered the living room, it would have dropped open again now.

Cupboards, countertop, appliances, and tiled floor, all hospital white, created a blank canvas for vibrant splashes of cobalt blue and lime green. An oversize handblown glass bowl in swirls of blue and white took up the middle of the table in a white-painted breakfast nook. A smaller bowl of the same color, filled with oranges, was the only object on the ceramic counter. Valances, striped blue and new-leaf green, hung over the nine-pane windows. Small pots of wheatgrass graced the sill above the sink.

She'd gotten the minimalist part right. The color was unexpected. And then a question mark poked its tail into her amazement. Had *she* done the decorating? Was this the touch of the almost-Mrs. Bachelor?

"Who did your decorating?" Her voice strained around the lump in her throat. Maybe he wouldn't notice.

Seth smiled. A smile that said he'd heard the question behind her question. He took the pan from her hands and set it on the counter, leaving nothing but air between them. His hands rested on her arms. "I did. Just me, all by myself. Alone. For me alone."

There was nothing she could do but laugh. "I'm really not that insecure." *Usually.*

"Remember what I said on the bluff?" His fingertips found the bottom of her chin. "A little insecurity is just as flattering as righteous wrath."

"I'll try to rememb—" Her words got lost in his lips.

His arms wrapped around her. Her hands reached up to his shoulders.

And the doorbell rang.

Chapter 14

I t's a college thing."

Denisha Williams rolled huge brown eyes toward the kitchen ceiling as Seth and Darren finished an elaborate and ridiculous high-five, low-five, under-duck-and-twirl handshake routine.

April shook her head. "Are they always this nuts together?"

"Always."

The two men contrasted like photograph negatives. Seth, in his black shirt with his arms barely tanned—Darren, his skin the color of strong coffee, wearing a white Harley shirt.

Leaning toward Denisha, April whispered, "I missed the memo about wearing Harley shirts."

Denisha's shoulder-length black curls swayed when she laughed. She rested both hands on the red blouse stretched over her extended belly. "It's eerie how often they dress alike. I'm convinced they're twins separated at birth." Her dark eyes sparkled as she laughed.

Light, running footsteps and a tumult of claws echoed from the hardwood floor in the living room. "Se. . .th." Wesley bounded into the kitchen, followed by Maynard, the grizzly bear Seth tried passing off as a dog. Both skidded to a stop in front of Seth.

"Make me fly, Se*th*."

"He's working on his *t-h* sounds," Denisha whispered.

Seth ruffled Wesley's thick black curls and picked him up by the back of his coveralls. "This plane's gonna be too heavy to get off the ground pretty soon."

Wesley made airplane sounds as Seth flew him around the dining room table twice and back into the kitchen.

"I think the men should make a quick trip upstairs to see my new telescope until the good little women call us for pizza. Right, Wes?" Seth winked in April's direction.

Darren planted a kiss on top of Denisha's head. "We'll do dishes."

As the men walked out of the kitchen, Denisha squeezed April's arm. "I'm glad we're getting a little girl time." She pointed toward the breakfast nook. "I gotta get off my feet." The bench creaked as she sat down, with no room to spare between her stomach and the table. "It's so good to finally meet you. I suppose it's cliché to say I've heard so much about you, but it's true." She leaned her forearms on the table. "I'm so sorry about your sister. Darren was devastated when he heard about it."

Angel held up her hand. "Seth and your husband blessed her with a wonderful day."

"Thank you. That's very gracious."

"So what have you heard about me?"

"It's all good." Denisha glanced toward the stove. "Okay, the oven timer's going off in seven minutes, so I'm just gonna plunge right in. Are things getting serious between you two?"

April blinked. She hadn't expected an interrogation.

A ladylike snort answered April's awkward silence. "I can see it on your face." She folded her hands. "Seth is special to me. He dragged my husband back to the Lord a few years ago and saved our marriage. So I'm pretty protective of him. You know he's been hurt in the past, and all I'm asking is that you promise me you'll be honest with him—about everything."

It wasn't something she needed to think about. April rested her fingertips on Denisha's bangle bracelet. "You have my word on that."

⨯

Wesley stood at eye level to the kitchen counter. "Can we watch tornado movies and eat in Man Room?"

April looked from Wesley to Denisha. "Man Room?"

"You'll see. If we're very, very good they'll take down the No Girls Allowed sign." Denisha handed a pizza pan to Darren and one to Seth and picked up a bowl of potato chips. "May we enter the inner sanctum?"

As if they'd practiced their routine, the men bowed simultaneously, ushering the way into the den with the hands that held the pizzas.

"You're right, it's eerie." April picked up paper plates and napkins and nodded to Denisha. "I'll follow you."

The hush in the dimly lit room was the first thing she noticed. As her eyes adjusted to the low light, she understood. Sound-absorbing plush black carpeting covered the floor, three walls, and the ceiling. Massive speakers and a flatscreen TV took up the fourth wall. Six recliners formed a curved row in front of a glass-topped coffee table that appeared to be at least five feet long.

Seth set the pizza on the table and opened a small black refrigerator. "Everybody help yourself to soda or water." He walked over to April. His fingers rested on hers before he took the plates from her. "Welcome to Man Room."

"It's an honor to be allowed in."

"Sit there." He pointed to the second recliner from the left end. "I'll hold your hand during the scary parts."

"The scary parts are the coolest!" Wesley grabbed Seth's forearm and hung like a little monkey. Turning to April, he said, "I chaseded a tornado today."

"You did?"

Seth raised his eyebrow and shook his head, and April bent down to Wesley's eye level. "What did it look like?"

"It was huuuuge and black, and it chomped houses like a T. rex, and I went right up next to it, and I wasn't scared even a bit."

"Well, maybe you can teach me to not be scared of tornadoes."

"Nah. I don't think so. 'Cause you're a girl like Mom and girls are s'posed to be scared of T. rexes and tornadoes. But when you watch my dad's movies, you just gotta keep saying 'It's only a movie. It's only a movie.' 'Cause even though it used to be real, it's not like it's outside right now. 'Kay?"

ℭℴ

"It's only a movie. It's only a movie." Seth whispered so close to her ear that his lips felt the cool smoothness of her silver and turquoise earrings. She'd been like a coiled spring for the past half hour.

Her eyes were riveted to the jostling footage that had been filmed through the windshield of Darren's van. A gray funnel swirled out of a black cloud and split into twin sisters. On the ground, lights flashed as the tornadoes flattened power lines and transformers. Darren's voice on the video shouted over the locomotive roar in the background. "I'm guessing wind speeds upwards of two hundred. An F3 for sure, maybe a 4. This storm is violent. Look at the action on either side. It's gonna do some damage if it doesn't change course. There's a subdivision just east of here. Let's hope the local weather guys got it right this time and gave them plenty of warning."

Seth tossed a crumpled napkin over April and Denisha, hitting Darren square on the head.

"Nothing personal, man." Darren's laugh said otherwise.

The scene changed to a different storm. This time, the sky was gunmetal gray, the supercell storm cloud white against the darkness. A shaft of lightning shot out of the cloud. Seth leaned forward, his pulse double-timing. This was footage he'd never seen. "Should be a funnel forming any minute," he said under his breath. Seconds later, a white snake dropped out of the cloud, sucking up trees like a vacuum hose. A barn, directly in its path, suddenly exploded. April jumped. Boards shot up into the cloud.

"Big tornado on the ground! I'm setting up the tripod!" Darren's voice yelled above the noise.

"Multivortex!" a second voice shouted. "You gettin' this on tape, Darren?"

"I got it. How many? I see three satellites."

"Four. One's pulling away. It's heading straight for us. Get in the car! Get in the car!"

The picture bounced. . .voices clamored. . .a shot of the inside of the car door. . .doors slammed. The car did a U-turn, and the camera panned to the rear window. "We can't outrun it! Let's try for the overpass!" A white funnel bore down on the speeding car. . .and the image froze on the screen.

Darren held a remote control in each hand. With his left hand, he slowly turned up the rheostat for the overhead LED track lights. "Thought April might need a break."

Wesley clapped.

April collapsed against the back of her seat. "You can't stop it there! What happened?"

"We made it to the overpass, which isn't really the smartest thing to do. I managed to loop one of the straps on my backpack over a piece of rebar. The guy who was driving wasn't so lucky. He got sucked out and got hit with a chunk of debris. Had to have a dozen stitches."

"Awesome." Seth didn't even realize what he'd said until he caught April's eyes drilling into him. "I mean. . .sure glad he wasn't hurt worse."

Denisha patted April's hand. "You'll get used to it."

The look on April's face clearly said she wasn't sure she wanted to get used to it.

Darren threw the wadded napkin back at Seth. "She won't need to get used to it unless Weather Guy leaves the station in somebody else's hands and starts doing what he really wants to do."

Seth felt his jaw tighten involuntarily. "Drop it."

"I haven't brought it up for months." Darren leaned around the women and pointed a remote at him. "I could still line up back-to-back tours all the way through July." He shifted his position to include April in his pleading gaze. "What we'd do is set up week-long tours for people. We'd take a caravan of three or four vehicles up and down Tornado Alley, from North Dakota to the Rio Grande. And this is an awesome year for storms, perfect for launching our business." His voice lowered as his hand came to rest on Denisha's belly. "But I can't be gone that long this season. I need a partner."

"I'm sure you can find one." Seth's body language was as tense as his voice.

"I want you. Get yourself a decent manager so the station can get along without you for a week at a time. You'd be reachable 24/7. And your puny little town doesn't need a live weather forecast. Give them daily feed from the National Weather Service. They'll get over missing your handsome face."

"Not interested."

"Liar."

"Give it up, Darren. You're boring the ladies."

Darren locked brown eyes on April. "I've heard your radio show. That dream list your sister made. . .you're all about living life to the fullest, right? Don't you think that if people can afford it they should spend their lives doing what they love to do? Can't you talk some sense into this guy?"

"What does—"

"I *can't* afford it." Tension knotted Seth's gut. This wasn't a conversation he wanted to have again, especially not in front of April.

"You could if you'd quit pay—"

"I said, drop it!"

❧

Sandals and empty cake pan in one hand, a list of storm-watcher gear in the other, April padded up the stairs, avoiding the two steps that creaked the loudest. Laughter and music drifted down to meet her. Good. Yvonne had company. She wouldn't have to worry about being chatty tonight. What she needed was a hot bath and a good book. Definitely not a romance novel.

A third sound joined in as she reached the top step. A vacuum cleaner. Strange thing to be doing when you have visitors.

But the sounds weren't coming from Yvonne's apartment. They were coming from hers. Cautiously, she opened the door.

"Ahh!" Midge jumped, eyes popping like a Pekinese, and shut off the vacuum cleaner. "I didn't think you'd be home so early."

Yvonne, standing on the couch, waved at her with a feather duster, sending dust bits raining onto Snow Bear. "How was dinner?"

"What are you two doing?"

"Cleaning." They answered in unison.

"I see that. Why?" It wasn't like she kept the place a mess.

Midge plopped down in the rocker. "I'm keeping my promise. You went out with Seth, so I'm cleaning your apartment."

"And I'm trying to make up for not telling you the truth about him taking you to *Riverdance*." Yvonne hopped down. "Even though it all worked out for the best."

Maybe.

"So. . .do you like Seth's friends?" Midge asked at the same time Yvonne said, "Do you want to chase a tornado?"

I want to take a bath. She dropped her shoes at the door and took the cake pan into the kitchen. Leaning heavily on the counter that divided the two rooms, she gave a halfhearted smile. "You didn't have to do this, but thank you. The place hasn't been this clean in forever."

Midge whisked away her thanks. "You're welcome, but you're not answering the questions."

"Dinner was good, the people are nice, and I kind of get the storm-chasing adventure thing."

"But. . . ?" Yvonne sat down next to Snow Bear.

"But what?"

"Something didn't go right. I can tell."

Unfastening her necklace, April walked around the counter and sank into the other end of the couch. "I think I finally figured it out. I just don't get men." She picked a fleck of lint off Snow Bear's ear. "Think about it. . .how could I? No brothers, no grandfathers or uncles, a father who was more out of my life than in it. Guys are. . .they're not like us."

Her audience of two erupted in laughter. Midge, who'd been—at least outwardly—happily married for twenty-five years, was the first to regain her composure. "No truer words were ever spoken."

April tucked her feet beneath her. "Tonight—we're in the middle of watching storm footage—when Seth and his friend Darren get into this argument. Not a quiet one. I was ready to get out of there when I looked over at Darren's wife. She's just sitting there munching on chips. Like she's watching a basketball game. But she knows these guys, so I stayed and watched; pretty soon their voices lowered, and in a couple minutes, they're talking about a sci-fi movie that's coming out next week. No 'I'm sorry.' It was like they both said what they had to say, and then it was over."

"Men are a lot like tornadoes."

"Midge! Did you just say something critical?"

Midge's shoulders rose to her ears. "God made tornadoes, too."

Yvonne nodded. "I've seen Kirk do that with his brothers a million times."

"It just scares me, knowing he's capable of yelling like that. When's he going to turn it on me?"

The rocking chair groaned as Midge bent forward, resting her hand on April's knee. "Probably never. I know I've said it before, but don't make the mistake of putting your father's sins on every man you meet."

"I know. But why can't they just be more like us? Quieter and—"

"Cattier?"

"Midge! What's gotten into you?"

"Just speaking the truth. I think I'd rather take my chances with a man who lays it all out on the table than some of the women I've met who quietly stab you in the back."

"Me, too." Yvonne stood then stuck her hands in the pocket of her cardigan. "Oh, here—somebody called for you about an hour ago. She said it didn't matter how late you called her back."

April looked down at the scrap of paper. And a chill skittered down her back.

555-784-0938
Brenda Cadwell

Chapter 15

Water thundered over the stair-step rocks. The spray above Middle Gooseberry Falls split sunlight into a halo of color. Sitting next to Seth on a hardened lava flow below the falls, April skimmed her bare heels along the surface of the icy water then pulled her feet back to the sun-warmed rock.

"You're doing that like a girl." With both feet submerged, Seth talked through gritted teeth, "Just stick 'em in all at once." He gestured toward Yvonne's fiancé, Kirk, sitting beside him, feet also under water.

"And look as miserable as you two do just to prove I'm tough? No thanks."

Yvonne shook her platinum curls. "You guys have more pride in your little toes than we have in our whole bodies."

With a painful gasp, Kirk yanked his feet out of the water. A split second later, Seth copied his move. Both men writhed, accompanied by female laughter. Kirk reached out for Yvonne's hand. "I concede. You're a better man than I am, Seth. Come on, woman, help me walk some circulation into my legs."

As Seth lay back on his elbows, a look of triumph mixed with pain on his face, April rested her bare feet on his.

"Ah. . .heat. Thank you." He lifted his sunglasses. In the bright light, his eyes took on a bronze tinge.

The warmth soaking through the back of her North Face polo was now met by the heat sparked by those bronze eyes. Suddenly her feet on his seemed way too intimate. She shifted and copied his posture, resting back on her elbows. Nearer than she'd calculated. Not touching but close enough to smell that musky, earthy aftershave.

A herring gull scudded to a stop several yards away, lifted its head, and called into the air. Seth's little toe touched hers. "Perfect day," he whispered.

"Mm-hm."

It seemed the ideal setting to tell him the news that had been percolating in her head since Friday night. The news that had stolen her sleep and filled half a notebook with heady, adrenaline-driven ideas.

"You won't believe who called me the other night."

Seth rolled his fleece jacket into a ball and used it for a pillow, stretching out on the flat rock. "Who?" His voice sounded sleepy.

"Brenda."

Bolting to a sitting position, he whipped off his sunglasses. "Brenda. . .who?"

Your Brenda. No, he wouldn't find that amusing. "Brenda Cadwell."

"She called you? Why?" Suspicion dripped from his words.

April grinned. "To offer me a job."

&0

How could five little words turn a perfect day into a nightmare? He'd been lying there, more relaxed than he'd felt in months, stringing words together in his head—words that would describe his growing feelings for the woman with the honey-blond hair who was so close to him he could smell the spicy, touch-of-vanilla scent of her.

And then she'd smacked him with a name that he was within weeks of never having to hear again.

She was effervescing before his eyes. Glowing like Sirius on a clear night. Her warm, lush radio voice painted the vision as detailed as an oil painting. A prime-time spot on a cable station three hours from Pine Bluff. She couldn't tell him what station, what town. The details were all being worked out. Her own talk show. Huh. . .where had Brenda gotten *that* idea? A Christian show on a secular station. What were the chances? April asked.

Behind his back, Seth's fist clenched on the green-tinged rock. *Slim to none.* Whatever Brenda Cadwell had up her sleeve, it wasn't good.

"It'll be an hour-long show, five days a week, to start with." April's fingers knit her hands into a ball. "And I get to pick the guests. Pretty much carte blanche, it sounds like."

"Hm. Where'd she get the idea for the format?"

Confusion wrinkled her forehead. He wanted to kiss it away, wanted to kiss away the last five minutes.

"She got the idea from you."

She certainly did. "She told you that?"

"Yes. She said you told her that I'd always dreamed of being a television talk show host. To be honest, it made me mad at first. I shared that with you in confidence."

Seth opened his mouth to defend himself, but she held up her hand.

"But then I realized that you'd told her about it because she's got the right connections. She's somebody who could make my dream come true."

Her eyes held his for a long moment. "I know the distance is an issue, but I'd be back here every weekend."

"When would you start?" His voice was as flat as his mood.

"In two weeks."

"Kind of soon."

"Well, it wouldn't air for another six weeks or so. I'd start out just lining up guests and working on promotion."

"And they'd pay you for that part?"

Her hands separated. She rubbed her palms on her knees. "I. . .assume so."

"What's your starting salary?"

"She couldn't say yet, just promised I'd have no complaints."

Promised. Brenda's promise. . . .now there was an oxymoron if he'd ever heard one. "When is your interview scheduled?"

She recoiled, just a fraction of an inch. "That was. . .my interview. . .on the phone."

"Oh. Don't you need to talk to a manager?"

"Brenda is. . .in charge of hiring."

"She is, huh?"

❧

Yvonne walked over and pointed at her watch. "Time to move on."

April nodded. Keeping the group on schedule was supposed to be her job. She picked up a sock, grateful for a reprieve from Seth's cross-examination. What was wrong with the man? Of course, she wanted him to express some sadness, but he seemed far more angry than sad. He knew how much this meant to her, didn't he? His barrage of questions was insulting. Didn't he know her well enough to know that she'd check it out carefully before accepting? The KOEK Web site said they were actively working to expand their programming and give the station a fresh, new image. She was going to be part of that new image.

Turning away from him, she used her purple bandana to dry between her toes and then slipped on her white liner socks. She yanked at the shoestrings of her dusty gray Raichle boots. Too tight. After tying them right, she stuffed her jacket in her day pack. As she zipped the pocket shut, Seth's hand jutted into the space between her and her walking stick. He blocked the sun, but the look on his face would suffice for sunlight. "Let's enjoy the day, okay?"

"Okay." Like a trained puppy, she held her hand out to him. It was becoming easier and easier to let his offenses slide. Was that a good or a bad thing? With her hand in his, she couldn't decide.

The seven of them scrambled across slippery rocks, climbed the outcroppings above the falls, and ended back on the shaded trail. April took the lead, with Seth right behind her, singing "Happy Trails." He'd rallied, but his mood still wasn't where it had been before she'd brought up the job offer. A few weeks ago, her response to his negativity would have been a cold shoulder, but she was learning to put a leash on her emotions, to let things play out. The more it sank in that the males of the species processed conflict in a whole different way, the more she was willing to think before she acted. And little by little, she was beginning to accept that not all—probably not most—men had hair triggers like her father.

So what part of her news had set him off? The mention of Brenda's name? After three years, was the hurt still that fresh? Or was it that he still had feelings for her? They'd been a day away from the altar, after all.

The thoughts got shoved aside as she picked her way across a shallow spot in the Gooseberry, jabbing the end of her pole into the river-smoothed pebbles. Seth had switched to "The Happy Wanderer," and the rest of the group joined in. Yvonne's clear, sweet soprano carried the melody. April added her so-so voice to the mix—"Val-deri, Val-dera"—glad there was no one in front of her to offend. It kept her mind off Seth's strange behavior until the last line. "*Oh, may I always laugh and sing*". . . . Something about it hit her strangely. Maybe it was the word "always." Had she made it clear enough to Seth that she had no intention of letting this job interfere with their relationship, that her weekends would belong to him?

If it wouldn't cause a seven-hiker pileup, she'd stop right there in the middle of the trail and wrap her arms around him, whispering things for his ears only. *This won't change what's starting between us. If it's God's will, we'll make it work. We'll find time to be together. I promise I won't put my career ahead of you.*

She stumbled on a tree root, caught her balance again. Was that true? If he asked her not to take the job, to stay at KPOG forever just to be close to him, would she? Should she?

A rustling sound up ahead stopped her. She held her hand over her head and heard footsteps halt. Two whitetail deer stepped into the path, looked at her, then went back to the thick grass on the side of the trail. Stealthily, Seth's arms wrapped around her from behind. His warm breath tickled her ear.

"I'm sorry. I'm really happy for you." His lips grazed her cheek. "It'll all work out."

&

Did he really believe any of what he'd just said? Seth's eyes tracked the doe and her yearling, but his mind was on the wisps of sun-kissed hair tickling his cheek. The paradox between the setting and his emotions spun his world off kilter. The rush of water over rocks in the distance, the dappled pattern created by sunlight filtering through the leaves, the smell of her hair, the camaraderie of a day with other believers. . .all clashed now with the havoc in his mind.

What was Brenda up to? He was so close to breaking all ties with her. Was this her parting shot? She wasn't happy, so she'd see to it that he wasn't either?

Behind him, Yvonne sneezed. The doe startled and skittered into the trees, her little one right behind her, taking with them his excuse for standing in the middle of the trail with his arms draped around the woman with golden hair. As they followed the trail east toward the lake, Seth went back to his brooding. Trying to make sense of Brenda Cadwell wasn't the best use of his brainpower, but he couldn't let it go. If he could figure out her motive, he'd know what to do. There was no way he was going to sit by idly and watch April get hurt.

He examined the possibilities as they came to him. Brenda had done some consulting work for television and radio stations over the years—"vision creating," as she called it. So maybe that's what this was. Maybe.

One thing he was certain of—she wasn't doing it altruistically to advance the career of the new love interest of the guy who dumped her at the altar. But she could be opening doors for April in hopes that other doors would slam in Seth's face.

It boiled down to two theories: She was either doing it to advance her own career. . .or to hurt him. And yet, it might still be the best thing for April. Until he knew more, he'd be the encourager she needed him to be.

∞

"I'm. . .happy for you."

April stared at Jill's pitiful attempt at a smile. Would everyone she told say those same words with equal fakeness? When she'd given her notice for the apartment, Sydney's enthusiasm had been just as artificial as Jill's. Yvonne, thankfully, hadn't even pretended to be happy for her. "Thank you."

"Your listeners will miss you. I'll miss you." Jill's usually perfect posture rounded to the curve of her chair. "You're building up quite a fan base in this little town, you know. People feel like you connect with them—and connect them to each other." Her red-nailed hand pressed against her black blouse. "You get to the heart, April."

Tears constricted April's throat. "Is this just you being weirdly emotional, or is this you doing your guilt-tripping manager job?"

"Both. I know I've always said I wanted to see you living up to your potential. Selfishly, I just hoped it would be right here. Have you prayed about this, long and hard?"

"Yes." The ghost of a doubt floated through her consciousness, but she shooed it away. She had spent much of the past week thanking God for opening this door and asking Him to help her put together a show that would honor Him and touch lives. She'd prayed her way through her tour of KOEK, through every word in the contract before she'd signed it. And yet, second thoughts had hovered for days. But that was normal. Anyone making changes this big would have a few doubts.

"Well then, I guess, like Scuffy the tugboat, you were meant for bigger things, and the rest of us will just have to live without you." Jill pulled a tissue from a carved black dispenser and blew her nose. "I'll get to work finding someone to fill your slot. I'm not going to say replacement, because I don't think we'll find anyone to do that."

∞

"Oh, baby, I'm so happy for you."

April pulled the phone away and stared at it before resting it back on her ear. Finally, a voice that actually matched the words. But from the strangest source. She closed her office door. "Thanks, Mom."

"It's what you've always wanted. My little girl, a TV talk show host! Wait till I tell my friends."

Friends? Was the woman whose words were bouncing off a satellite and into her office really her mother? "It's just a cable station. Not national syndication."

"But it's a start. And you'll have your weekends free so you can spend some time with me."

More guilt. April stared at the Itasca State Park wallpaper beneath the icons on her desktop. She didn't even remember telling her mother what her new hours would be. "Sure. . .some of the time. I'll be coming back here a lot."

Silence. A tight-sounding inhale. "It's a long drive from wher. . .ever you're going."

"I know." Only too well. Three hours hadn't seemed like much until she'd told Seth about the job offer. Six hours of driving every week. Would that get old? Would he get tired of only seeing her on weekends? Would she?

"Don't expect that man to wait around for you while you figure out your life." A tired sigh. "They never do."

Chapter 16

The new girl, the one Jill refused to call "April's replacement," was catching on faster than April would have thought. Chrissy Leibner was fresh out of school and as bouncy as Tigger. But her three-toned blond hair and fast, breathy words gave the wrong impression. After four days with her, April was astonished by her emotional and spiritual maturity. Jill had chosen well.

And it bugged April.

"Good job, Chrissy."

The Thursday afternoon spot, Chrissy's first solo on-air shift, had just finished. Her transitions had been smooth and witty.

"It's really an honor to work with you, April." Chrissy set her headphones on the desk." I looked up KPOG on the Internet. People love your show." Her pert little nose wrinkled. "That's not all they're talking about."

"I don't have time to read blogs. Do I want to know what people are saying?"

"They're talking about a guy who keeps calling your show and whether or not he's the Channel Five weatherman. Some people think there's a thing between you two. Is there?"

"Is that what they think?" April stood, hugging her laptop to her chest. "Let's call it a day."

❧

Brenda was eight minutes late.

April did a mini–drum solo on the tablecloth as she memorized the Sage Stoppe's menu. *Whole grilled lemon sole with lemongrass butter, roast cod with spring onion mash and soy butter sauce, rib eye steak with béarnaise sauce, and thin cut—*

"You must be April."

Dark eyes, olive skin, and thick, shampoo-commercial mahogany hair. The almost-wedding picture had not done Brenda Cadwell justice. April took the bangle-crowned hand and shook it, wondering as she did how the woman's fingers could be icy with the outside temperature nudging ninety.

"Thank you for taking the time, Brenda."

"My pleasure. It's so much easier to ask questions in person, isn't it?"

April nodded, suddenly wondering which one of them would be asking the questions. She'd been trying for a week to set up a meeting with Brenda and KOEK's station manager, who'd been out of town when she'd toured the station. When Brenda finally returned one of her many calls, she'd said it would work best for her to meet in Pine Bluff on Friday. She had some "business near there." The manager, apparently, was an extremely busy man.

April smiled, covering her irritation. "How was the drive?"

"Oh, you know how it is. Well, maybe you don't, living up here where there isn't any traffic."

"I went to school and worked in the Cities."

"You did, didn't you?" Brenda picked up the menu. "What's good here?"

"The fish chowder is to die for."

"Sounds heavy. I'll have a salad."

Their waitress, in a white apron and traditional Cornish bonnet, approached them and took Brenda's order first.

"I'll have the spinach salad with grilled chicken instead of the bacon. No croutons. Dressing on the side. And a glass of Perrier." She pushed her water goblet to the edge of the table.

"There will be an extra charge for the chicken."

Brenda's fingers fluttered. "Of course."

The young waitress nodded and smiled as she scribbled. "And how about you, Miss Douglas? Sorry we don't have chocolate fondue." She winked. "I heard you guys were getting serious," she whispered.

"My life is a fishbowl, Sherry." April winked back. "So the chowder would be fitting."

"Cup or bowl?"

"Make it a bowl. And can we have a bread basket with extra butter?"

Sherry headed for the kitchen, and April opened her notebook. Her lips parted, but Brenda spoke first.

"I bet you haven't been able to sleep a wink or talk about anything but your new show."

"I've got pages of ideas and questions. Some of them can probably only be answered by the people I'll be directly working with."

Brenda's thumbnail creased the crisply pressed fold of the cloth napkin next to her plate. "Mr. Palmer will be back next week. He took his daughter on a graduation trip to Italy."

"Seems strange that he'd hire somebody he hadn't met." There, she'd verbalized the loudest question in her head.

A corner of the cloth napkin bent under Brenda's finger. The long nail creased it, again and again. "He trusts me. So. . .is Seth excited about your new opportunity?"

I wouldn't exactly call it excitement. "Of course. He's even come up with some suggestions."

Brenda took a long draught of the lemon water she'd pushed aside earlier. "Knowing Seth, I imagine his vision is probably a little more 'out there' than what you'll be doing." She laughed and dabbed her lips with her napkin.

"What do you mean?" April rubbed her right thumb against her left.

"If Seth were to design a show for you, I don't think you'd have the kind of freedom you need, April."

"What do you think he'd do to squelch my 'freedom'?"

"He'd insist that your guests all be Christians whose stories have happy endings. As you and I know, that kind of format would turn away a lot of potential viewers."

April leaned forward on her elbows. "When we spoke on the phone. . . you. . ." She let the sentence trail off when she realized that Brenda's wide brown eyes were fixed on something other than her.

"Seth!" Though their tones were as different as night and day, both women spoke in tandem. "What are you doing here?"

℘

If protecting April meant making her mad, so be it. If protecting April meant making Brenda mad. . .he smiled extra-wide as he shook her cold fingers and pulled out the chair next to April. On the way to the restaurant, he'd thought back to the Sunday school lesson on the twelfth chapter of Romans he'd facilitated back in May—*Do not repay anyone evil for evil. Be careful to do what is right in the eyes of everybody.*

Lord, change my heart.

It was tempting to pretend he wasn't there for what both women knew he was. But that would have fallen short of doing what was right in the eyes of everybody. "I have a few questions about April's new job."

He'd known ahead of time that April's reaction could have gone either way, so he was disappointed, but not surprised, when her lips curved up but her eyes held no sparkle. He'd seen that look before. Brenda, wearing the smile he'd seen her practice in the vanity mirror in his car, turned to April. "Are you comfortable with him being here?"

"Of course."

She could have just said yes. She could have hesitated. "Of course" was a good sign. The waitress approached and asked in a giggly voice if he was ready to order. He asked for coffee and said he'd just order dessert when the women did, knowing full well that in Brenda's mind sugar was lumped in with the seven deadly sins.

April turned to him. "We haven't had a chance to get to my questions yet. Maybe yours will be answered at the same time mine are."

Was that a nice way of telling him to be quiet? Not a problem. He had no intention of monopolizing the conversation or making April feel inadequate in any way. He just wanted to be sure that Brenda didn't evade. Brenda was an expert evader. For the thousandth time, he wondered why he'd put up with that until it was almost too late. He smiled at April and then turned it on Brenda. "Great."

"What I want to talk about is format. Everything else was clearly outlined in the contract." April picked up her pen and pulled off the cap. "How involved are you in programming?" In a seemingly unconscious gesture, April shoved the cap back on her pen. "I called the station yesterday." She stared, letting her words sink in. "Until then, I was under the impression that you worked for KOEK."

A 100-watt smile beamed at April. "I do work *for* the station. I'm not employed on-site."

"So you're a consultant?"

Brenda took a sip—and then another—from her half-finished water glass. "Among other things, I'm a recruiter. When Seth told me about your idea for a show, I knew just where you were needed." The megasmile flipped from April to Seth and back again. "So let me hear your ideas, April. We need to start brainstorming about promotion."

Seth had had enough. His fingers closed around the handle of his butter knife, and he pointed it at Brenda. But just as his lips formed the first letter, April leaned forward. "I need some details. This is all way too vague for my comfort, Brenda. The pay is better than I'd expected, and the benefits are wonderful, but now that I know you're not employed at KOEK, I've got some huge concerns. I need to see in writing the things you promised—that I'll be in charge of picking my own guests, my own topics. And I need to know now."

Way to go, April. Seth high-fived her in his head. As soon as he had the chance, he'd apologize for barging in. Clearly, his presence wasn't needed at this meeting. This girl could hold her own.

Brenda nodded. "I'd have the same concerns if I were you." She bent down and pulled a tube of lipstick out of her purse, applying it without need of a mirror.

He'd forgotten how much that irritated him. "Brenda, just spell it out for her." April didn't need a knight on a white charger, but he couldn't help trying to play the role.

"I understand what—" Music blared from the floor near Brenda's feet. She closed the lipstick tube and picked up her purse, sliding her hand in and out. "Excuse me." She slid the cover up on her slim ruby red phone. "Hello. Oh no. Of course. No, not a problem. I'm on my way." Her lip did the fake pouty thing he'd once found so appealing. "I'm so, so sorry. I have to run." Her hand reached across the table to April. "I'll call you on Tuesday."

Her elegant hand reached out to him. "So good to see you, Seth. I'm so sorry I can't stay, but we'll talk soon." Her smile could melt lead. But it didn't touch him.

With her fingers in his grasp, he stared, letting her know he'd seen right through her. "Lots of big emergencies in the television business, aren't there?"

Her eyes glazed him before she pivoted on spiky heels and strode out.

The waitress appeared with their coffee and Brenda's bottled water. Seth stood up and moved to the vacated chair across from April and slid his coffee cup toward him as he asked the confused waitress what Brenda had ordered.

"Spinach salad, dressing on the side, no croutons, chicken breast instead of bacon." The girl in the apron and massive bonnet seemed to be struggling to rattle off the instructions in an even voice. Apparently, she'd sized up Brenda in short order.

"Heap on some bacon and pour the dressing on top, and I'll eat it." He turned his attention on April. "Mind if I join you for lunch?"

April looked as though she'd just stepped off the Tilt-A-Whirl at the county fair. "I. . .guess." Parallel lines formed above her nose. "That remark about emergencies was rude."

"Yes, it was. I had every intention of being polite, but. . . ." He lifted his coffee cup. "If I were a betting man, I'd bet there was nobody on the other end when her phone rang."

"Seth!"

It was the second time she'd used his name in half an hour. Was he ever going to hear her say it again without the exclamation point? "Brenda downloaded a program that rings your phone to get you out of sticky situations. She hit the 'hot key' when she reached for her lipstick."

"You don't know that for sure."

Oh yes, I do. "Did anything get settled in your mind in that. . .brief encounter?"

"No."

He didn't like seeing her embarrassed. He put both hands around his cup to keep from touching her hand in a gesture she might perceive as patronizing. "So what's next on the dream list?"

"Thank you." A genuine smile lit her eyes. So he'd been right to change the subject. "I have to put off anything that costs money since it's going to cost me something to move. . . ."

"Can we leave that little fact out of our conversation? I'm being an ostrich on that subject."

The waitress appeared with a bowl of soup, a bread basket, and Seth's salad. When she left, April reached across the table and held her hands out for his. "I'll pray."

Her warm hands hugged his. "Lord God, thank You for this food and this time. Thank You for the way You meet all our needs. You are in the details, Lord, and we trust You."

She opened her eyes and the deepness of the blue was once again too deep, but he couldn't have let go of her hands if his life depended on it—nor could he remember what they'd been talking about before she'd reached for his hands. He fumbled for a coherent sentence. "Will you make it home in time to watch the weather tonight?"

Her thumbs swept across his knuckles. "I always make it home in time for you."

Chapter 17

April's head felt like it was banded with steel straps. She kicked off her shoes and dropped her purse next to Snow Bear. With little to do other than supervise Chrissy, the afternoon had dragged. Her headache, which had started the moment Brenda walked out of the Sage Stoppe without answering a single question, had gotten worse with each jerk of the second hand on her office clock. And just to add to the stress, she'd promised to spend Saturday with her mother.

She turned on the window air conditioner in the bedroom and positioned a fan so that it would draw the cool air into the living room. Even Willy and Splash looked wilted. "Hard to fight in this heat, isn't it?" Neither of them looked especially anxious to grab the flakes she sprinkled over them. "I know just how you feel."

After changing into shorts, she rummaged through the refrigerator for something that wouldn't require heat or effort. Thanks to the generosity of a listener who worked for Bridgeman's, two pints of Wolf Tracks ice cream called her name through the freezer door, but she settled on a cold chicken leg and some cottage cheese.

Paper plate and iced tea in hand, she flopped onto the couch and turned on the news. Five minutes to Seth. The thought revived a little voice she'd been trying to silence all afternoon. Why hadn't he asked her to do something tonight? Not that she wanted to be locked into a Friday night date routine, but he hadn't mentioned any plans. She sank back on Snow Bear as she took a halfhearted bite of chicken. The bear's head turned when she squished him. He seemed to be staring at her.

"Tell me he's not with Brenda." Was Seth the "business" Brenda had in Pine Bluff?

A tap on the door kept her from waiting for an answer from a stuffed bear. "Come on in."

Yvonne's shift at the nursing home had ended more than two hours earlier, but she was still in uniform.

"What have you been up to?" When she didn't get an answer, April looked closer. Yvonne's eyes were red and puffy. "What's wrong?"

"We lost a resident a little while ago. A sweet little old lady." Yvonne dropped her purse on the floor and closed the door behind her. "And then on the way home, Michael W. Smith was singing 'Friends,' and I just started thinking about how nothing's for sure, you know, and nothing's going to be the same after you move. I know you'll come back here on weekends, but you'll want to be with Seth, and I'll be married in two months and—" A sob shook her shoulders.

April jumped up and wrapped her arms around Yvonne, triggering her own flood of tears. When she pulled away, Yvonne laughed. "Do I look as bad as you do?"

Staring at the streaks of black that ran from Yvonne's eyes to her chin, April shook her head. "You could never look as bad as me. Do you have plans tonight?"

"Not until eight. Kirk's having dinner with some guys from work."

"Have a seat. I know just what we need."

Seth was pointing at a radar map when April sat down beside Yvonne with two spoons and two pints of Wolf Tracks. Listening to Seth's smooth voice, April shut out the uncertainty of the day. "This is kind of the best of everything, you know? My headache's going away already."

"Just what the doctor ordered." Yvonne's raccoon eyes squinted when she smiled. "The guy's not hard to look at."

Seth's brown sports jacket matched his eyes. April tuned in and out of the weather report.

". . .line of storms headed our way that'll give us a break from the heat for the Fourth of July weekend, but we'll have to be on the lookout for possible severe weather. This is the kind of front that could develop. . . ."

"He's so sweet." April licked her spoon like a Popsicle.

"Told you so."

"Yes, you did." She pulled her attention off Seth's eyes and onto his words.

". . .All in all, it's a good night to do something in air-conditioned comfort. Something like the climbing wall at the YMCA in Coon Rapids, maybe." His dimple deepened. "This is Seth Bachelor for KXPB Weather. Have a blessed night." His index finger pointed at the camera. "I'll be over to pick you up at seven."

Yvonne gave a long, low whistle. "I told you so."

‰

The gym smelled of stale sweat and dirty socks. Oldies music and the triumphant yells of three teens who'd made it to the top rebounded off the cement-block walls. April stood at the bottom of the climbing wall in full harness, telling herself the dampness on her palms was irrational. One of the spotters had told her the wall was twenty-eight feet tall, only a fraction of the height of the water tower. But the water tower had ladder rungs, and it didn't have a four-foot overhang at the top.

"This'll be a piece of cake for you." Seth double-checked her harness.

"It's not only fear of heights I'm battling; it's fear of no biceps."

Seth pinched her upper arm between his thumb and fingers. "Hm.

You may be right."

"Thanks for the confidence."

He tousled her bangs the way he'd done with Wesley. "One step at a time."

"One step at a time. One step at a time." She whispered the words as her fingertips found a hold above her head and her foot left the floor.

Rock by rock, with Seth only two feet away, offering a constant flow of encouragement, she made it to the overhang. "I think this is far enough for the first time."

"You have to at least try it. Even if you do slip, you won't hit the ground."

"But I'll dangle like a spastic spider."

His laugh bounced off the rock face. "I think I have just the thing to get you over the top. Stay right there."

His left hand stretched toward a rock that jutted out just above her head. He found a foothold and shifted to his left until his arm touched hers. "I've been trying to figure out the best time to break this to you."

If he thought he was calming her jitters, he was way off base. "Break what to me?"

"Well, you see"—his lips grazed her knuckles—"it appears I'm in love with you."

&

"Take your shoes off." April padded up the weather-beaten outside stairs leading to her mother's apartment. Her stomach felt jittery. Maybe having Seth bring her to her mother's wasn't such a great idea after all. She wouldn't have a getaway car if things got tense, and she'd have to worry about Seth staying awake on the hour drive back to Pine Bluff.

Shoes in hand, Seth followed. "Are we gonna get in trouble for breaking curfew?"

"Shh! Want me to get grounded?"

"I thought you said your feet wouldn't touch the ground for days." He nuzzled her cheek with his nose as she fit the key in the lock and opened the door to the galley kitchen.

Seth set her gym bag on the floor. April looked up at him. Slits of light from a streetlamp sneaked through the venetian blinds and lined his face. She slid easily into his arms, feeling like she belonged there. "Thank you," she whispered against his shirt.

"What did I do now?"

"I was feeling so sorry for myself, sitting home alone on a Friday night after a lousy day, and here you had the whole night planned. The climb, dinner, the walk, the words. . ."

"Which words?" His chest vibrated as his words baited her.

"I love you."

"You do?"

"I do."

He pulled back several inches, one arm still around her waist. The fingers of his right hand glided into her hair. "Even if it means a three-hour drive, I'm going to keep filling up your Friday nights. If that's okay with you, of course."

"That's o—"The overhead light flashed on.

"April!" Her mother stood in the doorway in a faded pink robe, gray roots showing in her tangled hair, clutching a vacuum cleaner wand like a billy club. "What is *he* doing here?"

Pulling slightly away from Seth, April kept her hand on his back. "Mom, I'd like you to meet Seth. Seth, this is my mother, Lois Douglas."

Seth extended his hand and then dropped it to his side when the gesture wasn't reciprocated. "Nice to meet you, Mrs. Douglas."

"It's two in the morning."

April commanded her eyes not to roll. "I told you I'd be here late."

"You told me *you'd* be here late."

"We were at the Y, and then we had dinner at Solera."Why did she feel like a high school kid caught sneaking home after midnight?

"The couch is made up." Her mother turned and stepped into the dining room. "I doubt I'll be able to go back to sleep now."

Was that remark made to incite guilt or to say she'd be watching to make sure Seth wasn't staying?

Seth's hand slipped from her back. "Mrs. Douglas? Could I talk to you for a moment?"

April's mother stopped as if his words were a brick wall. "Nothing you can say will change a thing, Mr. Bachelor."

"I know that. I'm so sorry about the loss of your daughter. We never would have taken her if we'd known she was so sick. She turned in the permission slip, so—"

Lois Douglas's hands rose to her face. "I don't remember signing it. If I'd known she'd be outside, that she'd get wet and cold. . ." Her face distorted, and she turned away.

April covered the space in three strides and put her arms around her mother. She looked up into Seth's helpless face, and they stood like that, eyes locked, until her mother's sobs quieted. April guided her to a straight-backed chair and left the room to find a box of tissues.

When she returned, Seth was on his knees in front of her mother.

". . .anyone's fault, Mrs. Douglas. From what April has told me, Caitlyn was a pretty headstrong girl."

Seth's words were soft. Unbelievably, her mother responded with a smile. "She was that."

"Can I tell you about that day?"

Her mother took a Kleenex, wiped her face, and nodded.

April watched in awe as Seth, still on his knees, described driving toward the bank of dark clouds with three teens in the back of Darren's van singing Sesame Street songs.

"Your daughter was wearing this crazy elephant stocking cap."

Her mother nodded. "April bought it for her."

Tears stung April's eyes. Shortly before Caitlyn's diagnosis, they'd gone to see *Horton Hears a Who*. She could picture the floppy elephant ears so clearly. And Caitlyn's comical grin.

"When it started to rain, we pulled under an overpass and dug out the rain gauges so the kids could set them out. Caitlyn took one of the gauges and ran out into a field." He paused and looked up at April.

April hadn't heard this part, but she nodded encouragement.

"She was laughing and leaping over the rows of cut corn with the other kids following her. My buddy made a comment that they were acting as goofy as his four-year-old with his little friends. All of a sudden, Caitlyn stopped." Again, he glanced up at April. "She raised her hands in the air like she was worshipping. Even from the road, I could see her smile. And then...she took off her cap...and threw it into the wind."

A gasp slipped from April's throat.

"It was...beautiful. And until that moment, we had no idea she was sick."

Chapter 18

He'd given Brenda long enough. Not one of his e-mails, text messages, or phone calls had been answered. Seth had no doubt where he'd find her at six o'clock on Thursday morning. She'd be working off the guilt from eating pizza at her Wednesday night book club.

He rubbed his hand over his face as he turned onto Spring Street. He was a morning person, but setting the alarm for four o'clock wasn't his idea of fun. He scanned the Anytime Fitness parking lot. Three spaces from the front door, he spotted the silver Audi. But instead of opening the car door, he closed his eyes.

Lord, let my words be pleasing to You. You know my heart is not filled with grace at this moment, but let me listen to You before I speak.

Two minutes later, he stood face-to-face with a sweaty, disheveled, and extremely self-conscious Brenda.

As the blush covered her cheeks and neck, she greeted him with a smile and a hug that he didn't return. "What a surprise! What are you doing here?"

"I just have a few questions." He lifted the two envelopes in his hand as a shield. "Does this job you've offered April really exist?"

"Of course! What do you take me for?"

Lord, help. . . . His teeth clamped down on his tongue until he could trust himself with words.

"Is there any part of this offer that isn't exactly the way you described it to her?"

"She'll be on the air with her own show in six weeks, I promise." A manicured hand ran from his shoulder to his elbow. "You must be sooo proud of her."

Pins and needles prickled along his spine. "If you're lying about any of this, I'll be back." He hadn't intended to sound like the Terminator. Then again, he liked the sound of that title. That was, in fact, what he'd come to do.

"You'll always be back, Seth." Pink nails retraced the line from his elbow to shoulder.

Seth drew back. The muscles in his neck tightened like a vise. The envelopes in his hand felt suddenly heavy. He shoved the smaller one, the one addressed to her father, in front of her face. "This is the last payment. I need your signature on the deed, and this will all be behind us."

The color left her face. She blinked. And then her lips pulled tight across her teeth and her shoulders straightened. "There's no proof that you've given me a single penny for my half."

ༀ

The promised call from Brenda hadn't come. April had left messages five days in a row. She tossed her cell phone on her desk and her pencil holder in the cardboard box on the floor. She could recite the voice mail message by heart, flawlessly imitating the chirpy tone.

Plunking down on her desk chair, she stared at the KOEK home page, trying to picture her face on it. Picking up her phone, she did the thing Brenda had, with no explanation, told her not to do. She dialed the station and asked for the manager.

"Bud Palmer here."

"Mr. Palmer, this is April Douglas."

"Yes. I've been waiting for Brenda to set up a meeting with you."

April's shoulders lowered from their permanent place near her ears. He knew who she was. That eliminated her biggest fear, anyway. "Mr. Palmer, I've got tons of questions, and I imagine you have some for me. If you're busy right now, I'll call back when it's convenient."

"I'll make time right now. I'm excited about you coming. We put a half page ad in the *Winona Daily News* announcing the upcoming *On the Spot*."

"What's that?"

"Your. . .show." He sounded confused. "Brenda came up with the idea. Hasn't she told you anything? Yeah, *On the Spot*. Our tagline is 'Real People. Real Shockers.'"

April's throat constricted. "Wh. . .what is the format?"

"Just like it sounds. One guest per show. They sit there having coffee with you just like you're old buddies, and then *zam!* they let go a zinger, some buried secret or juicy bit of gossip about a friend, old boss, or ex—somebody they want to get even with." His laugh belonged in a circus sideshow. "And then you call that person on the phone and repeat what you just heard. The rest, as they say, is history."

Black splashes spattered across her field of vision. Her breath came in short, squeezed spurts. April lowered her head to her knees.

"April? Did I lose you? Hello?"

"Mr. Palmer. . ." Her fingers spasmed around the phone. "That's not. . .the job. . .I was offered."

ༀ

There was a note on her door when she got home.

April—I found someone to rent the apartment on the 15th. Stop
in to say good-bye and give me your address before you move.
Sydney.

She was jobless. In six days, she'd be homeless. She hadn't even found an apartment in Winona yet—not that she would have gone there now. April ripped down the note and kicked open the door. Bud Palmer's cackle echoed in her ears. *"Christian? You thought this was a Christian show? Where in the world did you get that idea?"*

Closing the door, she leaned against it. *Lord Jesus.* . . . It was the beginning and ending of her prayer, the same one she'd repeated over and over since breaking the phone connection with Bud Palmer. From the dim recesses of her memory, a verse whispered. . . . *"The Spirit helps us in our weakness. We do not know what we ought to pray for, but the Spirit himself intercedes for us with groans that words cannot express."*

Her purse dropped, her arms crossed over her waist. She hadn't yet shed a tear. Walking, driving, breathing sucked all her energy, not leaving enough to manufacture tears. She couldn't afford the luxury of giving in to self-pity yet. She should be doing something—making lists, searching the Internet, thinking. But thoughts wouldn't stick together in her mind.

Slowly, she opened her eyes and stared at the hodgepodge of boxes, bags, and baskets that cluttered her living room. Splash and Willy treaded water between two DVD skyscrapers. Snow Bear slept on a pile of folded blankets on the floor. . . like the street bear he was soon to be. Thin, late-afternoon sunlight hit the picture leaning against a box on the couch. Itasca. In the photograph, misty morning light filtering through the trees, reflecting in the water. The headwaters of the mighty Mississippi. . .quiet, serene. . .everything her life wasn't at the moment. A place of beginnings, a place to think, to sort through the remnants of what used to be her life. . .

She could pack tonight and be there by noon tomorrow. She'd miss her last day of work and the surprise going-away party everyone had been whispering about. But maybe they'd be willing to postpone it until Monday. It wasn't like she was leaving town.

Like a shot of caffeine, the plan jolted her into action. Mental lists made lines and columns out of the mess that had filled her head just moments before. *Call Jill, cancel Winona hotel reservation, call Itasca, tell Yvonne, Mom, Seth.* . . .

Seth. Earlier, with Bud Palmer's laugh still ringing in her ear, she'd picked up the phone to call him. And then it hit her. He'd feel responsible. He'd shared April's dream with Brenda, like handing her live ammunition. She had to tell him in person that she wasn't angry. He needed to see that she was doing okay.

Right.

As she bent to pick up her purse, a buzz sounded in the outside pocket. She pulled out her phone and stared at the caller ID. "Hi, Mom." She didn't have the energy to mask her mood.

"April?" Her voice sounded tight, strained. "I. . .heard you turned down the job in Winona."

Alarm bells went off in April's head. "Where did you hear that, and how did you know—"

"Did you get another job offer, honey?" Her voice bordered on shrill.

"No." Muffled sobs met her ear. *Not again, not now.* "What's going on, Mom? How did you—"

"It's all my fault!" A louder sob. "I thought it was the best thing. I thought it would be good for you to get away from. . .there."

Every cell in April's brain stood at attention. "What are you talking about?"

"I thought you'd love the new job. Brenda made it sound like it was perfect for you."

"*Brenda?*" April was yelling, but she didn't care. "You talked to Brenda?"

"It was weeks ago, before I met Seth. I was so worried about you. I wanted to know the truth about him, so I looked her up, and she said she had the perfect solution. . . ."

April's phone snapped shut.

∞

The last time she'd entered the doors of KXPB-TV, she'd been young and idealistic, with a head full of dreams. Before Caitlyn died, before she got a great job and then threw it away like a dog with a bone in his mouth looking at his own reflection.

She stepped into the dimly lit empty reception area. No one sat at the two desks behind the counter. The screen saver on a monitor rolled and transposed the call letters. *KXPB. . .X-ceeding X-pectations.*

From somewhere in the back of the long, narrow building came the sound of the current broadcast. The news was over, and the seven-to-eight slot was filled with spotlights on local organizations and school functions. *Prime-Time Pine Bluff.*

If she hadn't seen Seth's Camry in the parking lot, she would have left. The quiet was eerie, and she had no idea where to find him. A blade of light from a doorway sliced across the darkened hallway in front of her. She walked toward it, stopping when she reached the door. MERVIN FULLER, STATION MANAGER, the nameplate read. She tapped on the door.

"Come on in."

The voice startled her. She pushed the door open. With his phone in one hand, pencil in the other, and feet crossed on top of the desk, Seth looked as surprised to see her as she was to see him.

"April!" His feet arced over the corner of the desk and hit the floor at the same time his phone landed in its cradle. "Hi!" He stood and walked toward her, hands reaching out before she reached him.

She thought she was smiling. But the look on Seth's face told her otherwise. His hands clamped on her arms. "Sit down." He guided her to a chair and took the one beside her. "What's wrong?"

The sobs gave no warning. Racking, jarring, they emanated from some buried storehouse of hurt and fear and longing.

Like a fortress, his arms surrounded her. Her face pressed against his chest. He didn't talk, just held her tighter, stroked her hair. Never in her life had she been held like this. How many times as a little girl had she imagined a rescuer, someone who would step in and make things right, who would defend and protect her? God had been her strength, but still she'd craved the feel of strong arms around her. Over the thud of Seth's heart, she heard him whisper.

"Lord, comfort her, protect her, and fill her with Your love and the knowledge of Your presence." His fingers stroked her cheek. "Whatever it is, April, I'm here for you. We'll get through it. We'll work it out."

His words brought fresh tears. Finally, when his shirt was damp and her eyes sore, but there were no more tears, she told him.

§§

Seth eased off the accelerator when his headlights lit the sign for the 107A exit. He'd only been driving for about fifty minutes, but the muscles in his forearms ached from gripping the wheel. A sense of déjà vu washed over him. This was his second trip to St. Paul in fourteen hours.

But this time, he was hoping to *not* find Brenda.

As he turned onto the exit, his shirt pulled away from his chest then touched his skin again, cold and damp with April's tears. Saying good-bye had been so hard tonight. But the only way he could offer her any hope was to bring an end to his three years of bondage to the Miss-St.-Cloud-wannabe.

He took a right on 70th Street. Minutes later, he pulled into the circle driveway on Lone Oak Road and parked in front of two tall white columns. It was the first time he'd ever used the front door.

Chimes echoed behind double mahogany doors at the press of his finger against a lit button. The door swung open, and the woman who had almost become his mother-in-law stood before him. Openmouthed shock smoothed her face in a way Botox never had. "Seth!"

"Margaret."

Perfectly tipped nails ran through short-cropped, eternally blond hair. "Are you. . .looking for Brenda?" A spark of hope lit her gray eyes.

"No." *Absolutely no.* "Is Gil home?"

Margaret tugged at the bottom of her fitted blouse. "He's in his office." She opened the door wider and stepped aside for him to pass. "I have raspberry lemonade."

He stopped. The sadness in her voice turned him around. "That would be good." He gave her a quick hug. Though she probably deserved most of the blame for the way her daughter had turned out, he doubted that she had any clue.

She led the way across marble floors and handwoven wool rugs to the study, stopping on the way to fill a chilled glass with lemonade.

Gil Cadwell stood in front of an arched window with his back to the door. In his midfifties, he was still a striking man. Disdain for golf carts kept him in shape.

"Hello, Gil."

The man whirled. "Seth!" A grin lit his face. He covered the space between them in four long strides and engulfed Seth in a bear hug. "It's been too long. Sit down." He pulled away and gestured to two overstuffed leather chairs. As they sat down, he said, "Got your check this afternoon. By courier—you must have been anxious to make that last payment. I imagine that feels mighty good. You're a prince of a guy, Mr. Bachelor. More of a man than I would have been at your age."

"Thank you. But. . .there's a little problem." Just imagining the look that would soon harden Gil's features started his stomach churning. If he'd known any other way to put this to rest, he wouldn't have involved the man who had been more of a father to him than his own father. "Brenda is refusing to sign over her half of the business."

"What?" Gil's eyes glinted like steel.

"I have nothing on paper to show that I paid her off."

Gil rose to his feet. His hands coiled in tight fists at his sides. "I'll take care of it, Seth. Enough is enough. She'll sign. You've done more than anyone would have expected." His shoulders suddenly lowered. Shame and frustration wove through a heavy sigh. "I'm so sorry, Seth."

Standing and closing the gap between them, Seth put his hand on the older man's shoulder. They'd had too many conversations about Gil Cadwell's oldest daughter. "It's not your fault." He pulled his hand away. "I just don't know what game she's playing this time. She doesn't want the station, does she?"

"No. She doesn't." A sad smile lifted one corner of Gil's mouth. "She wants you."

Chapter 19

As she turned north onto Main Street, sunlight shot between two buildings, through the passenger window, around Yvonne, and behind the frames of April's sunglasses. Her eyes and head still hurt from crying, and she had no more answers than she'd had the day before. And yet, a vague sense of hope had begun to infiltrate her dark mood. All because of a man who knew how to listen. . .and hug.

And a best friend. She squinted at Yvonne. "This may be the most sacrificial thing anyone's ever done for me."

"That's pitiful." An undecipherable smile twisted Yvonne's lips to the side. "I take a personal day from work to walk in the woods with you, and you call it sacrificing? You ain't seen nuttin' yet." She pointed ahead to the right. "Pull up in front of Perk Place. I want to stock up."

April parked the car in the shadow of the coffee shop awning and opened her purse. "Get me a Polar Cap."

"Come in with me." In answer to the question on April's face, Yvonne added, "I've only got two hands."

Closing her purse, April got out and followed, muttering the whole way. "We're stopping for brunch in Brainerd, you know. You've got three bags of chips and half a dozen water bottles in the backseat. How much stuff do you need for a four-hour trip?"

Yvonne walked ahead of her to the counter, ignoring every question April aimed at her back. A boy with three earrings in one ear asked for her order.

"I'll have a large Polar Cap, a medium White Chocolate Mocha with a squirt of raspberry, a large Dolce Latte sprinkled with cinnamon, and a large Hazelnut decaf, cream on the side."

April folded her arms across her chest. "How many rest areas do you think there are between here and Itasca?" She turned away, staring at booth after booth of tourists with cameras, hats, and rambunctious children. Yvonne grabbed her elbow.

"Do you want a muffin or a scone?" Yvonne's finger jabbed the air in the direction of a glass-front case. "Pick one, my treat."

"I'll have a chocolate chip muffin."

"Make that four."

"Yvonne! You'll be a whopping size 2 by Sunday if you don't watch it."

Yvonne handed money to the earringed boy and took a white bag from

222

him. Motioning for April to wait at the pickup window, she waved. "I'll be in the car."

Rude. Something was eating at Yvonne. Probably some misunderstanding with Kirk. Before they got to Milaca, she'd wrangle the truth out of her. April took the cardboard holder with the four drinks and walked toward the door. With one foot on the sidewalk, she nearly dropped the cups.

Yvonne leaned against the side of April's car, holding the bag of muffins and smiling like a Cheshire cat. To her right was Kirk.

To her left stood a man with deep brown eyes. . .holding out a jar of jam and a package of Twinkies.

"Breakfast?"

&

Towering red pines, ramrod straight, stood like sentinels on either side of the needle-covered path. They walked past a cabin built by the Civilian Conservation Corps in the 1930s. Huge brown-painted logs stood on a stone foundation. A stone chimney rose from the roof. Cozy, romantic. . . A warm flush started at April's ears and spread toward her toes.

Pulling her sweatshirt off, she tied it around her waist, relishing the sun on her bare arms, the slight breeze drying her damp T-shirt. She slipped her hand back into Seth's. "Have I said 'Thank you' lately?"

"Not in the last three minutes. So we're forgiven for wrecking your girl time?" He pointed toward Kirk and Yvonne, walking hand in hand far ahead of them.

Why was it, again, that two days at Itasca with Yvonne had sounded so wonderful? *You can wreck my girl time any day.* "You're forgiven. I just feel bad about the dumpy motel you guys are stuck with while we're in the lodge."

"We guys is tough." He gave a manly grunt. "It's only one night. And we'll get our share of time in front of the fireplace at the lodge when that front comes in this afternoon. We're in for quite a storm." His thumb caressed the back of her hand. "How are you doing, for real? Or would you rather not talk about it?"

"I'm still a little numb. God's got this all figured out. I know that. I'm trying to look at this as an adventure into the unknown."

"That's my girl!"

She liked the sound of those words.

Inches off the path, a patch of sunlight illuminated a lady's slipper. Delicate white petals hung suspended over a pink-tinged pouch. A low hum drew her gaze to a circle of ferns. Low above the deep green fronds, a dragonfly hovered, its blue body held aloft by clear, black-veined wings that beat the air. All reminders to savor the moment.

Seth let go of her hand. His arm slid across her shoulders, unspoken encouragement for her to open up.

"I've had plenty of panic moments in the past twenty-four hours, but I don't think the full truth has sunk in yet. I don't have a job. I don't have a place to live. I'm going to end up sleeping on my mother's couch and busing tables at a greasy spoon, all because, once again, I checked my reporter instincts at the door."

"Please tell me you're not blaming yourself for this."

"I'm too trusting."

Pine needles absorbed the sound of Seth's laugh. "That's not a fault, April. You're not a cynic, and that's commendable. You were up against a master of deception. Believe me, I know."

They stopped at the sign for the headwaters. Kirk and Yvonne were already balancing on the rocks that crossed the shallow water. Acutely aware that Seth seemed to be gathering his thoughts, April read the sign half-consciously: HERE 1475 FT ABOVE THE OCEAN THE MIGHTY MISSISSIPPI BEGINS TO FLOW ON ITS WINDING WAY 2552 MILES TO THE GULF OF MEXICO.

"If I hadn't told Brenda about your dream, this never would have happened."

April pulled back and stared into his eyes. "Please tell me you're not blaming yourself for this."

A wink accompanied his smile. His hands rose to her face. "I helped get you into this mess. If you'll let me, I'd like to be part of the solution."

&

"Maybe we shouldn't go all the way to the top." Gripping the railings on either side of her, April yelled above the wind.

"Go on down if you want." Seth's voice came from behind her.

And give in to fear. She shook her head and nailed her gaze to the backs of Yvonne's knees. *I can do this*. She didn't dare look up but figured there couldn't be more than three more zigzag flights of stairs to the top of the eighty-foot Aiton Heights fire tower. The view at the top would be worth it. It would.

The wind seemed to pick up with each step. The tower swayed, slightly but unnervingly. Finally, she planted her feet in the green-painted, seven-foot-square roofed cab at the top. She walked across the platform and stood beside Yvonne. "Wow." Thousands of acres of trees spread in every direction. A blue lake rested like a sapphire amid the green. To their right, the sky was deep blue and cloudless, but black clouds rolled toward them from the southwest.

Seth came up behind her and wrapped his arms around her. "You stared down another fear. This could get to be a habit, you know."

The temperature was dropping, and his warmth was welcome. She nestled against his chest. "Next week, bungee jumping."

She felt, rather than heard, the rumble of his laugh. "I'll be the one on the ground taking pictures."

April pointed toward the mountain of steel gray clouds roiling and tumbling, growing taller and wider before their eyes. "It's moving fast."

"We'd better get back down." Seth's arms dropped. "Hold on. I've got a call."

April turned, watching the expression on his face as he answered the call.

His eyes glowed. "Uh-huh. You're sure? Okay, I'll ask her."

His eyes fixed on hers as he closed the phone. A ripple of fear swept over April, though she had no idea why.

"That was Darren." Seth's hand grasped her arm, as if to steady her. "About that fear-conquering habit. . ."

℘

The minute the van door closed behind her, she knew she'd made a huge mistake. By the time she found the words to explain her change of mind, Darren was peeling out of the gas station parking lot. April pressed her hand against the window, in final farewell to Kirk and Yvonne. She stared at her car, with Kirk sliding in behind the wheel, until Darren turned a corner on what felt like two wheels. She was trapped.

Next to her in the center of the middle seat, oblivious to her terror, Seth dug around in a camera bag, familiarizing himself with different lenses. Darren, his eyes more on the conglomeration of equipment in the passenger seat than on the road, jabbered with Seth in a language April didn't understand. Terms like "supercell," "radial velocity," "A-bomb," "agitated region," "wedge," "altocumulus," "knuckles," and "anvil" ricocheted off the van's interior.

April's fingers melded into her shoulder harness. They were heading west, barreling toward an enormous wall of gray. The sky took on a bile green hue. Wind rocked the van. Veins stood out on Darren's hands as he fought with the steering wheel.

Seth unfastened his seat belt and reached between the front seats. Swiveling Darren's laptop so that April could see the screen, he pointed to an angry blob of red and orange on the radar. "There's hail in there. Figuring in that updraft, I'm guessing it's big. Golf ball-size at least." The zeal in his voice made him sound more like a sportscaster than a meteorologist. He sat on the edge of the seat, hands folded, eyes darting between the radar and the windshield. "Yeah, baby. This is gonna be good."

Good? What planet were these guys from? Maybe the account in Genesis had been mistranslated. The thing God took out of man to form into woman wasn't a rib; it was common sense!

But that didn't explain Caitlyn. Though she'd been a basketball whiz, April's sister had also been as girlie-girl as they come. And yet, the only thing she'd underlined twice on her dream list had been "See a tornado." So what would Caitlyn be doing if she were here. . .sitting next to tall, dark, and handsome, speeding toward a whirling bank of violent clouds? The answer startled her. *Caitlyn would be laughing.*

So maybe April couldn't laugh, but she could make an effort to relax and to try to understand the man beside her. "What did Mark Twain say again?"

His lips parted in a look that she could only label "delight." " 'Courage is not the absence of fear but resistance to the mastery of fear.' "

"What's the rest of it?"

" 'Except a creature be part coward, it is not a compliment to say it is brave.' "
He laughed, wrapped both arms around her, and planted a noisy kiss on her
cheek. "You're amazing."

Her eyes opened wide. "Amazingly scared."

"Amazing *because* you're scared. And you're here."

∞

"Listen to the roar!" Seth lowered his window.

Pressure pounded against April's eardrums. The noise was like nothing she'd
ever experienced. Like standing directly beneath Niagara Falls.

On top of the roar, the heavens opened fire on them, on the acres of ripen-
ing corn on either side of the highway. Hail, bouncing like ping-pong balls, bombarded the van with a thundering volume that drowned out the voice of the radio
announcer.

The barrage lasted only moments. The deafening noise stopped as abruptly
as it started, leaving a silence equally disturbing. Darren turned north onto Highway 169. The greenish sky gave way to murky black. Beside her, Seth ducked
even lower for a better view through the windshield.

April crouched beside him, waiting, her heart pounding with something
that wasn't fear alone. Excited anticipation had somehow sneaked in. The realization stunned her.

"There!" She followed Seth's outstretched hand to a V-shaped cloud descending from a swirling, pewter gray mass. Suddenly, a white tube dropped like
a massive Slinky.

"What a hose!"

"That's a monster!"

"Look at the motion at the base. Huge debris cloud!"

Seth's and Darren's words overlapped. From the van radio, stern warnings
added to the chaos: ". . . long line of storms moving northeast at about thirty
miles per hour. We do not want you to be out looking at this potentially hazard-
ous storm. There are spotters on the ground, emergency management directors
and trained spotters. Stay indoors. Seek shelter. If you're out in this, do not stay in
your car. Do not park under an overpass. Find a low-lying ditch and lie flat until
the storm passes. The storm center is heading toward Hill City and. . ."

Shingles, branches, fence posts, and corn stalks spun out from the dust-
choked vortex that ripped across the open fields. Narrowing in the middle,
the tornado was shaped more like a bud vase than a funnel. April watched in
stunned silence, a sense of awe momentarily obliterating her fear. She glanced
at the speedometer. The needle edged toward eighty. Darren made a wide turn
onto a gravel road, barreling toward the next intersection where he again headed
north.

"Incredible! Turn off the wipers for a minute." Seth aimed the video camera at the white shaft that seemed to hover on the road about two miles ahead of them, churning a brown cloud of debris, spitting out trees like toothpicks. "Great shot. Great. . ." He lowered the camera, leaned forward. "Darren. . ." His voice was thick with warning.

"I see it." Darren slammed on the brakes.

"Back up! Get out of here! It's headed straight for us!"

April's hands clamped onto Seth's arm as the van sped backwards.

"We're okay. We're safe." Seth repeated the words, but his face told the truth.

A piece of PVC pipe smashed against the windshield. Seconds later, the brown cloud engulfed the van. Darren slowed. Something heavy crashed against the roof. Seth grabbed a jacket from the backseat and threw it over her. April knew instinctively why. To shield her from breaking glass. She squeezed her eyes shut and buried her face in his shoulder.

Just when April was sure she would scream, silence slammed down on them.

Dust settled. The twister had disappeared. A whoop from Darren shattered the stillness. Seth echoed the sound and then broke into laughter. As relief flooded her body, April pried her fingers from Seth's arm.

Darren did a U-turn and then came to a stop. Sunlight knifed through steel gray clouds. A swath of color arced from the split in the clouds to a field of gently fluttering corn.

Seth's lips brushed her ear. "I'm in love with one mighty brave lady."

Chapter 20

Seth stood at a distance, watching as April got down on her knees beside a little girl with windswept blond ringlets and spoke into the KXPB microphone.

"While her mom fills out Red Cross vouchers for food and new clothes, I'm visiting with three-year-old Zoe Lewis. Zoe and her mom and little sister moved into a mobile home park just outside of Hinckley only two months ago." April looked from the camera to the little girl and back. "In the wake of a series of tornadoes that touched down in Minnesota a week ago, Zoe's family is homeless, and Zoe's holding the only possession the Lewis family now owns." She jiggled the ear of the dirt-stained stuffed dog clutched in Zoe's arms. "Who's this?"

"Misser Peabody."

"I heard that somebody found Mister Peabody for you after the storm. Where did they find him?"

"He was stuck in a 'lectric wire high, high over the trees. On TV, they showed a pitcher of him stuck, and my mom called, and a man from the 'lectric company climbed up and got him and bringed him to me."

April stood with her hand on the little girl's shoulder and faced the camera. "Just one of hundreds of stories we've heard in the past few days, which is why KXPB is joining forces with local churches, businesses, and organizations to help raise funds for these families and. . ."

"She's a natural."

Seth jumped at the out-of-place voice. "Gil! What are you doing here?"

Gil Cadwell ran a hand through his hair. "I hope I'm here to bring you some peace."

No words came to mind. Seth settled for a raise of his eyebrows.

"I had a little talk with my daughter the other day." His eyes sparkled with mirth. "I informed her that I had no record of her paying off her credit card debt to me."

"What?" Seth couldn't believe what he was hearing. This was the man Brenda called "Old Softy" to his face.

"Yup. It felt awfully good, too. You should have seen the look on Margaret's face when I calmly stated that there were no papers that indicated that the monetary gifts Seth Bachelor had been sending me for the past three years had anything to do with what Brenda owed me." Gil winked and chuckled. "I said that I would, however, be willing to expunge her debt if she signed over her half

228

of the station to you, no strings attached." He pulled an envelope from his jacket pocket and handed it to Seth. "Be happy, son."

∞

"Are you sure I'm not stepping on some reporter's toes?" Picking her way along a sidewalk strewed with debris, April handed the microphone to Seth. "Is this really okay with your boss?"

"I. . .don't have a boss."

A sick feeling settled hard in April's stomach. Had he gotten in another argument? Or gotten fired for taking off last Friday? "You lost your job?"

The granddaddy of all patronizing expressions swept over Seth's face. Men! Why had she ever tried to understand this one? "What happened?"

"I don't have a boss, but I do have a job. More of one than I want, actually."

She was too tired for games. She'd spent most of the past week serving meals and reading stories to children at the emergency shelters set up in three church basements. . .and doing television interviews of the victims. This was the fifth day that her coverage would be broadcast on the six o'clock news, yet she still hadn't spoken to anyone at KXPB other than Seth and the cameraman. The whole setup struck her as odd. But she loved every exhausting minute of it. It didn't matter that she had no idea if she'd be compensated for her reporting time. The thought had occurred to her more than once that, if she'd still been working at KPOG, she wouldn't have been freed up to do this. God was in control. Raising public awareness of the needs of these people who were truly homeless was where she was supposed to be. And by the time she dropped onto Yvonne's couch around midnight every night, she was too worn-out to feel the lumpy cushions.

She aimed a lopsided smile at Seth. "I'm too brain-dead for riddles, Mr. Bachelor. Spit it out."

He handed the microphone to the cameraman. His hands rested on her shoulders, and he kissed the tip of her nose. "We need to talk."

"That sounds ominous."

"I hope it's not." His hand slid over hers, and they walked toward the road.

An elderly couple who April had interviewed earlier in the week stood beside a washer and dryer, the only things still intact in the pile of tinder that had once been their home. April waved, and the man held up a sheaf of crumpled papers. "We found our marriage license!"

His wife laughed. "We're still legal!"

"Congratulations!" April turned to Seth. "Why does it take losing everything to figure out what's really important?"

Brown eyes smiled back at her. "What have you figured out so far?"

"That God's plans don't have to make sense." She grinned at him. "And men don't either."

He laughed. "Thank you. That makes this next part so much easier."

"You're scaring me."

"Just hear me out. This is one of those Lots of Grace Required moments."

"O...kay."

Seth steered her around a dented microwave on the side of the road. "I haven't been completely...forthright about some things, and I'm hoping my reasons will make sense." He took an audible deep breath. "A few days before our wedding date, Brenda's father gave us a wedding gift. An unbelievable wedding gift."

He stopped to say hi to two men from the power company, giving April's imagination time to spin out of control.

"He deeded KXPB and his helicopter to the two of us."

"You *own* the station?" April stopped walking. "With Brenda?"

"I did. Until half an hour ago. That was her father I was talking to." Seth rubbed the back of his neck. "I made a deal with Brenda, a stupid deal, in retrospect. She didn't want to sell me her half of the station. Looking back, I realize I should have just walked away from it, but I offered to pay off her credit card debt and the debt to her father in payment for my half of the station. I didn't have a thing put in writing. I love her dad and trust him implicitly. I figured that with him involved she wouldn't try anything underhanded. But when I made my last payment, she refused to sign the deed over to me. Anyway...Daddy stepped in, and the deed is now in my name alone."

April's knees felt like jelly, like the feeling after a near miss on the freeway. "You *own* the station?"

"And my second order of business will be to fire my station manager, which will make me the temporary manager as well as owner." A sheepish look spread across his face. "I'm the man upstairs."

April's mouth opened, but what came out wasn't indignation. It was laughter. "You're the one who didn't hire me because I might move on?"

"Kind of ironic, isn't it?" His fingertips pulled a strand of hair off her cheek. "But I'd like to make amends for that mistake. I've been wanting to for weeks. That's the reason I shared your talk show idea with Brenda."

"I'm guessing she wasn't all in favor of the idea." An almost literal light went on in April's consciousness. "She's still in love with you! That's why she tried to get me away from here, isn't it? That's why she was so willing to join forces with my mother."

Seth's gaze dropped to the ground. "Apparently."

Rising on tiptoes, she brushed her lips across his forehead. "Who could blame her?"

He smiled, clearly relieved that she'd broken the tension. "Anyway, the strings are all cut, and I'm free to make executive decisions. So the first one I'm making is to offer you a daily talk show. Real people, real stories, with a real beautiful host. Interested?"

At that moment, KXPB's newly hired talk show host couldn't have put two words together if her life depended on it. Her tears answered for her.

Chapter 21

Thank you, John." April smiled at John Nelson, Pine Bluff's town chairman, sitting across from her in an overstuffed leather chair. Turning toward Camera Two, she was glad she couldn't see beyond the lights, or her gaze would have strayed to the man with dark brown eyes. The man who, every week for ten months now, had watched her from his chair beside the studio door. "Tomorrow night we'll be talking to Trace and Sydney McKay—a real-life 'prison to praise' story. Thanks for joining us."

April uncrossed her legs, shedding the tension that came with taping a show. "That was an amazing story, John. After this airs tonight, we'll get tons of e-mail."

Leaning forward and resting his elbows on his knees, John gave her a strange look. "You know, my heart attack not only brought me to Christ, it also left me with an insatiable desire to experience things I'd never done before. Legal things—not like climbing a water tower." He winked at April.

"This sounds like a topic for another show. What kind of things?" April picked up the water bottle that sat on the floor beside her chair.

"Hot air ballooning, for one. I wanted to try it, just once. But being up there, away from all the hustle and bustle, seeing this panorama of God's handiwork, I got hooked. The experience is. . .worship. That's the only way I can describe it. Especially right now with the trees all in bloom. So I got trained, and I bought a share in a balloon. I'm giving rides to everyone I know. Including you."

"It is on my list, John. Someday. . ."

"Today's as good as any. Gorgeous spring day and the air's still. Right about sundown would be perfect. Let's go."

As April responded with a nervous chuckle, Seth stepped out of the dark, holding out her jacket and a wrapped package, shoe box-size. Only then did she notice the cameras were still on.

≫

John cranked the burner, and April's fingers bit into the side of the wicker basket. Anticipating a stomach-lurching sensation at liftoff, she closed her eyes and buried her face in Seth's shoulder.

"Smile for the camera." His breath was warm on her cheek.

"I can't. Tell me when we're off the ground."

"We're off the ground."

"What?" Now that she concentrated on it, she could sense that the earth was no longer beneath her feet. Cautiously, she opened her eyes. The ground crew waved, a KXPB camera tilted up to track them. The figures grew small. A burst of noise drew her eyes to the flame spurting from the burner and the envelope of primary colors that towered overhead. "Amazing."

Pine Bluff and the St. Croix shrank beneath their feet as they drifted northwest on the air currents. April pointed out Main Street and the chamber of commerce building. Seth found his house. Soft pinks, luminous purples, and stark whites dotted the spaces between houses. In seconds, they were at eye level to the catwalk on the water tower.

Seth pointed toward the tower. "Remember a year ago when we shared a moment at the top of that thing?"

"I'll never forget it. Believe me, I've tried." Still gripping the side of the basket, she grinned up at him.

"Maybe I can make a moment you'll want to remember."

"You already are."

Seth bent down and picked up the box he'd taunted her with since they'd left the studio. "Now you can open it."

April turned slowly and anchored her back against the side. Behind Seth, John winked and turned away from them. Tearing through the paper, she handed the crumpled wads to Seth and lifted the cover. Two things sat side by side in the box. A book and a hat.

"It's a Mary hat!"

Seth took the tam out of the box and set it on her head. "I thought you might need something to throw from up here."

Leaning over the box, she took his face in both hands and kissed him. "I love you."

"Because of a measly old hat?" He reached into the box and turned over the thick, spiral-bound book.

Block lettering across the pale green cover spelled out *April's Dream List*.

"I thought it was time you made your own list." He pulled a pen from his shirt pocket. "And I was kind of hoping I could be on it."

Wiping a tear from the book's cover and another from her chin, April shook her head. "You already are." Taking the pen, she opened the book. . .and her mouth. The shoe box clattered to the basket floor.

A hole had been meticulously cut through the blank pages. And a small black box nestled in the space. With shaking fingers, she lifted the box and then held it out for Seth to open.

The setting sun glinted off the square diamond and the two little emeralds beside it.

"I love you, April Jean, and I want to spend the rest of my life sharing adventures with you."

Smiling through tears, April held out her left hand. "That wasn't a question, but the answer is yes." He slid the ring on, and she raised her hand to the peach pink sun. "You won't be a bachelor anymore."

"No." His arms slipped around her. "But you will be."

Laughing, she leaned into him. "Know what?"

"What?"

"I don't think I'm afraid of heights anymore."

୫

Behind Pastor Owen, the stone chimney stretched to the vaulted ceiling of rustic Douglas Lodge. Flames crackled in the hearth, adding their rhythm to the chords of two acoustic guitars. Outside the windows, red and white pines stood guard and quaking aspen leaves rattled in the September breeze.

April stared down at the silver band that nested with her engagement ring and then up at the man who had just placed it there. She willed the tears that balanced on her lower lashes not to fall on the white satin that rippled at her feet.

Pastor Owen raised his hands. "Ladies and gentlemen, it is my honor and pleasure to introduce to you Mr. and Mrs. Seth Bachelor."

Over the applause, "Ode to Joy" rose from the guitars. As Yvonne handed her bouquet back to her, she whispered, "I told you so."

"You sure did."

Seth took her hand, and they walked down the aisle.

When they reached the back, Yvonne, in floor-length rust-colored satin, took Darren's arm and walked toward them, blowing a kiss to her husband as she passed him.

Tissue wadded in one hand, the other swiping at tears, April's mother, looking stronger than she had in years, held her arms out to Seth first. She kissed her son-in-law on the cheek and turned to April. "Thank you, honey."

"For what?"

"For forgiving my meddling. And for ignoring my advice."

As her mother walked away, April allowed a few brief seconds to scan the reception line, looking for her father. She wasn't surprised he hadn't come.

Seth's parents were next. Rod Bachelor hugged his son in a gesture that didn't seem natural, but his smile seemed genuine. "We'll set four places for Christmas dinner this year." His wife nodded and kissed April on the cheek.

Denisha, holding the hand of a toddling girl in head-to-toe pink, prodded Wesley toward April. "He's having some problems with this big change. He needs some reassurance from you two."

Large brown eyes looked up at Seth. "Is there still gonna be Man Room?"

Seth squatted down to Wesley's level. "Absolutely. Your mom and April and baby Grace will stay in the kitchen where they belong."

A smile split Wesley's face. "That's Girl Room, isn't it?"

In spite of the toe of April's shoe connecting with his leg, Seth laughed. "It sure is."

Another furrow creased the boy's brow as he looked up at April. "Are you gonna be in Daddy and Uncle Seth's comp'ny and chase storms now?"

Seth's face turned up expectantly. "Now there's a good question."

April's eyebrow rose. "You know what? I just might."

"So you're not scared anymore?"

"Oh, I'm still scared. But being brave means doing things even when you're scared."

April hugged friends from college, coworkers, Seth's relatives, and neighbors from her childhood. And then Jill stood before her, tears in her eyes, her manicured nails sweeping along the lines of April's pearl-trimmed gown. "I think you've finally reached your full potential, girl. You look beautiful."

When they'd shaken the last hand and the guests had moved into the dining room, Midge stood alone, facing the fireplace. April walked across the room. "Midge? Are you okay?"

Her aunt's hairsprayed curls bobbed in affirmation, but it took her a moment to turn around. Eyes red, lashes smudged, Midge smiled. "I have something for you." She opened her lavender purse and pulled out a tissue. "Here, you'll need this." The next thing to come out of the clutch was an envelope. "I've been holding on to this for almost two years."

April's name was written on the front. In Caitlyn's handwriting.

Midge walked away, and Seth's arm slid around April's shoulders as she opened the envelope.

Hey Ape,

So this is the big day, huh? The one we always dreamed of. I'm so sorry I can't be there, standing by your side, making you laugh so your mascara doesn't run. Knowing how picky you are, this guy must be amazing. I know you wouldn't settle for anyone who didn't make you feel totally loved and safe and protected. After all you've been through, you deserve that. While you're floating on his arm tonight, think of me, but do it with a smile. I'm dancing with The Bridegroom now.

Love you forever,
Cait

Seth held her until her tears stopped and then took the tissue and wiped her face. "So, Mrs. Bachelor, what's next on your dream list?"

Standing on tiptoes, she brushed her lips against his cheek. "Just you."

STILLWATER PROMISE

To Becky Melby, Patti Haas, Nancy Johnson, and Diane Ross—
I am so blessed having been graced with your friendships
that are filled with love, laughter, and prayers.
Thank you! Cathy

To my father-in-law, Irvin Curtis Melby—the real storyteller in the family.
Thank you for entertaining three generations of Melbys and for painting such
vivid pictures of life in God's country. And in loving remembrance of Lillian
Irene Melby, the woman who raised the man of integrity I fell in love with
and taught me that love grows like a tree adding branches. . .
there will always be enough to go around.
Love, Becky

A special thank-you to JoAnne, our fabulous editor (and her assistant, Jodi),
and to Margie for her great eye. Thank you Bill, Cynthia, Jan, Tiffany,
Carrie, and the amazing Pearl Girls—Patti, Eileen, and Lee—for awesome
editing, ideas, and prayer support. And to Sara's husband, Brian, for Korgy.

Chapter 1

N ot every princess has a prince."

Sara Lewis laughed at the obstinate looks on her daughters' faces.

"Uh-huh. They do so." Zoe, her four-year-old, narrowed her eyes. Deep furrows creased her forehead, and her lips pressed together in a tight line. Snuggled next to her under the faded pink bedspread, two-year-old Sadie mimicked the expression.

Sara tweaked two miniature noses. "Let me tell my story."

"Will the prince be at the end?"

No, the prince will be at the beginning. And then he will fly away to England, leaving the princess all alone but not in a castle. "I promise the story will have a happy ending, okay?"

Zoe folded her arms across Mister Peabody—her worn, stained, once-pink stuffed dog. Sadie folded her arms across her purple pajamas. "Okay."

"Once upon a time, Lady Sara—"

"That's you!"

"Well, it's make-believe me."

Pale blond curls bounced. "Is make-believe Zoe and make-believe Sadie in the story?"

"Absolutely."

Sara stared into two pairs of sky-blue eyes. Her girls had her hair but not her green eyes. Those sky-blue eyes were too much like their father's. She swallowed, smiled, and began the story for the third time.

"Lady Sara and her two little princesses left their tiny little apartment in Pine Bluff and went out for a walk in the woods to pick wildflowers. They were so busy picking pink roses and purple violets and white daisies that they didn't realize how deep in the woods they had wandered."

Zoe's eyes widened. "They were lost, huh?"

"Well, they thought they were. But just then, Princess Sadie found a shiny diamond on the ground, and then, just a few steps away, Princess Zoe found another one and another one. The diamonds were leading them down a path, deeper into the woods."

"And they got loster!"

"Shh. Just listen." Sara tapped the tip of her finger to her lips. "All of a sudden, the path turned and there in front of them was a ginormous castle! All white and sparkly, with a green roof and green shutters and a great big porch with a swing and lots and lots of shiny white rocking chairs."

"Like that one!" Zoe pointed to the mural on the wall. "Is the castle far, far away? Is it in Myoming like Nana and Papa?"

"Is it by Babe?" Sadie sat straight up, white-blond wisps waving as she moved.

"It's pretty far from Babe the Blue Ox. The castle is in Stillwater, and that's *still* in Minnesota. It's about as far away as the Disney Store."

"The one at Mall of 'Merica?"

"Yup."

Sadie held up one finger, her sign for the world to stop and give her center stage. "We goed there with Grandma Connie one time."

Sara rubbed the muscle at the back of her neck that tightened reflexively at the mention of her mother-in-law. In just under twelve hours, Connie Lewis would descend upon her girls like an overcaffeinated toucan and whisk them away for three days while Sara went to work. After Sunday it would take Sara four days to get them back to some semblance of a calm routine, and then the circus would began all over again. "We *went* there with Grandma Connie," she corrected.

"Uh-huh. To Yego Yand."

Zoe gave an exasperated sigh. "Say L–L–Lego, Sadie."

"L–L–Yego."

Sara held up one finger. "It's almost time to turn out the light. Should I tell the story another time?"

"No. We'll be quiet." Zoe patted the pillow next to her. "Lie down, Sadie, and shut your eyes and 'magine the castle."

Sara stifled a yawn, thinking she'd give about anything to just lie down, close her eyes, and imagine her Stillwater castle.

&

Still sitting on the edge of the bed long after her girls had fallen asleep, Sara stared at her daughters in their hand-me-down pajamas. Outside, ice-laced snow pelted the window, gathering along the ledge. The wind whistled around the corner of the old building. Sara wrapped her sweatshirt jacket a little tighter but shivered anyway.

This was her last year of secondhand living. By this time next winter, she'd have a fireplace to curl up next to after tucking Zoe and Sadie into their canopy bed. By this time next year, she'd be decorating the Stillwater Inn for Christmas.

She pulled the shade down and began her nightly ritual. Books in the book basket, sorted by size. Plastic toys in the plastic bin, stuffed animals in the net that hung in the corner of the room. She straightened a picture, turned off the lamp, and picked up a dirty sock and a pair of 3T jeans on her way out the door.

Three bowls sat on the small, scarred table pushed against the wall between her kitchenette and living room. Remnants of Hamburger Helper, sans hamburger, covered the bottoms of the bowls. She cleared the table and wiped it off then took off her red-striped apron and moved a large cardboard box from the counter to the table. In it were ten white paper bags with snowman faces made from felt and yarn. Each bag was filled with Christmas cookies. She glanced at the clock on the stove. All she had yet to do was make the tags. From index cards she'd picked up at the dollar store, she cut five freehand snowflakes and printed names on each. She'd just finished attaching the tag labeled "Raquel & Allison" when there was a knock on the door. As usual, Mattie Jennet was on time.

Sara opened the door to find Mattie, in her heavy EMT jacket, shaking off snow like a wet puppy. "It's miserable out there. Two accidents since four o'clock."

"You could have waited until tomorrow."

Running fingers through her dark blond hair streaked with silver, Mattie smiled. "Neither sleet nor snow nor a daughter in labor will keep a Sanctuary mentor from her appointed rounds."

"What?" Sara held the door for Mattie. "Shouldn't you be with Sydney?"

"Nah. That's what husbands are for. I've delivered my share of babies, but I'd be a wreck with my own daughter." Mattie unzipped her jacket and pointed to a cell phone and a pager clipped to her belt. "So I'm on rescue squad *and* grand-baby call tonight. Are the girls asleep?"

Sara nodded. "They were exhausted after helping me bake cookies all day." She pointed to the box on the table. "Would you mind taking cookies to the Middletons and Gwyneth and the new residents?"

"No problem. That's so sweet of you."

"Hey, you paid for the ingredients."

"No." Mattie's voice held an undercurrent of maternal sternness. "We give you vouchers, but you make choices. You could have spent that money on candy bars or magazines."

Embarrassed yet quietly warmed by the praise, Sara stuck her hands in her pockets.

Mattie slipped off her boots, laid her jacket on the floor, and walked over to the box. "Do you have any idea how easy you make my job?"

Sara shrugged.

"Out of the twelve apartments in the Sanctuary program, yours is the only one I can walk into without taking a deep breath and praying for patience...and certainly the only one where the floors are clean enough to eat off and the soup cans are alphabetized!" Mattie pulled out a chair and sat at the kitchen table. "I've decided to create a new award. I'm calling it the Bounce Award. And you're the first recipient."

Sara let her look of confusion suffice for an answer.

"You bounce back faster and better than anyone I've ever met. Your husband walks out on you, and you bounce. You're smoked out of your apartment, and you bounce. A twister destroys your trailer. . .and you bounce back to us, still smiling and being a mom to everyone in this building. You're amazing."

"Amazing will be when I bounce out of here and your church is no longer subsidizing my food and rent." Sara wrapped her arms around her middle. "How about some tea?"

"That would be wonderful, but you're not going to get me off track that easily. You need to learn to take a compliment, young lady."

Opening the lid on the teapot and holding it under the faucet, Sara repeated the shrug. "It's. . .uncomfortable."

"You'll have to get used to it when your bed-and-breakfast starts getting rave reviews."

Sara laughed. "Only three hundred and forty-seven days until the Stillwater Inn is under the management of Sara Lewis. I'm planning a grand reopening." She took two cups from the cupboard and brought them to the table. After shoving the cardboard box toward the wall, she sat down. "Let's get the accountability questions out of the way in case you have to run to the hospital." She took an exaggerated breath. "I haven't smoked, gotten drunk, used illegal substances, been with a man, or broken the law in the past seven days. I have paid my bills, stuck to my budget, gotten to work on time, kept my apartment clean, disciplined my children. . .most of the time. . .and tried to be an asset to the community. And the spiritual stuff isn't mandatory, so I'm all good."

"Like I said, you make my job easy."

"I may take over your job someday."

Leaning forward, Mattie rested her hand on Sara's. "As soon as you figure out the spiritual stuff *is* mandatory, I'll create a position in the Sanctuary program just for you."

Sara shifted in her chair, wishing the teapot would whistle. This was the part of Mattie's visits she hated. She had no doubt that Mattie Jennet was the kind of person she was because of her religious beliefs. It worked for the Jennets and most of the people Sara had met from Pineview Community Church. But it didn't work for her.

Mattie patted Sara's hand. "Do you want to know what I pray for you?"

"I. . .guess."

"I'm praying that God won't leave you alone until you admit you need Him."

The sound of pressure building in the teapot brought Sara to her feet. What would an answer to Mattie's prayer look like? A pay raise? A new husband? Or another natural disaster?

"A letter came to the church for you." Mattie ripped open a tea bag packet.

"If it's a bill, you can keep it." After the tornado, before she'd known she'd end up back in a Sanctuary apartment for the second time in two years, Sara had arranged for her mail to be forwarded to Mattie's church. Some of it still ended up there. "Is it my Visa bill?" Mattie knew every detail of her finances. Her credit card bill, much of it racked up by the man who was still legally her husband, the man she hadn't laid eyes on since Sadie was eight months old, was the final hurdle she'd have to jump before realizing her goal.

A pensive look creased the lines around Mattie's mouth. "It's not a bill. It's a letter." Slowly she reached toward her back pocket, pulled out the envelope, and laid it on the table. "It's from London. . .from James."

⁊

"He thinks that's going to make everything all better? Just like that—*poof!*—five years of being a self-centered, immature, irresponsible lousy excuse for a man is just wiped away?" Sara's laugh teetered on the edge of hysteria. She kicked a stuffed pony, sending it flying at a fake green ficus tree. Mattie had left hours ago, so she ranted at the cracked living room walls.

The words of the letter were branded on her brain, burning and blistering, and no amount of raging at the walls was going to douse the pain. For the third time, she picked up the cell phone she shared with her neighbor because they were both clinging to every dollar they earned. For the third time, she slammed it back on the counter. If James were paying the bill, she'd make an overseas call in a heartbeat. But James hadn't paid a bill since Sadie was born.

> *Dear Sara,*
> *I can't possibly do justice to an apology in a letter, so consider this just my first step in the right direction.*

Sara stared at the spotted beige carpeting. *No, James, your first step in the right direction was out the door.* Not that she had seen it that way at the time, of course.

There were cookie crumbs on the carpet—cookie crumbs and red and green sugar and little chocolate jimmies. She walked into her bedroom, opened the closet, and took out the carpet sweeper.

> *I'm not the same man I was two years ago. I've given my life to Jesus Christ, and now I know that only God can save our marriage.*

Cookie crumbs ticked against metal as the roller brush whisked them into the sweeper. *Why didn't God save our marriage back when I still loved you? Back when I begged you not to leave us? Back when Zoe sobbed herself to sleep every night, crying for her daddy?*

> *I'm sending you a book that a friend recommended. It's called* Recipe for a Godly Wife.

Recipe? How about this for a recipe, James: one part commitment, two parts sacrifice, and a pinch of putting your dreams on hold for your kids? The carpet sweeper banged the leg of the couch, leaving a dent.

In the meantime, here are some tracts that explain the basics of what it means to be a Christian.

I know what it means to be a Christian, James. I've seen it up close in the people who gave me a place to live when you didn't, in the Sanctuary volunteers who aren't afraid to get close to recovering addicts and ex-cons and kids with AIDS.

Walking into the kitchen, she opened the cupboard under the sink and retrieved the tracts she'd shoved into the trash can. On one, fierce orange flames licked at the title—"Where Will You Spend Eternity?"

Mechanically she closed the cupboard door and stood next to the counter, tearing the tracts into minuscule pieces. Scooping the confetti into her hand, she turned and walked to the door. In worn-thin slippers she padded into the hallway and opened the front door.

Sleet stung her face as she stepped onto the porch, leaned over the railing, and opened her fist, scattering bits and pieces of angry flames into the wind.

Chapter 2

Grandma Connie's here!" Zoe flew into Sara's room in nothing but her Dora the Explorer underwear. "She has gernola."

"*Gran*ola." Sara caught Zoe and shoved an undershirt over her head. "Of course she does," she muttered. Her mother-in-law couldn't just feed the girls her homemade nuts and twigs at her house; she had to show up fifteen minutes early with her labeled zippered bags and plop them on the counter next to Sara's off-brand graham crackers and skim milk.

Sadie's squeal of delight sounded from the living room. That tone meant only one thing—Grandma Connie had brought something, probably something pink. Sara ran a brush through her hair and squared her shoulders. After practicing her smile in the mirror, she turned off the light. In her cheeriest voice she sang out, "Good morning!" as she walked into the living room.

"*Bom dia!*" Connie held Sadie by the armpits, swinging her around in a waltz pattern. "I'm practicing my Portuguese for our trip to Brazil." As they danced, something that looked like a neon rainbow bounced in Sadie's hands.

Smile glued firmly in place, Sara nodded at the plump woman in the crinkly all-cotton periwinkle blue jumper and fur-lined leather boots. Connie had been planning a trip to somewhere as long as Sara had known her, but the money in the vacation envelope always got diverted. One year it went to beekeeping equipment, another to a spinning wheel. The last Sara knew, both were gathering dust in her in-laws' private museum, otherwise known as their garage. "What did Grandma Connie bring you, Sadie?"

Connie stopped spinning. The clusters of hand-sculpted red cubes that dangled from her ears didn't. She set Sadie down. "Show Mommy what the poor people in India made."

"A Christmas dress! One for Zoe, too." Sadie held out a limp, crumpled sack dress.

Sara's smile tightened. "Ah. Purple and pink and yellow and orange. . .what Christmassy colors. Say 'thank you,' and go get the clothes I laid out, girls."

"Wait, Sadie! Wait, Zoe!" Wooden bracelets collided on Connie's pale, pudgy arm as she waved them back. She turned to Sara. "I just read on earthgrandma. com that you should never lump your children together by saying 'kids' or 'boys' or 'girls' but should always use their names. It gives them a stronger sense of personal identity."

"Fascinating." *And what do matching rainbow dresses do to their "personal identity"?*

"Oh, and you shouldn't always refer to them in their birth order. You don't want to establish a hierarchy in the family." She smiled at the girls. "Sadie, Zoe . . .I have an idea! Let's find the reindeer shirts I made you and get our pictures taken with Santa after we go to Grandma's t'ai chi chih class!"

"Um. . .wait." Sara's tinny laugh accompanied the finger she held in the air. "I think the shirts are dirty." The oversized sponge-painted shirts had, in fact, been worn just yesterday and were now folded next to the princess dresses and clown costumes. She didn't want Connie to know that her masterpieces had found a home in the dress-up box.

Her mother-in-law donned a quizzical look. "Dirty? How I wish you knew the meaning of the word. A little disarray would be so good for their souls, Sara."

"The sweaters I laid out will be just fine for a picture." Sara tried in vain to relax her neck muscles as she told the girls, for the second time, to go get their clothes then turned to Connie. "I thought you said they didn't have child care at your exercise class."

Connie laughed. "The boy who works at the front desk downstairs watches Sadie and Zoe for me."

Sara opened her mouth, but Connie flashed a smile like a little girl with a secret. "I had a wonderful conversation with the dean of admissions at the community college in Coon Rapids. I know his wife through the arts council, you know." She talked in a conspiratorial whisper. "And. . .he said. . .that just for me he'd guarantee that you can still get in for the spring semester! They have openings in the social work degree program, and you could take classes Monday through Thursday and still be able to keep your job."

Sara's fingernails pressed into the palms of her hands. "Thank you for checking on it." *Again.* "It's just not possible right now." *And it never will be because I DON'T WANT TO BE A SOCIAL WORKER!* Yelling in her head brought a smidgen of relief.

"Nonsense. If you had a degree, you could get paid for doing what you do anyway." Connie's hand swept toward the front door. "And you wouldn't have to live in a place like this to do it. With your low-income status, you'd qualify for a gazillion grants and loans. And"—her expression morphed into an unconvincingly sympathetic smile—"when the divorce is finalized, I'm sure you'd get even more."

The moon-shaped grooves in Sara's hands throbbed. "We haven't filed yet."

"Well yes, but when you do. . .how many times have Neil and I told you that we'd watch Zoe and Sadie? You know, if the gir—Sadie and Zoe were with us, it'd be a party every minute."

A party every minute. That was the philosophy that had turned James and his brother Brock into people who looked like adults on the outside but handled disappointment and responsibility like toddlers. When a wife and children disrupted James's dreams, he ran. When losing two friends—one to leukemia and one in a car accident—set Brock's world on end, he partied to avoid thinking and grieving.

"If I went to school for anything, it would be to finish my interior design degree."

"You'd end up decorating houses for snobby people in the Twin Cities and lose your passion for people and art. Take it from someone who tried. When I had my sculptures on display in that upscale gallery, I started thinking in dollar signs just like those people."

But your two-headed giraffes and elephants with wings didn't sell! "Interior design isn't quite the sa—"

"Art should be free. . .like air." Connie's fluffy black hair bobbed as her head shook.

Sara's tongue was sore from holding it in place with her teeth. "That's not the advice you gave James."

"Well. . ." Connie spun a wooden bracelet with a thick finger. "Music is a different story. And James is a different subject altogether." She looked up but not at Sara. Her eyes took on a glazed, faraway look. "My boy was destined to do great things."

※

"Hey, Lewis! Quit yer lollygaggin', and give me a hand with this amp."

James set down the pen that he'd been holding an inch above the paper for the past ten minutes and waited while a Metropolitan Police car sped past the window, siren wailing, blue lights flashing. Nights in this part of London were never quiet. Over the repetitive clunking of wooden chairs being upended on tables and the bartenders' after-hours chatter, James yelled to the drummer. "Be there in a sec." He folded the unfinished letter and stuck it in the pocket of the battered leather jacket he'd bought eight years ago.

Had the first letter reached her? Maybe he'd never know. It wasn't likely she'd answer—his wife had every reason to hate him.

But something was prodding him to try. No, not something. . .Someone. The first cracks in his denial had started in July. His best friend's nagging played a part. And the pictures his mother sent of his daughters—pictures intended to draw him home—not to his wife but to his girls—were wearing him down, too. His girls were getting so big. . .and looking so much like their mother. The conviction had been growing for months, but it had only been in the last few weeks that he'd felt the go-ahead to actually contact Sara. He'd plied his mother for details, but she was being tight-lipped about Sara's whereabouts. Her reluctance didn't surprise him—she'd never approved of Sara. He'd just about killed his mother by marrying a waitress. James was sure his little brother had the answers to all his questions, but Brock was silent for totally different reasons. Brock was protecting Sara. . .from James.

Where was she living since the tornado? What was she doing? For all he knew, she'd found someone to take his place—someone who fit the mold better than he'd been willing to.

Was he crazy to wish for another chance when Sara regretted giving him the first. . .and second?

It wasn't like he hadn't warned her. Five minutes after meeting Sara Martin, the chatty little blond behind the counter at Perk Place, he'd told her flat out that he and his band were on their way to Canada—which was just a stepping-stone to their dream goal—England. He'd warned her that she'd better turn those gorgeous green eyes on some other guy. She'd acted shocked at his comment, but James had her figured. The half can of whipping cream she'd mounded on his pumpkin pie told him all he needed to know. His buddy Reece, sitting right next to him, had gotten a dollop the size of a quarter.

If only she'd listened to him. If only he'd listened to himself.

No, Lord, I don't mean that. If she hadn't snared him with those startlingly green eyes, he wouldn't have those rumpled pictures in his wallet. And if it weren't for those two pairs of blue eyes staring up from the pictures, maybe he wouldn't have taken Reece seriously when he'd popped back in his life acting like a Jesus freak.

And if it weren't for Jesus, he was pretty sure he wouldn't have just applied for a job in Minnesota.

∞

Sara scraped the frost off her windshield with a cracked CD case as she watched the back end of Connie's Ford Escape turn the corner with Zoe and Sadie tucked in their car seats in the back. Something in her wanted to run after them, to pull the girls out of the car and hold them close for just another minute before being away from them for three days. She hadn't had a chance to ask details about the boy who watched her girls at the health club. She tried to tell herself that their grandmother wouldn't do anything to put them at risk, but it still didn't sit right with her. Unfortunately she wasn't in a position to call the shots. A stray tear hit the glass and froze as it rolled down the sloped window.

"Sara, wait up!" Allison Johansen, seventeen years old and six months pregnant by a boy who had fled the scene, waved from the porch and started down the steps, her jacket and long dishwater-blond hair flapping in the wind. "Can I hitch a ride to town with you?"

"Sure. Be careful on those steps, Al."

Allison was laughing when she reached the car. "Man, I'm sick of feeling like a cow." She pointed toward the corner. "Hey, I almost asked Crazy Connie for a ride just to see the look on her face."

Sara bit down on her tongue. She was the grownup in this conversation. Besides, anything she said to Allison would find its way to her brother-in-law. Who knew which recycled words Brock might use as ammunition against Connie in a mother-son fight? "She would have given you a ride."

"Yeah, right. It drives her wacky that Brock and me hang out. You shoulda heard her hulk out on him last week."

They got in the car, and Sara turned off the country music station. "Where am I taking you?"

"My friend Diana's house. We're just chillaxin.'"

"Translate, kid."

"Chillin' and relaxin.' You know, watching movies, talkin' about how lame Christmas is, and eating cookie dough all day. Just don't be a squealer, okay?"

"You really need to take your doctor's orders seriously. You don't want to end up with an emergency C-section like your mom had."

Allison blew her bangs out of her eyes. "Things have changed since back then. They have drugs for gestational diabetes now. Hey, did you know that your ex is a Bible thumper? Brock got a letter with a bunch of weird stuff in it." She widened her eyes and held her hands, fingers bent and wiggling, next to her face. "Where will yooooou spend eternity?" A wicked laugh followed.

"What does Brock think about it?"

"He thought it was funny, but. . .I don't know. He used to be into that stuff before that girl died."

"Caitlyn."

"Yeah. Hey, at least he's not into all that chanting stuff Crazy Connie does."

"Chanting? What do you mean?"

Allison shrugged. "Brock says she lights candles all over and sits on the floor in the living room, mooing like a baby cow."

Sara laughed, but the vision of Connie mooing triggered a flash of anxiety. What kind of nonsense was Connie exposing the girls to? "I think she's just doing her tai chi exercises."

"Yeah, maybe. Or maybe she's doing voodoo on you and me cuz we messed with her boys."

Nerve endings prickled along Sara's spine. Allison's perception of Connie's territorial nature surprised her. "Connie may be"—nothing positive came to mind for several seconds—"eccentric, but her heart is really in the right place."

A laugh, almost as evil sounding as the last one, came from Allison. "Who you kidding? I hear her talking to you. She's frontin' you with all that nicey-nice, girl."

"What do you mean?"

Allison's hands folded over her belly. "I mean she's scammin' to take your kids away."

Chapter 3

Working at Tippet House wasn't just a job; it was an apprenticeship. Today it was also an escape—from thoughts of James's letter and Allison's chilling words. Eight hours ago, as she'd driven up the drive lined with ice-crusted trees to the old Victorian covered in traditional "painted lady" nursery room colors, Sara had left most of her roller coaster emotions behind. In spite of only four hours of sleep, she was on task, ready to tackle three days of work, ready to pepper Bessie with questions and collect answers and instructions like a human DVR. Until Sunday night when she drove back down the winding lane, she'd do her best to put her mother-in-law and James and his newfound religion, on PAUSE.

Sara set a square pan of hot gingerbread on a trivet and pulled off the oven mitts. "How'd I do?" She beamed at the woman with the steel gray hair pulled back in a painfully severe bun.

"Perfect." Bessie Tippet dabbed at her temples with the hem of her apron. Bumpy arthritic fingers pulled a flour sack towel off her shoulder and began wiping a glass plate. "Better than mine, actually."

"Never."

Bessie held the plate up to the light. "Did you chill the beaters?"

Sara opened the double-wide stainless steel refrigerator. She took a pint of whipping cream off a shelf and pointed to the crockery bowl and beaters next to it.

"Good girl."

The front door buzzer sounded as she plugged in the mixer. The timing was just right. Bessie would show the first Friday night guests to the Tremayne Room. As soon as they were settled, they'd come downstairs and join their hostess for warm gingerbread and Devonshire tea in the spacious kitchen. And Sara would slip away to her pile of decorating magazines in the third-floor maid's quarters until nine, when it was time to fix the "Hearthside Hot Chocolate" and shortbread cookies Tippet House was famous for.

Bessie went to answer the door, and Sara did a quick mental tour of the house. She'd spent the morning scrubbing claw-footed bathtubs, making hospital corners on flowered sheets, and arranging lace-trimmed pillows in Glen, Penrose, Brae, and Tremayne, the four upstairs guestrooms. Since noon she'd cleaned five fireplaces and stacked them with fresh wood, baked four dozen shortbread cookies and two pans of gingerbread. There wasn't a single fingerprint left on the refrigerator or stove.

Stiff peaks topped the sweetened cream when Bessie walked back into the kitchen, dabbing her top lip with a tissue. Her face was flushed.

"Are you all right?"

"Right as rain." Bessie straightened the lunch cloth on the table. "I've got some paperwork to get to. Would you mind being the hostess tonight?"

Sara glanced down at her baggy-kneed jeans and the bleached spot on her purple sweatshirt. It could all be covered with the white apron that hung on the back of the door. "Of course."

"There will be two couples coming around six. The man who just came is a businessman headed to International Falls. Just here for the night. Doesn't seem like much of a talker." Bessie picked up a list of local restaurants and fanned her face with it as she examined the sugar spoon for spots. "Does that make you uncomfortable?"

"Finding words isn't a big problem with me. It'll be good practice."

"Then I'll see you in the morning."

Bessie walked into the back bedroom that doubled as her office, and Sara filled a cream pitcher. She'd just set it on the table when she heard footsteps descending the curved staircase and walking through the parlor. She grabbed the apron, slipped it over her head, and was just tying it around her waist when she froze.

"Reece!"

∞

The last time she'd seen the six-foot-plus sandy-blond bass player was just over two years ago. She'd handed her husband's ex–best friend an ice pack on his way out the door.

"Hi, Sara."

"What. . . ?" The last she'd heard, Reece Landon was in New York City.

"You're still the only woman I've met under eighty who wears an apron." He grinned and shook his head. "I'd say I was just passing through, but I don't imagine you'd believe that."

He'd come to see her. Just what was she expected to say to that? She couldn't deny it was a scenario she'd toyed with more than once. Sara pulled out a chair and sank into it, motioning for him to do the same. "Would you. . .like some gingerbread?" That would buy her a few minutes to figure out if she was glad to see him. Could Reece Landon possibly do anything but complicate her life even more?

"Did you bake it?" Reece shrugged out of his sport coat and hung it on the back of the chair. "Nobody bakes like you."

Sara nodded, pretending her face didn't feel like she'd just opened the oven. "It's still warm. And there's homemade whipped cream."

A gentle, rolling laugh accompanied Reece's "I'd love some." He stretched his long legs out under the table. "If you're not too stingy on the whipped cream."

Sara stood and walked over to the counter, relieved to have a reason to turn her back. She cut a larger-than-usual piece of cake and loaded it with whipped cream. As the spoon clattered back against the side of the bowl, she realized the gesture would send a message she didn't want to send. Or did she? It was too late to second-guess now. She set the plate in front of him.

"Thank you." His gaze latched on hers as he picked up his fork.

"Still take your coffee black?" She opened the cupboard and took down a mug. Reece Landon wasn't a teacup kind of man.

He nodded, smiled around his first bite, and winked. "Delicious."

Sitting down across from him, Sara didn't even try to disguise her curiosity. "You've changed." It wasn't just the haircut, the close shave, or sport coat.

"A little older." He rubbed his left hand across the knuckles of his right. "And much wiser."

"How is your hand?"

"It tells me when the weather's changing." He took another bite of gingerbread. Sara let the silence hang, sensing there was more he wanted to say. After he swallowed, he shook his head slowly. "Always wondered what would have happened if I'd hit his chin instead of your wall."

Sara allowed a fraction of a smile. "If his little girls couldn't keep him home, I don't think a fist in his face would have done it." She spread her hand on the tablecloth, not close enough to actually touch him. "I never got to thank you for trying to keep my family together. You lost your best friend over my marriage."

Reece shrugged. "Hey, I had a few principles even back then. I couldn't partner with a guy who'd leave his wife and kids." His hand closed over hers for a moment then dropped to his knee. "Have you managed okay, Sara?"

Trying to focus on anything but the brief warmth of his skin on hers, she told him about getting into the Sanctuary program and about the fire that had started in the apartment above hers. She described life with the elderly lady who'd taken them in and how she'd finally gotten out on her own in a tiny rented mobile home that was destroyed by a tornado just months later. "And here I am. Back to taking handouts. Back to waking up grateful but angry every morning."

She described her plans to take over managing the bed-and-breakfast in Stillwater. When his gently probing questions about how she was coping threatened to crack the veneer she'd worked so hard to layer over raw emotions, she turned the spotlight on to him. "What are you doing now?"

"I'm living in the Cities and managing the cabins our family owns in International Falls. We're building three more cabins not far from here."

"You. . .working for your dad? This is not the Reece I once knew."

A sheepish smile parted his lips. "I used to be ashamed of my family's money. But I've figured out that if you don't make it an idol, it's pretty handy stuff to have."

"Tell me about it."

"You know..." Reece leaned forward. "I might have a job opportunity for you."

"Oh, really."

"I need somebody local to show properties and take reservations. I may have one person, but I could use two." He smiled as if there were some inside joke attached to his offer. "I could use someone with your obsessive-compulsive list-making tendencies."

Sara wrinkled her nose. "What makes you think I'm still a list maker?"

Reece nodded toward the open spiral notebook on the desk behind him. "I recognized the handwriting. Are you for hire?"

"Thanks, but I love what I'm doing." She eased away until her back rested on the chair. "Are you still with a band?"

"No." Reece set his fork down. "Well, no and yes. I still play, but now it's with the worship team at my church."

Church? Worship band? *Reece?* A gear locked in Sara's brain, making another thought impossible.

He laughed. "I know. Who woulda thunk it, huh? I found the Lord about a year and a half ago." He set his napkin on the table and pushed his plate aside. "And a few months ago I had the privilege of leading your husband to Christ."

The gear dislodged, sending questions ricocheting in her head. The front doorbell buzzed just as she harnessed one fact and clung to it. One reality that made her stomach lurch.

Reece wasn't here to *see* her. He was here to convert her.

❧

They hadn't had another moment alone after the next guests arrived. Reece left for International Falls right after breakfast on Saturday yet still managed to follow her around all weekend. As Sara drove away from Tippet House just after four on Sunday, the look in Reece's eyes as she'd served hot chocolate, chatted with the guests, and set out the quiche-like *sformatino* for breakfast, still clawed at her insides. He'd stared at her the same way Mattie and her daughter Sydney and Audrey, the pastor's wife, looked at her—as if she were lost. It was straight-up pity, the kind of look Sara would give a toddler in the grocery store who'd strayed from her mother.

As if Reece setting up camp in her head wasn't enough of a strain, Bessie had acted weird all weekend, staying in her room much of the time and pushing Sara to do things she hadn't been trained to do. It had been good experience hosting breakfast, taking phone reservations, and being the go-to person for the guests, but Sara didn't appreciate the dump-her-in-the-deep-end education. Bessie was planning a trip to visit her sister in Arizona in February, and this was probably her way of being sure Sara could handle it all. But she could have given a bit of warning.

She turned onto the highway. Orange light flickered between the pines, stretching long, thin shadows across the snow-swirled road. Sara turned on the radio. Connie would bring the girls home at five on the dot, and she needed to have her head in a much better place by then. Kenny Chesney was in the middle of "Better as a Memory." The irony almost made her smile. Almost but not quite. *"Move on. . .Walk away. . .I'm just a dreamer. . . ."* James had made her "better as a memory" list long before he'd actually walked out the door. Maybe she'd add Reece to the lineup now.

Had it really been only five years since James and Reece had walked into Perk Place and rearranged her life? She'd been nineteen, overconfident, and way too flirty for her own good. She'd just finished her first year of interior design at the Art Institute in Mendota Heights and was home for the summer, holding down two jobs to earn money for tuition. Her mother had remarried and moved to Wyoming, so Sara was sleeping on a friend's futon on the floor. Her days were spent baking and waiting on customers at the coffee shop, her nights in the kitchen of the Sage Stoppe, Pine Bluff's only upscale restaurant, owned, at the time, by Bessie Tippet.

She could still see the two of them walking through the door in their leather jackets and faded jeans. There was something European about their appearance. Later she'd learned that it was a long-calculated look, designed to impress the agent they hoped to sign with.

Sara hadn't been the only one to take notice. The other girl working behind the counter had voiced out loud the sigh in Sara's mind. "I get the tall blond," she'd whispered. That was fine with Sara. Her eyes were riveted to the dark-haired one with the strong square jaw and sky-blue eyes. The men both ordered pumpkin pie. Funny how a little thing like whipped cream could turn a man's head.

Just like Kenny Chesney's song, James had let her know early on that he wasn't interested in anything serious. He had a dream—a dream that included an agent in Canada and gigs in Liverpool and London. A dream that didn't include a waitress in Pine Bluff, Minnesota. *"Move on. . .Walk away. . . I'm just a dreamer. . . ."* Instead of listening, the challenge only made the chase that much sweeter. And she'd won, for a while. . . .

The song ended, and Sara turned off the radio. She couldn't risk another memory fueler. She turned her thoughts to her girls. These weekends away from them were hard. Missing them was a constant ache. She didn't feel quite whole without their chatter. Sunday night supper was a celebration and always the same—generic frozen pizza with instant chocolate pudding for dessert. The girls fought over stirring the pudding, ending up with far more on them than in the bowl. Sunday nights ended with a bubble bath and scrubbing the kitchen from top to bottom.

She was smiling when she turned onto Wright Avenue. But it didn't last long.

Reece Landon stood on her front porch.

She'd given him her address. He'd said he wanted to keep in touch. This wasn't what she thought he had in mind. Her legs felt tired and heavy as she got out of the car and walked toward him.

He was smiling, but it didn't hide that look of pity. "I wanted to say good-bye before I head home. And I was kind of hoping to see the girls."

Sara nodded. She wasn't mad at him. He hadn't, after all, tried to preach at her. . .or given her a tract with flames on it. Her disappointment had come from her own foolish ideas when he'd walked into the kitchen and looked at her in a way that made her feel significant. In a way that made her feel like something more than just a mom. She opened the front door, and he followed her into the hallway. "I can't ask you in. It's stupid, but it's house rules. Brock is the only guy who can be here since he's family, unless there are other people around."

Reece pulled his stocking cap off and then his gloves. "That's a good rule." He *had* changed. "The girls will be back any minute."

In the awkward silence, Sara motioned toward the steps leading to the second floor. "Have a seat." She unlocked the door to her apartment. "I'll get some coffee." Raising her voice to be heard over the reverberating bass of rap music from one of the upstairs apartments, she pointed toward the source of the noise. "That's also against the rules."

His hands in air guitar position, Reece shook his head in time to the beat of the bass. Now this was the Reece she knew. When he stopped, he was laughing. "Don't bother with coffee. I can't stay long." His hand touched her shoulder. "I just can't leave without saying something face-to-face."

Here it comes. The salvation pitch. Sara closed her eyes and sighed, then she opened them and stared, waiting for the inevitable.

"Give James a chance. He's not the same guy who walked out on you. And he loves you, Sara."

Without warning, tears stung her eyes. Her throat tightened. *"He loves you."* Those were words she couldn't afford to believe. Tears slipped over her lashes, and she swiped at them with a gloved hand.

Reece's arms wrapped around her. He pressed her head to his wool coat. She felt the roughness of his chin against her hair—

The front door opened. Connie Lewis stepped into the foyer.

Chapter 4

Only one eye open, James groped for the insistent phone. In the red glow of his alarm clock—1:01 a.m.—he read the caller ID. His mother had never quite grasped the time difference between Pine Bluff, Minnesota, and London, England. It would be a nice respectable 7:01 p.m. back home.

"'Ello, Mother." He salted his greeting with a heavy British beat, just to irritate her. He was letting her off pretty easily for waking him up after only an hour of sleep.

"James." She said it like a reprimand. As usual.

"What's up?"

"I just got home from taking the girls back."

He sat up and flipped the switch on his lava lamp. "Are they okay?"

"I. . .don't know."

His eyes were wide open now. "What's wrong? What happened?"

"I caught your wife making out with Reece Landon."

Making out? Nobody says "making out" anymore. His brain stuck on the seventies vocabulary before wrapping around the scene she was describing—his once-best friend kissing the woman he was, at least legally, still married to.

"James. It's time to end this. File for divorce and full custody, and come home and take care of your children. They need stability. She's bounced them around from place to place, and who knows how many men she's had living with her. It's not healthy."

Questions churned and multiplied like a mushroom cloud. Other men? Did his mother know of others? Reece and Sara together? It shouldn't surprise him. They'd hit it off from the beginning. It wouldn't take much to turn it into something deeper. Sara had to be lonely, and she owed him nothing. But Reece? The guy who had come all the way to England to hunt him down? The guy who had shown him what a Jesus-following, changed-from-the-inside man looks like?

Sara's unfaithfulness he could justify. Reece's betrayal was a knife to the gut.

Then again, Reece had just called him about the job opening back home. What was that all about? Wasn't there a saying about keeping your friends close and your enemies closer? "What did you see?" He really only wanted an answer if it was better than where his thoughts were leading.

"You heard me. I walked in the door with the girls, and there they were—going at it, totally oblivious to the rest of the world."

Pressing his thumb and forefinger against his eyes didn't black out the vision.

Lord, I deserve this, I know I do, but. . . But what? But turn back the clock? Make it like it never happened? Like I was never so caught up in myself that I destroyed the best thing I ever had?

"Do you know anything more? Did Sara explain anything? Are they living together?"

"I assume so. She didn't explain a thing. After I'd watched your girls for three long days, all she could say was 'Get your hands off my children.'"

∞

Chocolate pudding splattered the table, the wall, the floor, and Sara, but the girls were clean, read to, and sound asleep. Rinsing the ragged dishcloth for the second time, Sara stared at the chocolate-tinted water rushing toward the drain. Slowly it turned milky brown then clear again.

Wash it away. Why couldn't she just wash it away? Zoe's fear-filled eyes as Connie pulled her back toward the car. Sadie's mittened hand stretching out to her. "Mommy!"

Never in her life had Sara moved so fast. Out the door, down the steps, one arm grabbing Sadie while the fingers of her other hand latched onto Zoe's jacket hood. But Connie didn't let go. She kept moving, her back to Sara, toward her car.

"Get your hands off my children!"

"No. You've crossed the line this time."

Sara folded the pudding-smeared cloth over on itself. *This time?* What other imaginary lines had she crossed?

With the flood of "what-ifs" rushing through the center of her brain, she couldn't grapple with that question right now. What if Reece hadn't stepped in to pull Sadie out of Connie's arms while Sara untangled Zoe's fingers from her mother-in-law's clutch? What if Allison was right and Connie really did want to take her girls away from her?

Icy tendrils of fear tightened around her chest. What could she say in court that would hold up against all that James's parents had to offer? Their old farmhouse on two acres between Pine Bluff and North Branch was equivalent to Disney World in her girls' eyes. Brock had built the most elaborate backyard playground Sara had ever seen—two sandboxes, a kiddie pool, three slides, swings of every height, rings and ropes, and a teeter-totter. Inside the house, the girls had their own room. Purple, pink, and sparkles. Nothing faded. Nothing secondhand.

Her girls were well fed, healthy, and secure, and anyone could see they were happy. Yet for the past few nights, Sara had awakened in a cold sweat after a dream that almost became reality just hours ago. Sometimes Connie stood at her door demanding her children, sometimes uniformed officers with guns. She'd rehearsed her lines over and over in her sleep. *They're mine! You can't take them! Get your hands off my children!*

Filling the sink with water and detergent, she watched three plastic bowls rise on the tide, slowly fill, and capsize. Bubbles swept across the surface of the water until the bowls were hidden from view.

"He loves you, Sara."

Only in the books that littered the floor in the next room did the prince come home to rescue the princess with his undying love. In real life, love dies.

"Give James a chance."

What if that was the only way to keep the girls?

"He's not the same guy who walked out on you."

Bubbles glistened, clean and pristine. Sara fished for a capsized bowl. Beneath the white froth, the water had turned murky brown.

Maybe not so different from a man who claims he's not what he used to be.

෪

A soft glow lit the room. The three-foot Christmas tree in the corner boasted two strings of colored lights and a dozen frosted sugar cookies hung by red yarn. Sara pulled a blanket off the back of the couch, wrapped it around herself, and sat down, wedging her feet between the cushions. No point staying in bed if all she was going to do was fight with covers and memories.

She'd drifted off for a few minutes, long enough to dream about James. Strange that her dreams of him were always good ones. In this one he'd brought her a small white bag with a snowman face on the front. She'd opened it and found a fresh sprig of mistletoe. His kiss woke her.

Sara breathed on cupped hands. The blanket wasn't doing a thing against the chill in the room. She picked up the tablet of paper she'd left on the arm of the sofa. Bessie had asked her to plan menus for next weekend's breakfasts. Meat-and-potato-stuffed Cornish pasties and raspberry-filled meringues were a better use of her time than thoughts of James. And mistletoe.

She heard the front door of the building open then close. Raquel, her neighbor across the hall, getting home from her second-shift job. Sara stared at the clock then at the Christmas tree. As the idea took shape, she threw off the blanket. Opening the apartment door, she ran across the hall and tapped her knuckles on the door.

"Who is it?" Raquel's cigarette-roughened voice came through the door.

"Sara. I want to ask you something."

The door opened wide. "Hey. C'mon in." Raquel pulled a rubber band from her ponytail. Rusty brown hair straggled to her shoulders. She smiled, deepening the laugh lines surrounding her lips. Life had aged her beyond her thirty-nine years. "Thanks for the cookies. I got a few before Allison nabbed 'em. She's eating like a horse these days. Oh, and thanks for the card last week."

"Six months sober is something to celebrate."

"Yeah." Raquel's chin lifted. "It is. So what's up?"

"I have a huge, huge favor to ask of you and Allison." Sara's mind whirled, thinking as she talked. She stared at the beige couch against the bare beige walls. "Remember how you said you wanted to paint?"

Raquel's confusion was accompanied by a yawn. "We'd be doing you a favor if we painted our living room?"

Sara laughed. "No. I'd be doing you a favor by painting your living room. And your bedroom and bathroom and Allison's room and anything else you can think of."

"And we'd be doing what?"

"Watching my girls on the weekends."

ℰↄ

James sat on the narrow, thin mattress of the iron-framed bed, staring at his checkbook register. The timing was perfect; finances weren't. With the money he'd get for playing his final night at the tavern, he could just squeak by without touching the check he'd been carrying in his wallet for weeks. As long as he didn't plan on eating along the way.

It wouldn't be the first time he'd traveled on empty.

Lord, stop me if I shouldn't be doing this. Throw a roadblock in my way if I'd just be making things worse.

He waited, listening to the traffic rumbling over the cobblestones below, feeling the low vibration from the Tube, London's subway, far beneath him. As usual at three o'clock, the cat lady in the flat directly above him began vacuuming her rugs. He didn't sense the voice of God in all the clamor. He picked up his phone and punched 2.

"Lewis residence. Brock speaking."

James rolled his eyes. Brock the chameleon. Enough of Brock's antics had leaked to James to let him know his little brother wasn't the sweet boy his mama bragged about, and yet, at nineteen, Brock was still playing the charade at home to ensure free room and board while he commuted to school. How could two people who shared so much DNA be so completely different? At nineteen, James had left home to see the world. . .and found all he wanted in a coffee shop in Pine Bluff. All he'd wanted for a while, anyway.

"Brock. I have a favor to ask."

"What?" His brother sounded wary.

"Pick me up at the airport on Saturday."

Chapter 5

The pale light of December dawn filtered through the thin pink curtain as Sara brushed feathery kisses over the girls' foreheads. This was going to be so much easier than waking them and listening to their sleepy whines as she prodded them to get dressed and ready for Grandma Connie.

Coffee mug in hand, she padded across the hallway and knocked on the door. "Allison? You up?" She kept her voice low. The single moms in the two upstairs apartments wouldn't appreciate their kids being roused.

The door creaked open. Allison hugged a pillow and blanket. Her hair looked like it hadn't made friends with a brush in days. Dark-smudged eyes blinked from her puffy face. "Morning."

"Are you feeling okay?"

Allison nodded. "Just a little queasy. I'll be fine by the time they wake up." She stepped into the hallway and shut the door behind her. "Anything I gotta know?"

"I left a note on the table about food and their bedtime routine."

"Okay." Allison rubbed her hand over her stomach. Her face looked pale. She nodded, shuffled into Sara's apartment, and flopped down on the couch.

Sara took a deep breath, then another. In spite of the cold wood floor beneath her socks, she felt clammy. *They'll be fine.* As long as her mother-in-law didn't decide to show up while she was at work and take matters—take her girls—into her own hands. The girls had asked why they weren't going to Grandma Connie's, but they'd accepted Sara's white lie about Allison wanting to play with them. Sara half expected to find Crazy Connie waiting on the porch.

She opened the front door just wide enough to stick out her arm. The sudden cold was a shock. Her hand darted toward her mailbox. For a split second, her damp fingertips stuck to the metal flap. She pulled out the bundle of yesterday's mail. It was thicker than usual.

Shutting the door and leaning against it, she slurped the last of her coffee and hung the mug on her little finger. She opened the top envelope and stared down at a picture of a squinty-eyed newborn. Inscribed below it was the birth announcement. *"Trace and Sydney McKay proudly introduce their son, Benjamin Eldon McKay. . . ."*

Tears prickled the rims of Sara's eyes. She wasn't quite sure why. Joy was part of it; new babies just did that to her. But maybe a smidgen of it was sadness. She'd probably never give birth to a son.

Shaking her head, she took another deep breath. Leaving the girls for three days was hard enough; she didn't need to start manufacturing new reasons to be sad. The next envelope was a letter from her mother and stepfather. She'd take that along to savor during her morning break. The third thing in the pile was a six-by-eight padded envelope. The minute her hand closed around the stack of mail in the box, she'd known what was in it. The book. The book that was going to teach her how to put on a string of pearls and her best little dress and light the candles and meet her husband at the door—*Recipe for a Godly Wife*.

I tried that, James. Don't you remember? Oh no, that's right, you wouldn't. That was the night you never came home.

଼ଠ

"Is there a good Bible-based church in the area?" The pewter-haired woman with the black pearls and crocheted pink sweater took a plate of scones from Sara and smiled sweetly.

Weren't all churches based on the Bible? Wasn't that the definition of a church? Sara took a dish of lemon curd off the tray in her hand and set it on the table. "Pineview Community Church is a good one. The people are very friendly." Not that she'd ever gone to a church service, but she'd met Pastor Owen and the Sanctuary volunteers.

"Is that where you go?" The pearl lady's expression seemed to combine both hope and pity, as if Sara's answer would tell her what kind of smile was appropriate.

"Actually, every Sunday's like today. I work until four." She realized that wasn't giving the woman the information she sought. There'd likely be a tract under the cup and saucer when she cleared the dining room table. She just hoped there'd be no flames. "I'll get you the brochure for the church."

She walked through the swinging saloon-type doors into the kitchen. Bessie stood with her back against the counter, a rose-covered teapot dangling carelessly from one hand. The other hand was clamped over her mouth.

"Bessie?" Sara set her tray down and made three quick steps, grabbing the teapot. "What's wrong?"

It seemed to take an effort for Bessie to focus on Sara. When she did, she took a tremulous breath. "I. . .need to talk to you. . .after they leave." She blinked then wiped her hands on her apron. "I. . .don't want to keep you right now." She nodded stiffly toward the dining room.

Sara's pulse picked up tempo, tapping on her eardrums. She nodded. "I'll fill the pot." Knees stiff, she walked to the stove. Steam dampened her bangs as she filled the rose-patterned pot with the kettle. Her mind whirled with questions. What had she done? Bessie had never given the slightest indication that she was unhappy with her performance. But what if. . . Steam stung her nostrils as she tried to breathe the thought away. What if Connie had talked to Bessie? Things like integrity and character mattered immensely to Bessie. If Connie had told her about finding Reece at her door, if she'd painted the picture she'd created in her imagination. . . Sara put the cover on the teapot, pulled a brochure from the rack over the kitchen desk, and fabricated a smile as she walked into the dining room.

"How is everything?" She made eye contact with each of the six people seated at the table—two sixty-something couples on a getaway weekend from the Cities and a couple on their honeymoon. Murmurs of approval came from all six. Sara pulled out the chair at the head of the table.

The young bride, Lydia, passed the plate of pasties to her. "Did you make these?"

Sara took one of the half-circle pies. The crust around the edge was perfectly browned and showed Sara's unique crimp, slightly deeper and more angled than Bessie's. The savory smell wafted from the vents she'd cut in the top. "I did. Do you like them?"

"I love them."

"Tradition claims that the pasty was originally made by the women of Cornwall for their men who worked in the tin mines. They'd be covered with dirt from the mines with no way to wash before lunch, so they would hold the pasty by the thick edge and eat the rest without touching it. The crust they threw away was supposed to appease the spirits who might otherwise lead miners into danger."

"That's fascinating."

"The Cornish who came to Minnesota to work in the iron mines brought their traditions with them. Bessie Tippet's great-grandfather was one of them."

"I love history." Lydia winked at her husband and turned back to Sara. "Are pasties hard to make?"

"Not at all. The trick to making the crust is to use real lard, and the secret to the filling is to dice the potatoes and rutabagas just the right size. I'll give you the recipe before you leave."

"I'd love that."

Love. It seemed to be the girl's only verb. No wonder, looking at the deep brown eyes adoring her, the arm resting protectively along the back of her chair. Sara cut into her pasty, needing something to do other than stare at the two who were in their own world even as they interacted with the other guests.

She remembered the feeling, remembered James looking at her as if she were his whole world. For a while.

The woman with the black pearls held out a plate of scones. "These simply melt in your mouth. I can't imagine why you're so skinny. You'd think you'd have to taste everything to cook like this." She patted Sara's arm and whispered, "You need to taste more. A stiff wind could blow you away."

"Thank you." Sara took a scone, leaving it to the woman to decide if she was thanking her for the scone or the comment.

Black Pearl's husband leaned forward. "Is there a book on the history of Pine Bluff?"

Sara nodded, wiping her mouth with her napkin. She got up and went into the kitchen. As she picked up the book—*Growing Up in Pine Bluff*—she glanced at Bessie's back. The woman stood, spine straight as a white pine, facing the window that looked out on the gazebo in the backyard, now covered with the four inches of new snow that had fallen during the night. Bessie didn't turn around.

Sara walked back into the dining room and filled the hour with stories she'd learned from the book in her hand and from the woman who stood silently in the kitchen, waiting to talk to her.

಄

It was just after noon when she pulled onto the highway. It seemed all wrong to be leaving Tippet House so early.

It was. All wrong.

Tears she'd held in for hours broke loose. Sara pulled the car to the side of the road and sobbed.

"Where is your God now, James?"

The question hung in the air with her breath. Cold, crystal, visible for a moment then gone. Was God watching her? Breaking her down, inch by inch? Waiting for the moment when she'd had enough punishment?

She flashed back to the night of the fire. She'd heard a noise, like crinkling paper, and then a loud *pop*. Out in the hallway she smelled smoke. *Please God, protect us.* She woke the girls, ran upstairs. Smoke seeped from under the door of the empty apartment above hers. Somehow she'd managed to get everyone out of the building, run across the street, and call 911. But God hadn't answered her prayer that night. The little girl upstairs had needed skin grafts, and smoke damage kept all of them from returning to their apartments.

The next scene filled the screen in her private horror show—huddling in the cement-block laundry building, covering the girls with her arms like a hen with chicks, listening to the roar of the approaching tornado. . . . *Please, God. . .keep them safe.* But their trailer had been flattened; their clothes scattered; furniture, appliances, pictures ruined.

Sara pressed the heels of her hands against her eyes. This time she wouldn't pray. This time, like the others, nothing could fix it. The movie in her head zoomed in on Bessie, staring out at the gazebo, talking in a strange and distant voice. . . . *"Rheumatoid arthritis getting worse. . .I can't do this anymore. . . . I'm moving to Arizona. . .already listed the house. . . . I'm sorry, Sara. . .so sorry."*

Heat whispered from the vents, and she could no longer see her breath. Sara put the car in gear. Snow crunched beneath her tires as she eased her rust-marred car onto the road. *We'll be okay. I'll find a job.* She still had two checks coming. The letter from her mother had included money for Christmas gifts for the girls.

She'd tuck it away just in case. *We'll be okay*.

At the gas station on Main Street, she picked up the Sunday *Star Tribune* and the weekly Pine Bluff paper. If she was lucky, Sadie would be ready for a nap when she got home and Zoe would spend her "quiet time" hour actually being quiet. And Sara could comb through the classifieds.

Throwing the three-inch-thick Minneapolis paper on the seat, she thought of Mattie's "Bounce Award." She had to bounce back one more time. Enough to get her credit card paid off so that her earnings at the Stillwater Inn could be put toward one thing alone—the land contract payments that would make the castle hers someday.

"One more time." She said the words but didn't feel them. She had to do it, had to find the drive to look for a job, to pare her budget. Again. Her back was against the ropes, but self-pity would weaken her. She couldn't, even for a moment, cave into it, because there was no way she was going to give her mother-in-law reason to take her girls. That thought dried her tears until she turned onto Wright Avenue and saw Connie's car parked in front of her building.

"One more time." Sara parked the car, got out, pulled her bags out of the backseat, and squared her shoulders. With determined steps, she walked up the porch steps and opened the front door. With her hand on the doorknob of her apartment, she stopped, took a moment to gather her resolve. Of all the people in the world she didn't want to see in this frame of mind, Connie Lewis topped the list.

She opened the door. . .and gasped. There was one name above Connie's on that list.

And he sat in her living room. . .reading a book to his daughters.

Chapter 6

S he was so thin. That was the first thing James noticed. The second was that she'd been crying. A sickening sense of déjà vu tightened his gut.

Brock had told him not to come to the apartment, but he'd also let it slip that Sara wouldn't be home until five. He just needed a few minutes with the girls to be sure they were all right. And he wanted to show up before Reece knew he was in town and had time to pack and leave. He had to know if any of what his mother had told him in the last twenty-four hours was true.

Sadie wriggled off his lap and ran to Sara, wrapping herself around her leg. Zoe waved. "We're reading *Goodnight Moon*."

The babysitter, who'd been watching his every move and refusing to answer his questions, stepped out of the kitchen. "I called Brock at work, and he said I could let him in."

Sara nodded. James knew that look. Every fiber of her being was fighting to hold herself in check. "Thank you, Allison. Tell your mom thanks."

The teen slowly gathered her things and ambled out of the apartment, probably hoping something interesting would happen before she left.

Sara didn't move. In one hand she held a purse, in the other a large canvas bag. She hadn't acknowledged Sadie, who was wrapped around her thigh like a firefighter sliding down a pole.

James bent his head toward Zoe. "Let's finish this later. I want to talk to your mommy."

"Okay." Zoe slid off the couch and ran into another room.

Sara finally dropped her bag, picked up Sadie, and hugged her, burying her face in the flyaway corn silk-colored hair. "I missed you, princess. Go help Zoe make placemats for supper."

"Pizza. . .pudding. . .pizza. . .pudding. . .pizza!" Sadie ran off, singing her made-up song.

James stood, took three steps, and stopped. After all the times he'd rehearsed this moment, he couldn't think of a thing to say. "Sara."

Her teeth bit down on her bottom lip. Her eyes burned into him.

"I should have called first." The words sounded so lame.

"Yes."

"Could—" He swallowed. His tongue felt like stone. "Could we talk?"

She walked toward a worn and faded chair. Her movements were robotic. She lowered herself to the chair and folded her hands on her lap.

James sat down on the couch and angled toward her, resting his elbows on his knees. Like her, he folded his hands. *Lord, tell me what to say.* To give her some emotional space, he looked away. His gaze landed on the book he'd sent her, lying open like a tent, pages bent, beside her chair. As if it had been thrown there.

He wiped his hands on his knees and refolded them. "The girls are beautiful."

Sara nodded. Her expression was no longer angry. It was vacant. Dead, unfeeling.

"You've done a wonderful job raising them."

Again she nodded, still with no emotion he could read. He'd rather deal with her anger than this.

"I know that saying I'm sorry isn't going to mean a thing to you. I don't have a single excuse for putting my wants ahead of you and the girls, and I can't ever make it up to you."

He looked at her blank stare and considered getting up and walking out the door—for her sake. She didn't need him stirring up old pain. He parted his hands and rested them beside him. One hand fell on *Goodnight Moon*. The feeling of holding his daughters on his lap came back with a wave of pain like circulation to frostbitten toes. "It would be wrong of me to ask for another chance. But would it be possible for us to spend some time talking? Just to see if maybe—"

Fear replaced her dead stare and silenced him. Nothing was coming out right. He studied the shadows under her eyes and her pale but still flawless skin. She wore no makeup and was dressed in faded jeans and a denim jacket that had once been black. Like her, the jacket was too thin. White lines showed on the edge of the cuffs where the fabric had worn away. So different from the clothes-conscious girl with the heavy eye makeup he'd fallen for five years ago. That girl had been spunky and pretty. This one was strong and hauntingly beautiful. In spite of the coldness in her eyes, everything in him longed to know this woman.

He held his breath, waiting for her answer.

Sara's eyes closed. Her shoulders rose in a heavy sigh. "What would that accomplish?"

&

His nod was barely perceptible. As desperately as Sara wanted to look away from the hurt on his face, she couldn't. His eyes glistened and he blinked. Bending down, he picked up his jacket. She hadn't seen it on the floor behind the coffee table. At the sight of the scarred brown leather, her pulse skipped. She tried not to remember the scent of it but couldn't block it out.

He stood up, slid his arms into the jacket. He hadn't said a word after her reply. Sara rose to her feet but couldn't have moved away from that spot if she'd wanted to. Her legs felt nailed to the floor. Reece had told the truth—this was not the same man who walked out on her. His body had filled out, and his face had lost its boyish look. A long-sleeved black T-shirt fit tight across well-defined muscles. She wondered how he could move his arms in the snug jacket. The sky-blue eyes she saw in her dreams seemed deeper set and held the look of a man who had lived hard for the past two years.

As he zipped his jacket, he looked at her with a slight smile that hinted of regret. "I'll be at Mom and Dad's until the day after Christmas if. . ." Leaving the sentence unfinished, he walked past her then turned and reached out to her. The back of his hand touched her cheek. His eyes gleamed with tears. "Sara. . ." His voice was soft and hoarse, just above a whisper. "I still love you."

He pulled his gloves from his pocket and walked out the door.

∾

Her hands shook. Her whole body vibrated with the shock of finding James in her living room, looking so natural, so comfortable with her girls.

For two years she'd imagined the moment she'd have to face him. For some reason, she'd always pictured it at his mother's funeral years from now. The girls would be grown and successful in whatever they chose to do, proving she'd been a good mom after all. She'd be the owner of the Stillwater Inn, the B&B with the five-star reviews in travel magazines. Rich, happy, maybe even married to a man who put her above his career; she'd offer James her tastefully jeweled and manicured hand. "Hello, James," she'd say. Her voice would have just a hint of condescension, but no anger. She'd let him know she'd forgotten him long ago and that she and her daughters had done fine without him.

At times, she'd envisioned him groveling at her feet, begging her to take him back. That wasn't James, of course, but once in a while she needed to picture him fully aware of how much he'd missed. It took the edge off her bitterness.

Not once had she imagined him the way he was tonight. Physically stronger, yet emotionally vulnerable, focused more on her and the girls than on himself. Her chest tightened as she realized how close she'd come to falling into his arms, to believing he'd changed enough to make it work, to make it last.

But had he changed in the ways that would matter to her? Even if James was nicer, calmer, maybe even more attentive to her, he was still a musician. He'd always be a musician. She didn't know what he was doing in London, most likely still with a band. Maybe now he was with a Christian group, but that wouldn't make any difference. He'd still be engrossed in practicing and writing. Every conversation would roll around to his next gig or their next song that was destined to be at the top of the charts. There'd still be time on the road. . .time away from her.

Zoe ran out of the bedroom, stopping several feet from Sara's chair. Her little hands flew to her hips in a gesture that mirrored Sara's often-impatient stance. "Where did he go?"

Sara stood, realizing for the first time she was still wearing her jacket. "He went home." She took off her jacket and threw it on the couch, covering the spot where James had sat. "He went home."

"But we didn't finish *Goodnight Moon*."

"I'll read it to you before quiet time." A question rose in her mind. "Do you know who that man was?"

"Uh-huh." Zoe's curls bobbed. "He's Uncle Brock's friend. Can we have pizza now?"

He hadn't told her he was their daddy. The knowledge rocked her. "It's a long time until supper." Her voice held a quiver she couldn't control.

"But I'm starving!"

"Didn't you have lunch yet?"

"Nuh-uh."

Scooping her up, Sara planted a loud kiss on her cheek. "All right, my drama queen. Go get a box of pudding out of the cupboard, and tell Sadie to come help me with the pizza."

Zoe ran a few steps then stopped. "Can sometime that man eat pizza with us like Uncle Brock does?"

As Sara bent to pick up her jacket, she saw something on the floor beside the chair. The book she'd chucked across the room on Friday. The one that would tell her how to be a submissive little wife and smile and nod when her husband packed his bags to travel with the band for months at a time.

"No. That man lives far, far away."

&

"Girls napping?" Raquel pulled out a kitchen chair and helped herself to a slice of room-temperature pizza.

Sara nodded, picking up a pudding-covered Winnie the Pooh spoon. "Zoe fell asleep, too. You must have worn them out this morning."

Raquel shrugged. "They went to Sunday school."

"*What?*"

"Yeah. Mattie picked us up. I'm kinda gettin' the 'higher power' stuff, so I figured I'd give the church thing a shot."

"But..." The spoon clattered into the sink. Sara turned. "I don't want them—"

"Cool it." Raquel rolled her eyes toward the ceiling. "They're too young to get brainwashed. They had a blast." She picked a chunk of green pepper off her pizza and set it on the counter. "So your ex showed up."

"My unofficial ex."

"I caught a glimpse. What a hunk. If Brock grows up that fine, Allison will be one lucky girl."

Sara's fingers tightened on the spoon. This wasn't the first time Raquel had implied that Brock had more than a platonic interest in her daughter. Since Allison had made it clear that she wouldn't be expecting anything from the baby's father, Raquel had set her sights on Brock. Though Brock and Allison had been friends for years, Sara couldn't imagine two people less suited to be life mates. Brock needed a woman with at least a little bit of ambition. On that one point she was sure she and her mother-in-law would agree. "They're just friends."

"Uh-huh." Biting into the pizza, Raquel grinned. "Wish I had a friend like that."

Before Sara could formulate a controlled answer, her front door opened. Brock walked in, knocking as he entered. Allison hovered behind him like a shadow. Brock's gaze swept the apartment. "He's not here, is he?"

"No." Sara threw her dish towel on her shoulder, walked across the room, and gave her brother-in-law a hug. "Missed you, kid."

"They got me working weird hours this month." Brock returned her hug with his right arm. More than a year after the car accident that killed his best friend, he was still in therapy for his reconstructed shoulder.

Allison sat on the couch, and Brock joined her, a little too close for Sara's liking. Without meaning to, she made eye contact with Raquel, who returned a look that clearly said, *See?* Sara looked away.

Brock tapped his fist against his knee. "I told James not to just show up. I knew you'd leave work early if you found out he was here."

Sara slumped into the chair. She didn't feel like talking about the real reason she'd left early.

"Did you kick him out?" Brock's eyes held a steely glint. Like Reece, he'd sided with her when James left for the second time. Young as he was, for two years now he'd been the father figure in her girls' lives.

Sara shook her head. "Do you think he's changed?"

"Yeah. Not for the better. He's off the wall about his religion. He sticks God into every conversation. It's weird."

Allison rested both hands on her slightly rounded belly. "He asked a lot of questions."

"What kind of questions?"

"About what you do and if you're seeing anyone and stuff like that."

Brock put his elbows on his knees and folded his hands, a posture that mirrored the man who'd sat in that same spot two hours earlier. "You know why he's here, don't you? Mom's been a raving lunatic since she caught you and Reece—"

"She didn't 'catch' us. We weren't doing anything."

Raquel jumped off the kitchen chair and perched on the end of the couch. "Who's Reece? What did I miss?"

Allison shifted to face her mother. "Crazy Connie walked in when Sara was kissing this cute guy who used to be a friend of Brock's brother."

Raquel clapped her hands together and winked at Sara. "What a life you got, girl!"

Sara covered her face with her dish towel and groaned. Knowing Raquel, half the town would hear an embellished version before the week was out. For a moment she teetered on the brink of laughter. Her life had become a soap opera. No, a country western song—lost her man, her job, her house. . .and now her reputation.

Chapter 7

D on't let Mom find out." Brock walked through Raquel's living room on Tuesday afternoon with one girl wrapped around each leg. While they giggled, his eyes were fastened on Sara.

Looking down at the paint she'd just opened, she began to stir. "Your mother doesn't need to know. . .and neither does your brother. Do you understand? I'll find a job."

"Good luck. I'd get you in at the store, but everybody's coming home from college."

"I'll find something." Her voice reflected her doubt. She'd made six calls the day before. Not one place had even told her to pick up an application. The offer from Reece was probably still open. That would give Connie enough evidence to bury her. *And now she's working with the man I saw her kissing. . . .* "I'll get a job."

"You better. Mom's just waiting for you to mess up."

Her knuckles whitening around the stir stick, Sara froze. Evidently Allison hadn't fabricated her prediction. "Have you actually heard her say that she wants to take the girls from me?"

Brock looked cornered. "Yeah. She makes it sound like they're starving and neglected and she has to rescue them."

Sara's teeth ground together. A weight settled on her chest. "What makes her think she'd get them? Even if she could prove I was an unfit mother, who says the state wouldn't step in and put them in foster care or award them to my mother? Does she really think James would leave his music and move in with her so they could raise my kids like a happy little family? Doesn't she realize that he gave up his chance to—"

"I'm ready." Allison pranced out of her bedroom with her hat, gloves, and jacket on.

Sara looked from her to Brock. "Ready for what?" Brock and Allison had promised to watch the girls in her apartment while Sara painted Raquel's living room.

A mix of embarrassment and frustration crossed Brock's face. "Uh. . .we were thinking maybe of taking them for ice cream or hot chocolate. . .you know. I. . .didn't tell them yet, but I figured you'd be okay with it, you know. . . ."

Taking her hand off the stir stick, Sara set both hands on her hips. "Brock?"

He stopped walking, looked at her then down at the girls.

Since Sunday night, Sara had been waiting—for what, she wasn't sure. "Is *he* involved in this?"

Wide brown eyes stared back at her. "*He?*"

Sara's laugh was hollow. "You're a lousy actor, kid." She glanced at the girls. Engrossed in tickling each other, they weren't listening, but she wanted to be careful. "You were going to take them to see him without telling me, weren't you?"

"He's only here for a few weeks. You gotta let him spend some time with them."

"He'll see them on Christmas Day." She'd made that decision for the girls' sake, not for James's. She wouldn't be there, but she wouldn't take that tradition away from them. And James would be leaving the day after Christmas. She narrowed her eyes at Brock. "I thought you were on my side."

Brock dropped into a sheet-covered chair, and the girls scrambled onto his lap. "Why do there have to be sides?"

Sara simply stared at him, feeling suddenly alone. She'd lost her only ally in the family.

"We had a long talk last night." He finally looked her straight in the eye. "The religion stuff is annoying, but that's not the only change in him. Ja—*he* is really sorry about leaving you, Sara. And I kind of understand what was going on in his head. It wasn't really all his fault, you know. It makes more sense now that I heard the whole thing."

The emotion that took hold of her felt more like fire than anger. Her nerves seemed to literally burn, from her shoulders to her fingertips. "It makes *sense?*" Zoe and Sadie stopped tickling Brock and stared at her. She heard the front door open, but she didn't care who heard her yelling. "It makes *sense* that he left me to raise two kids without a father? It makes sense that—"

Brock turned toward the door, and she followed his gaze. The door that had been partway open for ventilation opened all the way.

James stood in the doorway. "You're right, Sara. None of it makes sense."

ဆ

He hadn't been prepared for the intensity of her rage. He knew she wouldn't be any happier to see him this time than she had been on Sunday, but with the clock ticking, he had to give it a shot. Maybe he was crazy for hoping she'd listen, but one thing was sure: If he didn't try, the guilt that had gnawed at his insides for the past two years would swallow him whole.

"Can we talk?" The same words hadn't gotten him anywhere two days ago.

Without taking her piercing gaze from him, she spoke to Brock. "Put the girls down for naps."

"Let's go, ladies." Brock handed Sadie to Allison.

As they were walking out, Zoe waved at James. "You said Uncle Brock's friend lived far, far away, Mommy."

"He does." Sara's tone was hard, her voice strained.

Zoe ran to Sara and threw her arms around her waist. "I'm just gonna have quiet time, right? I don't hafta sleep."

Sara nodded. James watched as Sadie copied her sister, squirming out of Allison's arms and running to hug Sara. He'd missed so much. What would their life be like if he'd stayed?

When Sara Martin and her amazing green eyes had snared him, he'd told the other band members to go on to Canada without him, said he'd join them in a few weeks. And he had. Without telling Sara he was leaving, he'd made the trip across the border in the middle of the night. . .just hours after she'd told him she was pregnant.

For weeks, he'd poured himself into his music, sure he'd forget her, convinced that she didn't really love him and that she and the baby would be better off without a guy who wasn't even close to husband or father material. But it didn't work. He hitchhiked back to Pine Bluff, married Sara, and gave up his dream for the next two years.

But Sara had never acknowledged what he'd given up or what he'd put his friends through for her.

Brock and Allison carried the girls across the hall, and the sheet-shrouded room was suddenly quiet. James took off his leather gloves and stuffed them in his pockets. The apartment was warm, but he didn't dare unzip his jacket. Sara needed to be the one to decide if he was staying. "I don't want to hash over old stuff. . .unless you do, I mean." He ran his hand across his jaw. He wasn't saying it the way it played in his head. "I need to explain something."

Her hands were on her hips, a pose only too familiar to James. She pointed to the paint buckets and the room around them and sighed. "I have to finish this tonight."

He nodded. No way would he leave that easily. Not this time. "I'll help."

Green eyes sparked like backlit emeralds. She'd painted their townhouse, every room, without him. She had to be wondering why he'd never offered when it mattered. Sara lifted the stir stick out of the paint can.

He'd seen that shade before. "Nice color."

A wistful expression crossed her face. For the briefest of moments, he could almost have called it a smile. "Bittersweet." Her tone melted to a softness that made his heart skip. "It's the same color I painted our bedroom."

"I know. *Bittersweet.* The irony made him match her almost smile. "I should have helped you."

His admission seemed to catch her off guard. He spotted a hint of vulnerability before she bent down for something beneath the newspaper-covered card table that held the paint. When she straightened, she held two things out to him—a paint roller and a trimmer.

She was letting him stay. It took monumental self-control to not grin at her like a two-year-old offered a triple-scoop cone. A tempered smile escaped as he reached for the roller. "You're good at the detail work."

Sara's cheeks seemed to flush, but she turned away so quickly that he wasn't sure if he'd imagined it. Was she that unaccustomed to compliments? The obvious answer fed the guilt monster. Unaccustomed to compliments from him, certainly. When had that stopped? Long before Sadie came along, he guessed.

He unzipped his jacket, walked out to the front entryway, and hung it on the newel post. Pushing up his sleeves, he went back to the card table and poured several inches of paint into a tray. "Brock told me what you've done for Allison's mom."

With a shrug, Sara dipped the trimmer pad into the tray. "Raquel and Allison watch the girls for me."

"I know." He'd heard more than he wanted to about that arrangement. His mother had done some private investigation work. "According to Brock, Allison's mom wouldn't be living here and certainly wouldn't be sober if it weren't for you."

This time, there was no question about the color that tinted her face. "Brock told me a friend of his and her mom needed a place to live. I just let them know when there was an opening."

James knew she'd done much more than that. She'd driven the woman to AA meetings, fixed decent meals for her, and showed her how to clean and organize. *That's my Sara.* The thought came spontaneously and with it a jab of regret. "She must be a completely different person than when you first met her." He hoped it sounded like a casual statement. He also hoped it would have an impact.

Sara stared at him, set the trimmer on the edge of the paint tray, and took a deep breath. After several seconds, she pointed at the couch. "Maybe we should move that out a little farther."

Strange what a simple, ordinary sentence could do to a guy. "Sure." He grabbed one end while she took the other. Since becoming a Christian, he'd met people who saw symbolism in everything. He wasn't one of them, but he couldn't ignore the picture of teamwork.

They set the couch about three feet from where it had been. Sara looked down at the floor and actually laughed. "*Bus. . .ted.*" She bent over and picked up an open package of peanut butter cookies and a bag of peppermint patties. "Allison is supposed to be cutting back on sugar."

"I wonder if she eats licorice whips and rainbow sherbet in the middle of the night." James smiled at her, holding his breath, sure he'd gone too far.

Sara laughed. And James exhaled. She shook her head. "I still can't look at red licorice without feeling pregnant."

"But your red tongue was so cute." He winked at her then wished he hadn't. As jittery as a boy with his first crush, he was second-guessing every word. *Lord, guard my mouth.* Too scared to wait for her reaction, he turned and dipped the paint roller in the tray.

"A person who can eat twenty-six hot dogs has no room to laugh at pregnant cravings."

"Touché." James laughed and looked at her over his shoulder. He'd come in far behind the winner at The Midwest Hot Dog Eating Contest at Mall of America. He shook his head in mock sadness. "I trained so hard for that competition, and my wife didn't even stick around until I finished." Four months pregnant with Zoe, she'd run from the contest and left her lunch in the ladies' room.

Sara waved her hand as if pretending to slap him. "Can we get to work instead of talking about foods that make me sick?"

"Okay." He hated to stop the easy banter, but he needed to before he said something to burst the bubble that surrounded this moment. "Where should I start?"

She pointed. "Let's start in the corner to the left of the door and go clockwise." *That's my Sara.* She'd always had a system for everything.

Including him.

&

They worked in silence. Possibilities did a dangerous dance in Sara's head. She couldn't explain her change in attitude. Reece's words had suddenly whispered to her: *"Give James a chance. He's not the same guy who walked out on you. He loves you, Sara."*

James had asked to talk. What was the worst that could happen if she agreed to listen? She'd get defensive when he accused her of not being the kind of wife he needed? *Been there.* She'd find out that the most important thing to James was James? *Done that.* There was no way she'd let him spend time with the girls. She couldn't take the chance of Zoe finding out who he was and then having to say good-bye again. But as for herself, he couldn't hurt her any more than he already had. She really had nothing to lose.

She climbed three steps up the ladder and looked down at him. Muscles stood out on his forearm as he pushed the roller up the wall. His hair curled behind his ear. She swallowed hard. "Brock said you're not with a band anymore."

"Never really was, to be honest." He looked up at her and gave a brief shrug. "It never got off the ground. Maybe my heart just wasn't in it." He turned back to his painting. "I've been playing at a little tavern near King's College. It's not a rowdy place, kind of highbrow and quiet with law and med students discussing stuff that's way beyond me. Still, I don't like working in a bar. I'm starting a new job at a supper club on New Year's Eve. They've got an eighty-year-old mahogany Kemble I can't wait to get my fingers on." His right hand played piano keys in the air.

Music. Her old competition. James may have changed, but that part of him never would. "You. . .wanted to tell me something."

Eyes the color of summer sky stared up at her. He nodded and turned back to the wall, used up the paint in his roller, and refilled it. James, the self-assured musician, was afraid to talk to her.

"Can I ask you something?" he asked.

"I. . .suppose."

"Are you and Reece together?"

"Is that why you're here? To check up on me?" Her questions came out harsher than she intended. Considering what Connie had probably told him, she shouldn't be surprised that he asked.

His fingers tightened around the handle. "Partly. If you're serious about him, I guess there's no point—"

"I'm not." She couldn't explain her need to rescue him before he finished the sentence. "There's nothing going on, never was. He came to talk to me about Jesus, and he hugged me good-bye. That's what your mother saw."

James exhaled through his nose. "Okay." His shoulders lowered.

"Is that it? What you wanted to talk about?"

"No." He set the roller in the pan. "You know—probably better than anyone—that my mother raised me to believe that I could do anything I set my mind to." He shrugged, looking embarrassed.

Sara turned around and sat on the ladder step, facing him.

"I was barely old enough to reach the piano when she told me I was gifted and I should never let anything or anyone get in my way because I was going to be famous someday."

Sara nodded. She knew all this. She was the "anyone" who had gotten in his way.

James stepped back and perched on the back of the couch. "I'll save my list of lame excuses for another time, but the thing is. . .I actually believed her. I thought I was destined for something huge." He blinked several times. "You and the girls were interfering with my destiny."

Did he remember that he'd once screamed those same words at her? This time, though, they brought a different kind of hurt. This time, she wanted to cup his face between her hands.

"The real world smacked me hard. I should have learned that the first time I ran away. The first shock was when Reece ditched me because I left you. In my deluded state of grandeur, I thought he'd support my destiny." James shook his head. "I borrowed money from everybody I could and got to London with nothing but my inflated ego and my keyboard. Didn't have a penny or a plan, just that crazy dream of making it big in England where all my heroes started." Pain-filled eyes stared into her. "And. . .it was far enough from you to keep me from running back." He rubbed his hands on his jeans. "Anyway, the next year and a half I'd pretty much sum up as hungry and miserable. I washed dishes and swept floors and played in smoky little dives. That's where I was back in June when Reece showed up."

Sara's neck muscles tensed. She didn't like where this was going. "And talked you into becoming a Christian."

James smiled. "Yeah...but not quite like that. He didn't preach at me. I knew there was something different about him in the first two minutes. The amazing thing was that even a few months before that I wouldn't have been willing to listen. You know the story of the prodigal son, right?"

Sara gave a stiff nod. Her pulse hammered in her ears. She'd been "witnessed" to more times than she could count. Every Sanctuary volunteer had their defeat-to-victory "testimony." Some of them she could repeat verbatim.

"Just the week before, I'd taken stale bread from an Italian restaurant's Dumpster. Just like a scene out of *Oliver Twist*. So when Reece said that God had told him to find me and—"

"Stop." She held up her hand. "I'm happy for you that you found God. But I'm not there. I'm not desperate. I'm doing just fine without it, James."

Chapter 8

After Mattie left on Thursday night, Sara scanned the weekly Dollar Saver flyer, highlight marker in hand. The plywood factory where Raquel worked had a third-shift opening. The Sage Stoppe, where Sara had once worked as an assistant cook, was looking for someone to bus tables. Brock was right—this close to Christmas was not a good time to look for a job. College kids were home, and businesses had already hired their holiday help.

She folded the paper and tossed it onto the end table. It fell off, landing on a stack of magazines. On top of the stack sat "the book."

She stretched toward the table and picked it up. Curiosity had kept her from throwing it out. Just what was the recipe for a godly wife? A cup of submission, a spoonful of "Yes, dear"? Throw in a healthy dose of "Your slightest wish is my command"? She stared at the cozy couple on the front cover, wanting to make fun of their air-brushed happiness. But she couldn't. The woman had on a baker's apron like the kind Sara wore at work. Her husband's muscled arms wrapped around her from behind. . .and made it hard for Sara to breathe.

"Riley J. Schmidt" was the name splashed in black across the white apron. "Figures. Bet his little wife was thrilled when he wrote it." Yawning, she opened the back cover—and blinked twice. Riley Schmidt had shoulder-length blond hair and wore a diamond pendant with matching earrings. She looked neither male nor nineteenth century-ish.

Finding the table of contents, Sara scanned the chapter titles. "Stir in Laughter," "Spice It Up," "Study the Cookbook—Together," and "Are You Ready for the Banquet?" She let the pages flip until they fell open near the middle of the book, to a chapter called "Making the Most of Leftovers." She read the first paragraph her eyes focused on.

> If your man is married to his job and you feel, at best, like the mistress, you have to ask yourself one tough question: Why? What's driving your man? The need for approval or respect? A real need to generate more income? Are the requirements of his job beyond his control? Is it possible that God is asking you to graciously sacrifice time with your husband for a greater good? Or. . .the hardest question of all. . .is there a reason why your husband would rather be on the job than at home?

Sara slammed the book shut. She'd picked a random paragraph and found just what she'd expected—the guilt trip. "It all comes back to the little woman's fault, doesn't it?" She sent the book sailing across the floor for the second time.

The subservient Riley Schmidt had the right question—*why?* She just didn't ask it right. *Why* would a man with two precious daughters and a beautiful home give it all up for a pie-in-the-sky career? Sara closed her eyes and pictured the two-bedroom townhouse, the furniture she'd reupholstered, the color scheme she'd carried throughout the house. She remembered the paint colors. . . Pumpkin Pie, Eggnog, Plum Passion, Wild Sage, Bittersweet.

It hadn't been easy. They'd each held down two jobs, but they'd worked it out so that one of them was always home. There hadn't been money for extras like eating out or movies, but the sacrifices had been worth it. She'd made a home they could all be proud of, and with each paycheck, their Stillwater Inn fund grew.

In the soft glow of the dwarf Christmas tree, she scanned the shabby room and the ragged furniture. She hadn't done much with it. They were, after all, just passing through on their way to Stillwater. The thought eased her tension. She rested her head on the couch pillow and closed her eyes. The colors of her future home floated through her head. Dusky Violet, Antique Pearl, Victorian Mauve. . .

&

A loud knock woke her. Disoriented, Sara stared at the Christmas tree. It was still dark. She had no idea what time it was.

"Sara!" The sound of keys jangling accompanied Raquel's yell.

Shivering and heart pounding, Sara stumbled to the door. She opened it and stared at Raquel, in jacket and gloves, her hair a mess and her heavy makeup smeared. "What's wrong?"

"I have to take Allison to the hospital. I'm afraid she might be losing the baby."

"What can I do?"

Raquel shook her head, fear evident in her eyes. "Just pray and call Mattie. And we won't be able to watch the girls today. I'm sorry."

Sara nodded. "Call me at work when you know something." She walked back into the apartment and turned on the light. The wrought iron clock above the television said it was just after five. She needed to leave by six this morning. Two couples were arriving before noon, and Sara had left too many things undone when Bessie had sent her home early last week because they both "needed time alone." Not that she'd gotten a moment of alone time on Sunday.

Grabbing the key to Raquel's apartment, she ran across the hall. It took several minutes to find the phone on the counter in the bathroom. She dialed Mattie's number. Eldon answered. Mattie was out on a rescue call. Eldon promised to pray for Allison and have Mattie call when she got home.

Sara pushed the Off button. The women who lived upstairs both worked days, and she couldn't think of anyone else. This had never been a problem when Connie watched the girls. If she'd been busy, either Grandpa Neil or Brock was there. *Brock*. His days off varied each week. There was a chance. She dialed his cell phone number. There was no way she was going to call the house phone.

The phone rang three times before she heard Brock's groggy voice. "Sara?"

"Hey. Sorry to wake you. Allison's having some problems and—"

"With the baby?" Brock sounded suddenly wide-awake.

"Yeah. Raquel just took her to the emergency room."

"Whoa. Okay, I'm on my way. If you talk to her, tell her I'll be there in fifteen minutes, maybe less. Bye."

Sara stared at the phone, her tired mind trying to process what had just happened and what to do next. If she couldn't get to Tippet House this morning, Bessie would try to do her own work plus Sara's. Bessie simply didn't have the strength or energy for that. There was really only one option, and it involved admitting to Connie that she couldn't handle things on her own. Before second thoughts could take over, Sara pressed the numbers. For the first time ever, she hoped the voice she heard would be her mother-in-law's.

It wasn't.

James's sleep-heavy voice took hers away. Memories flashed like fireworks, and she had to brace herself on the bathroom counter.

"This. . .is Sara."

"Good morning."

Sara closed her eyes. His words slid over her like a caress.

"Sara? Is everything all right?"

Nothing is all right. You should be whispering good morning in my ear. We should be together and happy and— She turned on the cold water, held her hand beneath it, and splashed her face. "I'm sorry to wake you. I need to talk to your mother."

"She's not here. She and Dad went to pick up Granny. Is something wrong?"

The walls of the tiny bathroom pushed in on her. She opened her mouth but couldn't get enough air. Almost running, she strode through the apartment and out into the entryway.

"Sara? Are you still there?"

She opened the front door. The shock of cold helped her find her voice. "Yes." She hadn't realized until that moment that she was crying.

"Tell me what's wrong."

"I need—" A thousand things filled the blank. She pressed her fist against her forehead and took a long, slow breath. "I just need to find a sitter for the girls."

"When? I can watch them."

No. She couldn't let that happen. Not to Zoe and Sadie or to her. But they'd be safe with him, wouldn't they? And she could find someone else for tomorrow.

Maybe it would only be for an hour or two. Maybe Mattie would get home. . . .
"Now. I'm sorry. I have to leave for work, and my sitter can't—"

"I'll get there as fast as I can."

෨

Back in her own bathroom, Sara stared in the mirror while she waited for the water in the shower to get hot. Her face was pasty white. Sweat dotted her upper lip, and her mouth watered with a sour taste. When she was a little girl, her mother had told her to breathe with her mouth open if she thought she was going to throw up. After several breaths, the churning in her stomach calmed to merely rolling. She stepped into the shower and closed the lined eyelet lace curtain. It was the only thing she'd bought new since the tornado and would be the only furnishing she'd take with her to Stillwater Inn—her castle. Her castle that didn't need a prince.

But James was playing the part well. She turned the water temperature up until the spray hit her face like hot needles. He'd be in the car by now, probably speeding to get there. . .for her.

She should have said no. After this, he'd think he could come over anytime. The girls would get attached, and he was going back to London in fourteen days. It startled her that she knew that. Was something in her subconscious counting the days? She finished her shower and got out, racking her brain for any alternative. She ran a brush through her hair then wound it in a towel. After slipping into jeans and a bright green sweater with jingle bells stitched to the front, she flew back to the bathroom. With one hand she held the blow dryer, with the other she put on mascara and lipstick, something she didn't usually do. This morning she simply needed the added confidence.

෨

The door was ajar. Her boots and jacket were on. The fuzzy pink puffball attached to her Tippet House keys dangled from the canvas bag that waited by the door. The list of instructions and emergency numbers were taped to the fridge. When James walked in, everything was ready but her nervous system. He wore a snug-fitting gray thermal shirt beneath the leather jacket. A small duffel bag was slung over his shoulder. A day-old beard darkened the contours of his face. Finger tracks showed in his hair. Long ago she'd left lines in that soft brown hair. . .

Sara called on every ounce of will she could muster. "I'm so sorry I had to ask you—"

"You didn't. I volunteered, remember?"

The man had an infuriating way of interrupting her and messing with her train of thought. "Thank you. There's a note on the fridge with everything you need to know. Breakfast is cereal, soup for lunch. Suppers are in the freezer, all labeled. You just need to microwave them."

He smiled, the same grin that had once put the sun in her sky. "I have friends with kids. I'll figure it out."

"They have a bedtime routine. . .if you're still here then. My work number is next to the phone on the table. Call me anytime. I'm hoping to find someone to watch them, so maybe you'll only have to be here a little while."

"I brought clothes. I don't mind staying the whole time."

A thought hit like a fist. He was too tall for the couch. Would he sleep in her bed? "I already left a message for someone. I'm sure she can come over. . . ."

Appearing resigned, he nodded. "Will they be scared when they wake up and find me here?"

"I don't think so. Just tell Zoe you came to finish *Goodnight Moon.*"

"Would you mind if I took them sledding?"

Sledding. Zoe would be talking about it for weeks. If Sara said no, it would be for herself, not the girls. "I. . .suppose. You'll need their car seats."

James reached in his jacket pocket and pulled out a set of keys. "Let's just trade cars."

Her head was starting to hurt. If she took the keys, she'd be committing to letting him stay until Sunday. She stared at the gold *C* on Connie's key chain. The sour taste rose again in her throat. She opened her mouth and breathed. "O. . .kay."

"They'll be fine. We'll have fun."

She nodded. That was one of her biggest fears. She walked past him and picked up her bag.

"I didn't tell them who I was."

She stood statue-still, her back to him. "I know." *Thank you.* She faced him, feeling something close to a smile pull the corners of her mouth into a straight line.

James tossed his duffel bag onto the chair and took a step toward her.

Sara took a step back.

"Sara. . . I know it's killing you to accept help from me. You don't have to prove to me that you're a competent mom, that you don't need my help. I know that." His fingertips touched her sleeve. "I'm not doing this for you, okay? I'm doing this because I need to connect with my kids. Maybe you and I are over. I don't blame you for hating me. But the girls need a father, and unless there's someone else in the picture, I'm still it. I've screwed up big-time, but please. . . give me a chance to make it up to them. I won't tell them who I am until you're ready. Just give me a chance to be a dad."

Tears sprang to her eyes, and no amount of willpower would stop them. James stepped toward her, and this time she didn't back away.

His arms slid lightly around her. His breath brushed her cheek. "I won't ask you for anything more than that."

Chapter 9

James walked slowly through the quiet apartment. It was hard to imagine Sara living in this colorless space. He stopped at the girls' room and leaned on the doorjamb, staring at his sleeping daughters. Blond hair splayed across pink pillowcases; stuffed animals were snuggled in their arms. This room was the only place that showed any sign of Sara's creative touches. On one wall she'd painted a mural. Two little girls with jeweled crowns stood in front of a white house with green shutters and a wide front porch. Rocking chairs sat in a row behind carved spindles.

So Sara hadn't given up her dream even after all she'd gone through. Most likely that's all it was now—nothing but a dream.

James knew the place well. They'd spent their honeymoon, brief as it was, in this place Sara had dubbed "Stillwater Castle." Over breakfast on their last morning, Sara had told the owners that it was her dream to own a bed-and-breakfast. James remembered the rest of the conversation as if it had taken place yesterday.

"Come back in five years, and we'll sell it to you." Ingrid Torsten had smiled at her tall, Viking-looking husband.

Erik Torsten winked at his wife, and his huge hand clamped on James's shoulder. "We're planning our retirement. This place is kind of like our baby, you know? Don't want just anyone handling it. But we like you two. You start putting your pennies in a cookie jar, and we'll stay in touch."

It was all Sara had talked about on the way to their first night in the townhouse they'd just rented with the money she'd earned for tuition. "We can do it if we work really hard, can't we, James?" Just thinking about it now brought back the same gut-tightening fear. Her cheeks had flushed pink as she stared at him. "Promise?"

He couldn't say no to those amazing green eyes. In spite of the knot in his belly, he'd grabbed her hand and kissed it. "Promise."

∞

He was sitting on the couch, leafing through the book he'd sent Sara, when he heard the soft padding of little feet. In bright pink pajamas, Zoe walked toward him, her curls in a wild mess. Without a word, she handed him a sad-looking, furless stuffed dog, turned around, and walked out. Minutes later, he heard the toilet flush, the water run, and then she appeared again in the living room with *Goodnight Moon* under her arm. She crawled onto his lap and leaned against his chest.

James put his arms around her and opened the book, but it took several slow, controlled breaths until he trusted himself to talk. "Should I start at the beginning?"

Zoe's chubby fingers grabbed the stuffed dog's head and wiggled it up and down.

"Okay, the doggy says we start at the beginning."

"Misser Peabody. His name is Misser Peabody."

James put his thumb and forefinger on a threadbare paw. "Glad to meet you, Mister Peabody." He bent down to look in Zoe's eyes. "He looks like he's been loved a whole lot. His fur is rubbed off like the Velveteen Rabbit."

His daughter giggled. "That's just 'cause the ternado flew him round and round"—she circled the dog in the air—"and stuck him in a 'lectric wire, and a 'lectric company man went up on a ladder on a truck and rescued Misser Peabody, and he was even on TV, and so was I."

James took another slow breath. "Was the tornado scary?"

Blond curls bobbed against his shirt. "It was so, so loud you can't believe it! We hided in the washing machines building, and Mommy said the ternado couldn't get us there, but I cried, and Sadie screamed, and our house just went *squoosh!* like when you step on a bug."

Regret burned like acid. If he hadn't left, his wife and kids wouldn't have been living in a mobile home. "I'm glad that man saved Mister Peabody."

"Me, too."

A soft whimper came from the bedroom. James looked up to see a purple sleeve retreat behind the door.

"Sadie's awake. She's very shy. I'll go get her and tell her you're not a danger."

"What's a danger?"

"Bad people that you don't know that give candy to little children and tell them to get in their car." Zoe slid off his lap then turned to face him with a stern expression that was a carbon copy of her mother. "We don't talk to dangers. . . ever."

☙

Outside the window, snow sparkled in the sunlight. Dust cloth in hand, Sara stood by the bow window in the Tippet House parlor on Friday afternoon and tried to keep her mind on her to-do list.

"Why don't you invite James and the girls here?"

Bessie's soft words cut into Sara's meandering thoughts. She turned and smiled. Bessie appeared thinner and frailer than she had a week ago. "That's sweet of you. But—"

"No excuses. Our guests won't be back until after eight. There's a perfectly good sledding hill in back that's useless in a place that doesn't allow children.

If it weren't too late, I'd rethink that policy." Her chin jutted forward.

Sara picked up the handblown glass cardinal perched on the grand piano and dusted beneath it. She waved her hand across the room filled with glassware and antiques. "One of the charms of this place is that it's *not* childproof. Your policies are just fine, Bessie."

"Still. . .there are things I'd do differently. We all would, I suppose." She folded the hem of her apron between her fingers. "Call James. After all I've heard about him, I think I deserve to judge for myself what kind of man he is."

Running the dust cloth over the hinged door that covered the piano keys, Sara sighed. "I think you'd like James."

"You say that like it's a bad thing."

Staring at Bessie's gnarled fingers, Sara shook her head and lifted the lid, exposing the keys. "The two of you have a lot in common. You should hear him play. . . ."

"I'd like to." Bessie smoothed the lace doily that sat beneath a Tiffany lamp and an antique candlestick phone. "It's the musician in him that scares you, isn't it?"

"Scares me? I'm not afraid of him."

"No. But you're afraid of *it*—the music that pulses through his veins, the thing he needs to feel alive."

The protest stopped before it reached Sara's lips. Bessie's red-rimmed eyes focused on the open keyboard. Did she even realize she was talking about herself as well as James? "You miss it, don't you?"

"It was like air to me." Her words were soft, maybe meant only for herself. "When it became too painful, Warren thought it would be easier for me if we sold the piano." She smiled at Sara then wiped her eyes. "I couldn't even entertain the thought. Once in a while I have to grit my teeth and plunk out a tune in spite of the pain. It refreshes the music in my head."

Sara touched the ivory keys, not sure what Bessie had said that had caused her throat to constrict. "I guess I never did understand it. Maybe I didn't really try."

"Musicians are strange folk." Bessie picked up the candlestick phone and handed it to Sara. "Maybe it's not too late to understand him."

"You're a conniver, Bessie." The phone wasn't functional, but it made the point. "If I do—and I'm not saying I will—he can't know anything about me losing my job, okay?"

"Okay. Sara, what I said about doing things differently. . .marriage is one of those things."

"But I thought. . ."

"I know, I know. You haven't heard me say anything but good. But I have a lot of regrets." Bessie walked over to an arrow-back chair with a needlepoint cushion and sat down. "I was very good at getting my way."

Sara pulled out the piano bench. "Is that a trait of all musicians?"

A reproving eyebrow raised in response.

"Sorry," Sara said. "I was pretty good at getting my way, too. What do you regret the most?"

"Not pursuing adoption. We were promised a child once, but it fell through. I couldn't face going through that again, so I got my way. . .and Warren suffered for it. He would have been a good father." Bessie rubbed her wedding ring against her apron then tilted her head slightly. "Learn from my regrets, Sara. Call James."

ॐ

"Don't crash us!" Snow-crusted mittens slapped over Zoe's eyes.

James laughed and tightened his grip on her. "Here we go! Give us a push, Mommy."

Sara's hands pressed against his back, and the sled flew down the forty-five-degree slope. Zoe squealed until they tumbled off at the bottom. Giggling and breathless, she scrambled to her knees and waved to Sara and Sadie. "Let's do it again."

"I think it's your mom and Sadie's turn to use the sled." He held his hand out to her. "Help me up."

Shaking snow off her mittens, she looked at him then narrowed her eyes. Her eyebrows bunched together above her freckled nose. "Are you my daddy?"

"What. . ." James swallowed hard. "What makes you ask that?"

"Grandpa Neil showed me pictures of my daddy. You look like him."

"Oh. . ." He stood and picked up the sled. "Want to race up the hill?"

"I'll win. I'm fastest." Zoe's boots dug into the packed snow, and she darted ahead of him. James took one step to her three but didn't even try to catch up with her. He felt like he'd just dodged a fastball.

Like her mother, Zoe talked with her hands. She was gesturing wildly to Sara when James reached the top of the hill. ". . .and we falled off, and my face got smooshed with snow!"

Sara's hair framed her face beneath a red knit cap. Her skin was pink from the cold, and her eyes sparkled as she laughed at Zoe. James set the sled down and held it while Sara sat on it with Sadie tucked securely between her legs. He put both hands on the back of the sled. "Ready? Okay, here you—"

"So *are* you my daddy?" Zoe stood with her hands on her hips, head cocked to one side.

James pulled back on the rigid purple plastic and locked eyes with Sara. Her lips pressed together, her eyes closed, and she shook her head. "What did you tell her?" she whispered.

"Nothing."

"Go down!" Sadie reached behind her head and patted Sara's face. "Go down!"

Sara nodded toward Zoe, her gaze still fixed on his. "Stall her."

James pushed, and the sled slipped away from him. He watched it careen down the hill, only too aware of the wide blue eyes waiting for an answer. "So . . .Mrs. Tippet said we can have hot chocolate when we're done. Have you had enough sledding?" Cautiously he turned his head toward Zoe and was relieved to see her clapping for the sledders who had stopped at the bottom of the hill. Maybe he wouldn't have to try stall tactics. How long could a four-year-old's attention span possibly be, anyway?

Zoe waved at Sara. "They didn't fall off like us. . .did they, Daddy?"

&

Sara carried a thermos, four plastic mugs, and a bag of shortbread cookies out the back door and down the walkway to the gazebo. Her legs trembled. Maybe learning who James was wouldn't radically impact the girls. Sadie was too young, and Zoe didn't fully understand the definition of "father." She wasn't in school yet and didn't know many kids with fathers who lived at home with them.

No, the real problem was Sara's. How would the revelation impact the life she was trying to build for the three of them? With a smile she didn't feel, she walked up the gazebo steps and held out the treat to the threesome bundled under a blanket on the bench that circled the perimeter of the six-sided structure. "Who wants a winter picnic?"

"I do!" Three voices answered. One seemed to hold the same forced cheer Sara struggled to sustain.

Pouring hot chocolate and passing out cookies ate up the first five minutes. When she ran out of distractions, Sara looked at James and nodded. His smile was sympathetic—not the victorious look she'd expected. He turned his hand over in a gesture that said it was all up to her.

Clearing her throat, Sara pressed her gloves together. "I have a surprise for you, girls."

"Chalocolate?" Sadie smiled up at her with a cocoa mustache.

James laughed, and Sara matched it, staring at the lines that spoked away from his eyes. They hadn't been there two years ago, but she had to admit she liked them. She pulled her gaze away and back to the girls. "You've had enough chocolate for one day, sweet stuff." She leaned forward and waited for both sets of sky-blue eyes to stare at her. "You know that James is a friend of Uncle Brock's, right?"

The girls nodded.

"Well, he's really more than just a friend. He's Uncle Brock's big brother." The news didn't seem to matter in the least to either of them. "And. . .James is also. . .your daddy."

Sara's pulse pounded. In spite of the cold, her shirt clung to her skin beneath her jacket.

Sadie smiled around a mouthful of shortbread. Zoe grinned and looked at

James. "I told you so!"

A shiver started in the small of Sara's back. "But he lives far, far away across the ocean, so we won't get to see him very often."

James zeroed in on her eyes like a heat-seeking missile. "I could change that in a heartbeat. . .if I had a reason."

Chapter 10

S oon it will be Christmas Day. . . ." As James sang, his fingers stroked the keys. He smiled at the four couples sitting on couches and cushions in front of the fireplace. Candlelight reflected off the polished black top of the baby grand, and the room smelled of cinnamon and pine.

Sara walked in with a silver carafe, and for a moment James forgot where he was in the song. Watching her move. . . The way she glided silently around the room, refilling cups and bending with a fluid motion to pass a tray of cookies, made it too difficult to concentrate on anything else. He looked away and caught Bessie Tippet's smirk. Now there was a woman with an agenda. . .and James was already beginning to love her for it.

The girls sat on a huge round pillow on the floor. Sadie, barely keeping her eyes open, appeared mesmerized by the fire, but Zoe craned her neck to watch James's hands. Partway through "The First Noel," she stood up and walked over to him. He kept playing as he slid over to make room for her to climb up beside him. She rested her fingers on the board in front of the keys. James finished the song, and his audience clapped. Over their thank-yous and murmurs of "Wonderful" and "Beautiful," he turned to Bessie. "Thank you so much for letting me play. This is an amazing instrument."

Bessie nodded and walked slowly toward him. "Thank *you*." She ran her hand along a curve in the black wood. A tender caress. "You have no idea what that meant to me, James. These old walls have sorely missed music." Bessie touched a tissue to her eyelashes. "What a gift you have." She folded her hands on the reflective top. "And it seems you've passed it on to your daughter."

Zoe touched the keys, not pressing down, just caressing them lightly with the tips of her fingers. James looked up and caught Sara staring at them. She'd learned something in the past two years—the art of hiding her feelings. He couldn't read the expression on her face, and the realization settled heavily against his chest. Looking down at Zoe, he pushed down on an ebony key. "Now you."

Wonder-filled eyes turned up to him. "Can I, Daddy?"

It was at least the tenth time she'd called him that. She'd found ways to insert it while asking him to pass something at supper, while he helped Sara and Bessie clean up the kitchen, and while he'd kept them quiet by drawing snowmen and Christmas trees so Sara could prepare the tray of goodies for the guests. "For a few minutes, and then we have to go home and put you two to bed. Just be gentle, and don't pound on the piano."

Blond curls jiggled. "I'll be very careful." Slowly she pecked one key at a time, first randomly then starting at middle C and moving to her left.

Goosebumps raised on James's arm. He remembered being just about Zoe's age, playing each note, trying to memorize the sound each key made. For a moment, his hand rested on her shoulder, then he stood and let her have the bench.

Several of the guests were heading up the stairs. Sara had left the room, but Bessie still leaned on the piano. "Don't give up on her."

James looked at the woman with the stern-looking face but compassionate eyes, then he touched the top of Zoe's head with his hand. "I won't. I think she's got the gift."

"She does." A soft smile created rows of concentric curves on Bessie's cheeks. "But I was talking about Sara. Be patient and listen to the things she's not saying." A gnarled hand touched his sleeve. "Let her stay mad while she's figuring out how to forgive you."

§

Zoe had already kissed her good-bye and was dancing around outside in the glow of the porch light, but Sadie's arms wrapped around Sara's neck like a vise. Sara whispered in her ear. "Tomorrow you're going to get out the craft box and make Christmas ornaments with...James." After two years of pretending that he didn't exist, she couldn't easily make the shift to calling him Daddy. Sadie's face burrowed into her neck. Maybe inviting them to Tippet House hadn't been such a good idea. Once Sadie got into a clingy mood, nothing would change it. Sara looked at James. "This isn't going to be pretty."

James squatted down and put his mouth near Sadie's ear. "Hey, Sadie Lady, kiss Mommy good night, and you can walk on the sky all the way to the car."

Sadie giggled and raised her head. "Can I walk on the stars?"

"And the moon and the planets."

A wet kiss banged into Sara's cheek. Sadie reached out to James and jumped into his arms. Sara's chest felt cold.

"Watch, Mommy. I can walk upside down."

James flipped her over and held her by her knees...big hands, wrapped around skinny legs. Sadie's stocking hat fell off. Sara bent to get it, but James was lowering Sadie so she could pick it up herself. Giggling, Sadie jammed it back on her head. "Let's go!"

Sara folded her arms. "I only let them have two stories before bed."

James smiled, moving Sadie's legs back and forth like scissors. "I know. I read the rules on the fridge."

"And even if they're tired, they have to brush their teeth after all the sugar they had tonight."

"Will do."

"Sometimes chocolate gives Zoe nightmares."

A slow smile curved his lips. "I remember."

Sara stifled the "Oh. . ." that formed on her lips. At a year and a half, Zoe had only let her daddy comfort her after what they'd come to call her "Oreo Dreams."

"Well, I'd better get Skywalker home." Without warning, James leaned over the bottom of Sadie's boots and touched his lips to Sara's cheek. Instinctively she drew back. James pulled away, too. "I'm sorry, Sara. I don't know why. . ." He turned and opened the door wider with his foot. Turning back, he gave her a sad smile. "It just seemed so. . .natural."

℠

Something a hundred times larger and fiercer than butterflies played havoc with Sara's insides as she drove Connie's car home through heavy, blowing snow on Sunday. Anxious about the girls, she'd finished stripping beds and cleaning bathrooms in record time, but now that she was headed home half an hour early, she wasn't at all sure she was ready to face what waited there—James, laughing with her girls, playing sugar daddy to the children he'd deserted.

If the weather had looked better, she might have stopped at Mattie's. In the two on-and-off-again years that Mattie had been one of her mentors, they'd had innumerable conversations about how Sara should handle it if James showed up in Pine Bluff again. Yet, after all those hours, Sara was having a hard time recalling much of anything. Fragments of a talk on healthy anger and conflict resolution flitted across her consciousness like the snow that blew horizontally in front of her windshield. "Hold hands and look into each other's eyes" was one of the rules for fighting fair in marriage. Hot tears stung her eyes.

A bizarre thought shot at her from a blind spot. Maybe *she* should leave. Maybe, in reality, she was the one who was all wrong. Not James, not Connie, but Sara. She couldn't compete with either of them on the entertainment scale. James had always nagged her about loosening up and having fun. Well, maybe she'd just get out of the picture altogether and let them make every day a party. What would it hurt if her children lived like the boys of Pleasure Island in Pinocchio? Bedtimes and schedules were overrated. Kids didn't need sleep as long as they had fun! Her foot pressed harder on the accelerator; her gloves squeezed the steering wheel. It dawned on her that she was driving a Ford Escape. How fitting.

Squinting and leaning forward, she searched for the corner that couldn't be far ahead. Her hand was poised on the turn signal lever when the stop sign came into view. At the last second, she pushed the lever up instead of down, announcing to the lonely white countryside that she was not going home.

Not more than thirty feet into her northward flight, rational thinking took over—crazy thoughts banished by a vision of Sadie singing her Sunday night "Pizza-pudding" song. Stepping on the brake pedal, she cranked the wheel to the left. Antiskid brakes shuddered, but the tires couldn't find traction on the slick road. Around the wet snow collecting on the windshield wipers, Sara saw a road sign—way too close to the passenger side. She cranked harder, felt the back end swerve, heard the tires dig down to gravel, and her Escape thudded to a stop.

The sport utility vehicle sat at an angle, leaning toward the ditch but not in it. Shaking, heart thumping, Sara put the vehicle in PARK and wrapped her arms around the steering wheel, her forehead pressed against the hard plastic. She wasn't hurt, not physically, the car wasn't stuck or dented, but that didn't prevent the tears that dropped to her lap. It struck her that this was a point where someone like Mattie would pray. But Mattie was the kind of person God would listen to.

She straightened up and pushed the FOUR-WHEEL-DRIVE button, something she should have done when she pulled out of Bessie's driveway. All she wanted now was to get home, say good-bye to James as quickly as she could, and wrap her arms around her girls. The smell of their hair, the baby softness of their skin, like an elixir, had pulled her through much worse things than running her mother-in-law's car off the road. She swiped at the tears that blurred her vision and shifted into REVERSE. As she swiveled to look out the rear window, something on the middle seat caught her eye. A frayed black backpack. . .the same one James had slung over his shoulder on his way out the door two years ago. Sticking out of the pack was a corner of a book. Only the bottom of the spine was visible, just enough to show the author's name. Schmidt. As in Riley J.

James had his own copy of *Recipe for a Godly Wife*? And he'd brought it with him? He'd probably memorized it on the flight over, just waiting for the moment when Sara would fall to her knees and beg him to teach her how to become a sweet-talking, slipper-carrying, master-serving little woman. And just what else did he tote around in that ugly bag? Bibles? More fire-breathing tracts? Maybe he'd already bought the pearls and heels that would complete Sara's domestic goddess image. Teeth grinding, she put the car in PARK, unfastened her seat belt, and stretched over the back of the seat.

The pack was heavy enough to hold a case of Bibles. Hefting it onto the passenger seat, she opened the flap slowly, as if it might be filled with scorpions or tarantulas. Grabbing the book with thoughts of hurling it into the snow-filled ditch, she yanked it out then stopped and stared. It wasn't the same book. . .or the same author. This one was written by Caleb A. Schmidt. And the title was *Blueprint for a Godly Husband*.

A teaspoon of conviction mingled with curiosity as she opened to the table of contents and scanned the chapter titles. "Under Construction. . .Always," "Read the Specs," "Solid Footings."

Once again she let the book fall open. The pages she stared at were marked with notes and underlined sentences. As heavy snow plastered the side windows, Sara read out loud from a chapter called "Plan B. . .or Z": " 'The two-by-four is a quarter of an inch too short, the oven won't fit in the space you made for it. . .

what's your first reaction? Let the hammer fly along with a toolbox full of expletives? That was the extent of my coping skills a few years back—on the job and across the kitchen table. Let me tell you, guys, it doesn't work. Then again, maybe you're the kind who screams "I quit!" as the hammer sails through the plate glass. . .or your wife dissolves into tears. If that describes your MO, I have to ask: *How's that working for you?*'"

After the last sentence, which was underlined in ink, were penciled two words in all caps: *"IT DIDN'T."*

&

The sight of Brock's car parked behind hers in front of the apartment peeled off several layers of tension. He was probably breaking Sanctuary rules once again, alone with Allison, who had been sent home with instructions not to lift or climb stairs. But Sara would borrow him for a few minutes, just long enough not to be alone with James. Her reasons changed with each swipe of the windshield wipers—because she was scared to death of falling into his arms, because she might say something she'd regret, because maybe now wasn't the time to tell him he couldn't just jump back into his role without paying penance or serving time for desertion.

She walked up the front walk and took a deep breath as she stepped onto the porch and opened the front door. Muffled laughter and a familiar smell met her in the foyer. Her stomach twisted as she opened the apartment door.

"Surprise!"

James, Brock, Allison, Zoe, and Sadie sat at the kitchen table. In front of them were two baked pizzas and six bowls of chocolate pudding.

With a strangled sob, Sara ran to the bedroom and slammed the door.

Chapter 11

D o something!" Brock shot daggers at James, as if Sara's meltdown was his fault.

Allison's accusing gaze zigzagged between the two men then parked on James. "What was that all about?"

"Daddy, why is Mommy crying?"

James closed his eyes and took a prayer breath. *Lord, help!* It had been too long since he'd tried to figure out what to say to a crying woman. From past experience, "I'm sorry" was usually the place to start. But what came next? With four expectant faces locked on his, he stood and walked on unsteady legs to the bedroom.

The door was open several inches. Sara had certainly used enough force to shut it, but the latch hadn't caught. His hand formed a fist, and he raised it to knocking position then froze. In the three days he'd been in the apartment, he hadn't set one foot on the other side of this door. Though the couch was too short and too lumpy, it was a neutral zone for thoughts.

In the fear-filled silence, he heard her crying. His hand lowered to his side. Maybe she needed time. Maybe *he* needed time. Time to prepare for launched pillows and lacerating words. A line from the book he'd read for the third time on the plane came to mind. *"Let her get it out."* The advice dovetailed perfectly with Bessie's counsel. *"Let her stay mad while she's figuring out how to forgive you."*

When he was little, his father had bought him a blow-up clown with a weighted bottom. A punch to the big red nose would send it to the floor, but the stubborn thing would always pop back up again. He could be Bop the Clown for her, rebounding after every blow. . .at least for a while. Without knocking, he opened the door and stepped over the stocking cap and boots she'd most likely fired at the wall.

Still in her jacket, Sara lay on the bed. The face that turned toward him didn't much resemble the funny little blond he'd fallen for five years earlier. Her hair was electrified from tearing the hat off. Her nose was Bop the Clown-red. Wild, puffy eyes narrowed to smoldering holes. "Get out."

"Sara. . ." He took a step forward. "Sara, what did I do?" He suddenly realized how large a door that question would open. "What did I do. . .just now? What's wrong?"

Her head lifted from the pillow. "What did you do? You ruined ev–ry–thing, that's what you did! You made pizza and pudding with *my* girls!"

291

A smile threatened to move his lips from their tight hold. This is where he'd gone wrong way too many times. He had to take her seriously—even when she was overreacting, even when she looked so adorable with her face all scrunched and angry. He'd found out the hard way that saying "You're so cute when you're mad" wasn't the way to disarm the bomb. This one had to be disassembled wire by wire. And to do that, he had to see pizza and pudding through Sara's eyes.

"I'm sorry." Man, this wasn't easy. Sorry for leaving her, yes. Sorry for being an insensitive, self-absorbed idiot, yes. But sorry for baking a pizza? *Lord, show me....* "That's your special thing to do with them, isn't it?"

"Yes." The word came out rough and gravelly.

"I should have realized that."

"Yes, you should have." She smashed her face into the pillow.

"I'm sorry." Enough, already! He was sorry. Brock had told him about the Sunday tradition; he should have realized that having supper ready for her when she walked in the door wasn't a help. But there were just so many times a guy could use those two words without feeling like a total slug. He needed to save them for the really vital things. "Sara? Can we talk?" Where had he heard that before?

"Talk? Sure." She leaned on one elbow. "Let's talk about how I had to quit my jobs and get out of *our* lease and move into subsidized housing. Or maybe you want to know what it feels like to apply for food stamps and medical assistance. Or how about all the choice little names I've thought up for you in the past two years?" She laughed, cold and biting. "Do you really want to hear what I have to say, James?"

He took a deep breath, another step, then made a move that was certain to hurt him in one way or another. He sat on the edge of the bed. "Yes."

Sara sat up, clawed at the buttons of her jacket, and ripped it off, hurling it at the floor. She drew her knees to her chest like a protective fortress. His one-word answer seemed to have created a lull before the storm. Raw pain, more than anger, blazed in her eyes.

"Do you have even the slightest idea what you put me through?"

"No." James held her gaze. He knew he needed to hear her out without defending himself, but he wasn't going to cower from her. Beyond the shadow of a doubt, he knew that his sins against her had been paid in full. It had taken a lot of late-night talks with a small group of God-honoring men and hours on his face before God to bring him to the point of accepting that he no longer needed to be punished for what he'd repented of. He did, however, need to face the consequences like a man of integrity. *"A soft answer turns away wrath."* "I can't imagine."

Sara turned to face the wall, her knuckles pressed against her mouth. A silent sob shook her shoulders, and James commanded his arms not to reach out. "I'm listening."

Red eyes blazed. Her fist lowered. "You. . .can't. . .do. . .this." Her words snapped out a staccato beat.

"Do what?" Try as he might, he didn't have the sixth sense she'd always wanted from him.

"You can't just walk back in acting like two years was nothing. You can't use the Jesus card on me, James. I'm not that stupid. You can't tell me that in six months you've become this—this perfect, sensitive guy who's suddenly going to be an attentive, responsible father. It doesn't work that way. You forget. . .I know you. I know that the only thing that really matters to James Lewis is James Lewis."

Bam. Hit the floor. Get back up. *Lord God, I can't do this*. James rubbed his hand across his eyes. "I'm a work in progress, Sara. I'm a million miles from perfect, but I am different." He hammered his defensiveness back down where it belonged.

"For how long? Your brother went through a Christian phase, too. Remember? It lasted until Caitlyn Douglas died of leukemia after all her friends had prayed around the clock for weeks. What's going to turn you away, James? Do you honestly think I'd let you move back in like old times and just sit around and wait and pretend that everything's wonderful until something gets too hard for you again and off you go to Canada or England or Timbuktu?"

James dug his fingers into the dark blue bedspread. "I'm not asking to move in. I'm just asking for a little patience, Sara. I don't expect you to believe I've changed just because I say so. But the only way I can prove it to you is if we spend some time together and—"

"And you worm your way into my girls' hearts? No! I can't let you do that." She pointed to the door. "Just get out, James. Go back to your music and your roadies and quit pretending to be something you're not."

James released the fabric balled in his hands and stood up. "This isn't about the girls and you know it. This is about you. And if you ever decide to be mature enough to carry a conversation all the way through, maybe we'll actually get around to talking about your side of this. I didn't just walk out on a whim. I left because I finally caved in and agreed with you. I finally believed that you were right, that you could do it all better than me and better without me. My goals were getting in your way big-time, and running my life on top of yours and the girls' was just a bit too much of a strain on you, wasn't it? So I finally decided to just get out of your way." He turned, took two steps toward the door, and looked back. "You win, Sara."

☙

The door slammed and ricocheted off the loose frame. Sara stared as it wobbled to a stop halfway open. So it hadn't taken long at all for him to do exactly what she'd predicted. He'd walked out on her once again.

It shouldn't bother her. With all the scar tissue left from the first two times, her sense of pain should be calloused over. So why did it hurt to breathe? She heard the apartment door open and close. Her next breath wasn't quite so tight. She massaged the shoulder muscles that tension had turned to steel. He was gone now. Life would return to normal. . .except for the fact that she didn't have a job, and if she did get one, she didn't have a full-time sitter.

Her feet had just hit the floor when Allison stuck her head in the room. "Um. . .we're gonna take the girls over to my place. You can come get 'em whenever." She pulled her head back out.

"Allison! Wait!"

"Yeah?" The girl looked annoyed.

"Did they have time to eat?"

"We're gonna take a pizza with us. Give you time to. . .you know. . .chillax." She was gone again.

Chillax? Maybe the kid was right. Sara needed to regroup before she got the girls. Take a shower, grab a slice of pizza. Her eyes stung at the thought of pizza, but she didn't have the energy to get upset about that all over again. Her head hurt, her eyes burned. She flopped back on the bed.

James was gone. She said it to herself twice then again, feeling the tension drain. But the ache in her chest was still there. Scenes from Saturday popped in her head unbidden. James and Zoe pulling the sled up the hill. James and Sadie huddled together in the gazebo. Guilt, like an old shoe molded to fit, slid around her.

"This isn't about the girls and you know it. It's about you."

How dare he! Just like always, he'd twisted the facts and dumped it all back on her. He'd accused her of running his life. Well, somebody had to. If she'd left everything up to him, he'd have been gone every weekend, playing gigs from here to Liverpool.

If only he'd been able to tailor his ambitions to fit a family. She would have been fine with him doing an occasional concert on the road or even a regular Friday night job in the Cities. But right from the beginning, he'd been adamant about pursuing his fantasies of fame on the other side of the Atlantic. Why hadn't she walked away before letting her heart and brain get so enmeshed?

James had stayed in Pine Bluff when the rest of the group headed to Canada. *"I'll stay until you and I are solid, Sara,"* he'd said.

"And then I'll go with you. I'll follow you to the ends of the earth, James."

An inaudible gasp slipped through Sara's lips. She sat up. Why had those words surfaced now? Was it a false memory, or had she really said it?

There'd only been a few weeks between the time he'd told her he loved her and the day she found out she was pregnant. She tried to put herself back in that place, tried to think like a starry-eyed girl in love with the guy who mesmerized her with his music and his compliments. Only five years had passed, but it seemed like forever. A dim memory came into focus. . .standing backstage at Pine Bluff's Veterans' Hall, watching the crowd as they sang along with the words her man had written. Imagining a stadium full of fans. . .

But all that changed with a pregnancy test.

Memories served no good purpose. Sara stood up, kicked her jacket out of the way, and walked toward the living room. She'd eat her pizza alone, take a long, hot shower, and—

Her mental list disintegrated.

James was not gone.

Chapter 12

He stood in the middle of the living room, hands on his hips. Sara braced herself on the archway leading from the hall, feeling like a dog caught in a bear trap. He'd waited. . .just to finish her off. She stared, daring him to blame one more thing on her.

His hand reached toward his back pocket. "I came home for three reasons." He pulled out his wallet. "To see the girls—yesterday was a day I'll never forget. To have an open and honest dialogue with you—I guess until I get on the plane I'll still be hoping for that. And to give you this." One stride brought him just close enough to hand her a check. "I didn't want to mail it. I had a feeling you might not be opening my letters."

Sara looked down. She knew immediately what it was. It surpassed the running total in her head by 10 percent—two years of back child support plus interest. Brock had researched it and told her several times he'd sent James a bill on her behalf. She'd convinced herself she didn't want his money anyway, yet the imaginary tab continually multiplied in her head.

Reactions bubbled like a stew pot. Disbelief, relief, anger. This would pay off her credit card bill and tide them over for weeks if she didn't get a job right away. But she could have used it months ago after they'd lost everything. She thought of his story about digging bread out of a Dumpster. Was that all it was—a story? "Have you been saving this up all along?"

"No." James looked down at the floor. "If I'd made any money, I would have sent it."

"Then how. . . ?"

He gave a quick shrug. "I sold some equipment."

His voice was so quiet on the last two words she wasn't sure she'd heard him. He looked up but not at her, with eyes that spoke of hopelessness. Her insides twisted. "What did you sell?"

Again he shrugged. "Korgy." A thin-lipped smile accompanied the word.

Suddenly chilled, Sara hugged her arms to her waist. James had sold his keyboard—the 88-key Korg OASYS—the "synthesis studio" that did everything but make his coffee. She thought of the things she'd called the extravagant purchase—his baby, the other woman, the real love of his life. The thing that spawned their worst fight. Later she'd found out that his mother had paid for much of it. Armed with that new knowledge, Sara had been just as mad that James hadn't told her that up front.

He stuck his wallet back in his pocket. "She was getting old."

Tears stung her already sore eyes. James had sold his baby. For her.

"Give James a chance." It was almost an audible voice in her head. She closed her eyes, opened them, and motioned toward the couch. "Sit down."

&

Sara laid the check on the coffee table between them and sank to the edge of the chair. She rubbed the spot that throbbed above her right eye. What now? What were the rules for fighting fair?

She stared into crystal blue eyes and took a shaky breath. "Thank you. . .for the money. The timing is—"

"I know. I should have been sending something all along. I—"

"No." She offered him a hint of a smile. "Yes, you should have, but that's not what I was going to say. James, I lost my job. The bed-and-breakfast is closing."

James leaned forward. "I'm so sorry, Sara."

"Thank you." She ran her fingers along the frayed seam near the knee of her jeans. "But maybe the timing is. . .a God thing." She held her breath, hoping he wouldn't take her inch and turn it into a mile.

"Maybe it is."

She waited, but he didn't add anything more. Now what? She felt like she was holding her finger on a hand grenade pin. One wrong word could blow away any chance of real communication.

She remembered another rule. *"Speak the truth in love."*

She took a deep breath. Then another. "I'm scared."

James groaned. "Sara. . .so am I."

"I'm scared of trying and then finding out it's too late."

James nodded. "I know. But I'm scared to walk away without trying."

"I don't think we can talk without hurting each other."

"Then we need some help."

"I know a couple." Mattie and Eldon would probably consider it an honor to counsel them; that's just the way they were. "They've been married over thirty years, and they've gone through some bad times." She watched his expression, wondering why he seemed to hesitate. And then it dawned on her. "They're Christians. . .*real* Christians."

Blue eyes lit with a kind of glow Sara wasn't sure she'd ever seen. "Thank you," he said.

Was he thanking her or God? Maybe both. She needed to lay down some rules before she got cornered by three people with a God agenda. "The only way I'm going to agree with this is if you can promise not to push your religion on me anymore. No more books or tracts or guilt."

James sat back on the couch. The clock above the TV ticked louder than Sara had ever heard it. "I can promise not to push or give you tracts or books. . . but I won't promise to never talk about God."

In a strange way, Sara was satisfied with his answer. It was pretty much the same thing Mattie had said when Sara had asked her not to preach to her. She could accept James talking about what was important to him as long as he wasn't shoving it at her.

Leaning forward, James rested his elbows on his knees. "Do you think maybe you and I could do something fun together? Something unserious and unthreatening. . .just the two of us?"

Unthreatening. Looking at his eyes, at the dark hair splayed across his forehead, Sara knew that his very existence was a threat to the guard she'd put on her emotions. After today, after knowing the sacrifice he'd made for her, he'd still be a threat if. . .*when* he flew back to London. "Like what?"

"Like lutefisk."

"*What?*"

"Bessie slipped me two tickets to the lutefisk dinner at the Lutheran church on Friday."

"But I work on Friday."

"Not between six and eight. Boss's orders."

Sara hated the jelly-looking Norwegian delicacy, but a crowded codfish-smelling church basement would, like James had said, be an unserious environment. "I'm only eating the Swedish meatballs."

"Is that a yes?"

Her sore eyes and dull headache wouldn't let her forget what she'd been thinking about James just minutes earlier, yet his hopeful grin made her laugh. How in the world had her pendulum swung so far so fast? And was she crazy not to push it back? "Yes."

∽

"Can I ask you a question?" Mattie spoke through the cinnamon-scented steam floating from her mug of tea.

Sara laughed. "Since when do you ask first?"

"Since we started talking about your marriage in the present tense."

"You can ask me anything. By now you know more about me than I do."

Mattie took a sip of tea, set down her cup, and pressed brownie crumbs with her fingertip. "Why didn't you stop wearing your wedding band when James left?"

A bite of still-warm brownie gave Sara a reason to stall. She chewed, on her dessert and on her answer. "People look on single moms differently. I don't want to be pitied or judged. . .or hit on."

"Is that all?"

"I suppose, deep down, I love the idea of marriage."

"Is that all?"

Sara wrapped her hands around her mug and sipped the hot chocolate spiked with coffee. "I know what you're trying to get me to say. I thought I'd given up, but maybe. . . I would have told you a month ago—I probably *did* tell you a month ago—that I never wanted to see his face again. If I was holding out hope that he'd come back and sweep me off my feet, it was buried deep in my subconscious."

Unbidden, her dream popped into her mind—the mistletoe in the white box and the kiss that followed—maybe her hopes weren't as buried as she thought.

"But he's changed enough that you're willing to get swept now?"

"Yes. Maybe." Sara set her mug down. "I'm afraid to believe it's genuine. Can being a Christian really change somebody that much?"

Mattie laughed. "What do you think I've been trying to tell you for the past two years? Change is what it's all about. There's an old saying in the church— God loves you just the way you are, but He loves you too much to leave you that way." Mattie reached across the table and touched Sara's arm. "I'm not sure what's holding you back. Either you feel that God doesn't care because of all the bad stuff that's happened to you, or you feel like you've done too much bad stuff for Him to *want* to care—"

"Or all of the above."

Mattie smiled. "All of the above is false. God loves you, Sara. It might not be evident right now, but He does. And when you finally surrender to that fact, you'll find out that people really can change that much. But God isn't a magic potion. You can't just say all the right words, and suddenly life is beautiful. It has to be a real commitment." She pointed at her chest. "In here. You don't have to have it all figured out, but you have to be sure in your heart that Jesus is who He says He is and that you want to give Him every part of you."

"James seems to think that if I just become a Christian, everything will be easy."

Again Mattie laughed. "Oh how I wish it were that simple. Marriage can be hard, and following Christ can be even harder. If James has been following Jesus for six months he knows that by now. One of the ways God changed me years ago was by making me realize that difficult doesn't mean bad. It just means difficult. I started looking at my marriage as a challenge instead of a hopeless mess. And years later, as an old married grandma, I can honestly say life is beautiful. Tough but beautiful." Her thumb wiggled the back of the ring on her hand. "Did you ever do the climbing wall at the Y?"

"Years ago."

"That's my marriage analogy. One precarious step at a time, you work your way to the top. Sometimes you feel stuck, lots of times you want to quit, but there's always another rock to grab or plant your foot on. And, for me, Jesus is my safety harness."

Sara laughed. "You sneak that little hook into every conversation, don't you?"

"That's who I am, Sara."

"I know." *Is that who I want to be?* "Maybe I need a safety harness."

୨୦

Kitty-corner from Sara, the man sitting next to James wore a sweatshirt with a picture of a Viking in a horned helmet on the front, and the words LIFE IS SIMPLE: RAID. PILLAGE. BURN. REPEAT AS NEEDED. Suspenders in the red and blue of the Norwegian flag secured the pants of the potbellied man who brought their coffee. From a platform in the corner, a singer with a three-piece band sang "The Lefse Song" to the tune of "Camp Town Races." *"Norsky ladies sing dis song. . .Uff Da! Uff Da. Bake dat lefse all day long. . .all da Uff Da day."*

Sara looked down at the whitefish and boiled potatoes swimming in butter and cream sauce on her plate next to the meatballs slathered with brown gravy. She hadn't had the heart to tell the rotund little woman with the big red spoon that she couldn't stomach fish that had been dehydrated and soaked in lye. She took a bite of meatball. "These are great."

A huge forkful of fish hung from James's fork. "Try this. It's perfect. It only gets like jelly when they overcook it." He inched the fork closer. "Come on. You love fish."

Her eyes crossed as the fish drew closer. It would end up on her lap if she didn't open her mouth. One bite wouldn't kill her. She could hold down one bite. She opened her mouth and was shocked to find the fish flaky and not nearly as fishy tasting as she'd remembered from a childhood experience that had catapulted her to the bathroom. "Not bad. But even cardboard would be good with enough butter and gravy."

"Cardboard's not so bad with spaghetti sauce either."

She laughed and then remembered what he'd said about hunting for food behind an Italian restaurant. "Were you serious about stealing bread from a Dumpster?"

"Not the kind of thing I'd joke about."

He looked embarrassed. Clearly he hadn't expected her to delve any deeper into his comment. Sara picked up the piece of potato flatbread that was folded on her plate. She didn't want to open it up on the table the way she did at Christmas and Thanksgiving at the Lewises, but she'd watched James skillfully butter his in his hand. "Will you fix my lefse for me?"

"My pleasure." He laid the soft tortillalike bread across one large hand, spread it with butter, sprinkled sugar over it, and rolled it tight. With a slight bow of his head, he handed her the cigar-shaped roll. "Always ready to help a damsel in distress." His face reddened on the last word, but he smiled. "I mean that. . .now."

I believe you. She couldn't say it out loud, but at least in this moment, she did believe.

୨୦

"These things are messy." James reached across the table and wiped a drop of whipped cream from Sara's chin. *Krumkake*—thin, crispy cones filled with whipped cream and lingonberries—was only one of the dessert offerings passed around by the teens of the Norway Lutheran Church youth group.

"That's what makes them good." Sara looked at him with a smile that momentarily banished five years of misunderstandings.

"But you make them better."

A half smile quickly slid behind Sara's napkin.

"You should open your own bakery." *Or bed-and-breakfast*. He hadn't asked her yet about the Stillwater Inn. Knowing he'd been the one to shipwreck her future made it a topic he really didn't want to approach. "Brock says you still bake a lot."

A wistful look drew her gaze to some distant place, but she smiled and nodded. "I bake. . .*baked*. . .at work, and Brock still gets his macaroons when he begs for them."

James took a drink of thick coffee from his Styrofoam cup. "I'm glad you and my little brother stayed friends."

"He's been a huge help, and he's so good with the girls." Her eyes came back to his, her expression slightly accusing, but James didn't sense anger.

This might have been a good place to insert another apology, but he couldn't form the words. "The mural in the girls' room is amazing." Where had that come from? Sara would see it for the subject shift it was, and it would probably lead to talk of Stillwater, a topic he'd narrowly avoided moments ago. He scanned the outside walls until he found his escape. "Think I'll hit the restroom before we leave." Crumpling his napkin, he stood and jockeyed around folding chairs and gray-haired Lutheran ladies until he found the men's room.

Cold water and a rough paper towel reddened his face but gave him the clarity to think. He'd been the one to suggest the guidelines for this date. Unserious and unthreatening. He was beginning to realize that was close to impossible. There were things that had to be talked about, and so many more reasons to say "I'm sorry." He walked back through the noisy room. The band leader was introducing a children's song called "Paul and His Chickens." It was time to leave.

Sara was on the same wavelength. She stood and grabbed her jacket before James had a chance to ask if she was ready. When they walked out the back door, Sara pointed down the hill toward Founders' Park, where pineapple-shaped lamps lined the west bank of the St. Croix. "Let's walk down by the river."

Only a sliver of moon hung over the water. Stars sprinkled the expanse above them like salt spilled across a black tablecloth. James watched the frozen vapor of their breath hover and then vanish as they walked along the sidewalk, close enough for hand holding. He stuck his gloved hands in his pockets. "Have you talked to the Torstens lately?" He kept his eyes on the poorly shoveled walk.

"Not for a few months. But I'm counting down the days."

He stopped. "You're still considering it? I thought that. . .when you had to quit your other job and—"

Her hand on his arm interrupted him. "They're offering me a land contract, no money down. Instead of retiring, they're moving to Southern California to help some relative run a vineyard, and they'll give me five years to come up with a down payment and get a conventional loan. Erik says I have a positive aura or something, and they want me to have it. To be honest, I think they feel sorry for me."

"Wow." *Thank You, Lord.* Of all the things that had haunted him in the past two years, Stillwater Inn was one of the worst.

"So that brings up a question, James." She pulled her hand away and tied her scarf tighter. "If we were to. . .work things out. . .could you handle that kind of life?"

Lord, help me here. An old familiar tightness gripped his throat—a caged feeling. Could he? So many conversations in his small group of men who were trying to let God put their lives back together had centered on sacrifice. Sacrifice and priorities and dying to self. "I won't make promises I can't keep, Sara."

෨

On Sunday afternoon Sara walked through the upstairs rooms of Tippet House for the last time. She took a moment in each bedroom doorway, as if saying good-bye to old friends. In the Penrose Room, which faced west, she pulled back the lace curtain. The storm that caused two cancellations last night had painted the countryside like a Christmas card. Rounded globs of snow decorated pine boughs, and cone-shaped mounds made swirled finials on fence posts. The sun had sunk to the treetops, like a bright orange ball speared on the tip of an arrow. Long shadows striped the snow-covered lawn, tinted pink by the setting sun.

At this time next year would she really be looking out the window of her own bed-and-breakfast? There were so many details yet to be addressed. She hadn't spoken to the Torstens in months. A larger question overshadowed the rest. If she found herself standing at a window of the Stillwater Inn, staring out at a winter sunset, would she be alone or with James?

He'd said he wouldn't make promises he couldn't keep. But would he make any promise at all?

Friday night, after James had dropped her off and ended the night with a restrained hug, she'd stared at the ceiling in her third-floor garret for hours. Wrestling against hope had proved impossible, and once again she'd come to the conclusion that he couldn't hurt her any more than he already had. She couldn't possibly end up worse than before James walked back into her life. Their relationship would either begin to heal. . .or would end for good.

Now, two days later, as she waited for James to pull up the drive in his mother's car with their girls in the backseat, she knew beyond the shadow of a doubt that her middle-of-the-night conclusion had been totally false. If the fragile hope growing inside her shattered, this time she wouldn't bounce.

She let the lace slide back into place and picked up the basket of sheets at her feet. Rosy light patterned the wall and spilled into the hallway. She closed the door behind her and walked toward the stairs.

Halfway down, she saw Bessie sitting at the piano in tears. Sara set the basket on the floor, slid onto the bench, and put her arm around her. "I can't imagine how hard this is."

"What will I do in Arizona?" Bessie's shoulders shook with sobs. "This is all I've known for so long. . . ." She blew her nose, shook her head, and stared at Sara. "I need a purpose. I need to be needed, Sara."

"I'm sure you'll find things to do with your sister." Sara knew her words lacked conviction.

A soft huff preceded another blow of her nose. "My sister plays canasta and golf. That's her whole existence."

An idea began taking shape. "*I* need you, Bessie. I have a huge, huge favor to ask of you."

"What's that?"

"Would you use your tape recorder and make tapes for me of all your secrets? All the little touches that make this place so special—like the spices you boil on the stove at Christmas and what you put in the gift baskets for anniversaries and birthdays. I've taken a ton of notes, but you do so much behind the scenes during the week. It would really help."

Bessie sniffed then gave a weak smile. "I'll do that." She patted Sara's hand. "You know, if I hadn't taken out a second mortgage to pay for Warren's hospital bills, I'd just give this place to you." Her eyes filled again. "I hate to think of the house in anyone else's hands."

"Thank you. That means so much. And don't you go doing the guilt thing on me, you hear?"

As Bessie wiped at her tears, they heard snow crunching beneath tires on the drive. The engine stopped, and a car door slammed.

"That's James."

Bessie nodded toward the window. "Don't let that man get away, Sara."

"We're trying."

"You know, I'd stay in Minnesota if I could make a career out of saving marriages with church dinner tickets."

Sara laughed and touched her cheek to Bessie's. "You'll get all the credit if we work this out."

Chapter 13

While he waited for Sara to get her coat and gather her things, James picked up a shovel and cleared off the porch and the back steps, grateful for a way to channel nervous energy. In the car was a surprise he hadn't mentioned to Sara. Not a pleasant surprise.

The door opened just as he started shoveling the steps to the gazebo. Sara poked her head out. "All set."

James hugged Bessie and stacked bags and boxes, months of accumulated magazines, books, and toiletries, under each arm. As they stepped onto the porch, James took a long sideways glance at Sara, trying to gauge her mood.

"What are you staring at?" she asked.

My wife. "You. How are you doing?"

"Kind of sad." She fell in step behind him on the sidewalk.

Probably not in the mood for a shift from routine for the second Sunday in a row. "I bet." He slowed his steps and turned to face her. "Um. . ."

"Um *what?*" Sara stopped, peering over a pile of white bakery boxes filled with Tippet House gingerbread and shortbread cookies. "That look scares me. I already don't like what you're going to say."

"I know." James tried on a smile then cast it off. "My mother's in the car."

"Oh."

Whatever Sara was thinking, it wasn't on display. Was it good or bad that her thoughts no longer scrolled across her face like a teleprompter? "She needed groceries, and I had her car. . . ."

There. For a split second, like a window opening and slamming shut, he read the words in her head. *Groceries? On Sunday? She couldn't have sent you?* Or maybe he was just tuning in to his own thoughts, because Sara was actually smiling. Sort of.

They rounded the corner of the house in time to see his mother slip out of the backseat and into the front, leaving the back door open for Sara. *Could you be any more blatant, Mother?* From the first day he'd brought Sara home for dinner, he'd hated the crackling tension that spit like sparks whenever the two women were in close proximity.

Sara said hello first. His mother repeated the lifeless greeting. Sara slid into the car and transformed before his eyes. As he closed her door, hugs, kisses, and giggles filled the backseat. By the time he'd filled the trunk with Sara's bags and boxes and gotten in on the driver's side, the girls were singing "Mommy's home!

Hurray for pizza! Mommy's home. . . ."

Beside him, his mother sat in chiseled stillness, staring at the gazebo as if it were a cinema screen. An outsider would have thought her deaf and mute. A dim light of understanding flickered in James's consciousness. His mother was jealous. All along he'd assumed the whole issue was that he'd married below her expectations. But maybe the problem was simply that he'd married.

Oddly, the realization made him smile. He put the car in gear and followed the drive that circled around the back of Tippet House. "Where to, Mom? Health food store's closed on Sunday."

Like a statue touched by a good fairy, his mother came to life. "Let's go out for dinner. My treat." Her hand patted his knee, and she turned toward the backseat. "Let's celebrate your last day, Sara."

Celebrate? "I'm not sure Sara's really feeling like a celebration."

"Well, she should be." His mother turned back to the front, then she opened her vanity mirror and adjusted it to get a view of Sara and the girls. "It's all about the way you perceive things. Dark thoughts are like toxins that poison your body and clog your spirit."

An image of a toilet plunger came to mind. Wouldn't jealousy count as a dark thought? James glanced in the rearview mirror at Sara's frozen expression. "How do you feel about going out for supper, Sara?"

Zoe nodded like a bobblehead doll. "Can we get pizza?"

The ceramic grapes hanging from his mother's ears swayed back and forth. "Absolutely not. The Sage Stoppe has pumpkin soup this week just for Christmas. Wouldn't that be a nice Sunday supper?"

Three faces fell in unison. James stifled his laugh. Sara looked beyond miserable. Little did she know she was about to witness firsthand the miracle of a life transformed. James stopped at the end of the driveway and fixed his gaze on the rearview mirror but spoke to his mother. "Mom, Sara has a tradition of pizza for Sunday night supper. If you'd like to treat, I'm sure they'd love it. Otherwise, let's pick up what you need at the store and then I'll take my girls home."

The blinking, incredulous stare from the woman with the amazing green eyes warmed him to his toes.

&

A girl could get used to this.

James kept his hand on the small of her back as the hostess ushered them to a rounded booth in the corner of Mama Gina's Pizza. The girls crawled to the middle of the bench seat, and Sara followed, which left room for one person next to her and one next to Zoe. Connie took a step toward Sara's side, but James set his hand on his mother's shoulder. "Why don't you sit next to Zoe, Mom?"

Without waiting for her answer, he sat down and scooted close enough to Sara that his leg touched hers. Could he feel that? Sara's sweater was suddenly heavy. How deliciously absurd to be so off-kilter over her own husband! *"He's not the same man who walked out on you."* James had sold his keyboard and stood up to his mother. . .twice. Sara's doubts were dissolving like the snow on her boots.

As their waitress set down water glasses, the assistant manager walked up behind her. Sara had known Tom Wilkes since high school. "Hi, Sara." Tom nodded at James and Connie then turned back to her. "If you're still looking for a job, we've got a place for you as a server after the college help leaves. I know you applied to work in the kitchen, but we just don't have openings."

Waitressing was not what she wanted to do, but it was a job. And the look on Connie's face made her want to accept the offer on the spot. Connie knew people who came to Mama Gina's. What would they think if the wife of her gifted son was waiting tables? "What are the hours?"

"Weekends mostly. Four to twelve."

Not good hours for a babysitter. "I'll let you know in a couple of days. Thanks, Tom."

Connie shook her head as Tom walked away. "James, don't you think Sara should go back to school and get her degree?"

His eyes on the menu, James chewed on the inside of his cheek. "I think Sara should do whatever Sara decides to do. She makes good decisions."

A girl could get used to this.

James ordered a large pizza—half deluxe, half ham and pineapple for "his girls." Connie ordered a salad, ate it with her eyes on the pizza, then picked at a leftover piece of deluxe, leaving it a barren crust. As she popped the last pepperoni slice into her mouth, she smiled at Sara, the kind of smile that triggered a silent *Uh-oh.* "We need to talk."

Uh-oh.

"I spoke to my spiritual director about you two." Though her words included James, her eyes didn't.

Sara prodded the corners of her mouth upward. "Oh? What, exactly, is a spiritual director?"

Connie appeared annoyed at Sara's ignorance. "Padma is my life coach. She has amazing abilities. She can tell everything about a person just by their handwriting."

James rested his chin in his hand and arched his left brow. "Oh really?"

"Yes." Connie shot her son a glance and refocused on Sara. "I showed her your list of rules." Her mouth puckered on "rules" as if it left a bitter taste in her mouth.

A woman I've never met read my kids' bedtime and toothbrushing rules and now knows all things about me? "Fascinating. What did she discover?"

"That you are a diamond."

Sara blinked. An affirmation from her mother-in-law?

"You retain your luster under adverse circumstances."

The statement was so unexpected that Sara didn't know how to respond.

Connie leaned forward. "However. . .diamonds also make excellent abrasives. A diamond person is often inflexible and can rub others the wrong way."

James's hand found Sara's—on her knee, where it was squeezing the life out of her napkin. Sara stretched her lips, baring her teeth. "How interesting."

"Isn't it? After Padma analyzed you, she looked at a letter from James." A full-out smile blazed on her son.

"And. . .?" Sara and James asked the single-word question in unison.

"And. . .James is a star sapphire."

Of course he is. Sara choked her napkin. James tightened the pressure on her hand.

Connie laid her right hand on the table, all four fingers pointing at her star sapphire son. "Asterism. That's what they call the starlike phenomenon in a sapphire when it's exposed to a source of light."

Zoe and Sadie whispered and giggled over their Polly Pocket dolls. That was the only sound at the booth in the corner. James withdrew his hand, laced it with his other one on the table, and sat, in this prayerlike position, staring at his mother. Sara waited. The old James would have laughed nervously and suggested it was time to leave.

James cleared his throat. "Jesus said, 'I am the light of the world.' There isn't any star quality in me without His light, Mom."

"Oh, James. . ." A sound like a slowly deflating balloon leaked from Connie. "Embracing a religion can make you a happier person—though you'll soon find Christianity is far too restrictive—but it doesn't change your destiny. I knew you were a star from the moment I laid eyes on you."

As indignant as she felt at the moment, Sara couldn't resist humming the first few bars of a song from the Disney movie *Hercules. . . .* "*Shout it from the mountaintops. . .a star is born. . . .*"

James laughed. Connie flashed an annoyed look then manufactured an Oscar-winning look of despair. "Unfortunately, there's more."

"Brace yourself," James whispered, not loud enough to carry over the noise the girls were making. "What else, Mom?"

"I'm afraid. . ." Connie looked genuinely crestfallen. "I'm afraid that diamonds and sapphires are not spiritually compatible."

A warm hand slid back over Sara's. She glanced at James, tracing the strong line of his jaw with her eyes. Under the pressure of his touch, her anger melted into mere annoyance.

James shook his head. "So it's hopeless for us?"

"I'm afraid so."

He dropped his shoulders, hung his head, and gave a ridiculously exaggerated sigh. "What do you think we should do?"

Sara used her right hand to pull the napkin from her left then took great pains to wipe her mouth while covering her smile. How James was controlling his, she couldn't imagine.

"Diamonds do best with other diamonds."

"So Sara should be shopping around for another diamond?" James twisted the plain silver band on Sara's ring finger.

"Don't make it sound so crass, James. You should both be searching for your soul mates."

Sara dropped her napkin on the table. "Don't you think we should be trying to work things out for the girls' sake?"

Connie looked up at the ceiling, as if she'd been about to roll her eyes and then decided against it. "Do you really want to spend the rest of your lives *working* at a marriage? What kind of a message does that send to your chil. . .to Sadie and Zoe?"

Picturing her father-in-law, parked in his favorite recliner, only the top of his balding head visible over the newspaper, Sara had her first-ever twinge of empathy for James's mother. Did she categorize the past twenty-five-plus years as simply "work"?

Was it her imagination, or did James lean just a fraction of an inch closer to her? He pulled his straw out of his empty soda glass, sucked on the end of it, then pointed it at his mother. "Nobody has a good marriage without work."

This was not the same man who walked out on her.

"It's good that you're talking now. Children need the security of parents who are at peace with each other, but just because you can be friends doesn't mean you should be married."

James tapped the end of his straw on the table. "Actually, Mom, I think that's exactly what it means. If Sara and I can manage to respect each other and communicate like we should have long ago, there's no way I want to settle for just being friends."

Sara's face warmed, and another song skipped through her mind—the one that said, "*I love you too much to ever start liking you.*" She felt the warmth of his leg against hers and looked over at the dark lashes that haloed sky-blue eyes.

She couldn't imagine ever wanting to "just be friends" with this man.

Chapter 14

Well hat drew you to Sara the first time you met?" Eldon Jennet crossed his long legs and rested his arm along the back of the love seat. His fingertips played with the ends of his wife's hair. The seemingly subconscious gesture roused a sense of longing in James.

Fingering a loose thread on the Jennets' couch, James tried to dispel his fear of the unknown. He'd entered the comfortably worn living room feeling like he was walking into a dentist's office. In truth, he would have chosen a throbbing abscessed tooth over marriage counseling. But the first few minutes had passed without pain. What had first drawn him to Sara Martin? He glanced at Sara and smiled. "Whipped cream."

Eldon laughed. "Dare I ask?"

James told him about the pumpkin pie.

Mattie pointed at Sara. "That girl was sending signals."

"Oh yeah."

"Describe her." Eldon bent over and picked up a notebook and a pair of bifocals from the coffee table. "Tell us everything you remember about your first impressions."

This should be easy. He'd replayed that day so many times since he'd left. But with Sara sitting just inches away, it was awkward. He was about to use glowing superlatives to describe the woman he'd deserted. . .twice. "I noticed her eyes first. Her uniform was bright green, and her eyes just sparkled. . .like emeralds. The next thing that grabbed me was her voice." James smiled self-consciously. "I'd just heard a guy on the radio describing a woman's laugh as root beer fizzing over ice. That's what Sara Martin's laugh was like. It bubbled."

He'd never told Sara her laugh reminded him of root beer. He slid a finger under the collar of his sweater, wishing he'd worn something else.

"Very poetic." Eldon raised his eyebrows. "What else?"

"Am I allowed to say I noticed her body?"

Mattie laughed. "You're allowed."

"Well, okay. . .I noticed. . .curves. Maybe I noticed that before her eyes." He laughed, fully aware that he sounded about fourteen. "And her hair. . .it kind of looked windblown, not stiff, you know?"

Eldon wrote something on the notebook. "What else?"

Was everything he said going to be recorded? Maybe Eldon planned on giving Sara a copy to remind her of the good stuff when they got to the inevitable bad. Or maybe it would be James who needed the reminder. "She asked questions—tons of questions, mostly about music and what kind of songs I wrote."

"And you liked that?"

"Of course. What guy wouldn't like a gorgeous woman wanting to know everything about him?" He took a quick, shy look at Sara, who was covering her mouth with her fingertips. "She fed my ego big-time."

&

"What else?" Eldon chewed on the end of his glasses.

Sara was getting used to that question. "I felt special. Our honeymoon was the first time I had his full, undivided attention."

Up to this point, Mattie and Eldon had steered them toward good memories. Sara hadn't known until tonight that they'd been trained as lay marriage counselors. They knew what they were doing. Mattie curled her feet beneath her. "What did James do, specifically, to make you feel special?"

Mattie's casual posture relaxed Sara. The tension that had started building when the spotlight turned from James to her began to ease. Her spine conformed once again to the back of the couch, and her breathing slowed. "He listened, and . . .he looked at me."

"That was unusual?"

"Yes. I mean, he was always looking at me, but while we were in Stillwater, he gave me eye contact. And. . ." She hadn't wanted to be the first one to bring up negatives. "I didn't have to share him with his music. For three whole days, it was just us."

Two feet away from her, she sensed James stiffen. He wasn't allowed to argue or voice an opinion during this part. This was Sara's turn to express herself without interruption.

Eldon scribbled something in his notebook and nodded. "What did you do, other than the obvious, on your honeymoon?" He winked at James, causing Mattie to roll her eyes.

Sara thought back to those three near-perfect days in Stillwater. How many times had James told her he loved her more than anything? How many times had he apologized for running when he found out she was pregnant and for thinking he could be happy without her? "We took walks, and we talked about the baby and how—" She reached for the coffee mug she'd set by her feet. The coffee was room temperature, but maybe it would coat the sudden rasp in her voice. "I remember James saying that he or she was going to be the luckiest kid in the world. . .because we were going to be the best parents ever."

&

"Hi, Cal. Is Mom around?" Sara pulled flour, baking powder, and powdered sugar from the cupboard as she waited for her stepfather to find her mother. The hand that held the phone was clammy. She dug out measuring spoons and cups and two mixing bowls.

"Sara?" Her mother sounded breathless and worried.

"Hi, Mom. How are you?"

"What's wrong?"

"Nothing. I just wanted your Russian tea cake recipe."

The second hand jerked out four ticks. "I'll add minutes to your calling card, honey. I'm fixing myself a cup of hot chocolate, and I'm settling in. You know that recipe backwards and forwards, so tell me why you really called. Is it James?"

Tears blurred the words on the back of the sugar sack. "Uh-huh."

"Are those good tears I hear or bad?"

"I don't. . .know." Sara threw the ring of plastic spoons at the bowl. "We met with Mattie and her husband for counseling tonight."

"How did it go?"

Again she wanted to say she didn't know. "We spent an hour talking about how we met and everything that we admire about each other and skirting around all the garbage."

"Seems like a good way to start."

"At the end they asked us if our relationship was worth fighting for."

"How did you answer?"

"James said yes. I said maybe." Sara stared at the ingredients that lined the counter like soldiers waiting for orders and shut off the kitchen light. Pulling a blanket off the back of the couch, she "settled in" by the Christmas tree.

"What would it take for you to say yes?" A whiff of impatience floated on her mother's voice. There were times they could be two adult women and times when Sara was locked in little-girl mode. Tonight she'd been hoping for a friend instead of a mother.

What would it take? "A guarantee."

Her mother laughed. "Buy a dishwasher, honey."

Sarcasm was not what she needed right now. "I can't take a chance on him leaving us again. If anyone should understand that it's you, Mom." She hadn't intended it to sound mean, just honest. Adult.

Four. . .five. . .six clock ticks. "I've come to the conclusion that we have so much more control over that than we want to think."

If this conversation was leading to guilt, Sara wanted no part of it. Her mother and Don Goode, Sara's biological father, had never married, never even lived together. They'd continued to "see each other" until Sara was a freshman in high school, when her father married one of the other women he'd been "seeing" for years. The news barely caused a ripple in Sara's life and surprisingly seemed to set her mother free to finally find a man who respected her. "Explain."

"One of the older ladies in my quilting circle summed it up perfectly: 'Even a lizard won't leave a sun-warmed rock.' If I'd been warmer, he might have stayed."

Laugh? Cry? Scream? Sara ricocheted among the three, landing on a sound that combined them all. "But he'd still be a lizard! And I don't want to be any-body's rock!"

Her mother laughed. "I'm just saying that it takes two."

"James left me, Mom. I didn't kick him out. Don wouldn't marry you. His choice—not yours."

A soft sigh. "You can't fix something if you can't admit it's broken."

Sara's fingernails raked a path in a champagne-colored throw pillow. "You're talking about me—not the marriage—aren't you?"

"You. . .and me. I couldn't have fixed your father, but I could have changed me. What was your part in James leaving, Sara?"

Fingernail tracks crisscrossed the pillow. "I didn't call to get a guilt trip."

"But you called for honesty."

She'd never gotten anything less from her mother. Still, she bristled against it. "Do you want to tell me what my part was?" Not too many years ago her sassy tone would have gotten her grounded.

"Do you want to hear it?"

Sara covered her legs with the blanket and lay down on the pillow that looked like a fresh-plowed field. "I'll listen."

"You clipped his wings, honey."

Her mother's words crunched into a fist, finding their mark just below her sternum. Instead of a comeback, all she had were tears. "I have to go."

"Call me back when you have your own answer to the question. I don't care what time it is. Even if you're mad."

Sara closed the phone. Maybe she'd call back. Definitely she'd be mad.

&

"Married men aren't supposed to have wings!"

Sara glared at her tear-reddened face in the bathroom mirror. Two inches of toothpaste squirted from the tube; some landed on her toothbrush, the rest in the sink. Once again, James was costing her money.

I didn't clip his wings, Mother. Sara watched the image in the mirror scrub at her teeth with the same rhythmic motion she washed the kitchen floor. She washed floors on Monday. James had hated her schedules. James wasn't a sched-ule person. He was a fly-by-the-seat-of-your-pants person.

Fly. . . What was her part in James leaving?

She spat in the sink, rinsed her mouth, rinsed the sink, dried the sink. . .a system for everything. When had that started? She'd always been organized, always liked things clean, but when had the craziness started? She stared at the toothpaste cap, and the answer materialized. When she couldn't control the rest of her life. When James was unpredictable, when she didn't understand the free spirit she was married to, when he had dreams that didn't match hers.

"You're afraid of it—the music that pulses through his veins, the thing he needs to feel alive."

Maybe Bessie was right.

છ

Music woke Sara early. She'd set the radio alarm for six, giving her at least an hour and a half before the girls woke up. One way or another, by the end of this day, she would have a job.

Her hand groped for the snooze button before her eyes opened, but a voice stopped her.

"Top o' the mornin' to ye, Pine Bluffers! This is Nick Joplin opening December 23 with a song and a prayer. We're an hour and fifty minutes from sunrise, but it's already a beautiful morning because we're starting it with Jesus. Next song we're going to—"

Sara hit the SNOOZE button. The girls must have been playing with the radio knobs. Or James. He could have sneaked in and changed the station. The first time she'd started her car after he'd used it, some preacher had screamed at her in stereo about bringing her tithes to the storehouse. At least the volume on her clock radio had been low. She slipped back into a heavy sleep and woke nine minutes later with a heart-thumping start, to the deejay's absurdly cheery voice.

". . .love that song. Always makes me think of Psalm 139—'Search me, O God, and know my heart; test me and know my anxious thoughts. See if there is any offensive way in me, and lead me in the way everlasting.' I don't know about you, friend, but that's a hard one for me. I'm not too quick to ask God to point out the offensive stuff in me. But I have to wonder why David talked about anxious thoughts and offensive ways in practically the same breath. I'm thinking that maybe if we let the Lord search our hearts and dredge up the junk we need to pitch out, we won't be so anxious. Well, ponder that on your way to—"

Sara smacked the OFF button and sat up. Was God orchestrating some kind of conspiracy against her?

"I'm praying that God won't leave you alone until you admit you need Him."

Mattie's prayer. Sara rubbed her eyes. Was that what this was all about? Was God using Bessie and her mother and James and the hyper guy on the radio to pester her until she caved in? Caved in to what?

Instinctively she knew the answer to her own question. Caved in to Him.

But what did that mean? What would that look like? Would God really take away her anxiety, fix her marriage, protect her girls, find her a job? Or would He make her content without those things? She'd heard Mattie and her friends say things like "Give it all to Jesus" and "Leave it at the cross." One of Mattie's favorites was "Have to surrender that one." Mattie spoke of answered prayer the way Sara talked about gingerbread. Stir it up, pop it in the oven, and wait. Mattie expected answers—"His way, His time."

Sara didn't know where to begin or if she even wanted to. It wasn't that she didn't believe there was a God. Any doubt she'd ever had was erased the moment the nurse laid Zoe in her arms. The perfection of her rosebud mouth, the delicate curve of little fingers that Sara knew even then were destined to play a piano. . . Zoe was not a product of chance or evolution or pure biology.

Sara believed in a Creator. And she'd learned enough from Mattie and from the few times she'd picked up a Bible to be convinced that, as Mattie would say, Jesus was who He said He was. What she couldn't wrap her brain around was a song she'd learned from a neighbor when she was only four: "Jesus Loves Me." She could believe He existed, but why would He want anything to do with her?

"Search me, O God, and know my heart. . . ."

She clenched the edge of the blanket, drew her knees to her chest, and closed her eyes. "God, I don't know what You want from me," she whispered. "I'm tired. . .of doubting James. . .and You, but I don't know where to go from here."

Not even sure if her words constituted a prayer, Sara threw off the covers, got out of bed, and went in search of the phone. Unless that, too, had changed, there was one person she was pretty sure would be awake before the sun. She found the card in the silverware drawer and dialed the number.

"Minnesota Cabins. How can I help you?"

"Hi. This is Sara. I wanted to talk to you about that job offer, Reece."

Chapter 15

Two things were penciled on Sara's calendar for December 23. Shopping with James was first. It was her idea to use a little bit of the money James had given her to take the girls for lunch and Christmas shopping. The second thing on the calendar was counseling with Eldon and Mattie. Just looking at their names next to "7:00" in the neat white square hatched creepy-crawly things under her skin. The first session had uncovered good memories, but she had no illusions about tonight. To add to her stress, she'd agreed, in a weak moment, to let the girls spend the night with the Lewises. This time it wasn't just Connie who Sara was worried about. It was the man who would be dropping her off at her empty apartment sometime after ten o'clock tonight.

Keeping anxiety under lock and key all day would be a major undertaking.

By noon Sara had only one thing left on her to-do list. The girls were bathed and dressed and their backpacks filled with pajamas, stuffed animals, and gaudy tie-dyed Christmas dresses. The apartment was dusted and vacuumed, and her second round of Christmas cookies for Sanctuary residents was bagged and ready to go. She had only minutes until James would come by for her and the girls, but before she left, she needed to call Mama Gina's Pizza and tell Tom she wouldn't need the job.

Allison had come over around ten and taken the phone. "Zoe, run across the hall and get the phone."

"Me, too!" Sadie reached the door first, her dimpled hand poised on the handle, waiting for Sara's nod.

"Okay. Just come right back. . .and no treats. We're going out for lunch."

Minutes later they returned, shirts and faces peppered in Oreo crumbs but no phone. Zoe licked her fingers, doing her best to look guiltless. "Allison is crying happy tears, and she has a s'prise for you on Christmas, and she's gonna bring the phone here in just a minute."

"Don't move!" Sara took her policeman stance. "Hands in the air!" She ran to the bathroom and grabbed a damp washcloth. When she returned, James stood in the doorway.

"Are they being arrested?"

"Yes. They're cookie thieves." The girls giggled as Sara wiped mouths and fingers and blew at the crumbs on two pink shirts. Brushing would smear the chocolate. She took longer than she needed to and realized it made her look like exactly what James had so often called her—a clean freak. In reality she was far less concerned with Oreo bits than with the scent of Corduroy aftershave wafting her way from the man in the navy blue shirt and leather jacket. Her eyes—and hands—simply needed a hiding place.

"Do they need to make restitution?"

Sara looked up into eyes that glinted like moonbeams on Lake Superior. "I think we'll give them a pass this time. They kept a few carbs out of Allison's mouth."

"Mmm." The moonlight left James's eyes. "You ladies ready?"

Trying to read the sudden shift in his expression was futile. For some reason just the mention of Allison's name had set him on edge. "Have to get boots and jackets and hats and mittens. . .and probably make a potty stop. Other than that, we're ready."

The sparkle came back, turned on like a light switch. James let out a long, exaggerated sigh. "Women. . .so high maintenance." He winked at her. "Put me to work."

"Jackets are on the hook behind the door and—" A giggle floated through the open doorway. James stepped into the room and turned around.

Allison, wearing a skintight maroon maternity sweater and with her hair actually clean and brushed, held the phone out to Sara. James stared at Allison then reached behind the door for the jackets. Taking both girls' hands, he led them to the couch. The tension in the room was almost palpable. Sara narrowed her eyes at Allison. "You're looking cheery today. What's up?"

"It's Christmas, and I'm having a baby in two months!"

"The last I heard, Christmas was lame and you were sick of feeling like a cow."

"Yeah, well. . ." Allison smiled smugly. "Things change, you know? Gotta split." She turned, not too gracefully, and lumbered back to her apartment.

Sara closed the door. "She's acting weird."

"Yeah." James's voice sounded muffled. Sara turned to see him nuzzling Sadie's ear.

God, if You're listening, please make this work. My girls need their daddy. The prayer wasn't premeditated. It felt strange yet natural. The thought that followed it startled her. *And what do* I *need?*

That wasn't a question she dared answer.

&

Speakers mounted above the chamber of commerce building, the confectionery shop, and the Ben Franklin dime store flooded Main Street with Bing Crosby's rendition of "White Christmas." Tiny white lights lit up store windows and two-foot-wide silver stars glittered from every street lamp. Zoe stood on the sidewalk holding Sara's hand, eyes wide with wonder. "It's sparkly!"

James unbuckled Sadie's car seat and set her on the sidewalk next to Sara. Sadie's eyes looked like giant blue cat's-eye marbles. "So pretty. Princessy pretty."

"How come it's not prince pretty?" James picked her up and brushed his lips across her warm cheek.

Sadie giggled. Zoe answered, "Princes don't like sparkly things. They like swords and horses and stuff." She stared up at him then tilted her head to the side. "Mommy says every princess doesn't hafta have a prince. Is that true?"

James stared at Sara, who immediately opened her purse and rummaged through its contents, probably looking for something that didn't exist. So his absence had altered fairy tales. He took a deep breath. "Well. . .it's true that some princesses don't have a prince. But I think that God made most princes to want a princess, and they're very, very sad without one."

Appearing contemplative and more like fourteen than four, Zoe nodded then glanced at Sara. "I think Mommy's wrong."

If only we can convince her of that. He watched Sara close her purse then lock eyes with his in a look of chagrin. He winked at her, and the tiniest of smiles tilted her lips. Had his legs buckled like licorice whips when they'd first met? Apparently "weak kneed" wasn't just an expression. She'd curled her hair and put on more makeup than he'd seen her wear yet. For him. Beneath the faded denim jacket, she wore a high-neck sweater that matched her eyes. He was in trouble here. Over his head in love with his own wife.

Setting Sadie down, he took her hand then reached out for Sara's. Linked like paper dolls, the four of them crossed the street to the Ben Franklin store. Before opening the door, he said, "The first present on our list is a jacket for Mommy."

"I don't need a—"

He stopped her protest with two fingertips to her mouth. Her lips were warm. His head was fuzzy. "Do it for me. If you get sick, I'll end up doing laundry and dishes." He grinned at her but cringed inside. He was leaping over her boundaries. The drawbridge could rise and slam shut at any moment.

Sara's face twisted into an adorable combination of stubborn pout and shimmery-eyed surprise. "I have a better idea," she said. "Let's buy Daddy a new jacket, and I'll take his." She fingered the flap that covered the zipper on his jacket. "This one is too small for you now."

That must be the reason he wasn't able to expand his lungs. She wanted his jacket? The one she used to use as a pillow when they went for picnics on the bluff? The one she said smelled like him and gave her good dreams?

"White Christmas" ended, and Tony Bennett crooned "Winter Wonderland." James looked to his left then his right. He squeezed Sadie's hand then let go. "Did you know, girls, that Mommy knows how to swing dance?" Laughing at the look of terror on Sara's face, he grabbed her other hand, pulled her several feet away, then swung her in a circle. As he drew her close again, her look of fear morphed into a smile.

And then she laughed. Clear and root beer-sweet in the cold, crisp air as

Tony Bennett sang, "...to face unafraid the plans that we've made...."

ଚ୬

Sadie clutched her very own shopping bag as James carried her to the car. Sara, walking behind them with a tired four-year-old leaning against her, waved at her youngest and snapped a picture with the disposable camera James insisted she buy. Sadie gave a halfhearted wave and rested her head on James's shoulder.

It had been a day of scrapbookable moments. She didn't know when she'd laughed so much. Actually she did know. In the first twelve months of their marriage. Twirling on the sidewalk, holding onto James's hands had brought it all rushing back. In the first year, in spite of the growing clumsiness of her pregnancy and then an infant to care for while working two jobs, she'd felt strangely carefree...and madly in love. Memories came back more as feelings than pictures, leaving her light-headed and sad. Over the past two years she'd blotted out the good. It was so much easier to focus on the bad. Today had reminded her of what had been and what could be.

But the fun part of the day was almost at an end. Not only did she dread the counseling session, but at some point she'd have to talk to James about her new job and hope he didn't see it as a threat.

They rode in tired silence to the Lewis Ranch, as Brock and James referred to it. Both girls were sleeping when they got there. Sara carried Sadie, and James picked up Zoe. They laid them on their own beds in their own room, and Sara tried hard not to care that her daughters would wake up with happy squeals in a princess room in a cluttered house with a ten-foot Christmas tree surrounded by a moat of presents they didn't need. Tomorrow night Grandma Connie would dress them in their ridiculous dresses, and there would be too much food and too much wrapping paper strewed about...and Sara wouldn't be there to watch her girls have more fun than they'd had in months. She wouldn't be there, but so far she was the only one who knew that.

When they got to the car, James opened the door for her. She slid in and looked up at him as he leaned over the open door, haloed by the garage light. He reached down and lifted her chin with his index finger. "They'll be fine."

Tears stung her eyes. "I know." Just before he closed the door, she whispered, "That's the problem."

She didn't think he'd heard, but after starting Connie's car and backing down the gravel drive, he stopped and stared at her. "This is hard for you."

Not a question but a statement of fact. He got it. Sara nodded. "I hate that I resent her." She forced a swallow. "I never had a chance with her, did I? I can't ever do anything right in her eyes. She shows me up in everything." She bit down on the inside of her bottom lip. It was the only way to stop the flow of words once the lid was off.

James backed the car onto the road. The headlights arced across snow-covered ditches and a barren cornfield. "If I say she means well, it sounds like

I'm sticking up for her, but I'm not. It's just that whatever phase she happens to be going through and whatever wacko philosophy she's embracing at the moment is ultimate truth in her eyes. She's convinced it's her calling to enlighten the world to feng shui or iridology or high colonics or raising emus...."

Sara had no choice but to laugh. *Crazy Connie.* "She's...eccentric." Once again it was the nicest thing she could think of.

"She's a nutcase, Sara!" He said it with so much force that she had no idea if she should laugh or stay silent. The set of his mouth told her there was more to come. "She has no clue how many people she's hurt."

This wasn't the first time Sara had heard him criticize his mother, but in the past his comments had been sarcastic at best, often vicious. This time it felt more like regret. "How has she hurt you?" Sara could have made a list, but she wanted to hear it from him.

"I told you about the whole 'destiny' thing. I'm serious when I say that I really believed it. I feel so stupid. When God started opening my eyes to what a wretch I was, it made me sick."

Wretch? Isn't that right out of "Amazing Grace"? Did Christians actually use that word? "That's a little strong." Did she really just say that? "Wretch" was tame compared to the names she'd hung on him.

James smiled. "I'm guessing you used worse on me."

Was he in her head? "I did. Much worse. But it's hard to hear you saying things like that about yourself. You've changed." The one thing she knew he'd been waiting to hear—and it had slipped out like butter in July.

A car passed, outlining James's face, showing the smile her admission had birthed. "My mother's a product of a bizarre family; you know that. How can I blame her for not knowing how to be a mom? She was raised by a stoner and a sitar-playing gypsy! I had to make myself look at all that when I started trying to forgive her for raising me without any discipline or direction."

"You're disciplined in your music. Your mom encouraged you in that." Defending Connie was foreign territory.

James laughed. "She couldn't have kept me away from it. Music comes under the category of obsession not discipline." He glanced at her. "I don't have to tell you that, do I?"

No. But she wasn't in the mood to say it out loud. In fact, she wasn't in the mood for much of anything other than staring at her husband's profile in the red glow of the dashboard lights...or walking hand in hand by the river....

The last thing she was in the mood for was spending the next two hours digging up pain.

Chapter 16

"What consumes your thoughts, James?" Eldon offered him a second snickerdoodle from a mounded plate.

James shook his head. The cookies were heavenly, but he barely had enough saliva to swallow the first one. "Maybe later." If the night ended on a good note and the inside of his mouth no longer felt like a dirt road.

"Other than Sara and the girls, what's important to you?"

He didn't need to think about that one. "God and music. I try to keep it in that order."

Eldon grinned. "Appreciate your honesty. Can you elaborate?"

"Sure. For a long time my thoughts about the Lord were mostly worship. I'm still in shock that He came after me. It's all still new, and my head's kind of spinning with learning something about Him every day." He ran his hand through his hair, needing something to do with his jitters. "I think I'm in the housecleaning stage my buddies warned me about. I went through all the remorse, looking at what a mess I'd made of my life, and then once I finally got it—that I'd really been forgiven—there was sort of a honeymoon period."

"Kind of a weightless feeling, isn't it?"

"Yeah, that's a perfect description. But lately God's been making me deal with some stuff that isn't so easy." James was only too aware of Sara's every move. As he talked, she tugged at the bottom of her sweater then folded and unfolded her hands, yet her eyes seemed fastened on him. *Lord, let me say what You want me to say.* "Attitudes, mostly, and thoughts. I've been really convicted of how stuck on myself I've been."

" 'Be transformed by the renewing of your mind,' " Eldon quoted.

Mattie nodded. "He's refining you. It gets painful at times."

"I'm not really liking this part, but I wouldn't turn back for anything."

ജ

Though she sat just a few feet from the flames that blazed in the Jennets' fireplace, Sara pulled a throw blanket from the arm of the couch and covered her legs. No one else seemed to feel the cold. In fact, they all seemed warm and cozy, eating cookies and chatting like old friends. Mattie sat with her feet propped on the coffee table, sipping her chamomile tea and smiling at James. Sara felt so distant she could have been standing outside the window, chilled by the wind, staring in at the Christmas tree heavy with homemade ornaments, the six stockings that hung from the mantel, and the three people who shared a language she didn't speak. It wasn't that she didn't understand the words. It was that she'd never experienced the emotions that went with them.

Eldon asked James to talk about his "love of music." Sara pulled the blanket to her elbows.

"I feel guilty sometimes that I get paid for playing. I'd sure like to get paid more, of course." The Jennets laughed along with James. Sara made herself smile. "Music is pretty much like food to me. It feels like a basic need."

Bessie's words reverberated in Sara's mind. *You're afraid of it—the music that pulses through his veins, the thing he needs to feel alive.* Even now, just talking about it, James's demeanor became more animated. Was she really afraid of it, or was she—

"Sara, how does it make you feel to hear James talk about his music with such intensity?"

The question jarred her, pulling her from her isolated place outside the window. She'd vowed to be as honest and transparent as she could. "It makes me sad." She scanned James's face. He nodded, apparently not surprised. "The truth is, I've always been jealous of his music."

Mattie took the pen from Eldon and scrawled something on the notebook. "Because of the time it took away from you?"

"That and. . .he talks about the songs he writes like they were. . .lovers." Her face burned, but she was determined to press on with the truth. "I wish. . .I used to wish. . .that I could stir as much passion in him as his music."

James looked away. His body language changed. "Rigid" was the word that came to Sara's mind. Her words hung in the air for several too-long moments before Eldon pointed his pen at James. "That's not sitting well with you, is it?"

Silence. The fire crackled. James brought his hands down on both knees then crossed his legs. The *whish* of denim brushing denim amplified in the strained stillness. "It's not sitting well because it's not true. It's true that music took up more of my. . .more of me than Sara. But it didn't have to be that way. If she—"

Holding his hand up just like Sara did with her girls, Eldon stopped James. "Talk to Sara. Remember the rules, and tell her how you feel."

Bitterness scalded Sara's throat. *This should be interesting.* There was no way James could follow the rules—use only "I" rather than "you" messages, avoid "always" and "never," stick to the topic at hand, and don't bring up old disagreements unless they pertain. She stared at the Americana colors in the braided rug beneath the coffee table and waited. James shifted, and she sensed his eyes on her. With a shaky breath, she faced him and waited.

"I. . .wanted you to be the center of my universe, Sara. There was a window of time when I would have given it all up for you."

"A very small window. I guess I missed it altogether."

Her biting tone made James cringe visibly. His fingers curled into his palms.

"Think back. Just a couple of days before you told me you were pregnant. We were riding bicycles up on the bluffs, and we stopped for a picnic. Remember it?"

Sara's necklace was too tight, forcing pressure into her head. She'd shoved that day far back in the archives. Cool air scented with leaf smoke, the leaves turning colors along the river. Their lunch was fresh bread, apples, and cheese. They pretended they were overlooking the Seine or the Thames. A perfect day. It was only later that she realized it was all a lie. "Yes." It was more of a hiss than a word.

"Do you remember what I said?"

"Of course." The tension in her face made it hard to talk. "You said you wanted me to go to Canada with you, but if I didn't want to go, you'd stay right here with me." Darts shooting from her eyes didn't feel like a metaphor. "And four days later, you left."

"Whoa!" In one swift motion, James swiveled on the couch to face her. "If you're going to tell that part of the story, tell the whole thing, Sara. Tell about the day you called and told me you were pregnant." His glare pinned her to the back of the couch. "The day I came over to ask you to marry me."

"What?" Time had warped the story in James's mind. There had been no proposal. "You did not."

"Oh yes, I did. I walked into your kitchen, and you were on the phone in the living room, talking to your friend Kim."

Sara sucked in air, but it wasn't enough. She needed to get outside. He'd heard that conversation and never told her? Heard it just days after pledging to leave everything behind for her. Heard it and walked away for three months. What had she said that night? She remembered crying hysterically, pacing the living room, yelling about her life falling apart, her plans shattered. Tears blurred her vision as she forced herself to stare at James.

His eyes smoldered. "You said, 'And now I'm pregnant by a guy I'm not even in love with.'"

∞

Their dance in front of the dime store seemed a lifetime ago. James stared at the blotchy red face of the woman who shared the couch with him as if she were a stranger. His arms no longer ached to hold her, nothing in him wanted to draw her close and stop the sobs that shook her. He simply waited, cold and emotionless, for her to respond.

Maybe this whole counseling idea was a mistake. Was it really necessary to dredge up the ugliness of their past? Couldn't they have just made a fresh start? An unexpected picture dropped into his consciousness—the wall beneath the single window in his tiny London apartment. The landlord had painted just before James moved in. Painted right over the damp, bulging plaster where water leaked in every time it rained. In the two years James had lived there, the paint had peeled and the wet, moldy plaster had crumbled, little by little, onto the floor.

Lord, be my strength.

Sara took a long shuddering breath. "I was scared. I questioned everything. But the moment I knew you were gone"—glittering, pain-filled eyes pleaded for understanding—"I knew. I knew absolutely that I loved you and I wanted to spend the rest of my life with you. But. . ." She wiped her face with a wet tissue, and Mattie got up and handed her a new one. "But then it was too late to tell you that I'd move to Canada—or anywhere—with you."

She'd never told him that. Never. How could two people live under the same roof and leave so much unsaid? That one sentence could have changed the course of their marriage. A silent groan vibrated his chest like an oncoming train. Arms that had felt leaden just moments before crushed Sara to him. Only vaguely aware that they were not alone, he kissed the top of her head over and over.

The Jennets gave them a respectable time, then Eldon quietly asked, "What made you come back, James?"

Swiping at his damp eyelashes, James looked over the top of Sara's head and pressed his lips together in a straight-lined smile. "Life just seemed flat without her." Sara convulsed with a muffled sob, and he held her tighter. "I decided I was going to make her love me if it killed me." *Just like I'm doing right now.*

"What was her reaction when you returned?"

James laughed. Sara reared her head and glared at him, making him laugh even harder. "She was spitting tacks. Slashed me up one side and down the other then fell into my arms sobbing. Kind of like this." He pushed wet strands off her face. "And then I asked her to marry me, and she said yes. My mother was irate, of course, so we ran off and got married in a quaint little chapel in Stillwater, and we had a tough but wonderful first year."

Sara pulled away slowly, as if she hated to leave his arms but needed her space for safety. "It was a good year," she whispered.

Mattie cleared her throat. She seemed in danger of adding her own tears to the mix. "We may want to get back to that first year, but tell us when things started to break down."

"Our first anniversary." James looked to Sara for confirmation, and she nodded. "I get the insensitive-oaf award for that one."

Sara's smile came quick and natural, and James breathed a pent-up sigh.

Sara cleared her throat. "James announced over candlelight and spaghetti that he'd taken a job with a band that was leaving in two days for a three-month tour."

A lopsided grimace twisted Eldon's mouth. "Not the brightest move."

James shrugged. "Now you tell me." He took Sara's hand and squeezed it. "It wasn't quite as awful as she makes it sound. I hadn't officially accepted the job, and I would have been gone for nine days at a time then home for five. I was already working two jobs and not seeing Sara and the baby. The band had a following, and the money would have been double what I was making. And the five days I'd be home, I'd actually get time with my family." He looked from Eldon to Sara. She appeared almost startled, as if something he'd just said surprised her.

"You didn't take the job?"

"No." James clenched the hand that wasn't holding Sara's.

"Did you talk it over?" Mattie aimed the question at him first, then Sara. "Did you discuss possible compromises?"

He could have laughed at that one, but his mood had shifted drastically in the past few minutes. He simply shook his head.

The leather jacket that now belonged to Sara was wedged between her and the arm of the couch. She picked up one sleeve and ran her hand along the leather as if she were petting a kitten. "That was my fault." The same surprised look creased her forehead. "I. . .didn't. . .see it that way." Her hands shook. "All I could see was that you wanted to leave again. I didn't see anything good coming out of it." She looked at Mattie. "It was the first time I ever screamed at him. Not the last."

"She changed. . . ." James remembered the rules and squeezed Sara's hand. "Something changed in you after that."

Sara nodded, brushing away tears. "I knew you wanted to leave. It was just a matter of time, so I had to start thinking like a single mom. I had to be ready."

Sap bubbled on a pine log in the fireplace, filling the room with a quiet, high-pitched whine. The log snapped apart; red sparks shot up the chimney. Mattie pushed the box of tissues across the coffee table. "How did she change toward you, James?"

Shoulders shaking, Sara raised her stop-sign hand. "I became a. . .dictator." Her voice was ragged. "I made him turn in every receipt and keep track of every penny he spent. I'd always made to-do lists for myself, but after that, I made lists for James, too. I made sure there was no time in his schedule for his music. I yelled at him if he played too rough with the girls and yelled more if he didn't spend enough time with them. I told him what books to read them and. . ." She stopped, covered her eyes with one hand. "It was like I needed everything in neat little boxes."

Mattie's maternal smile poured grace on Sara. "You felt threatened, and you needed to control whatever you could."

Eyes wide, like Zoe staring at the lights on Main Street, Sara slowly nodded. "Even decorating was a way of controlling my environment. *My* colors, *my* fabrics to decorate *my* townhouse. It was just another way of making neat little boxes." She took a ragged breath. "I felt driven. . .to create a safe place for the girls. I thought I was just being a good mom, being prepared for what I was sure would happen. . .and in the process I made it happen."

James felt his throat tighten. She pulled her hand out of his and stared into him. The green eyes that had captured him and pulled him back every time he left looked suddenly rainwashed, unveiled. "I made your life miserable, didn't I?"

Chapter 17

James guided the steering wheel with one hand. Sara encased his right hand in both of hers. Her face felt tight from salty tear tracks as she nestled against the back of the seat, enveloped in a worn brown jacket. Heater vents shot warm air, but for once Sara wasn't cold. She looked over at James. "I have to call my mom and admit she was right."

"About what?"

"She said I clipped your wings."

James laughed. "I don't need wings. I'm not going anywhere."

"But you need to flap around a *little* bit. I didn't give you any room to flap."

Again he laughed. "You're cute."

"That's what I did to God, too, isn't it? I mean, nobody can stop God from being God, but maybe I didn't let Him be God for *me*. Does that make sense? I couldn't see how He could want anything to do with me, so I didn't allow room for Him."

"Everybody's got their own way of resisting. I ran from Him the same way I ran from you, Sara Bear."

Fresh tears threatened. Like a wobbly top, she hovered between crying and laughing. Sara Bear. That was a name she thought she'd never hear again. "I'm sorry."

James's laugh was a soft exhale through his nose. "That's number eight hundred and forty-six tonight." He extricated his hand and ran the backs of his gloved fingers across her cheek. "I'll say it one more time—it's not all your fault. I wasn't the husband and father I should have been. I was immature and looking for excuses to run. Both times. Can we agree, at least for this moment, that we've forgiven each other?"

She reached up, turned his hand, and kissed his palm. Once then again. "Okay."

"And you do understand, don't you"—his voice had a breathless edge—"that Jesus is just standing here waiting for you to surrender it all to Him?"

Surrender. This time she was ready to hear it.

James stretched his arm across her shoulders, and they rode the rest of the way in silence. Sara filled the minutes with unspoken words.

Dear God, I'm not holding back anymore. I don't want to hide from You or fight anymore. . . .

&

James stopped the Escape in front of her apartment and reached for her hand.

"I want to pray with you."

Mesmerized by the softness of his voice, Sara could only nod.

"Lord God, You alone have brought us to the beginning of healing. Thank You for loving us in spite of our selfishness. We're imperfect people who will make mistakes in the future, but You know our hearts. You know we want our family to be together and our marriage to be strong. Please save us from our own foolishness and guide every step we make together. Amen."

"Amen."

Reaching above her, he opened the mirror on the visor, triggering the vanity light. "I need to see you," he whispered. In the soft glow, Sara stared back, drinking in every angle of his face, the hair that curled over the collar of his new ski jacket, the creases that framed his mouth. The tenderness in his eyes tampered with the cadence of her pulse.

James pulled off his gloves then slowly removed hers. Warm fingers traced a path from her ear to her chin and followed the outline of her mouth. He leaned toward her until she could feel his breath on her ear. "I love you, Sara."

His words were almost buried beneath the hammering of her heart. Sara raised her hand and did something she'd visualized since the day he'd helped her paint. She slipped her fingers through dark brown waves and let them trail to the back of his neck. "I love you, too."

Feathery kisses covered her face, brushed across her lips and lingered there. He kissed her then in a way he'd never kissed her before, in a way that made her feel not only desired but cherished, protected, and sheltered. His mouth hovered just millimeters from hers. "It's kind of cold out here."

Her eyes were closed, but she heard the smile in his voice. She smiled back. "I'm plenty warm."

"There aren't any children inside."

"There aren't any children out here." She rubbed her nose against his. "Besides, there are rules."

"Whose rules?"

"Sanctuary rules say I can't have any man in my apartment."

James laughed, leaned across her, and opened her door then kissed her again. It was a clumsy kiss, made awkward by his grin. "I'm not any man, sweetheart. I'm your husband."

&

Laughing like teenagers, they ran up the snow-dusted sidewalk. James opened the door, scooped her in his arms, and carried her into the foyer while Sara fished in her purse for her keys.

"What's that?" James pointed at a square of yellow paper taped to her door.

"Probably a phone message. Allison's my social secretary." She laughed and nibbled his ear. With a mock groan, James dipped her toward the door so she could stick the key in the lock and turn the handle. As the door opened, she ripped the paper off the door and read it.

> *Sara—*
>   *Some guy named Reece called for you. Isn't he the cute guy you were kissing?*
>
>   *Al*

Feeling her face warm, she stuffed the note in her jacket pocket.

"Anything important?"

"No."

"Good." James closed the door with his foot and carried her to the couch, sitting down with her on his lap. "Have I told you lately that I love you?"

"That's a Rod Stewart song. You can do better than that, Lewis."

"You're right. I can. Have I told you lately how grateful I am that we have another chance to make something beautiful out of us and that I want to take care of you for the rest of our lives and be the best dad I can possibly be and help you manage the Stillwater Inn and make it a huge success and—"

"Shhh. . ." She held up her hand.

He wove his fingers into hers. "You don't believe me?"

Sara shook her head. "We need to talk about the Inn. It's my dream not yours."

"But if it makes you happy. . ."

"What will make me happy is when we find some way for us both to do what we love. I don't want you to give up your music."

James closed his eyes, just for a moment, as if stemming tears. "Thank you."

"We don't have to figure that out right now."

"Are there more important things we should be concentrating on right now?"

"I. . .think so. . ."

He touched the tip of her nose. "Like what?"

The glint in his eyes unraveled her last shred of reserve. "Like this." Sliding off his lap, she stood and held out her hand to him.

∞

Sara cracked four eggs and beat them with a wire whisk to the rhythm of the tune that had circled in her head since her eyes opened and she'd realized that, this time, James was not a dream.

"Have I told you lately. . ." Snippets of the lyrics filtered in, and words she'd never before paid attention to slowed her rhythmic beating—*"There's a love that's divine. . .we should give thanks and pray to the one. . ."* She had no idea if Rod Stewart was referring to God, but that's what the words now meant to her. She remembered Mattie telling her months earlier that God could use anything to get his message across. Apparently even a rock song.

God, thank You for my husband.

As the simple prayer formed in her mind, she poured the eggs into a hot frying pan—and strong arms slid around her waist. "Merry Christmas, beautiful." Mint-scented breath tickled her ear. "You saved an extra toothbrush and razor just in case?"

"I always have extras. You know I'm all about being prepared." Looking down at his bare arms folded tightly across her holly-leaf apron, she laughed. They could be posing for the cover of *Recipe for a Godly Wife*. Maybe she'd curl up with the book with the bent spine and wrinkled pages after James left for London.

If she hadn't been held tight against him, she would have doubled over at the thought of his leaving. They hadn't talked about that yet. He had a job waiting in London.

Turning in his arms, she laid her face against his chest. James reached behind her and shut off the burner.

రు

As soon as he started making some money, he'd buy her a new bathrobe. Something green and warm that flattered her figure better than the shapeless orangey-pink thing that had probably been donated to the Sanctuary program when some ninety-year-old nursing home resident died.

James stared across the table as he chewed slowly on a piece of bacon that was done to perfection. "This is delicious." He hadn't had bacon done right in two years. And he hadn't had breakfast with a woman in just as long. That was something he was immensely grateful for. Considering the crowd he'd hung with, it was nothing short of God's miraculous intervention.

"It's nice to have a man to cook for." Sara topped off his coffee.

He took a careful sip from the murky green Pine Bluff Community State Bank mug. "I'm buying you new dishes with my first paycheck."

"You? Shop?"

"Me? Shop? Not a chance. Me *pay*."

"I thought you'd changed."

"I have. All the bad stuff is gone. The good stuff stayed."

"Mattie says we need to compromise."

James made a show of squirming in his seat. "Uh. . .yeah. . .okay, so if I give in and endanger my reputation as a man's man and start shopping, what would you do?"

"Eat a hot dog."

He'd picked the wrong moment to take another sip of coffee. Tiny brown spots spewed from his mouth and spattered the housecoat. He grabbed a napkin, first for his face, then, sliding to his knees in front of her, he dabbed at her robe. "You are *not* getting by that easily."

She ran the fingers of both hands through his hair, sending shivers along his arms. "Fine. Name something."

"Go to church with me tonight." James held his breath.

"That's all?"

"I thought you'd have a problem with that."

Her nose wrinkled. "You think you're the only person God can change? I mean, don't expect me to start quoting Bible verses or anything, but I'll go to church with you. What else?"

What else? Church was huge, but he wasn't above taking advantage of the situation. "Take me to the airport on Monday and don't cry."

He hadn't factored in Sara's instant tears. It was his turn to hold up his hand in a gesture that once annoyed him. "I have to go back and get out of my lease and give away some stuff and sell some things and give notice on the job I'm not going to take." He'd tell her about the new job once he knew more about it. He used the belt on the tacky robe to dry her tears. "And then pick me up again on Saturday."

☙

Connie's hairless cat screeched from its wobbly perch on a high bough of the ten-foot Christmas tree. Sadie, in her rainbow dress with a purple crown on her head and a yellow plastic canteen filled with cranberry punch around her neck, clambered onto an end table and reached out to the cat. Her stocking feet slipped, juice splattered onto the pile of coats on the floor, and Sara screamed. Grandpa Neil grabbed the cat with one hand and caught Sadie just as her face grazed a sequin- and pearl-covered Styrofoam ball. Over Sadie's cries and Grandpa Neil's deep laugh, Granny Charity thundered on the piano and Connie, sitting beside her, sang "Grandma Got Run Over by a Reindeer."

Sara kicked a path in the wrapping paper and got to Sadie just as James took her from his father. She locked eyes with him and couldn't do anything but laugh.

"I told you you'd be glad you came!" he yelled over the din.

Her protest was drowned by the doorbell chiming out "Jingle Bells." Brock, who happened to be standing in front of it, opened the door, and Allison stepped in. The singing stopped. Connie clapped her hand down on her mother's, halting the music. One by one, every aunt, uncle, and cousin stopped talking, and the room became funeral home quiet.

Brock took Allison's coat, folded it over one arm, and put his arm around her. Smiling like he'd just returned from multiple root canals, he cleared his throat. "Mom, Dad, everyone...I've been watching James the past couple weeks and listening to him talk about God and what it means to be a man of integrity, and he finally got to me. Or I don't know...maybe it was God who finally got to me. Anyway, I made a decision. . . .Allison and I are getting married. My baby needs his daddy."

A *thud* echoed in the deathly quiet room. Sara turned to see Connie, white slits for eyes, wedged between the wall and the piano bench.

Chapter 18

Monday morning dawned without a hint of sun. Fitting, James thought, for the mood at the ranch. He rolled over, twisting in the crazy quilt like a worm in a cocoon, wishing he was waking up in a double bed instead of a single. They'd decided not to confuse the girls by having him stay for two nights and then leave for a week. At the moment, it didn't feel like the right decision. But then, not much of anything felt right.

His bedroom beneath the east gable still smelled of charred ham from what should have been Christmas dinner. Yesterday, after coming home from whatever it was she was doing in town on Christmas morning, his mother had labored, with long, loud sighs of martyrdom, over ham and scalloped potatoes then locked herself in her room. James left to spend the day with Sara and the girls, taking Brock with him. When they returned for dinner, the table in the dining room was set with Granny Charity's best dishes. In the middle of the table, next to lit candles in silver holders, two black, brick-looking objects were smoking on china platters with serving forks. His mother stood at the head of the table, pointing a carving knife at Brock and seething, "This is all your fault."

They went out for Chinese.

James tugged his pillow over his face but couldn't block out the smell of blackened potatoes and petrified ham. Still under the pillow, he groped for the lamp switch and then his Bible. *Lord, this is going to be a hard day. I have some tough questions for Brock. Grant me wisdom when I talk to him. And I don't want to say good-bye to Sara, even for a few days. Please give me something to hang on to.*

Propping on one elbow, he opened to Psalm 28 and read a passage he'd highlighted in yellow. *"The Lord is my strength and my shield; my heart trusts in him, and I am helped. My heart leaps for joy and I will give thanks to him in song."*

Song. They'd missed church on Christmas Eve because of all the drama. Withdrawal symptoms were setting in after three weeks of no communal worship. He got up and pulled on the jeans and sweater he'd worn the day before, scrunching his nose at the burned memories floating up from his clothes.

In the corner of the room, right where he'd left it two years ago, was the ten-year-old Gibson Hummingbird guitar he'd sell to a buddy back in London to pay for his one-way ticket back to Minnesota. And there'd be money left to buy Sara some clothes and dishes. . .and maybe a real wedding ring. He picked it up and sat down on the bed to tune it. He was good—not great—on the guitar. Music didn't seem to flow through his fingers to strings the way it did on ivory. He played a few chords until a tune took shape. A Kutless song— "Strong Tower." As music filled the garret room, he prayed. *You are my strong tower, Jesus. My shelter and my fortress. . .*

He heard the phone ringing and then his mother's footsteps trudging up the stairs. Setting down the guitar, he opened the door to his mother, perpetual tears clouding her eyes. She held out the phone. "It's Reece Landon. Though why you'd want to talk to that man, I can't imagine."

Because "that man" holds the key to my immediate future. James took the phone and then, surprising himself as well as his mother, wrapped her in a quick hug. "It's all going to work out, Mom."

"Right. That's what you said when *you* got married."

෨

The patch of sky Sara could see from her kitchen window looked dark and heavy on Monday morning. Even an hour after turning up the heat, cold air seemed to lurk in the corners. She tiptoed into the girls' room and laid another blanket over them.

As she pulled a second sweatshirt from her dresser drawer, it occurred to her that maybe the feeling of cold was merely the absence of the warmth she'd awakened to on Saturday morning. She slipped the sweatshirt over her head as she walked down the hall.

She'd gotten out of bed earlier than usual to face a to-do list as long as the pencil she wrote it with. Allison was coming over to watch the girls at nine so that she could drive out to meet Reece and tour the cabins his family owned on Whitebark Lake. After that she'd meet James and Brock for lunch. She and James had agreed on some "intervention" questions to find out if Brock was acting out of sheer obligation or genuine love for Allison. After that she'd drive James into the city for his four o'clock flight. . .and do her best not to cry.

She peeked in on the girls again. Sadie's hand rested on Zoe's forehead, but both were sound asleep. Relieved, Sara picked up a clothes basket. She needed to go downstairs to the washing machine and get James's new jacket, hoping the cranberry-juice stains she'd pretreated had vanished. She opened the door to the foyer just as Raquel opened hers.

"You're up early."

"Yeah. I need to talk to you." Raquel hadn't worked on Sunday yet looked as though she'd been up all night.

"Come on in." Disappointment settled on Sara's chest. Raquel appeared to have been drinking.

Raquel sat at the kitchen table, and Sara poured the last of the coffee into a mug and slid it in front of her. She didn't smell alcohol. "What's wrong?"

"Your mother-in-law paid me a little visit yesterday."

"On Christmas Day?"

"Yeah. Merry Christmas." Tears balanced on Raquel's mascara-clumped lashes.

"What did she say?"

"In a nutshell? She said, 'Your daughter's worthless, my son's not going to marry her, and if anyone's gonna raise Brock's child, it's me.'"

Sara slid her chair closer to Raquel and put her arms around her. She desperately wanted to say that she must be exaggerating or there must be some misunderstanding, but she couldn't. "She can't do that, Raquel."

Raquel pulled away. "Oh yeah? Tell me you're not scared to death she's gonna find a way to take your girls. I've heard you say it! You're scared she's gonna have you declared unfit. And look at Allison. She's still in high school, she doesn't have a job, she's living on handouts, and her mother's an alcoholic. What chance does she have against that lunatic woman?"

This wasn't the time to talk about all that had transpired with James in the past week, not the time to mention that she no longer harbored those fears. "It'll be okay. Nobody's going to take that baby."

Raquel wiped her face on her sleeve. "This is what I get, isn't it?"

"What do you mean?"

"My punishment. If I hadn't messed up my life, Allison wouldn't be pregnant and—"

Latching onto Raquel's shoulders, Sara waited until she looked up. "Listen to me, Raquel. I don't know much yet, but I know one thing. Jesus loves you and Allison and that baby, and He's got good plans for all of you. He's just waiting for you to surrender...."

శ్రీ

"What do you think?" Reece swept his hand toward the great room. "Just imagine leather couches and rustic tables."

Sara stared at a vast expanse of newly varnished hardwood floors then moved on to granite counters, black kitchen appliances, and a stone fireplace that spanned two stories. This was the second cabin they'd looked at. The first, right next door, had a hot tub in the finished basement.

"When you said 'cabins,' I was thinking *Little House on the Prairie*."

"My family doesn't do small."

"I guess. You're sure that cleaning isn't involved in this job?"

Reece laughed and glanced at his watch. "You're just the scheduler. I'm hoping to hire someone today to manage things here. You'll be answering the phone, checking e-mail, making reservations, and taking credit card info. We'll supply you with a BlackBerry and a laptop and train you on our computer system." He pointed toward the window. Huge drops of icy rain splatted the glass. "Let's get out of here. There's someone I want you to talk to. We'll take the car to the third house; it's a hike. We call this place North Point because..."

Sara listened but couldn't concentrate. Her mind was on the leaden sky and the sleet that had the power to ground James's plane and give her one more day with him. Reece held the door open, and she walked out onto a wide front porch. She looked up at the pewter clouds and smiled.

"Watch your st—"

It didn't happen, like people often say, in slow motion. It was instantaneous. One moment she was stepping onto the first step, staring at the ominous sky, a heartbeat later she stared at the same sky from a totally different angle. Her bottom sat on a step, her head on the porch.

"Are you okay?" Reece kneeled beside her, his face distorted by so much concern it made her want to laugh.

"I'm fi—" Little white stars danced in the corners of her field of vision. The back of her head throbbed, and something else hurt. The pain seemed distant; she couldn't quite focus on where it was coming from. "Help me get up."

"Are you sure you should?"

"Yes." She shivered. "We're getting wet."

Reece helped her to a sitting position. At the end of the long, rutted driveway that swayed before her eyes, his yellow BMW swung like a giant banana on a string. Sara clenched her eyes and fought nausea. The dizziness passed, and she opened her eyes. "I'm okay. Let's go."

"I'm taking you to the hospital." Reece looked at his watch again then toward the car, a good hundred yards on the other side of the frozen ruts that would be a paved drive next spring.

"Just get me up. I have to meet James."

Reece draped her arm across his shoulders and slowly raised her. A gasp ripped from her throat. "My ankle!"

The little white stars came back, and one by one turned black.

✂

James hummed "Strong Tower" as he navigated the narrowing gravel road. The windshield wipers played backup. Glancing down at the directions Reece had dictated over the phone, he wondered if he'd missed something. It was hard to believe there were luxury cabins at the end of this skinny winding path. Thankfully he was a good half hour early. If he had to turn around and hunt down a phone, he could probably still make the meeting on time. It wouldn't do to make a lousy first impression on the other staff members or Reece's dad or whoever he was meeting with this morning.

A crack of thunder shook the car. The wipers swiped a clean view as he rounded a bumpy bend in the road. A blurry streak of yellow took on the form and shape of a BMW. James breathed a sigh and eased on the brake. Another swipe revealed Reece, leaning against the car.

With Sara in his arms.

ᏽ

"James?"

Was that really her voice? She sounded like Sadie, helpless and whiny. Kettledrums banged a solo in Sara's head. Opening her eyes was not an option. "James?"

"It's me. Reece."

Why. . . ? Oh. . .the cabins. . .the ice. . .the rain. It came back to her in chunks. "What time is it?" Would she have time to change before driving James to the airport?

"Five to four."

Sara's eyes shot open then squinted at Reece and against the light. Where was the cabin? The yellow car? Five minutes to four? Panic rose like a flood surge. She tried to sit up, but the room spun. A room with pale blue curtains for walls. "Where am I?"

"The ER. You sprained your ankle, and you've got a mild concussion."

"Is James coming?"

Reece had a strange look on his face that turned up the volume on the kettledrums.

"You called James, right?"

A shoulder shrug and upturned hands were her answer.

"Call him and tell him he can get a later flight, but he has to come and watch the girls and"—a tear rolled from each eye onto the paper-covered pillow—"and tell him I need him to take care of me and tell him—"

"Sara." Reece put his hand over hers. "James doesn't have a phone."

ᏽ

James whizzed past every other vehicle on I-494, picking them off like clay pigeons. *Bing. . . Bing. . .* His mother probably had no idea her Escape could do ninety. At what point would they call out the helicopter to televise his escape in an Escape? The irony made him smile. His hollow, fun-house laugh bounced off the dashboard.

Traffic slowed ahead and forced him down to only seven miles over the speed limit, but his thoughts passed a hundred.

Sara could explain away the hug his mother witnessed as a gesture of friendship, but no one would call what he'd seen two hours ago a friendly hug. Sara had faced away from Reece, her head tipped back on his chest—just the way James had held her in the kitchen on Saturday morning right before. . . He pressed his fingers against his eyes until they hurt, and colored sparks shot like sparklers. But it didn't block out the picture of Sara, eyes closed, face raised to the rain. And Reece's arms, wrapped around his best friend's wife.

He opened his eyes and swerved to avoid the side mirror on a pickup. A whisper of common sense invaded his rage. In the state he was in, he could hurt someone. He got off at the next exit and pulled up to a gas station. A cup of hot coffee might take the edge off and let him think. By the time he turned off the ignition, second thoughts plastered his conscience. He'd just done what he'd vowed not to do. He'd run—again—without getting all the facts. There had to be some explanation. He knew Sara. She loved him. Maybe he hadn't seen what he thought he'd seen. Maybe the rain had distorted his view more than he realized.

He pulled the keys out of the ignition and slipped them into the pocket of the leather jacket. . .Sara's leather jacket. Something stuck to his fingertips. The yellow sticky note Sara had found on her door.

> *Sara—*
>   *Some guy named Reece called for you. Isn't he the cute guy you were kissing?*

James no longer needed coffee. His thoughts no longer chased each other like rabid dogs. He knew exactly what he needed to do. The key slid into the slot, starting the Escape.

Starting the escape. . .back home. . .to England.

∞

Sara opened her eyes in a princess room. Sparkly purple shades restrained the morning. Glow-in-the-dark stars lit the lace-trimmed violet canopy above her. On the bedside table, Cinderella circled the base of a night-light to the tune of "A Dream Is a Wish Your Heart Makes." Sara groped for the switch. Cinderella wouldn't finish her waltz this time.

Because Sara Lewis didn't believe in dreams.

At first, she'd worried. Lying in the emergency room, her head competing with her ankle for a ten on the Visual Analog Scale, she'd imagined dozens of gruesome reasons why James hadn't met Brock and hadn't gotten to a phone to call him. Reece had intensified her anxiety by explaining that he'd planned a surprise—James was to meet them at the third cabin so that Reece could offer the two of them the job of managing all the cabins on Whitebark Lake. The salary he quoted her while she lay shivering on the gurney was more than Sara had made in her life. It would have solved everything but meant nothing until she knew what happened to James. Was he out there in the sleety rain at the bottom of a ravine? Somewhere on the mud-slick, twisty-turny road to the cabins? Injured? Unconscious? Or worse?

Her panic finally earned her a shot in the hip, which made her less frantic but not less fearful. When Brock showed up in the room with blue-cloth walls, he danced around the truth, but Sara stopped him, just like she did Cinderella, and made him tell her. Made him tell her that James hadn't answered his page at the airport, that James had gotten on the plane, leaving only an eight-word phone call behind: "The keys are under the seat. Sorry, man."

Twenty-four hours later, she was here, surrounded by pixie dust and magic wands, listening to her girls playing hide-and-seek with Connie, smelling homemade corn bread, and feeling like Sleeping Beauty before she awoke. Cold, numb, lifeless.

The drums in her head were muted now, but the muffled beat was relentless. It pounded out a single word. Why? Why? Why? Why had he changed his mind? Christmas Day had been perfect. Too perfect? Is that what scared him? Why hadn't he said good-bye? Even if he'd changed his mind, even if he'd decided they couldn't work it out, why hadn't he said good-bye to the girls?

This time she wouldn't bounce. This time she would follow James's example—as soon as she could walk, she would run.

Chapter 19

"S he had extra toothbrushes and razors in the bathroom. Did I mention that?" James sat on the floor of his two-room apartment and stared at his friends. "She always used to just in case of company, but this time I know it was in case Reece—"

A meaty hand on his shoulder stopped his rant. "We need to pray over James, guys." The burly, bald-headed man with a cockney accent tightened his grip, and the other four members of the accountability group surrounded James. "Lord Jesus, our brother here is in an awful state. He's mightily in need of guidance and a touch from Your merciful hand. Show Yourself real to him and. . ."

James felt rigid muscles yield to the weight of their hands and their words. Blessings and petitions flowed over him like a Mozart concerto. With these rough, life-scarred brothers, he didn't pretend to be strong. When tears spotted his faded jeans, their grip on his arms and shoulders only grew stronger.

In the three days he'd been back in the damp cold of London, he'd leaned on their strength and welcomed their counsel. Tonight, however, their prayers came after an hour of grilling James like a crime suspect beneath an interrogation lamp. They'd questioned his reasons for leaving and challenged him to go back and be the father his children needed, even if he could never be a husband to Sara. Knowing they spoke the truth, he'd fought them with everything in him. He missed his girls with a physical pain that made it hard to breathe, but he didn't possess the kind of strength it would take to go back to Pine Bluff and compete for their attention with the man who had won Sara's.

After the men went home, James flopped back on his thin mattress, staring at the cracks that surrounded the single lightbulb like sun rays. The Tube rattled the bulb, and the rays shimmied. His phone rang, but he didn't get up to answer. Three days' worth of calls filled his voice mail box—mostly from Brock, a few from his mother. Amazingly, even three from Reece. Not one from Sara.

He hadn't listened to a single one.

James tried to pray, but his pleas seemed to go no further than the brittle plaster. From behind a barred door in the shadows of his consciousness, a voice prodded him to listen to the wisdom of his friends. James reached across the bed for his mp3 player. He didn't care what he listened to, as long as it was loud.

The song that blared through his earphones wasn't one he'd downloaded. His country-loving little brother had been messing with his stuff.

Josh Turner sang "Another Try." And James pressed the heels of his hands against his eyes.

"Let her go without a fight. . . . Next time I'll hang on. . .if love ever gives me another try. . . ."

છ

Just one more day.

Sara hobbled through the Lewises' cluttered living room, passing Granny Charity snoring in Neil's recliner. Barbies and Legos scattered out of her way with a swat of a crutch tip.

Voices rippled like rain from the kitchen. She didn't have the strength to witness yet one more example of "every day's a party," but she needed coffee to brighten her voice before making the phone call that could begin her independence.

The sink overflowed with dishes from breakfast and last night's supper, and the kitchen floor was sticky from the applesauce Connie and the girls had cooked days ago. Two hours after lunch and the girls were still in their pajamas. Three days ago, when Brock had brought her home, Connie had taken command. "I'll take care of everything, dear. I don't want you lifting a finger."

But someone needed to.

"Good morning—I mean, afternoon—lazy bum. That was a long nap." Connie drew out the "loooong." Hula hoop earrings banged against her cheeks as she clucked at Sara. "My girls are making *Mother Earth* suet holders for the birdies."

Your girls? Sara glared at the jumble of twisted coat hangers, birdseed, suet, and pinecones that littered the kitchen table. Sidestepping Connie, she kissed Zoe and Sadie on the tops of their heads. "The birdies will be very happy."

"Yook what we got. . .yickyish!" Sadie waved a rope of red licorice under Sara's nose.

"Ewww!" Just the sight of it made her feel pregnant. She looked over at Connie. Surely her mother-in-law knew her quirky relationship with red licorice—that what she craved during pregnancy nauseated her any other time. Was the woman that calculating?

"It's all natural, dear. It's good for them."

"Mm-hmm." Sara backed away from the smell.

Zoe grabbed her sleeve, bed-head curls scampering across her forehead. "Know what? We're going on a long ride to take Granny Charity home today."

Sara lifted an eyebrow and aimed it at Connie. "Oh, really?"

Raising peanut butter and sunflower seed-covered hands, Connie shrugged. "Well, Neil and Brock are working, and I can't leave them with you. We'll start out in an hour or so and be back in the morning, unless the weather gets too bad."

Not on her life.

Sara still had occasional dizzy spells. Her ankle was sore and swollen and throbbed with every beat of her pulse. But it wasn't broken. She could walk if she had to. Sara opened her mouth to argue but was saved from words she might regret when Brock kicked a plastic tiara through the door from the dining room. "I'm off until tomorrow night. Allison and I can watch the girls."

Fire shot from Connie's narrowed eyes, but she didn't say a word.

Brock ignored the fire. "Why don't you wait a couple days, Mom? It's gonna start snowing before dark, and it's not like Granny has to get home for anything."

"I've had enough of her." Connie's voice lowered, and her head dipped toward the living room. "I need to take her home. Today."

Brock's gaze latched onto Sara's, passing a restrained smirk.

Sara returned the look. Clomping back to the counter, she reheated morning coffee in the microwave and stared out the window while she drank it. Shadows lanced the snow-covered yard like javelins. As Sara sipped the Costa Rican coffee that Connie assured her was grown on a small organic farm in volcanic soil, she did something that didn't make sense, even to her. She prayed. *Lord, I know I don't know You very well yet, but I'm trusting You to get me away from here and do what's best for my girls.*

She didn't know where the fragile trust came from. It wasn't simply desperation. As soon as she could manage things at home, Reece would set her up with everything she needed for her new job. She was grateful for that, of course; yet, by her choice, it was only temporary—a bridge to the one dream she still clung to. Maybe, just maybe, God would answer this one prayer and move her farther from her mother-in-law's clutches.

She limped back to the living room. Picking up the phone, she dialed the number she hoped would be hers before long. While it rang, she prayed again.

"Stillwater Inn. *God morgen.* This is Ingrid."

"Hi, Ingrid. This is Sara Lewis."

"S–Sara. How are you, dear?"

"I'm fine." There was no need to tell her the truth. "I just hadn't touched base with you for so long, and I wondered if we could get together and talk. I've been thinking that it would be a good idea for me to work with you. . .um, *for* you. . .for a while before you actually turn things over to me." She rehearsed her next line, how she'd offer to do the books, answer phones, or even bake while she couldn't walk. But it would only be a week or so until she could change beds or clean or whatever they needed. And the single room at the end of the hall would be just fine for her and her girls. Her very quiet, well-behaved girls.

Ingrid Torsten was silent. A squeal of laughter came from Sadie in the kitchen. The room seemed suddenly dark. "Ingrid?"

"Umm. . .Sara. . . We've been meaning to call you. Erik and I have changed our plans. We're going to buy a campground in New Mexico with my brother. So we'll be selling the house outright. Like I said, we were going to call you. . . ."

Brock picked up Allison, and the two arrived less than five minutes after Connie left. Sara imagined them waiting at the crossroad for the Escape to pass. They fixed a snack for the girls then bundled them in snowsuits.

Sara watched from the couch. Shifting the ice pack on her ankle, she propped it once again on a stack of pillows. Just one more day. Her plan was to be home in her apartment tomorrow before Connie got back. Allison had already promised to spend the night on her couch or whatever she needed.

She felt eerily calm and strangely relieved since talking to Ingrid. Her future was no longer a mystery. She would work for Reece. Every day would not be a party. There would be no castle at the end of the path. But she would save, and maybe someday she would buy a house. And she would be all her girls needed.

Brock put on his jacket and sat down next to her. "We're going to hit the hill behind the house before it gets too bad out there. It's snowing pretty hard, and the wind's supposed to pick up."

Sara's eyes burned. Losing her last dream had produced a numb sense of resignation—not tears. But watching Uncle Brock with her girls reduced her to mush. She put her hand on Brock's. "You guys will make good parents."

Brock snorted, his eyes sparking. "James said you were going to try talking me out of marrying Allison."

"I was. You guys are still babies yourselves, you know. I'm worried about you. But seeing how sweet you are with Allison and watching you two with my girls—I don't know—maybe I was wrong."

"It took me awhile to figure out if I could be a decent husband and father."

Sara's eyes closed for the space of a breath. "You just have to. . ." Her voice squeezed to a whisper. "Just be there."

A look of pain twisted Brock's features. He stood then bent and kissed her on the forehead. "Take a pain pill, and go to sleep while it's quiet."

"I will."

Allison walked through the dining room with an armful of hats and mittens.

"Al, will you have a car tomorrow to give us a ride home?"

"Not till four. Mom's working a double shift. I could bring your car. . .if it's not buried in the snow by then."

"That'll work." Sara sat back. She had an escape strategy.

Allison wiped Sadie's nose and tied her hat. Sara motioned for Allison to come closer. Grabbing her hand, she squeezed it. "Thank you."

"It's nothin'. I'm almost their aunt, you know."

"I know." Sara put a hand on Allison's belly. "And I get to be Aunt Sara to this little person. We're going to be sisters, Al."

Self-consciously Allison giggled. "Yeah, we gotta watch each other's backs."

She glanced at Brock and whispered, "Gotta protect each other from the wicked witch."

❧

Sara stood in the middle of the Mall of America, staring up. Four stories above her, James leaned over the railing, dangling his leather jacket. "Catch it!" The jacket took flight, soaring like a hawk, and landed at her feet. She put it on. It smelled like James. Looking up, she giggled. "I'm getting dizzy!" she yelled. "Come down."

He reached toward her. "I can't. I can't find Zoe, Sara. Where is she? Is she in here? Is she with you, Sara? Sara. . .Sara. . ." His voice blended with the howling wind and the sound of snow pelting the windows. Four stories of windows . . .so loud and echoing. "Sara! Sara!"

Rough hands shook her.

"James?"

"Sara! Wake up. Is Zoe in here?" It was Brock, standing over her, dripping snow on her face.

Her head felt funny. She was dreaming, just dreaming. The pain pills gave her strange dreams. She closed her eyes, but Brock tapped her cheek with cold hands.

"Sara! You have to wake up. We can't find Zoe. Did she come in here?"

Fear shimmied from the base of her spine. Her eyes snapped open. "What do you mean you can't find her?"

"I mean I can't find her!" His voice rose. He paced, his hands on his head. "We've covered every inch of the yard and the house and looked up and down the street."

"Weren't you watching her?" Sara sat up, grabbing for her crutches.

"She went down on the sled. Allison and Sadie and I were at the top of the hill. Zoe got off, but instead of coming back up, she ran around to the front of the house. I called her, but she didn't come." His words came faster. "I've looked . . .everywhere. She just. . .disappeared."

❧

It was just after twelve when James crawled into bed. He was almost asleep when the phone rang. That would be Brock. That was his trick, calling every day after supper when he knew it would be midnight in London. The ringing stopped then started up again. "Not a chance, little brother." James pulled the blanket over his head and prayed he'd sleep through his dreams.

It felt like he'd just fallen asleep when a rap on the door woke him. "Mr. Lewis?"

"Who is it?"

"Metropolitan Police, Mr. Lewis. Open up."

James scrambled into jeans, his brain inventing scenarios as he stumbled toward the door. He imagined his car—smashed or missing tires—or one of the guys bleeding from a fight. He opened the door and nodded at the man in the dark blue hat with a silver crest. "What is it?"

"Mr. Lewis, your daughter is missing."

Chapter 20

Afternoon light crept around the corners of the sparkly purple shades. Sara stood in front of the open closet in the darkened room. She'd come in here to get away. Away from Sadie's incessant questions, from her mother calling every half hour, from the ringing phone that brought no answers and a roomful of eyes asking how she was doing. She came in here to keep from screaming. But she couldn't get away. The closet floor was strewed with dress-up clothes. "Zoe. . . Oh God. . .my baby girl. . .where is she?"

She picked up a pink leotard and a glitter-coated high-heeled shoe and pressed them to her chest. Her lips were dry and cracking, her eyes hot. Her throat ached. And yet there were still more tears. She threw her crutch and folded to the floor.

Mattie walked in and sat beside her, wrapping one arm around Sara. "They've posted the Amber Alert."

Sara pulled one knee to her chest.

"The storm's dying down. The roads will be cleared soon."

Not fully comprehending what that meant, Sara nodded.

Mattie placed a hand on Sara's head. "Lord Jesus," she whispered, "You are all we have. Hope is what we cling to—"

Brock walked in, sat on Sara's other side, and held out the phone. "Honey, James is on the phone."

Sara stared at the phone then looked at Brock. Fresh tears tracked along her chin. She didn't care what he'd done or why he'd left her again. She needed James here. "I. . .okay." She took the phone. Mattie and Brock left. "James?"

"Sara. . ." His voice was rough, gravelly. "I'm in Chicago. We're waiting for the runways to be cleared in Minneapolis. Eldon's going to pick me up. I'll be there soon."

Sobs jarred her. "I. . .I. . .can't. . ."

"I know. I know. Is there anything you can tell me? What are you thinking, Sara? Do you think my mother took her?"

"Ye. . .yes. But where would she leave her? The police picked up your mother at Granny's, and Zoe wasn't with her. She won't tell them, James. She won't admit to anything, not even to your dad. And what if she comes back for Sadie? And what if it wasn't her? There was a guy. . .at the health club. . . . Your mother let him watch the girls and. . .and. . .I should have told her no. What if. . .what if he—"

"We'll find her. And. . .Sara. . . ? I don't care what you've done. We're going to get through this together, okay?"

Sara rocked, still hugging the shoe. "What? What do you mean? What have I done?"

"I saw you, Sara. I saw you with Reece. . .at the cabin."

"*What?*"

"We'll talk about it later. When this is all over."

"No!" Glitter bit into the palm of her hand. "What did you see? Is that why you left?"

"I saw the two of you by the car." His voice caught. "His arms were around you and—"

"I sprained my ankle, James. I had a concussion. I fainted. Reece dragged me to the car and. . .we were waiting for you. He was going to surprise us by offering us the manager job. . .together."

The sound he made was part gasp, part groan. "Sara. . ."

"You didn't stop. You didn't trust me enough to find out the truth?" Her words formed on short, tight breaths. "If you'd been here. . .I wouldn't be at your mother's, and Zoe. . .wouldn't. . .be. . .gone."

&

An hour and twenty-one minutes to Minneapolis, the pilot announced. Minutes stretched beyond sixty seconds. Time distorted. He leaned his head next to the window, not taking his eyes off the clouds and glimpses of snow-covered land. *Zoe. . .where are you, baby?*

Guilt, regret—the old demons he'd almost defeated—embedded their claws. *Lord, I'm so sorry. I wasn't there for her. Find my little girl. Bring her back safe.*

&

God, find her. Find her. Bring her back to me. Sara sat on the edge of the couch, staring at the plow on the front of Neil's truck, widening the straight-walled tunnel to the road. The phone rang again, as it had all day. Sara closed her mind to false hope and kept her eyes on the plow. Fourteen inches in less than twenty-four hours, plus drifting and blowing. Drifts licked at the top of the split rail fence and the bottom of the mailbox. Fourteen inches. . .high enough to cover a little girl. Deep enough to—

Allison screamed. Sara whirled around to see her break into tears, clutching the phone.

"She's okay! Sara, she's okay. Zoe's with my mom." She held the phone out.

Sara grabbed the phone and sank onto the couch. "Raquel?"

"Sara. . .I'm so sorry. Zoe's fine. I'm so sorry. I. . .I took her. Just for a little while. . ." Her voice quaked and convulsed with sobs. "I wanted Brock's mother to know what it felt like to lose a grandchild. I was on my way to my sister's. . .just ten minutes away. I was going to call you as soon as we got there. . .I was going to ask you to go along with it to give that woman a good scare. But we went into a ditch, and the car got stuck. I couldn't open the doors, and I didn't have the phone. They're just digging us out now. I called the police when the tow truck got here. I told them everything. I'm not a kidnapper, Sara. I didn't want to hurt you, not you. . .but when Brock's mom came to see me again and said such awful things about keeping Allison's baby and taking us to court and. . .I'm so sorry. It was so stupid. I can't imagine how scared you were. I'm so, so sor—"

"Let me talk to Zoe." She couldn't listen to another word from Raquel.

"Hi, Mommy."

"Baby. . .are you okay?" Dark spots dotted Sara's vision. The room swayed. She closed her eyes and bent over the phone. "Are you okay?"

"We had a sleepover in the car, Mommy. We played games and ate candy, and I got cold, but Raquel had a blanket, and now the police is gonna take me home. Is that okay? He's not a danger, is he?"

"No, baby, he's not a danger. He'll give you a ride and. . .Daddy will be home when you get here."

☙

Bundled in James's new blue jacket and balancing on one crutch, Sara stood shivering on the back step, watching Eldon's car navigate the Lewises' driveway. Before the car came to a complete stop, James jumped out and leaped over the snow bank. Ignoring the shoveled path, he hurdled the fence and ran toward her in knee-deep snow, his gaze locked on hers. His eyes were red and swollen.

"Sara. . ." Several feet in front of her, he stopped. "Sara. . .I'm so sorry. . ."

The sound that came out of her was half laugh, half cry. She held out her free arm. "Just shut up, and give my jacket back."

In a breath, he stood beside her, engulfing her in the familiar smell of leather and Corduroy. He lifted her chin. His lips skimmed her wet cheeks and brushed over her eyes. The sound of tires on hard-packed snow pulled him away. The squad car drove up. Before Sara knew what was happening, James had lifted her off her feet. The crutch fell to the snow, and James carried her down the sidewalk. An officer opened the back door, and Zoe jumped out, blond curls springing from her stocking cap. "Mommy! Daddy!"

Sara slid down, stood on one foot, leaning on James's arm while he scooped Zoe up in the other.

Zoe put one arm around James's neck and one around Sara's. "Why are you crying?"

Burying her face in Zoe's hair, Sara sobbed. "Because we missed you, sweetie." Pink mittens stroked her wet cheeks, making her cry even harder.

"Can we go home now to our real house?"

Sara stared at James. His eyes asked the question she'd answered in her head hours ago. "Yes."

"Do I get to keep my Daddy now, for real?"

James blinked back tears. "If Mommy will have me in spite of my stupidity."

"Mommy, do you want Daddy's spidity?"

"Yes. I want Daddy's 'spidity' if he can handle all my silly rules."

"Yay!" Zoe wriggled out of their arms and ran down the path, toward the crowd gathered by the back door. "Sadie!" She waved at her little sister, wrapped in a blanket in Brock's arms. "Sadie! We get to keep our daddy. . .forever and ever and ever!"

∞

While James talked with Pastor Owen by the front door, Sara occupied the girls in the foyer of Pineview Community Church. She watched James gesturing with his hands. The music director had just gotten a job transfer, and Pastor Owen wondered if James would be willing to lead the worship team. *Lord, You are so good.*

Raquel came out of the sanctuary, squeezed Sara's arm, and headed for the exit without a word. Her face was streaked with mascara. Good tears, Sara hoped.

For the third time, Zoe held out the picture she'd drawn in Sunday school. For the third time, Sara bent to admire it. "Tell me about it."

"It's Nowhere and the ark. And these are the aminals. . . ."

As Zoe rattled on, a woman approached and stood a few feet away. When Zoe took a breath, Sara turned and smiled at the woman. "Good morning."

"Hi, Sara. I don't know if you remember me. I'm April Bachelor. I interviewed you. . .twice actually. . .after the Sanctuary fire and after the tornado."

"Oh, I remember you. I've been watching your TV show, but seeing you in person again makes me a little nervous. I kind of associate you with disaster."

April laughed. "I hope I can change that." Honey-blond hair skimmed her shoulders as she shook her head. "I just met Raquel. She told me what happened with your daughter. Talk about grace in action."

Sara shrugged. "We understood Raquel's motives." *Only too well*. After they'd gotten over the initial anger, she and James had been in agreement about not pressing charges. Ironically it was still harder for Sara to extend daily grace to Connie than to Raquel. But little by little, she was working on it.

"I was also talking to Mattie Jennet this morning. I'm doing a special Valentine show next week called 'Marriage Miracles.' Mattie says you two have a story you might be willing to share."

Sara pointed over April's shoulder. "Here comes my miracle now."

April turned around and introduced herself to James before Sara had a chance to. She explained the premise of her show. "Would you two be interested in telling your story?"

James rubbed his hand across his jaw. "I don't know. I think our story needs another chapter first." He looked from April to Sara and back to April. "April, I know I just met you, but could I impose on you to watch my girls for about five minutes."

Sara narrowed her eyes. "James. . . ?"

His mysterious smile quickened her pulse. He grabbed her hand and led her down the hall to the music room. Vibrant chunks of gold and blue from the stained-glass windows formed mosaic patterns on the dark red carpet. James pulled her into a swirl of sun-born color.

And dropped to his knee.

"Sara Lewis, will you marry me. . .all over again?"

∞

Hundreds of votive candles lit the small stone Stillwater Chapel. Sara stood alone at the back of the church and watched her girls walk hand in hand down the aisle, long white dresses swishing, tiaras ricocheting candlelight. When they got to the front, James reached for their hands and turned the girls to face Sara. The music changed to a piece written by James. . .and played by Bessie. In spite of her pain, Bessie had insisted.

Sara smoothed the front of Mattie's Juliet-style gown, fingering the pink satin ribbon that trimmed the empire waist. Something borrowed. This time, wearing secondhand was an honor.

In black suits, James and Brock waited at the front of the chapel. Mattie, wearing a pale pink dress picked out by Zoe and Sadie, stood on the other side. The small crowd rose to their feet, and Sara walked down the same aisle she had five years ago. She glanced at Connie's profile as she passed her. The look on her mother-in-law's face as she stared straight ahead at her star sapphire son could almost be construed as a smile.

Sara took her place between James and Zoe, and the four of them turned to face Pastor Owen. The music ended, and the pastor prayed then lowered his hands for the congregation to be seated.

"On behalf of James and Sara, I want to welcome you all to this celebration of marriage. Our God is a God of second chances, and this couple. . ."

His encouragement and wisdom surrounded them like sunlight. When he finished, Sara gave her bouquet to Zoe and held her hands out to James. His were shaking, but the look in his eyes told her it wasn't from second thoughts.

Pastor Owen closed his Bible. "And now we have the privilege of being witnesses to James's and Sara's vows of renewal. James?"

"Sara Lewis, your amazing green eyes stole my heart years ago. And even though I've tried. . .many times. . .to run from them, I'm afraid I'm simply stuck." He waited for ripples of laughter to subside. "I promise, before our Lord and the people gathered here, to put our family before myself, to protect and provide for my girls, and to be there when you need me. I promise to go to marriage counseling every week for the rest of our lives if that's what it takes." He winked at Mattie. "And I promise to be your prince forever and ever and ever." He smiled and whispered, "Zoe made me say that."

James held his hand out to the side, and Brock placed a ring on his palm. James slid it on her finger, next to the plain silver band she'd worn for five years. Two stones in a silver setting. Sara gasped.

"The star sapphire represents the light of Christ. The diamond is for the strength we'll need to finish the race set before us. . .together."

"Thank you." Her mouth formed the words, but no sound came with it.

"Sara?" Pastor Owen nodded to her.

"James, you are the love of my life. I have hurt you in so many ways over the years, and I know it is only by the grace of God we stand here today. I promise to never stop growing in my knowledge of the Lord and never stop learning how to be the woman He made me to be. I promise to read *Recipe for a Godly Wife* over and over until I have it memorized. And from this day forth, I will never again make a honey-do list or tell you how to father your children."

When the laughter faded, Pastor Owen held his hands over them. "Father, please hold this family in the palm of Your hand. Strengthen and protect them, and let Your light shine through them.

"James, you may kiss. . .your girls."

ഇ

When they reached the back of the chapel, James stopped her by the door. "I got you a little wedding gift." He pressed something into her hand but didn't let her open it. "It's not the castle you've dreamed about, and it won't really be yours for a few years."

Sara's mouth dropped open. She tipped her head to the side and stared into sky-blue eyes. The thing in her hand felt sweetly familiar. Her fuzzy pink puff-ball. . .with a key attached. Her tears were instant. "Does it come with a grand piano?"

James nodded. "And with a live-in assistant who's been miserable in Arizona."

"That will be"—she wiped her tears with the back of her hand—"a huge help. Because I have a little. . .a very little. . .gift for you, too." She held her bouquet in front of him. From the center of the flowers, she pulled a single red-licorice rope and took a bite.

Creases formed between James's brows. "You hate lic—unless you're. . ."

"Unless *we're*"—she placed his hand just below the pink ribbon—"having a baby."

348

A Letter to Our Readers

Dear Readers:

In order that we might better contribute to your reading enjoyment, we would appreciate you taking a few minutes to respond to the following questions. When completed, please return to the following: Fiction Editor, Barbour Publishing, Inc., P.O. Box 719, Uhrichsville, OH 44683.

1. Did you enjoy reading *Minnesota Moonlight* by Becky Melby & Cathy Wienke
     ❏ Very much. I would like to see more books like this.
     ❏ Moderately—I would have enjoyed it more if _____

     _____

     _____

2. What influenced your decision to purchase this book?
     (Check those that apply.)
     ❏ Cover   ❏ Back cover copy   ❏ Title   ❏ Price
     ❏ Friends   ❏ Publicity   ❏ Other

3. Which story was your favorite?
     ❏ *Walk with Me*   ❏ *Stillwater Promise*
     ❏ *Dream Chasers*

4. Please check your age range:
     ❏ Under 18   ❏ 18–24   ❏ 25–34
     ❏ 35–45   ❏ 46–55   ❏ Over 55

5. How many hours per week do you read? _____

Name _____

Occupation _____

Address _____

City_____ State_____ Zip_____

E-mail _____

HEARTLAND HEROES

Three-In-One-Collection

Three courageous women brave love in the heartland. Ravyn is determined never to have money worries like her ministry-driven parents. So what's her chance of a future with Mark Monroe, a doctor headed overseas as a medical missionary? EMT Cadi Trent only wants to help in a local crisis. So why is the attractive, but rude, Deputy Frank Parker giving her such a hard time? Ciara Rome is out to prove in her Master's thesis that no one needs love or God to survive. To what lengths will Luke Weston go to set her straight? With God in the driver's seat, anything can happen.

Contemporary, paperback, 352 pages, 5⁵⁄₁₆" x 8 "

OZARK WEDDINGS

THREE-IN-ONE-COLLECTION

Love disrupts the lives of three women in the Ozark Mountains. Larkspur Wendell's spontaneity and zeal for life is getting on the nerves of her new neighbor. Will Lark draw this recluse out of his shell or drive him out of town? Painfully shy Clair O'Neal is totally out of her element when two men vie for her attention. Can she trust either of them with her heart? Nori Kelly's biological clock is ticking away like a time bomb. Could her only hope be a member of the "geek" squad? Will these women dare to take a chance at romance?

Contemporary, paperback, 352 pages, 5¾₆" x 8"